the *Love* Startup

MÉLISA RYUN

Published in the United States by Create Mode Media, LLC. All rights reserved. Printed in USA. First edition 2024. Cover design by Lisa Kubja.

CREATE MODE MEDIA LLC

7925 W. RUSSELL ROAD #401103

LAS VEGAS, NV 89140

eBook Edition ISBN-13: 9781947775091

Paperback Edition ISBN-13: 9781947775107

For permission requests contact:

info@melisaryun.com

www.melisaryun.com

TRIGGER WARNING: This book contains explicit sexual content, reckless driving, extreme profanity, and references to the death of a parent and alcoholism.

To every "difficult woman" who's been told to "smile more".
Your patience is legendary, your dreams are valid, and your
time is coming.

PROLOGUE

ZACK

TEN YEARS AGO

SAME SHIFT, DIFFERENT DAY.

It's a total snoozefest at Gadget Galaxy tonight. I fiddle with my name tag 'Zack Hanley, Trek-tacular TV Sales Guru.' Okay, I might've added some Star Trek flair to my title, but hey, gotta show a little personality, right? Can't just be another sales drone in the sea of polos and khakis.

I'm chillin' in the TV section of this electronics megastore, pretending to study the specs of the latest 8K displays, when there's a commotion at the Geek Genius Counter.

"Be careful, lady! You're gonna break it. Maybe I should help you," the rude customer says aggressively.

And there she is, Maddie Denton, the girl I've been crushing on hard since day one at this soul-sucking job.

"Sir, do you know how to fix a Non-Volatile Memory Express SSD hard drive?" Maddie asks calmly.

"Well, no," the customer admits.

"Then how could you possibly help me?"

She coldly turns her attention back to the ailing hard drive, her delicate fingers working magic on the tiny components. She disconnects the cables with intense focus and perfect precision. It's mesmerizing. What this clueless redneck doesn't get is that he has zero chance against Maddie's intellect.

I watch and admire her in action. Her brown, medium-length hair sways to the side when her head tilts, revealing smooth skin and gorgeous lips. Adorable tortoiseshell glasses sit on her slender nose, highlighting her deliciously dark brown eyes.

She's wearing what we all have to wear: a neon orange polo uniform. But whereas the rest of us look like goofy traffic cones, Maddie's got that fabric working for her like Michelangelo with a chisel. It's as if the fabric has been tailored to fit her curves perfectly—the way it hugs her waist—how the collar highlights her tender neck—it's enough to make any dude's jaw drop like a broken elevator.

With his scruffy beard and weathered baseball cap, the disgruntled customer stands over her, exuding an imposing presence, but she's unfazed.

"You're staring again, Zack."

I nearly jump out of my skin at Kevin's voice beside me. My fellow TV huckster *(and occasional wingman)* is grinning like he knows exactly what's up.

Kevin chuckles. "Dude, half the guys here have a thing for the Maddinator. But a smokeshow like that is in her own stratosphere. Plus, we're all too scared that she'll rip our balls off if we try anything."

I wince, instinctively protecting myself. "She is intense for sure... and blazing hot. But it's not only her looks I'm into, Kev. It's that she's so smart... so fearless."

"She's too smart. That's a problem for me. I can't date someone who'll instantly realize what a dumbass I am."

"Bro, we can all tell you're a few beers short of a six-pack."

He's got a point, though. She's definitely out of our league. I first spotted Maddie in our shared Feminism 401 class last semester at Northwestern. She caught my eye right away with her hourglass figure and drew me in with her powerful debates and unapologetic attitude. The way she confidently took on our professor and classmates, her brilliance and passion on full display—I'd never witnessed anything like it.

She was captivating.

I did a little snooping *(not in a stalkerish way)* and discovered she was a computer science whiz with a serious reputation around school. Maddie: coding boss, feminist powerhouse, and destroyer of fragile male egos. That's why I'm both impressed and low-key scared of her. And also why I've never found the courage to make a move.

I'm dying to ask her out. But what do I even say? 'Hey, I'm Zack, and you're a legit genius who's also insanely hot. Wanna come kick it at my frat house?'

Yeah, that'd go over real smooth.

"Listen, princess, I've got some sensitive material on that drive, and I need it back," the rude customer snaps. "So go find a man who can handle the job."

"It's Maddie, not princess," she corrects him. "I'm the only tech available right now. Everyone else is out on calls, so it appears we're stuck with each other."

"What a dick," I tell Kevin.

"You gonna let him disrespect your fake girlfriend like that?" Kevin teases, elbowing me.

An elderly woman walks over and asks, "Excuse me, is this where I buy the Netflix? My grandson said he wants 'Netflix and chill' for his birthday."

Kevin pats me on the back. "I got this one, bro." He turns to the woman and says, "Ma'am, I know exactly what he needs. Let me show you our TV massage chairs."

"Hold on a shit pickin' minute, missy!" the pissed-off shopper shouts. "I won't be talked down to by a dumb little girl with a puffed-up badge that says Geek Genius. Get me your manager, now!"

Maddie picks up the phone receiver and speaks into it, her voice distorting through the store speakers. "Steve, assistance needed at the Geek Genius Department."

Seconds later, our on-call manager Steve comes to the counter. He pulls his trademark harassment move, squeezing past Maddie to get behind her, grinning as his crotch brushes her ass. *Fucking douchebag.*

Steve runs a hand through his oily hair. "Hi, I'm the manager. What seems to be the problem?"

"Well, this mouthy little bitch must be on her period because she's acting crazy, and she's taking it out on my hard drive," the angry client shouts, and then lowers his voice to continue, "There's over five years of exotic porn on there, and she doesn't respect that I'm paying good money to get it back."

Maddie's eyes fixate on the man, her voice steady and resolute. "Sir, I've been entirely professional. I'm simply trying to explain the situation with your hard drive and the steps to fix it."

"Maddie, the customer is always right, sweetheart," Steve says, brushing her off. "Sir, I'm sorry for the trouble. This gal's had a few run-ins with customers before if you know what I mean."

"Steve, are you kidding me with this garbage?" Maddie retorts. "I've closed more service tickets than every guy here combined."

"There's that tone again. You're being aggressive," Steve says, his words dripping with condescension.

The dipshit customer smirks at Steve. "I know companies are forced to hire chicks for diversity and wokeness and shit... and I can appreciate a nice set of knockers, but for Christ's sake, you gotta train this girl to smile more and talk less."

Maddie stews silently.

Steve doesn't say a word, and they both gawk at Maddie's breasts, sharing a gross, creepy nod of approval.

That's it. I march up to the counter, ready to defend Maddie. Just as I open my mouth, she beats me to the punch.

"Listen up fuckwads!" Maddie fires back. "Having boobs doesn't neutralize my brain. I've got more skill in my pinky toe than both of you have in your wrinkly ass, out of shape, midlife crisis bodies."

"Yeah, pricks!" I snap. "You're treating this highly skilled tech like she's nothing more than a set of boobs on legs? Show some freaking respect."

Maddie looks at me, surprised at my solidarity. Then she faces the angry man again, her voice firm and commanding. "You've come in here with a problem that I can still repair *if* you can stop your chauvinist manifesto bullshit. So either let me fix the shitty computer that won't let you jerk off 24/7, or grab your ancient hardware along with your antiquated, sexist, dehumanizing ass and go the fuck back to the fifties where you belong.

The man's face turns an alarming shade of purple. "Well, I never—"

"Never what? Had your limp dick handed to you by a female half your age before?" Maddie cuts him off. "Welcome to the 21st century. So what'll it be, ya dirty schmucker?"

I mean, damn. I bite back a grin.

"Enough, Maddie. You'd better stop being so hysterical, or you're fired," Steve says, his voice low and threatening.

"You're seriously siding with the porn king?" I demand. "Be better than him, Steve. We've all seen you trying to cop a feel on Maddie. This is your chance to be a decent human being. Just do it... lift a finger."

"You both want to kiss your jobs goodbye?" Steve barks, his face now red.

"I'll make it easy for you pervs. I quit," Maddie announces, her voice sharp. "I'm a goddamn rockstar tech, and I deserve better."

She turns to me, smiling. "Thanks for having my back, Zack. It means a lot."

Holy crap. I made Maddie Denton smile!

Maddie grabs the hard drive and smashes it onto the floor, breaking it into smithereens. "Oops. Good luck retrieving your spank bank now, shitnugget!"

"What she said! I quit, too!" I declare. "Let's bounce. This place blows."

And just like that, we strut out the door.

We catch our breath in the parking lot, still high on adrenaline. Then Maddie lets loose with a mighty roar. "Goddamn motherfuckers! I'm so sick of eating shit and smiling at assclowns like that."

"You okay?" I ask, knowing it's a stupid question.

"You didn't have to quit, Zack," she replies. "It was a nice gesture, but maybe you should go back in, apologize, and get your job back."

"I can't work for a company that allows jagoffs like Steve to run the place. It's not right," I say decisively. "Letting a customer treat you like that, it's barbaric and unprofessional. But don't worry about me. I've got this winning personality and handsome face. I'll bounce back." I flash her a smirk.

"Ooh, so cocky now." She chuckles. "Wanna grab a bite to eat, Hanley? I'm buying."

"It's a date."

"Not a date, just a meal... between two former coworkers."

I must be dreaming because I've gone and landed myself a non-date with the unbelievable Maddie Denton.

***

WE'RE AT A POPULAR HOLE-IN-THE-WALL DINER near Northwestern University, celebrated because it's one of two 24-hour joints in Evanston, Illinois. Like so many others, I come here when I'm wasted and need some greasy food and thick coffee to absorb the alcohol. I would never bring a date here.

Good thing this isn't a date.

We've been cracking up for the past hour, swapping her most epic *(and my embarrassing)* college stories.

"... so this drunk jackwad is straight-up chatting with my boobs... like they're his BFF's. And the funniest part is, when he finally looks up, I swear to God, he gets spooked that I have a face."

"Call me old fashioned, but I like a face with my floating tits," I snort.

Maddie chuckles. "That was my first and last time at a frat party. My IQ couldn't take the abuse."

"Your breasts don't like small talk. Good to know. Must be introverts."

We're hanging out in this booth, and it's like we've known each other for years. It's crazy how easy our conversation flows, especially considering how badly I've been crushing on her.

"You're a good time, Hanley. Sucks we never chatted in feminism class," she says, inhaling half her cheeseburger.

"Hold up, you clocked me in class?"

"Zack, every pair of ovaries in that class would've thrown their feminist convictions out the window if it meant locking lips with your pretty face. At least that's what my mom said."

"Your mom?" I shift, and the worn vinyl cushion squeak-farts.

"Uh, excuse you, Hanley," Maddie giggles, mock fanning her nose. "Yeah, Professor Taylor is my mom. She hyphenated her last name when she got hitched to my dad. Cheryl Taylor-Denton, feminist crusader."

"That totally explains your fiery attitude. You really spoke out in class."

Maddie jams a couple of fries in her mouth. One fry goes soaring as she talks, and I find it strangely endearing.

"Yeah, I'm naturally sassy, and it's not just me. I'm one of four sisters, and let me tell you, our mom raised us to be some kick-ass feminists. You wouldn't believe the debates that happen at my house."

"Your dad must be one of those super secure in his manhood kind of guys."

"Huge, cuddly teddy bear. He's a principal at an elementary school. My dad's all about lifting up the ladies in his life. Total hype guy."

"Your family sounds tight. My parents are more... formal. Growing up it was just me and my trusty dog, Tootie."

"Did he fart a lot?"

"Yeah," I admit, chuckling at her bluntness. "Give me a break. I was only five. I thought the name was hilarious."

"It's cute."

"I'm an only child, so Tootie was my partner in crime. And let me tell you, he took a lot of heat for me." I look up at the ceiling with a grin. "Thanks, Tootie. May Mom and Dad never know about the squirrel. RIP, buddy."

Maddie's eyes light up. "Seriously, don't leave me hanging here."

"Sooo, I thought Tootie needed a friend. I rigged a trap in my backyard, which surprisingly worked! My fatal mistake was bringing the squirrel inside. The feral creature flipped out when he saw the walls. He was desperate to escape, and Tootie was in hot pursuit, knocking over plants and chairs. I was caught in the middle, still trying to get them to bond."

"And your parents were...?"

"On a walk. Tootie chased the squirrel onto the kitchen sink and somehow turned on the faucet. When my parents walked in, the rodent bolted for the front door, and the kitchen was a swimming pool."

"You pinned this on your pooch! That's some top-notch sibling sabotage right there. Devious. Please, please, please tell me you named the friggin' squirrel."

I sigh. "Mr. Nuts. Works two ways because he was male. I think."

Maddie unleashes a belly laugh, and I immediately want to replay it.

We settle down, catching our breath. She finishes off her strawberry milkshake with a loud slurp that would make most girls cringe. But not Maddie, she's unapologetically herself.

Man, I'm totally falling for this girl. She's got it all—smarts, looks, and a killer sense of humor.

Then, either she picks up on the vibe change, or my heart-eyes give me away because she snaps me out of my love-struck daze.

"Let's play a game!" Maddie blurts out. "I invented it, and there's only one rule: make the other person laugh. Whoever gets the most laughs wins."

Maddie gestures to a nearby couple. The awkward dude chats nonstop and is laying it on thick, but the woman is just not interested. She fake smiles back, but bro can't take a hint.

"Those two people are on a first date. Roleplay!" Maddie commands, her voice leaving no room for argument.

Before I can even ask what the hell she means, Maddie lowers her voice, taking on the persona of the man on the date. "So, uh, have you ever been handcuffed?"

I jump in with my best high-pitched girl voice, pretending to be his date. "Like sexually or by the police?"

Maddie snickers and I mentally score a point for myself. *That's right, Hanley for the win!*

I continue my girly voice, "So, what do you do?"

"Meth. Lots of meth," Maddie deadpans in her low, matter-of-fact tone.

I chuckle. One point for Maddie.

"I meant for work. What do you do?"

"I get paid to post pics of my hairy-ass feet. People love it. But my secret dream is to start posting pictures of my ears."

"Aww, I can see why. They remind me of that elf guy from Harry Potter," I quip. "He's hot."

Maddie snorts a laugh, trying to hold it in. I raise my voice to an even higher falsetto, determined to win. "I'd invite you back to my place and pretend to have an orgasm, but I'm only on this date to make my dickwad boyfriend jealous."

Maddie fires back with her deepest, grittiest voice yet. "Well, that's a relief because you do not want to see what my penis looks like. It'll haunt you. Er, at least that's what my mother says."

I explode with laughter, pissing off the couple in the booth next to us.

"You're the champ, Mads. Can't beat that!" I concede, still laughing and wiping my eyes.

"Mads, huh? You think you're on nickname level with me now?"

"I held my own in your game, so yeah, we're bonded," I add with a playful wink. "What's next for you after graduation, Mads?"

"It's all mapped out. I've already snagged a starter job coding at Schmoogle. That's the first step. Then I'm hustlin' up that corporate ladder while hoarding all my cash so I can start my own company."

"What kind of startup?"

"Still working on that part. But here's the thing: we need more vajayjays in the coding game and more estrogen in CEO chairs. I'm on a mission to shake things up in the dude-heavy tech world."

Whoa. Of course she's got major aspirations. I doubt she'll be impressed I'm considering getting my MBA. And if I'm being honest, that's only to avoid the real world a little longer.

"How about you, Zack? What's in your future?"

"Time out. Are you in my head right now? Because that's my life plan, too," I say, chuckling. "Quick, no time to think. You have to choose. Star Wars or Star Trek?"

"Star Trek, duh. I'm a coder. I don't buy into fate or the force. You create your own destiny."

"Perfect answer. If you'd said Star Wars, I would have had my crew beam me up faster than you can say 'lightsaber.'"

"Same! And I would've taken the rest of your fries with me."

I push my plate towards her and for a split second, our hands touch. A jolt of electricity zaps through me, my heart racing and my stomach fluttering. I suddenly have this urge to hold her hand—to touch her—to do what people do on dates. I'm completely consumed by the desire to do something... anything to show how much I'm into her.

"Don't mind if I do," Maddie says, grabbing a handful of fries.

I'm too busy watching her lips move to process what she's saying. The way her eyes sparkle under the crappy diner lights; I'm so far gone for this girl, it's ridiculous. I feel stupidly in love.

This is it. This is the make-or-break moment. Either I spill my guts now, or I'll be friend-zoned for life. It's easy; I'll ask her out on a real date, and she'll know where I stand.

I inhale deeply, only for her to cut me off mid-breath.

"This was fun, like... way more than expected, no offense," she says, straightening up. "Listen, I don't want it to get weird and shit, but I gotta be upfront about something. This can't turn into anything. I'm not saying you're catching feelings, but you need to know that I've taken a vow to stay single."

The words bitch slap me in the face.

"Like for now?"

"Forever," she says, completely serious. "It's not like I'm becoming a monk or anything, but I've seen too many women throw away their aspirations for some dude or family or whatever. Not me. I've got important shit to do. Love is off the table."

Fuck. She means it.

I did not see this coming. *Can you do that... just completely remove love from the equation? What am I supposed to do?* I don't want to be the guy who gets in the way of this single-by-choice ambitious force of nature—someone with wild, passionate pursuits of world domination. But there's no denying that I like her, a lot.

So, I do the only thing I can think of. I lie.

"That's a relief because I was gonna warn you not to fall in love with me," I say, grinning. "I'm going for my MBA. I won't have time for relationships."

"Is that so?" she says, trying to read my eyes like Tarot cards.

She goes to speak and pauses as if working out a difficult equation behind those stunning eyes.

"Okay. Friends it is, Hanley," she says, offering me her hand. "I don't have many of those."

I shake her hand, locking in our friendship, trying to ignore the way she makes my skin tingle.

Did a part of me just die? My gut is telling me that if she's not in my life, I'll be missing out on something amazing. So, even if it's the wrong move, I'm not letting go of Maddie Denton.

CHAPTER ONE

MADDIE

PRESENT DAY

"SWIPING ON TINDER IS LIKE MASTURBATING IN PUBLIC. It's embarrassing; everyone knows you're doing it, but you just can't stop swiping left and right." I pause, waiting for the imaginary laughter to subside. "Online dating can be a cringefest, but not with LoveScore. Our new dating app is here to shake things up; wait, no... to flip the script... hold on, that's not right."

"Bitch, motherfucker, shit, what's the damn line?!"

I stare at my naked reflection in the dirty bathroom mirror, practicing my business pitch for the thousandth freaking time. Public speaking has never been my strong suit. Give me a complex coding problem, and I'll solve it faster than you can say "algorithm." But ask me to explain our dating app to a room full of investors and I'll choke harder than a nun at a hotdog eating contest.

But that's the price you pay when you're the co-CEO of a startup. You've got to be the friggin' brains and the beauty—the coder and the charmer. Let's face it: I'd rather be chilling with my computer than dealing with a bunch of humans. I don't know why these wealthy investor douche-holes need to see my social awkwardness. My brilliant thoughts should be enough.

I check out my tired-as-hell face in the mirror. My tortoiseshell glasses don't hide the dark circles under my brown eyes. My messy brunette hair is as disheveled as ever, and I spot a piece of cheesy popcorn that's been livin' in there. Don't judge, but I'm eating it.

I glance at the Post-it note stuck to the mirror, a message from my bestie and business partner, Zack. "You've got this, Mads! You're a brilliant boss babe, and a coding superstar! LoveScore's gonna blow them away! Let's gooo!"

A smile tugs at my lips. Zack knows just what to say to boost my confidence. He's the avocado to my toast, the boba to my tea. Without him, I'd be a shut-in, surviving on a steady diet of java and JavaScript.

I crank on the shower, ready to power wash my nerves. I clip up my mess of brown hair as steam fills the tiny bathroom. Call me quirky, but wet hair on my back feels like a bunch of slimy slugs having a rave. No thanks. Hair washing comes last, always.

I've got a solid hour before the big investor meeting on Zoom. No sweat. I grab my razor and step into the shower, ready to tackle my armpit fur.

Oh the irony of my life. Here I am, a single woman in her thirties, making it her mission to help people find their soulmates while simultaneously swearing off love like it's a goddamn curse. For the last decade, my career has been my number one priority, and everything else, especially my social life, can suck it.

And let's be real, I know the ugly truth about love.

Love is sacrifice.

Love means giving up parts of your identity, bit by bit until you no longer recognize who you are. Having it all? Yeah, that's a freakin' fairy tale for women. We get to choose who we are, so I guess I'm a workaholic, girl boss, she-E-O, and whatever else you wanna call it. I don't need some dude to 'complete me.'

I'm married to my work.

LoveScore is my baby.

And that's all I need.

Boom!

I drop that razor like a mic. I bend down to grab it, and I'm greeted by my overgrown lady jungle.

Damn, I've let that shit go wild.

With a hardcore feminist mom and three equally outspoken sisters, body hair discussions are as common as passing the salt. Growing up, dinner chats revolved around the suckiness of bras, the myth of workplace gender equality, and every friggin' aspect of the 'Free The Nipple' movement.

But hairy pits? That's where I draw the line. *My body, my choice. Right, mom?*

I slather up my loofah and scrub, mentally running through the pitch's key elements. Right now, I gotta focus on the game plan: surviving this investor meeting without making a colossal ass of myself.

Suddenly, the water feels like liquid ice. "Cum nuggets!"

Goosebumps erupt across my skin. I twist the knobs in vain—the hot water is gone—and so is my patience for my crappy roommates.

Teeth chattering, I poke my head out from behind the shower curtain, scanning for a towel. I pound on the bathroom wall, yelling,

"Hey, morons! Cosmo! Wes! Reid! Which one of you brainiacs stole my towel?"

Silence. Those man-children I call coworkers are too engrossed in coding to acknowledge my existence. I've trained them well.

Scanning the disgusting bathroom, I spot the ratty olive-green bath mat. It's not ideal, and it has a mildew stench that could make a skunk cringe, but I've got no choice. I wrap the shaggy rug around my soaking body and bolt out the door, leaving a trail of wet foot-prints.

Oh, the glamorous life of a startup founder.

***

"WHICH ONE OF YOU DICKWEEDS used all the hot water?"

I storm into the dining room, drenched and rocking the bath-room rug. "Ahem, geniuses, do I need to remind you that my huge investor meeting starts in one freaking hour?"

Cosmo, our resident coding savant (and secret gym rat), halts his typing and lifts his gaze.

Imagine the unholy lovechild of a Nordic Viking and an alien robot, that's Cosmo. With his pale skin, perfectly styled short brown hair, well-groomed beard, and penchant for all-black ensembles, he looks more "sexy cologne ad" than "nerd dungeon mastermind." But don't let the pretty packaging fool you—underneath those muscly tattooed arms and black-framed glasses—lies the soul of a true basement-dwelling hacker.

"Apologies, Mads. I had to shut down the water heater and reroute power to the server farm in the basement. There's an interface glitch in the app that needs squashing before the pitch meeting," he says, sporting his signature "I void warranties" T-shirt, which pairs perfectly with his deadpan, sarcastic demeanor.

At the word 'glitch,' I'm hit with an adrenaline spike. I dart over to my workstation, not caring that the soggy rug is barely holding in my cannonballs. I plop my ass down in the chair and scramble to log in, my damp fingers slipping on the keys.

"A glitch? What kind of glitch? Why am I just hearing about this?"

"Maddie, I like the new outfit. It really breathes," jokes Wes, our eccentric front-end developer from across the table. "You trying to set a new trend for Casual Fridays?"

"Psh, clothes are just society's way of keeping us down," I fire back, my eyes already scanning the lines of code on my screen. "And I don't take fashion advice from a guy who looks like a reject from an '80s workout video."

I glance up, taking in Wes's outrageous outfit of the day: a fluorescent orange Hawaiian shirt paired with leopard-print skinny jeans and mismatched Converse high tops (one red, one purple). He calls his wild style "peacocking," while the rest of us call it "struggling." Still, his unruly chestnut curls frame his youthful mug and highlight his blue eyes, epitomizing adorable dorkiness. And while he's severely lacking in style and shame, he's our irreplaceable class clown. Sitting next to him is Reid.

"Wes, buddy, don't be scared, but this is what we call a naked woman. I know you've never seen one in real life before," Reid teases.

"That's not a woman," Wes deadpans. "That's Maddie."

"Thanks," I say, sincerely happy that my all-male team sees me as one of the guys.

Reid sips smugly from his boob-shaped coffee mug. He's objectively handsome with dark cocoa hair, soft brown eyes, and his on-point earth-toned wardrobe. But don't be fooled, he's no ladies' man. Back in college, the guy bought himself a "World's Greatest Lover" trophy, and it's been gathering more dust than memories ever since.

I would applaud him for being such a productivity powerhouse if he wasn't always wearing that shit-eating grin.

"Fret not, my coding compadres. The Reidalicious Rainbow is here to save the day," Reid declares.

"Is that what you're calling your dick now?" Cosmo deadpans. "Cause, I'd call it one nasty yeast infection waiting to happen."

I high-five Cosmo before my fingers return to my keyboard. This is how we operate—equal parts banter and brilliance. Our insults are as much a part of our workflow as actual coding.

"Come on, guys. First person to fix the code will earn the glorious recognition of having the biggest swingin' dick in the nerd den." I say, my eyes still scanning the screen.

"Better Maddie's dick than Wes's," Reid scoffs, taking another sip of coffee. "We all know where that's been."

Reid turns to face the tattered blow-up sex doll propped up by Wes's desk. The infamous Linda—her plastic mouth gaping in a permanent "O" of surprise. Or maybe just existential dread.

Linda and Wes have been in a committed long-distance relationship since our college days at Northwestern. And by long-distance, I mean she lives at his desk chair while he lives in a fantasy world where a plastic girlfriend is brag-worthy.

Spoiler alert: it's not.

"Don't drag Linda into your trash talk," Wes scolds, tenderly wrapping his arm around Linda's shoulders. "She's a classy gal."

"Classy?" Cosmo snorts. "That's rich. The last classy thing Linda did was get patched up with a bike tire repair kit instead of duct tape."

That one gets a chuckle out of everyone except for Wes.

He pouts, "You're just jealous 'cause Linda and I have a deep, spiritual connection. Right, baby?"

Wes makes kissy faces at the doll, who stares back with dead eyes. The room shifts from cackles to soft clacking as our fingers return to a steady typing rhythm.

Welcome to The Coding Cave *(aka the dining room)*. It's a full-blown nerd invasion up in here—cables creeping along the floor—hard drives piled up like some sort of chaotic electronic shrine. Every square inch is covered in the aftermath of our takeout binges and soda can towers. Comic book movie posters and action figures look down on us from the walls, while the kitchen is a war zone of filthy dishes and suspicious stains.

I can't really point fingers here. My workstation is a wasteland of coffee cup corpses, crinkled candy wrappers, and scatterbrained sticky notes reminding me of thrilling tasks like "Restock Ramen," "Call the Momster," and "Shave? LOL." I could pretend like I'm not part of the problem, but hell—I'm a slob extraordinaire—and probably the worst offender out of the bunch.

This is the nutso world of startup life. We share a roof, a dream *(the LoveScore app)*, and an unhealthy dependence on screens, snacks, and stimulants. And as bonkers as it is, I fucking love it! Even when the guys are pushing my buttons... which is like 90% of the time.

The codebros treat me like a bossypants big sister they can't escape, and I manage this madhouse with an iron fist. Or, more realistically, a fist made of pool noodles. We're a lovable, dysfunctional work family, and I wouldn't have it any other way.

While I'm deep in code-mania, I crack open my Costco-sized tin of fancy-ass popcorn and begin shoveling it in, creating a cheddar-caramel mashup on my fingers. Reid tries to snag some, but I swat his hand away like a game of whack-a-mole.

"Hands off, pretty boy. This is my brain fuel."

Reid pouts, cradling his wounded hand *(more like his ego)* as if I know kung fu.

Drama queen.

"Gotcha, you little shitwad!" I shout, spotting the rogue line of code, "Cosmo, can you put eyes on this?"

Cosmo leans in, his gaze dissecting every pixel. He gives a quick, decisive nod. "Impressive find. I'll have this remedied momentarily."

His long fingers dance over the keyboard. Seconds later, he grunts with satisfaction. "Finished. Interface officially unfucked."

Crisis averted. I spring up, instantly back into Momzilla mode. "Hot water, pronto! And seriously, who stole my clean fucking towels?"

Reid grins. "Pretty sure I saw Wes violating one last night."

"Lies!" Wes objects, "I was merely cleaning up Linda after she graciously serviced me."

I glare at Linda's freaky plastic eyes, and we're locked in a blank stare for a moment. My stolen red towel hangs across her body like an unearned beauty pageant sash.

Are you kidding me? I feel my eye start to twitch.

"Boundaries! We've talked about this. No jerking off into communal towels! No sex doll shenanigans in shared spaces! I swear, you are all animals."

Wes offers the crusty towel back to me. I wince.

"Burn it. Burn the whole disgusting chair."

"Don't listen to her, baby," Wes coos, petting Linda's plastic head. "You keep the towel; it looks better on you."

I dash toward the kitchen, narrowly avoiding a broken neck as I trip over a rat's nest of cords. I'm met with a mountain of nasty-ass dishes in the sink and some *WTF-is-that* grime smeared over the counters. I'd love to tear into them, but a quick peek at the time reminds me I've got more urgent business.

I grab the paper towel roll, giving it a cautious whiff. "Look at that, no disgusting human secretions!" I loudly proclaim.

"The paper towel may be uncontaminated," Cosmo interjects. "But I'd wager the bathroom rug you're wearing is drenched in piss."

"Seriously?" I groan. "I curse you guys with the power of a thousand Karens who just found out their favorite Starbucks drink is discontinued."

"Nah, you love us!" Wes grins.

I turn on my heel and march towards the bathroom, the ragged edges of my rug toga flapping in my wake. Halfway down the hall, I glance over my shoulder.

"Hey, dorkwads!" They look up at me, eyebrows raised. I allow a small smile to curve my lips. "Thanks. You know, for being my ride-or-die nerd herd. Even if I fantasize about setting you all on fire at least twice a day."

Reid quips, "Right back at you, Mads!"

"That woman could crush your dick with a single glare," Cosmo says. "And you'd probably thank her."

"Damn straight." I give them a jaunty salute. "Now, if you'll excuse me, I'm getting my well-deserved shower. If I'm not out in forty, avenge my death."

***

FORTY-SEVEN MINUTES TILL THIS MEETING kicks off, and I'm sitting pretty with time to spare.

I reach into the shower and tentatively test the water. Yep, still frigid enough to make my nips pop like champagne corks on New Year's Eve.

"Hey Cosmo!" I yell through the door. "I thought you were fixing the hot water!"

"It's not like flipping a switch, your highness!" Cosmo shoots back. "Shall I mansplain to you the science of water heaters?"

I grumble, contemplating my options. I could suffer through a glacial shower, turning my vajayjay into an ice sculpture. It's not like it's getting any lovin' lately, anyway. Hell, even booty calls are too much hassle, which is why it's just me and my buddy, the Pleasure Penguin—my trusty vibrator—named for its ability to bring me instant wide-eyed wonder.

The Pleasure Penguin: Slide, Glide, and Enjoy the Ride!

Hey, don't be a hater! I didn't come up with the slogan.

I shiver, pulling the shabby rug tighter. No time for cooch excursions! I'm a woman on a mission, and that mission is world domination... or at least app store domination.

"With LoveScore our algorithm... no, that's not the line, shit!" I clear my throat, plastering on my best fake smile. "With our LoveScore app, you'll never have a bad first date again. Hopefully, if it works like it's supposed to."

Ugh, pitch meetings are the actual freaking worst.

I test the water again. "Annnnd we're still in the Arctic Circle," I mutter right as my phone blares to life.

Riinnggg! Rriiinnngggg!

I close the gross toilet seat and sit down, still wrapped in the grubby rug toga.

Video chat.

Fantastic.

Sissy's smiling face fills the screen.

"Hey, Sissy, I'm actually kind of busy—" I start, but she cuts me off.

"You're always swamped, Madeline! But we scheduled this sister call weeks ago," Sissy's smile remains warm, yet I catch the slightest hint of her emerald eyes narrowing.

With her strawberry-blonde hair framing her ageless face, Sissy exudes the effortless elegance of a Lululemon-clad angel; the kind that sips organic green juice while doing sun salutations and communicating telepathically with woodland creatures. She sure as shit's got her life together, and worse... she makes it look easy.

Sissy is my older sister—her actual name is Simone—but I couldn't wrap my toddler tongue around that sophisticated symphony of syllables. All that came out was a gurgled "Sissy," and the nickname stuck like gum to the bottom of her designer shoes.

I groan and sneak a glance at the clock. I've got 43 minutes until my investor meeting. I'll just have to hurry this sisterly bonding along. I can totally multitask.

The screen splits as another face pops in. "Hello, hello! What did I miss?" my younger sister Nora chirps. She angles the camera down, proudly displaying an immaculately decluttered kitchen drawer. "But first, check out my new spatula organizational system! Impressive, right?"

I stifle a snort. Of course Nora, my equally-Type-A but way-more-uptight younger sister, would arrange her cutlery like penises, organized in descending order from length and shape to girth and sheen.

Her shiny blonde hair is pulled into a tight ponytail, and her blue eyes gleam with the manic energy of someone who enjoys jogging at 5 a.m. She's like the love child of Martha Stewart and the IKEA home catalog, a hyper-organized control freak who color-codes the shit out of her daily planner weeks in advance. Her enthusiasm is both admirable and exhausting.

"Yeah, thrilling stuff, Nor," I deadpan.

"Ha, ha. I've seen your kitchen, Maddie. You desperately need my help." Nora's eyes widen as they flicker down to my rug-swaddled form. "Wait, are you naked?!"

"Very freaking astute, Watson. Are you like a detective super-hero?" I snark. "Yes, and as I was telling Sissy, I'm in the middle of prepping for a big meeting, so—"

"Mads, I know you're crazy busy, but we're all busy," Sissy jumps in, her voice as soothing as a spa day. "I'm worried you're not leaving enough time for our sisterly chats. It's important that we connect."

Ugh, she's right. I haven't been there lately. Sissy, the oldest and the nurturer, wants to wrap me in cashmere and cure my stress with comforting mac n cheese. Next, there's me, the "odd nerd out" in our little estrogen quartet. Then Nora, the perfectionist, who organizes my life into neat little piles and always lifts me up like the perfect bra. And last, there's Abby, the wild child, who wants everyone to loosen up, get buzzed, and make questionable decisions in the name of YOLO.

My sisters mean well, but their love can feel like another set of expectations to juggle. I know they want me to be happy, but they don't get that my version of happiness is not a picture-perfect life in the suburbs with a wardrobe full of Chanel. I'm content wearing hoodies as my daily uniform, building something from nothing, and knowing that I'm leaving my fucking mark on the world, one line of code at a time.

Whenever my sisters gang up on me, I've learned the only winning move is to not play. So, rather than arguing or explaining, I take a back seat and let them dive into their agenda.

Suddenly, two cute smiling faces pop into view. It's Violet and Hazel, Sissy's six-year-old fraternal twin troublemakers. Violet, the blonde one, wears a hot pink dress and pushes her face into the camera, while Hazel, a brunette in glasses and a black Minecraft shirt, stands behind her. Hazel's my little clone, so yeah, I have a favorite.

"Hi, Auntie Maddie! Hi, Auntie Nora!" they chorus.

"Hi, sweeties," Nora coos.

"Hey, munchkins!" I wave. "Did your mean mommy let you play Roblox this week?"

Sissy sighs, a rueful smile tugging at her lips. "They get thirty minutes of screen time a day. That's plenty. They can choose gaming or videos, but no budging on the time limit!"

"I get twenty-four hours of screen time a day," I stage-whisper. "You guys should grow up to be cool coders like me!"

"Yayyyy!" Hazel and Violet cheer as Sissy shoots me a tired glare.

Nora pipes up, "Oh my gosh, guys. While we wait and hope Abby shows up, can I vent about my date last night? It was a total trainwreck!"

Here we go. Another Nora rant about the pitfalls of modern dating.

Honestly, I can't complain. Her perpetual hunt for the flawless man is the reason my LoveScore app exists.

"Mads, I swear. I need your app up and running ASAP so I can report guys like this. He lied on his profile! Said he was into fitness but couldn't even make it through our jogging date. The man literally collapsed on our run! I had to call 911!"

I laugh. "Hold up. He faked a medical emergency to bail on your date? That's a new one."

Nora looks positively horrified, her hand fluttering to her heart. "Wait! You think he faked it?"

I want to feel sorry for her, but it's hard. My sister is famous for her bad dates. She's like some D-list actor who goes on hundreds of auditions, but never lands any roles.

Sissy shoots me a warning glare before turning back to support Nora.

"Eleanor, honey," Sissy says, "I'm sure he didn't fake it. But I wouldn't rush to reach out for a second date just yet."

I'm ready to crack a joke about a 'thanks for the heart attack' gift basket when another face appears on the screen, looking groggy and disheveled.

"Damn, it's hella early," Abby grumbles, rubbing the sleep from her bloodshot eyes. "What's the deal with the wake-up call?"

"It's two p.m. you sloth," Nora chirps. "The rest of the world has been up for hours."

Abby's still in bed—tangled up in red satin sheets. Her long platinum hair is all over the place, and last night's smokey eye is still smudged on her face. Abby's the wild one in the family, always chasing the next thrill, whether it's a new tat, a new boy toy, or a new way to get high. She's the kind of sister who'll hold your hair back while you puke, then help you plot revenge on the asshole who did you wrong. I freaking love her, but sometimes I wanna shake her and be like, 'Girl, get your shit together!'

Annnnd right on a cue, a muscular, tattooed arm snakes across her bare shoulders. "Gonna hit the shower, babe." A gravelly male voice mumbles from off-screen. Abby giggles, nuzzling into the unseen beefcake as he stands, exposing his bare butt.

That butt is tight. Muscular. Impressive.

Sissy quickly covers the twins' eyes with alarm. "Girls, go get a snack. The grown-ups need to talk."

"But mooooom!" Violet whines, straining to look past Sissy's fingers. "We wanna see the naked guy with squiggles on his arm!"

"They're called tattoos, dum dum." Hazel corrects her as Sissy ushers them away, hissing at Abby to keep it PG.

Abby yells to the twins through the phone, "Girlies, naked is natural. Set your own boundaries for your bodies!"

Only Auntie Abby would accidentally flash her one-night stand's dong to a pair of kindergarteners. But hey, at least someone is getting a shower... *oh wait, my shower.*

I check the water temperature. It's warm-ish—not the soothingly hot shower I longed for—but slightly above human popsicle temperature.

Sissy clears her throat, refocusing our attention. "So, I'm talking to you guys because Mom and Dad's thirty-fifth anniversary is in six weeks. We need to do something special for them, like plan a party!"

Nora's eyes sparkle as the word "plan" triggers dopamine into her brain's pleasure center. "Ooh, yes! I can create a detailed to-do list and a schedule!"

Abby groans, flopping back on her pillow. "Ugh, no way. I don't have the cash or the vibes for some lame-ass party for Mom and Dad's geriatric friends."

I hesitate, caught between my love for my parents and the increasing stress of running this business. "Look, Sissy, I'm not sure I should commit to anything at the moment. Can't we just buy them gift cards?"

Sissy's eyes narrow, and I know I've made a fatal mistake. "Madeline and Abigail Denton, we are throwing this party to demonstrate our love and gratitude for our parents. And you will both be there. No iffys, ands, or buts."

I cringe at the use of my full name. Sissy only brings out the big guns when she means business. "Nora, you're on decor and invitations. Abby, you're in charge of music and booze. I'm in charge of the venue and food. And Mads, you're handling the slideshow and tech stuff. Everyone clear on their roles?"

Before I can object, I hear a welcome gurgle from the showerhead, the pipes creaking to life with the promise of blessed heat. "Oh, thank fuck," I mutter. "Sissy, you can keep issuing orders, but I'm jumping in the shower. This rug smells like a frat house dungeon."

I prop the phone on the shelf, angling it to preserve what's left of my modesty. I yank out my hair clip, letting my chaotic brown locks tumble down to my shoulders, readying myself for the unpleasant sensation of wet hair on my back. As I step under the steaming spray, I hear a frantic pounding on the door.

"Occupied!" I yell, scrubbing my scalp furiously. "Go piss in a potted plant!"

The door flies open, and Zack barges in. "Mads, why the hell aren't you answering your texts?"

I stick my head out from behind the shower curtain. "Oh, I don't know, maybe because the Sisterhood of the Traveling Pants is ambushing me?" I snark, holding out my phone.

Zack blinks, finally registering the curious faces peering back at him. "Oh, uh, hey guys." He greets the camera sheepishly, offering an awkward wave.

"Zack!" Sissy beams, her smile stretching wide. "I'm so glad you're here. We're throwing our parents a thirty-fifth anniversary party. You simply must come! No excuses!"

Zack, the ultimate charmer, flashes a grin and nods eagerly. "Wouldn't miss it, Sissy."

I clear my throat pointedly. "Um, hello, girl trying to freakin' shower here. What can't wait, Zack?"

His eyes widen, snapping back into business mode. "Whoa, my bad! The investors bumped up our pitch. Video call now! No time to dry off. Throw these on." He chucks my clothes on the floor and then bolts out the door.

I groan, crank the water off, and spring out of the shower. My phone slips from my grasp, hitting the ground with a thud. My sisters' cackles fill the steamy air.

"I think I saw her butthole. Is that a normal amount of hair, or—"

"Pretty sure the '70s called. They want their bush back."

"It's like you're smuggling a small animal down there!"

I snatch up the phone, glaring at their gleeful faces. "I'm telling mom you made fun of my body hair."

"That forest would make her beam with pride," Sissy says with a playful grin. "Now go show 'em what you're made of!"

"Love you, losers." I smirk, jabbing the "End Call" button.

Time to break the record for the fastest outfit change in history.

CHAPTER TWO

MADDIE

I BURST INTO ZACK'S OFFICE, looking like a hot mess express. My clothes stick to my damp skin, and my sopping wet hair is yanked up haphazardly into a shoddy clip. My face is completely bare, not a trace of makeup. And the white button-down shirt Zack gave me? It's wrinkle city and barely hiding behind the pastel green blazer I threw on in a pathetic attempt to appear "professional."

I could wring out my hair and easily fill a bucket with all the water it's holding. I'm literally top-heavy.

Sexy, right?

Of course Zack is annoyingly put-together in his chinos and stupidly crisp gray button-down. I mean, seriously, how the hell does he always look like he just stepped out of a freaking GQ magazine? It's some next-level bullshit.

"So I said, who needs Google? I got the command prompt right here!" Zack chortles at his own joke, motioning for me to sit. On his laptop screen, two very serious-looking men in suits stare back at us. "Gentlemen, I'd like you to meet my partner and co-CEO, the brilliant Maddie Denton."

"Uh, hi, hello there!" I chirp with manic enthusiasm, unsuccessfully trying to match Zack's confidence. The investors, whom Zack introduces as Oscar and Ted from NovoNex Capital, give curt nods.

"We're thrilled to share our vision for LoveScore today," Zack begins smoothly before looking at me.

Right, my cue!

I clear my throat. "People say that love is in the air, but I say... it's online. Which translates to money because my coded ones and zeros will make you financial ones and zeros. Lots and lots of them." I flash a cheesy grin and double thumbs up.

Zack pats my leg under the desk, his polite way of saying, "Please shut up now."

He takes over effortlessly. "You may not think the world needs another dating app, but that's because you haven't seen what we've created."

Suddenly, I feel it—a cold, slimy water drip slithering down the back of my neck.

Fuckballs!

This is bad... like really, really bad.

I have major beef with water drips.

I squirm, discreetly trying to shake off the water droplets while still appearing engaged. Zack is explaining our development timeline, unaware of my aquatic agony.

"Maddie, tell Oscar and Ted about our current beta version," Zack prompts.

I hold up my phone, displaying the app interface. "Right, so the beta version has most of the core functionality..." I trail off as another frigid bead of water assaults my spine. Unable to take it anymore, I blurt out, "I'm sorry. Did I accidentally walk into a car wash or something? Because I'm getting hosed over here."

Zack jumps in, side-eyeing me viciously. "What makes LoveScore revolutionary is our first-date feedback system. It matches users based on—"

I try to adjust my hair clip casually but accidentally unleash a gushing waterfall down my back. I twitch, letting out this super ungraceful yelp. "Wow! You're spot-on, Zack. It's mega exciting!"

The investors look perplexed by my outburst, but Zack forges on. "After each date, users simply swipe to rate—"

"Totally, and listen, here's the deal," I interrupt in an anxious ramble. "I know about this stuff because my sisters can't seem to find 'the one', especially Nora with her ridiculous, insane list of deal-breakers. She'll probably end up dying alone and becoming a feast for a bunch of feral, wild cats. And Abby, she just wants a hot sugar daddy. Not that she's a gold digger. At least, I don't think she is. So there's definitely a market for it. Not that I need it because I'm married to my work, but I'm all for other people falling in love... I think I'll shut my mouth hole now."

Silence.

Painful silence.

I sense Zack's murderous glare.

"As you can see, Maddie is a true creative," he says through gritted teeth. "What sets LoveScore apart from other dating apps is our unique approach to matching. We have users rate their first dates, so our algorithm can find someone compatible with their preferences and lifestyle."

Zack fires up the PowerPoint part of his pitch. "Did your date show up on time? Did you feel a spark? How would you rate your first date overall on a scale of 1-10? That data is compiled to determine the users' LoveScore."

As Zack keeps blabbering on, I vow to just deal with the frickin' water drips. I casually reach back and try to use my shirt collar as a makeshift towel. But as I stretch the material, I hear a loud-ass ripping noise. And then, out of nowhere, buttons are flying everywhere. To my horror, my shirt bursts open, exposing my bra to the awe-struck investors.

SMACK! I carelessly hit Zack in the face, trying to cover up.

"Oopsie-crap! Sorry 'bout that. I'm like, straight-up Ariel from *The Little Mermaid* right now. Trying to act all sophisticated at dinner but totally fumbling it. You know the scene, right? Ted? Oscar? No? Coolio, coolio..."

I force a manic laugh.

Zack points to my wardrobe malfunction, his eyes screaming, "Fix it NOW!" I quickly clutch my shirt closed and start subtly wiggling. I feel my slimy hair. *Slugs! Gah!*

"Apologies, gentlemen," Zack says smoothly. "Maddie's been coding nonstop to prepare for this meeting. She's a tad over-caffeinated." He flashes his billion-dollar smile. "Now, as I was saying, we're on track for a full launch in six months."

Oscar, stone-faced as ever, cuts in. "Miss Denton, I need one thing clarified. Is this a dating app or a social network?"

All eyes are on me. I freeze.

Dating app? Social network? Uh...

I glance at Zack, but his eyes are glued to the screen, willing me to pick the right answer. "It's, um, well," I flounder. "Both?"

Ted's bushy eyebrows shoot up. "Both? That's a red flag. You need to have a clear value proposition. Are you trying to be the next Tinder or the next Facebook?"

I feel my palms start to sweat. "Well, see, the thing is… we're kind of like a mashup. You know, swipe right for love, but also connect with friends." I'm jabbering, and I know it.

Oscar sighs heavily. "I'm not sure I understand your target market. Is this for serious relationships or casual hookups?"

My mind goes blank.

Serious relationships? Casual hookups? What the eff should I say?

I feel the heat coming off Zack right now. He's so pissed.

"Our app caters to a wide range of dating preferences," Zack interjects, "but our core focus is on facilitating meaningful connections."

I'm nodding like a monkey on meth. *Come on brain, get it together!*

Ted leans forward, his eyes narrowing. "What about monetization? How do you plan to generate revenue?"

Shitnuggets!

I knew this question was gonna pop up. We've talked about it a million times. "Um, well… we've got a few ideas in the pipeline. Like, uh, premium subscriptions and maybe some in-app purchases. Yeah, that could work. Right, Zack?"

Zack clears his throat. "We're exploring several promising revenue streams, including targeted advertising and partnerships with local businesses. However, our primary focus is on building a robust user base."

Oscar and Ted give each other a look that says these two are in over their heads; they don't have a clue about business.

I'm drowning in my own suckiness. What the hell was I thinking, trying to pull off this business crap? I'm a coder, not some fancy-pants executive. I don't know jack about spreadsheets and corporate buzzwords and power suits. More importantly, I don't care.

Poor Zack, he's still trying to save this sinking ship of a meeting, but I can see the life and color draining from his face. The investors are grilling him like a cheeseburger, their doubt hanging in the air like a fart.

Yup, I majorly boned this one. Epic fail.

Zack finally pulls the plug. "Well, gentlemen, we've covered a lot of ground today. Thank you for your time. We'll integrate your insights and get back to you."

Oscar and Ted mutter some nice-sounding nothings, clearly disinterested. They can't wait to get off this Zoom meeting from hell.

***

AS SOON AS THE ZOOM WINDOW BLINKS OUT, Zack turns to me, his jaw tight. "Maddie, what the cringefest was that? I thought you were prepared."

I wince. Zack rarely loses his cool, so it's never good when he does.

"I know, I know. I screwed the pooch," I deflect with humor. "In my defense, it's hard to be on your A-game when experiencing a personal Niagara Falls."

Zack doesn't crack a smile. "This isn't a joke, Maddie. Those guys were ready to write us a check. I had a good feeling about them."

"I get it. I'm sorry. But let's hit pause on the verbal smackdown, yeah? I need a towel before I drown in my own hair."

I notice Zack's mouth tightening, but he nods. We make our way to the other side of his perfectly organized room. When we first moved in, we agreed that he'd take the largest bedroom so it could serve as both his personal space and an office.

"You know, this wouldn't be a problem if the guys didn't keep snatching my towels to crank one out in," I grumble as I head into Zack's pristine bathroom.

I grab one of his fluffy blue towels, marveling at how freakishly organized his toiletries are. Everything is lined up with military precision—toothbrush, toothpaste, floss, all arranged by height. It's like a serial killer's medicine cabinet.

As I emerge, Zack's waiting, arms crossed. "Well, if you had agreed to rent the bigger house with more bathrooms, you wouldn't have to deal with the, uh, towel borrowers."

I glare at him, but there's no real heat behind it. We both know why we're stuck in this cramped house with five people. Our company is hanging on by a thread, and every penny counts.

We've busted our asses and spent every last dime on this app, which means I'll keep on sharing space with the disgusting code monkeys and suffering their crunchy-ass towels.

Blech.

"You know, if this whole tech startup thing doesn't work out, you and Nora should go into business together doing holistic bathroom feng shui," I say, wrapping my hair in a towel. "Seriously, your Pinterest-level attention to detail is... kind of scary."

"It's called having standards," Zack quips. "You should try it sometime."

I plop down on his perfectly tucked-in comforter. "Alright, I made my bed, and now I'm lying in it. Tell me the ways I royally fucked up."

Zack sighs, rubbing his temples. "Maddie, we talked about this. When an investor asks you a question, and you're unsure how to answer, you should use the agreed-upon response."

Ugh. Not this again.

The "agreed-upon response" is Zack's way of idiot-proofing me. Because apparently, I'm a loose cannon who can't be trusted to speak freely.

"Yeah, yeah, I know," I mutter.

"Do you? Because I didn't hear you use it once in that meeting."

I say in my flattest, most sarcastic robot voice ever, "That's an interesting question. We would want our potential investors to have a say in that decision."

"I don't appreciate the tone, but exactly," Zack nods. "You're the one who wants to be seen as an equal co-CEO. So step up and act like it. Be professional."

I scoff. "Professional? Have you seen Zuckerberg? That guy is a legit freakazoid. Yet no one's trying to reform him."

"Zuckerberg is a billionaire. When you have a billion dollars, you can be full-on manic Maddie."

"Okay, Mr. Professional. What if, hypothetically, you were at an in-person meeting and accidentally zipped up your pubes before it started?"

Zack's eyebrows shoot up. "What are you talking about?"

"I'm saying, what if your short and curlies were being tugged on and ripped out, one by one, but you couldn't show any discomfort because it would be unprofessional?"

"Mads, I can say with absolute certainty that I would never find myself in that situation."

"But if you did," I press. "You're telling me you'd just sit there, stone-faced, while your man-hairs were being yanked out by the roots?"

Zack groans. "Yes, Maddie. If, by some insane twist of fate, I ended up in a meeting with my pubes caught in my zipper, I would keep a poker face. Because looking uncomfortable signals weakness. And weakness is the kiss of death with investors."

I burst out laughing. The image of Zack stoically enduring a zipper vs. pubes deathmatch is too much.

"I'm impressed, Mr. Pubes of Steel," I gasp between giggles. "Zack Hanley: unflappable in the face of testicular torment."

Zack cracks a smile and shakes his head. "You're impossible. You know that, right?"

"Part of my charm," I say breezily.

I ball up the damp towel and lob it at Zack's head. He catches it with a scowl.

"Hamper," he says, pointing to the wicker basket in the corner.

I make a big show of getting up, plucking the towel from his grasp, and dropping it in the hamper. "Happy now, clean freak?"

"Ecstatic," Zack deadpans.

"You know, studies show that creative badasses excel in chaos. A cluttered environment gets the wheels turning. It's science."

Zack snorts. "Oh, is that what we're calling it now? Science? I thought it was just, you know, run-of-the-mill laziness."

"I'm not lazy. I'm... selectively motivated." I say as I reclip my damp hair.

"Uh-huh. Sure." Zack glances at his watch and curses. "Shit. I gotta change. I have that press thing downtown, and then my date after—"

"Ooh, a date! Spill the deets! What lucky gal gets to hear your fascinating insights on Picard versus Kirk tonight?"

Zack gestures to his Star Trek: The Next Generation poster. "You know that Picard oozes dick swagger all over Kirk... wait! You know what I mean."

I giggle. "Oh man, she thinks she's snagged a suave businessman, but little does she know she's got a date with a huge dorkbag."

"I don't have high hopes for tonight. The girl seems nice, but kind of boring."

I gasp in faux horror. "Not nice! Anything but nice!"

"I'm serious. Nice is code for dull. No spark. Trust me on this one."

I make my way over to Zack's closet, flipping through the hangers. "Well, either way, you need my help. Then maybe, just maybe, you'll pass for a somewhat-cool dorkbag."

I pull out a couple of shirts and hold them up to Zack's chest. I settle on the royal blue button-down.

"This one. It'll make you look like the belle of the fucking ball," I tease.

Zack takes the shirt from me, grinning while giving his head a playful shake. "What would I do without you?"

"Crash and burn," I say sweetly. "Obviously."

Zack strips off his shirt and tosses it in the hamper. His toned abs and broad shoulders are on full display. Damn. The man is cut.

He catches me looking and smirks. Zack flexes theatrically, striking a ridiculous beefcake pose. "Like what you see?"

"Please. I've seen what dairy does to those chiseled abs. It ain't pretty. Cheese farts for days."

"My cheese farts are majestic, and you know it," Zack smirks as he buttons up his new shirt.

I mean, yes. Zack is a total banging hottie. It's no wonder women turn into horny little hoes around him. He's tall and muscular, with a strong jawline and a square chin. His short, messy brown hair, and facial scruff give him a chill vibe, while his polished wardrobe screams sex appeal. Combine that with his warm, inviting brown eyes and tanned skin; I'd have to be a fucking idiot not to see he's a total vag magnet.

But to me, he's always been... Zack.

My bestie.

My bro.

My confidant.

The dude who's seen me at my absolute worst and still sticks around.

We may bust each other's balls about my finicky family and his gas attacks, but our friendship runs deeper than that. Underneath all the jokes, there's trust, loyalty, and an unbreakable bond. Even when we want to strangle the shit out of each other.

So yeah, Zack's a total smoke show... like, damn. But that's not what I see when I look at him. I see the guy who has my back, even when I doubt myself. The man who puts up with my quirks and calls me out when I'm full of crap. My BFF, who loves me, flaws and all.

"We still need to chat about your little... wardrobe malfunction," Zack says, pointing to my chest.

I glance down and wince. "Ugh, seriously, don't rub it in," I mutter, stripping off my now-trashed button-down. "That was mortifying."

I straighten up, hands on my hips, wearing nothing but my navy sweatpants and old ratty tan bra. Zack raises an eyebrow.

"Gonna code with the guys like that tonight?" he quips.

"I haven't done laundry this week... okay, this month. Anyhoo, I'm hijacking a hoodie."

"Like hell you are," Zack grumbles, reaching past me to grab his Northwestern hoodie. "That's my favorite."

I snatch it out of his hands and dance away before he can take it back.

"Too slow, sucker!" I sing out, wriggling into the soft, worn fabric.

Zack sighs, allowing me my plunder. His eyes meet mine, suddenly serious. "Maddie, real talk. We need funding. Either dial up the charm, or in a few months, we'll all be living in this hoodie."

My gut clenches. "I'm sorry. You're right. I'll step it up, I promise."

Zack's stern expression melts into a smile. "I know you will." He eyes the hoodie, now engulfing my frame. "I'm expecting that back, clean and folded."

"Oh, Hanley. We both know that's never going to happen."

***

"HOW'D THE PITCH GO? Are we rich yet?"

Reid's head pops up from behind his monitor like a meerkat on high alert.

Zack shifts awkwardly. "Well, um, parts of it were solid, but uh—"

"Let me guess, Maddie shit the bed again," Cosmo interrupts, his voice flatter than his gym-honed abs.

Bless Zack's heart for trying to stand up for me. But the guys already know I'm a nightmare at pitching. I'm about as persuasive as a vegan trying to sell bacon-wrapped hot dogs.

Zack does a one-eighty, throwing me under the friggin' bus. "Maddie walked in dripping wet and rambling. It was like... ya know that girl from *The Ring?* She was like that, except way more terrifying. Pretty sure Maddie made at least one investor piss himself."

They all laugh. Of course Zack is going to drag me to look cool in front of the fellas. *Bros before co-CEOs, I guess.* But I don't mind; I can give as good as I get.

Wes gives me a sympathetic look. "It's okay, Mads, pitching just isn't your thing. Maybe Linda should take your place next time. She only opens her mouth when she's supposed to."

I laugh at his ridiculous blow-up doll and fire back, "It's Linda's damn fault I didn't have a towel. You did this, you plastic towel-hoarding skank."

Wes hugs Linda. "Don't listen to that cruel woman. Hurt people *hurt* people."

Reid puffs out his chest, always eager to stroke Zack's ego. "Bro-migo, I'm telling you, the next pitch is ours for the taking! Just two swole bros, slingin' dick and getting the job done."

I just can't with this guy, not today.

Reid constantly tries to be Zack's bestie. What Reid has failed to realize is that the position has already been filled—by yours fucking truly.

"Oh please, Reid. The only thing you know how to get done is jerking off to your own reflection."

The guys all *"ooh"* and laugh, and even Reid is busting up. "I gotta admit, that was a good one."

Cosmo snorts. "Gentlemen, let's agree. Maddie will out-dick Reid every day of the week."

I grin. "That's right; you're all damn lucky to be working with this genius and my metaphorical schlong!"

Beneath my snark, my stomach is actually tying itself into knots. I hate how much I suck at pitch meetings. One-on-one, I can banter with the best of them, but stick me in front of a crowd—with their judgmental gazes—I'd rather deep-throat a cactus.

Ain't nobody gonna deny that Zack's charm is freakin' magnetic in the spotlight. He's a natural-born hustler. The dude could sell dial-up internet to a Twitch streamer. And I'm totally cool with Zack stealing the show while I'm back here doing jazz hands like a failed theater kid with no lines.

In the shadows of my brain, though, those sneaky little whispers creep in. Zack's all like, 'Relax, Mads, it's just part of the game. Tons of meetings, blah blah blah.' But I can't help but feel like my screw-ups are gonna be what brings this whole thing down. What if my sucky public speaking is the kiss of death for LoveScore? If we can't get the moolah, it sure as hell isn't Zack's fault. So...

I plunk my butt down in the chair, eager to lose myself in the comforting embrace of code. Maybe if I fixate on the screen long enough, I can pretend my awkward striptease for the moneybags never happened.

The bros switch gears to a more pressing matter—bragging about their Friday night testosterone-fueled shenanigans.

"Well, Single-tons," Cosmo says smugly, "I've got a hot date tonight with my man."

"Nice!" Zack chimes in. "I've got an exciting date lined up for myself," he adds, then secretly shoots me a hilarious-as-hell worried grimace.

"Oh yeah? What's her name, Zack? And more importantly, is she DTF? Down to friend me on Instagram if you guys don't work out?" Reid asks, half-joking.

I snort. "Ha! I mean, seriously, Reid. Who'd pick you up after getting a taste of Zack? That's like going from a gourmet meal to a half-eaten bag of chips you found in the trash."

Reid playfully flips me the bird. "FYI, duderinos, Wes and I are scoping out a fresh joint in the city tonight. It's said to be the perfect spot for mingling with single, desperate ladies." He highlights his point with a dorky, yet amusing, little shimmy.

"Just please, for the love of God, don't bring them back here to bump uglies," I beg. "I do not need to hear you getting your freak on through the walls."

Wes nods solemnly. "Agreed. I don't want Linda to see me with another woman."

Reid turns to me, smirking. "What about you, Mads? Doing the usual... nothing?"

I give him my sweetest smile. "Oh, you mean busting my ass to make this company a success while you chucklefucks go off and play?"

It's not like I'm bitter about their social lives or anything... okay, maybe just a smidge. But let's be real, being a woman in tech is like trying to swim with sharks while wearing a meat suit. I've had to claw my way in and make serious sacrifices for just a fraction of the recognition those dudes get for showing up.

My entire existence revolves around LoveScore. Dating? Yeah, right. My personal life has been thrown in a blender, pureed, and then chugged down by this all-consuming dream.

And the messed up part? Even if we fail, the guys will be fine. Zack will just bounce back and charm his way into a cushy corporate gig. Cosmo, Wes, and Reid have the coding chops to score jobs anywhere.

But me? I'll be back to square one, busting my hump for some shitty salary in a cubicle dungeon. There are no second chances for female trailblazers in this industry. I have to create opportunities and find my path to the top. Nobody's looking at my cringe-worthy social skills and thinking, "Give that weirdo a chance."

So, if that means putting my entire life on hold, well, them's the breaks. I'll do whatever it takes for my company.

I watch the guys shrug into their jackets and head for the door.

"Don't forget your condoms, boys!" I call after them. "Wrap it before you tap it!"

"Thanks mom!" they sing.

And then there were two.

Zack hovers by my desk, his brow creased. "You good, Mads? I could easily cancel my date, come back, and hang with you. We could order Thai, watch some Star Trek. It would honestly be way more fun."

My heart clutches a little at his thoughtfulness, but there's no way in hell I'm going to cockblock Zack's search for his soulmate.

"I'm fine," I assure him breezily. "I've got a frozen dinner begging to be sprung from freezer jail. It's gonna be a wild night."

Zack's face scrunches up. "I hate that you stay cooped up here while we're out, letting loose. You deserve to kick back and have a good time, too."

I shrug, aiming for nonchalance. "Don't worry about me. I've got a thrilling evening of coding fixes ahead. Now go, have an awesome night. I want to hear all the juicy tea tomorrow."

Zack grins, snagging a handful of my popcorn from the oversized tin. "Alright, Mads, if you're sure. G'night."

"Night, Hanley," I reply, watching him walk away with a strange twinge in my chest.

Then silence.

Until my clacking keyboard echoes through the empty coding cave. I glance over at Linda, Wes's blow-up girlfriend, whose lifeless-ness suddenly feels unsettling.

"Looks like it's another wild night for us sexy-ass ladies," I mutter, throwing a kernel of popcorn in her mouth.

Ever the engaging conversationalist, Linda says nothing, and I realize I'm only talking to fill the oppressive quiet, drowning out the unwelcome thoughts that come when I'm alone.

This is the sacrifice. The grind. The unglamorous reality of chasing a dream bigger than yourself. I know in my bones that it'll be worth it. That every late night spent hunched over a keyboard, every passed-up party invite, every potential relationship left unexplored—it's all leading to something greater.

The odds are stacked against me—90% of software developers are men, for fuck's sake—but this is the fight I've chosen. Women need representation in STEM. We need a seat at the table, a voice in the room. And if I have to sacrifice my personal life, my social life, and any semblance of work-life balance to make that happen? So be it.

"Isn't that right, Linda? Us unstoppable ladies have to stick together!"

Linda, predictably, stares off into the void.

"Don't look at me like that," I say to her, narrowing my eyes, "I'm not alone."

I grab another fistful of popcorn, brushing the crumbs off Zack's old Northwestern hoodie. The soft fabric smells like him, like home, like comfort, and everything else I deny myself.

Sighing, I turn back to my computer, my fingers flying across the keys—the code blurs before my eyes, a tangled web of my own making.

But I'll untangle it. I'll make it work because that's what I do. That's who I am.

CHAPTER THREE

ZACK

"COME ON PUSSY" I shout as I sprint down the tree-lined Chicago street, the crisp morning air filling my lungs.

Maddie jogs up beside me, shooting me a glare that could castrate a lesser man. "Slow down, you crap sandwich. I haven't jogged in weeks."

We settle into a steady pace and I fill her in on yesterday's events. "So I had drinks with that reporter last night to get some press for LoveScore. It went well."

Maddie raises an eyebrow. "Great! And how was your date after? Did you kiss her or give her the Klingon Forehead Tap?"

"Neither. As predicted, she was mind-numbingly dull. I considered stabbing myself with a fork to end the misery."

Maddie's laughter fills my ears, and it's pure magic. Ever since we met, she's been my dream girl. In contrast, the girl from last night isn't even in the same solar system. Damn, Mads is adorable, even drenched in sweat. This view of her incredible body in her sports bra and leggings is a rare sight.

Usually, she conceals her beauty under her hoodies. It's not just her feminist ideals that make her mask her femininity, though. It's her ambition to be viewed as an equal, to be judged for her mind and not her looks. And I get it, I really do. She's put up with more than her fair share of creepy dudes in this industry; men who only see her as a pretty face with a nice ass.

Her smile would light up a room if she didn't always hide it behind a wall of sarcasm. As her friend, I get to experience the version of Mads with her guard down, not dulling her shine. I'm able to see this person who is beautiful, inside and out. She effortlessly leaves me in awe, and I'd have run screaming from the friend zone long ago if she hadn't made it clear that she'll only ever have bandwidth as friends, nothing more.

Thank God I've mastered the art of suppressing my feelings.

Sure, I still have the occasional dirty fantasy about her. I mean, come on. She's smoking hot, and I'm a guy. Do the math. You can't blame me, especially with her giant breasts bouncing around in that tight sports bra as we jog side by side. But hey, that's what compartmentalization is for, right?

"You should just give up on dating for good, like me," Maddie says between labored breaths. "Embrace the single life."

"Or maybe," I start, knowing I can get a rise out of her, "I should just marry your sister Nora."

Maddie starts cough-laughing. "Oh my God, I just pictured it. Your poor marriage counselor, listening to you two bicker about the proper way to store toilet paper and whether or not to alphabetize your spice cabinet."

This is one of the things that makes Maddie special. She's got zero filter. You always know where you stand with her. And through all life's ups and downs, she's always been there for me, my snarky, foul-mouthed guardian angel.

Like when I struggled to get through my MBA program, she stayed up all night quizzing me on financial concepts, fueled by nothing but coffee and pure stubbornness. Or when I went through that unfortunate frosted tips phase, and she dragged me to the salon to fix my hair, lecturing me the whole time about how chicks don't want to screw a guy who looks like a rejected member of *NSYNC.

But the moment that sticks out most in my mind is when my parents dropped the divorce bomb after thirty years of marriage. I was blindsided, gutted, and my whole world turned upside down. I holed up in my apartment for days, ignoring calls and texts from everyone—everyone except Maddie.

She showed up at my door armed with a take-no-shit attitude, ready to drag me out of my wallowing. She listened as I poured my heart out—I raged and cried—I questioned everything I thought I knew about love and family—while she kept up a steady stream of gut-busting stories that had me laughing through my tears.

And when it came time to clean out my childhood bedroom before my parents sold the house, Maddie was right there beside me, helping me sort through the memories and the pain, cracking jokes about my old Pokemon card collection and the unfortunate bowl cut I rocked in middle school. She held my hand as we visited Tootie's grave in the backyard, the silly pup who'd been my loyal childhood companion.

We're both huffing and puffing in a full jog now. Maddie's breathing has become more uneven and ragged, so I slow down slightly, hoping she doesn't notice.

When she invited me to team up and make her LoveScore app a reality, there was no way I could refuse. She needs me, even if she would never say it out loud. I've seen firsthand how hard it is for her to be a competitive woman in tech. Walking away from my corporate job was a no-brainer. Plus, having "co-CEO" on my resume is pretty sweet.

"Stop!" Maddie hunches over, her chest heaving as she gasps for air. She staggers to a nearby bench and collapses onto it dramatically. "My lungs are staging a mutiny."

I chuckle, plopping down beside her. "Wow, you are so out of shape."

"We can't all have your freaky cyborg stamina."

I wait for her to catch her breath. My gaze falls upon a group of people at the nearby dog park. "Roleplay, go!"

Maddie perks up instantly, her exhaustion forgotten. She zeroes in on a prissy-looking woman with a fluffy white poodle, putting on a snooty accent.

"Oh, Mr. Fluffington!" she trills. "Do hurry up. We mustn't be late for your anal gland surgery! Can't have you scooting your poop-ie tooshie at the gala, now can we?"

I stifle a laugh. Trust Maddie to go straight for the crude.

Not to be outdone, I spot a meathead with a bulldog, and I lower my voice to a caveman grunt. "Yo, Butch! Quit sniffing that poodle's ass! You're better than that. You're a purebred, goddammit!"

Maddie snorts out a giggle.

"Excuse you, sir! Keep your savage beast away from Mr. Fluffington's genitalia. We can't have any more scandals popping up on his Instagram account."

"He wishes," I scoff. "Butch here is a real dog. His balls are bigger than your mutt's whole body."

Maddie gasps, scandalized. "How dare you! Fluffington's balls are perfectly proportioned. In fact, the vet said they're the most symmetrical he's ever seen!"

That does it. I break. Laughter bursts out of me in a booming guffaw, startling a nearby Shih Tzu.

Maddie smacks my shoulder. "Zack! Stay in character!"

"Right, right." I take a deep breath, schooling my features. "No disrespect, lady, but your dog's symmetrical balls are small as hell. What you gotta do is buy them doggy ball implants I saw on Shark Tank. That'll take Fluffington's nad game to the next level."

She stares at me for a beat before collapsing into giggles. "Doggy ball implants? You're so messed up."

"Says the chick who led with anal gland surgery," I retort, setting her off again. "And hey, why aren't *you* staying in character?"

Maddie's phone dings repeatedly. "Time out!" She fishes the phone out of her sports bra *(seriously, how does she even fit it in there?)* and swipes to read the message.

I watch a rapid succession of texts flood the "sister text thread" on her screen.

Nora: *I was thinking we should have a theme for the party. How about famous couples throughout history? We could dress up!*

Abby: *Hell no.*

Sissy: *Hmm. A theme seems a bit much. We don't want to impose on the guests.*

"You should screw with them," I say, nudging Maddie. "Tell them you're down for a theme." She grins wickedly and starts typing.

Maddie: *Dungeons and Drag Queens. Dad in drag would be hilarious!*

Abby: *Fuck yeah. I change my vote.*

Nora: *Would I get to wear a medieval princess costume?*

Maddie: *Of course! Complete with one of those dildo princess hats.*

Sissy: *Can we please be serious?*

Abby: *I'm dead serious. I want to see Dad in drag.*

Maddie's sisters are a force of nature, a hurricane of hormones and hair products. Each one more extra than the last. But underneath all the bickering and sarcasm, these ladies would bury a body for each other.

I love Maddie's family like my own. Her mom, Cheryl, the formidable Denton matriarch, takes no shit and gives great hugs. Her dad, Jerry, and I bond over our mutual love of bad puns *(he's a master of the art form)*. And Sissy's twins Violet and Hazel—pint-sized agents of chaos—have me wrapped around their catsup-stained little fingers.

Being part of Maddie's family almost makes up for the dysfunction of my own. Almost.

Sissy: *I've got one. Seniors and Swingers.*

Nora: *Ew! Gross.*

Abby: *That's nasty.*

Sissy: *What... I thought we were all being funny?*

I snatch the phone out of Maddie's hands and take off running. "Come on, Mads!" I call over my shoulder. "Last one home has to give Linda a bath!"

Being Maddie's best friend is like being granted a wish to be near the most extraordinary person. The only problem... never being able to wish for more.

***

"YOU'RE A BADASS, ZACK. You're a fucking shark."

I stare into the rearview mirror of my Tesla Model 3, giving myself my usual pep talk. "You're gonna make LoveScore the next big thing. Nothing's gonna stop you."

I've been reciting this speech since Maddie and I started this crazy venture. I grab my golf clubs from the trunk, ready to schmooze, and swing my way to startup success.

See, all the big-shot CEOs seal deals out on the green. So, back in college, I learned to play. And not to brag, but I've gotten pretty damn good. It's just part of the gig, being in the CEO club.

Sure, LoveScore isn't a Fortune 500 company, but hey, it still counts. I'm a CEO! Maddie thinks it's ridiculous for our little start-up to shell out for a country club membership, but she doesn't get it. This is where handshake deals turn into big fat checks.

I stride up to the clubhouse at Platinum Greens, an oasis for rich tech bros and finance types. The fairways are much greener than our bank account, but not for long, not if I have anything to say about it.

Today, I'm golfing with Roland McBurney himself, CEO of McBurney Financial Group. This guy is a serious whale who could fund our overhead with a single check and not break a sweat. I spot him by the first tee and give him my most alpha handshake.

"Zack, good to see you," Roland says, his eyes crinkling in a grin. "I've been hearing great things about your business."

I puff up my chest, returning his smile. "Thank you, sir. That means a lot coming from you."

"And I see you're a fellow Northwestern MBA," he continues, nodding at my purple polo. "Good man."

I beam. "I can only hope to achieve half the career you've had, Mr. McBurney. You're a legend."

We hop into the golf cart and zip off to the first hole. Time to dazzle him with the LoveScore vision.

"So give me the pitch," Roland says, waving a hand. "What's all the buzz about?"

I launch into my schpiel. "Picture this: a dating app that lets users rate their dates like a Yelp review. How was the conversation? The chemistry? The restaurant? LoveScore is going to revolutionize online dating by adding accountability. No more catfishing. No more duds."

We pull up to the tee box, and Roland chuckles. "If my wife had rated our first date, I probably wouldn't be married right now."

He grabs his driver and takes a practice swing. "I was so damn nervous, I spilled gravy all down her dress at dinner." He shakes his head ruefully. "Take it from me, kid. Never order meatloaf on a first date."

I grin at his self-deprecating humor. Roland lines up his shot and crushes it, the ball soaring down the fairway.

"Interesting concept," he muses as we watch his ball land. "Dating has certainly changed since my day. It's all swipes and DMs now."

I nod eagerly. "Exactly, and Maddie, my brilliant Co-founder, is the one who cracked the code on this killer idea. She's got the smarts and the instincts to sense what's hot before it sizzles."

His eyes light up. "Tell you what. Why don't you two swing by the office later today and pitch it to my team? We've been looking to get into the dating app game for a while now, so this could be a good fit."

My heart leaps into my throat. This is it. Our big break. *Don't fuck it up, Zack.*

"Absolutely!" I say calmly, as if billionaire pitch meetings are an everyday thing for me. "I'll have my team set it up."

Never mind that my "team" is just me, myself, and Siri.

I line up my shot, riding high on adrenaline and premature visions of success. I'm about to show Roland that I'm not a peon selling a pipedream; I'm Zack Hanley, startup wunderkind.

I pull my club back, ready to drive this thing home, and then it hits me. Maddie...

Roland wants Maddie at the pitch. Anxiety knifes through my triumphant haze.

Mads, in all her unfiltered, smartass glory.

Maddie, who blurts out whatever pops into her chaotic brain.

Madeline, who is 100% going to tank this if I bring her.

I whiff the ball completely, nearly twisting my ankle as I swing. It dribbles sadly off the tee, mocking me.

Roland claps me on the shoulder, chuckling. "Let's hope the pitch goes better than that swing, eh?"

I force a weak laugh, my stomach churning. We're doomed.

***

I BURST INTO THE HOUSE, shopping bags in hand, my heart pounding. "Emergency all team meeting!" I yell to the guys. "Where's Maddie?"

Cosmo, Wes, and Reid all hold out a finger and point down the hall. "Shower," they chorus.

Not hesitating, I charge down the hall and burst into the bathroom. "Life-changing meeting. Happening now!"

Maddie yells from behind the shower curtain. "Are you freaking kidding me, Zack?"

"No time! Get out. Our future is on the line. Come on!" I order.

Minutes later, Maddie stands in front of us, dripping wet and once again wrapped in nothing but the bathroom rug. Her dark hair is plastered to her head, and fury flashes in her deep brown eyes. She looks like a pissed-off burrito—a sexy, pissed-off burrito.

"This better be fucking good," she growls. The rug slips a little, and I force my eyes back up.

"Oh, it is," I say, buzzing. "This morning, I had a meeting with Roland McBurney. I think we've found our Series A funding!"

The guys whoop and holler, exchanging high fives, except for Cosmo, who holds up a hand. "Not so fast. What details are you withholding?"

"Yeah, what's the problem?" Maddie grumbles. "I'm freezing my tits off here."

"Soo... Roland wants Maddie and me to pitch to his team of investors... at 5 o'clock today."

Cosmo, Wes, and Reid fall silent, then start walking back to their computers.

"Well, that was a nice dream while it lasted," Cosmo mutters.

"Hey!" I snap. "Have some faith. Maddie can do this. She just needs a little... finessing." I hold up the shopping bags. "Starting with wardrobe."

Ten minutes later, Maddie emerges from my room in a royal blue pantsuit. The guys see her and snicker.

"Holy shit," Wes says. "It's like Hillary Clinton and Jokey Smurf had a baby."

"I was thinking more Avatar," Reid muses. "Like if the Avatar got a soul-crushing office job."

Cosmo squints at her. "Nah, I'm getting Sonic the Hedgehog vibes. She's going to verbally spin dash her way through the pitch, leaving carnage in her wake."

"Guys, we're here to support Maddie's potential," I say sternly. "For God's sake, can't you suspend your disbelief for a second?" I encourage her with a smile. "Maddie, you're channeling a badass Blue Power Ranger right now."

That cracks everyone up, even Maddie.

"Fine, let's try option two."

Maddie disappears and returns in a tight, canary yellow dress. She tugs at the neckline. "I can barely breathe in this thing. No way I can sit down."

"Sweet Jesus," Wes breathes. "It's like Pikachu got a boob job."

"If Lisa Simpson and Big Bird had a baby," Cosmo agrees.

Reid snaps his fingers. "I'm getting sexy minion energy."

Maddie looks ready to murder them all. I take her arm and steer her into my room, away from the guy's laughter.

"Zack, I don't know," she hisses. "I feel like an idiot. I can't friggin' breathe, I can barely take a step without tripping. How the hell am I supposed to pitch in this SpongeBob straightjacket?"

I sigh. *So much for encouragement.*

Am I the only one who sees her rocking a Belle vibe from Beauty and the Beast? A woman who's smart, classy, and fully capable of handling whatever the world throws at her.

"Mads, no worries, we're just warming up," I assure her, feeling confident about the next outfit. I grab a lacy white push-up bra and hand it to her. "But, uh, you'll need to slip into this first."

Maddie's eyebrows shoot up as the underwire garment dangles between her fingers. "Seriously? Do you think this overpriced boob-hiker is gonna save the show? And my girls aren't that big."

"Your boobs are massive, Mads." I sigh, pinching the bridge of my nose. "We can't have the investors catching sight of your old raggedy bra through this thin white blouse."

"Oh, but I'm sure those crusty corporate dudes will be sporting their ancient tighty-whities and decades-old undershirts," she scoffs, arms crossed defiantly. "Hypocrisy at its corporate finest."

"We aren't going to solve sexist double standards in the workplace today. It's a messed-up situation, I agree. But if we want the money, we've got to play the game."

"Fine, I'll wear the contraption of patriarchy." Maddie groans, reaching for the zipper on her dress. "Now, help me out of this banana!"

When she finally emerges, the whole room falls silent. Then, the guys stand up and burst into uproarious applause.

Maddie exudes total boss energy in dark, high-waisted jeans that hug her curves. She flaunts a crisp white blouse tucked in and a fitted black blazer with rolled-up sleeves. Her typically messy hair is sleek and straight, and she's swapped her tortoiseshell glasses for bold purple frames that make her eyes pop.

"Whoa… you're a total knockout," I say, sounding a smidge too captivated. She is stunning, savvy, and sexy as hell.

"Alrighty, then," she says, busting out a lil twirl. "You think this kick-ass, 21st-century Cinderella can slay it?"

"Definitely," I say firmly. "Together, we're unstoppable."

Cosmo smirks. "If you let Zack do the yapping, we might just have a shot."

***

YOU'RE A TOTAL BOSS, ZACK. Focus on the endgame and crush it.

I'm psyching myself up as we wait in the McBurney Financial Group's lobby. This could be the most important meeting of our lives, and Maddie looks like she's moments away from a full-blown panic attack.

"Hey, Mads," I say lightly, "you okay over there? You're looking a little… moist."

"Never say that again," Maddie growls, shooting me a withering glare and fanning herself like a maniac. "I'm fine, Zack. Peachy freaking keen. It's just a little pitch, no biggie. Only our entire future. But hey, who the fuck needs a future?"

Maddie is a powerhouse most of the time, but if she's put in front of a crowd, it's her kryptonite. I slap on a smile, pretending she's not on the brink of self-destruction.

"I got your back," I say, touching her jittery knee. "You're gonna blow them away. Just show them the same excitement you had when you first pitched me this idea."

Maddie rocks back and forth as she mumbles, "I'm gonna tank this presentation so hard. I'm gonna ruin everything. I'm the fucking weakest link!"

Time to change tactics. When Maddie spirals into self-doubt like this, I know what to do.

Distract her.

"Roleplay, go!"

I point out a middle-aged guy in an expensive-looking suit standing nearby. Adopting a nasal voice, I say, "Oh man, this hemorrhoid cream is not doing the job today. I'll be doing Cirque du Soleil poses in my chair to get through this meeting."

Maddie grins, encouraging me to go bigger.

"You should see the swelling! My rectal area is out of control."

She snickers, the tension leaving her shoulders.

"I'm just one fart away from my whole anus falling out!"

Maddie bursts out laughing. Mission accomplished. But then I hear a sultry voice behind me.

"Sorry to hear about your anus."

I whirl around and find myself face-to-face with a gorgeous blonde bombshell. This girl is like Scarlett Johansson times ten in the hotness department. She's tall and curvy in all the right places. Her eyes are stunning sapphires, and her lips—red velvet cushions begging to be kissed.

Maddie lets out an undignified snort as I scramble to stand up straight, my face burning. "Uh, hi there," I stammer. "Um..."

"Hi, I'm Lexie," she says, extending a perfectly manicured hand. "I'm the investment analyst assigned to your pitch. I work closely with Roland."

"Zack, co-CEO of LoveScore," I say quickly, shaking her hand. Am I tripping, or did she let her fingers linger on mine for a sec? "It's great to meet you."

I'm so distracted by Lexie's smoking hotness that I forget to introduce Maddie. She clears her throat loudly, breaking the charged moment.

"Oh, and this is Maddie Denton, my co-CEO," I say, gesturing to Mads.

"And best friend," Maddie adds, giving Lexie a tight smile.

"Roland's told me about your company," Lexie says, her blue eyes twinkling. "I'm excited to hear your pitch."

I flash her my most charming grin. "We can't wait to show you our vision."

As Lexie leads us to the elevators, I can't resist checking out her perfect ass in that tight pencil skirt. Damn. "We'll meet in the main conference room on the top floor," she says with a flirty smile.

If this pitch doesn't work out, I will get her number. Win-win.

I close my eyes.

Cut it out, Hanley, get your head in the game!

A few minutes later, Maddie and I are standing at the head of a long conference table, surrounded by a sea of Armani suits. Behind us is a spellbinding panoramic view of the Chicago skyline. I take in the sleek room—all glass and chrome and achievement. This will be our company someday.

I glance at Maddie and give her a little wink. She smiles back weakly, and I see it. *Uh oh.*

There's a stringy chunk of something green in her front teeth.

Shit! Stupid deep dish pizza.

"You have some basil in your teeth," I whisper discreetly.

Roland strides into the room with power and authority. "Alright, let's see what you've got," he says, taking a seat at the head of the table.

I jump right in, pulling up our PowerPoint. "Introducing LoveScore," I say enthusiastically. "Never have a bad first date again!"

I glance over at Maddie. She's frantically running her tongue over her teeth, trying to dislodge the chunk of basil.

Oh fuck.

She's gonna blow it.

There's panic in her eyes.

I barrel on with my pitch, citing stats about online dating and target demographics, hoping to keep all eyes on me.

She holds a piece of paper up in front of her face, pretending to reference her notes, but I can see her picking at the basil with her finger. I nudge her foot, willing her to stop.

Maddie lowers the paper, but then she grabs a pen and starts fake-tapping it against her lips as I keep talking. With horror I realize she's trying to use the pen to dislodge the food. This is a disaster.

"Can I get my co-CEO a glass of water before she pitches the app interface?" I interject smoothly. Maddie plays along, clearing her throat.

I steer Maddie to the refreshment station in the corner. "You have to stop," I hiss under my breath as I pour her a glass. "You can do this."

Maddie nods and takes a big gulp. Then she flashes me a huge smile. "Did I get it?"

I hide my wince. There's still basil stuck between her teeth... and now her front teeth are tinged blue from the pen ink. But I can't let her confidence crumble. "You look perfect," I lie. "Now go kick some ass, Mads."

Maddie strides to the front of the room, smiling confidently as she projects the LoveScore interface onto the screen. And miracle of miracles, she's NAILING it. She walks through all the key features and differentiators like a pro.

Then Roland throws her a curveball. "So, is this a dating app or a social media platform?" he says, leaning back in his chair.

Oh fuck oh fuck oh fuck.

Maddie takes a deep breath and meets Roland's gaze.

"That's an interesting question," she says slowly. "We would want our potential investor to have a say in that decision."

Boom.

Mic drop.

I could kiss her.

The meeting wraps up, and Roland gives us a curt nod. "We'll be in touch depending on what we decide."

Everyone starts filing out, and Lexie corners me. "I think that went really well," she says, handing me her business card with a wink. "I'm your point person on this, so don't be a stranger."

The second we're alone in the elevator, I lift Maddie in a huge bear hug. "I'm so damn proud of you. We're taking the whole team out tonight to celebrate."

Maddie's beaming until she catches the reflection of her face in the elevator doors.

"You LIAR!" She smacks me on the chest, staring at the newly discovered blue stains on her teeth. "I look like a crackhead Smurf!"

"You're welcome. It worked, didn't it? Now, come on, Blue Man Group. I'm buying you a beer."

CHAPTER FOUR

ZACK

"A TOAST TO MADDIE for not screwing up."

I raise my beer, the amber liquid sloshing dangerously close to the rim.

Maddie deadpans, "Gee, thanks. I appreciate you all for barely believing in me."

Cosmo chimes in, dripping with sarcasm. "It's true, you exceeded our incredibly low expectations."

The Whispers and Whiskey Lounge is packed tonight, a sea of well-dressed techies nursing craft cocktails while bonding over start-up war stories. It's fun and chaotic, and it's just what we need to blow off some steam after the last few stressful weeks. Our table is by far the loudest.

"You're all a bunch of dildos," Maddie grouches while still clinking her glass to ours.

"But we're your dildos," Reid smirks. "Without us, you'd be a crazy coding hermit living in her bathrobe 24/7."

"Bathrobe? Please," Maddie retorts, rolling her eyes. "We've established I'm more of a bathroom-rug-as-a-towel kinda gal,"

Wes snickers. "I should get Linda a bathrobe. Her nips get cold when I take her out of the washing machine. Ya know, for her, not me."

Maddie playfully smacks Wes on the arm.

"Seriously, guys, Maddie crushed it today," I say, laying my hand on her shoulder. "She was witty, well-spoken, and she won over the whole room."

The guys nod in agreement, and she lights up.

"If we do get the money, it'll only be because Zack eye-fucked the hot investor chick into submission," Maddie jokes, arching her eyebrows flirtatiously.

"I didn't eye-bang Lexie!"

"Oh please, we've all seen your eye-fucking game. It's amazing," Reid laughs. "Hell, I'd let you eye-fuck me, and I'm straight."

"I second that, and I'm gay," Cosmo deadpans. "Ocular intercourse from you would be both arousing and intimidating."

The entire table explodes in laughter, and despite my embarrassment, I join in.

"Ha ha," I deadpan. "I may be ready to roll on this deal with Lexie's firm, but for the record, I won't be making any moves on her. You guys know that I'm a stickler for business ethics."

I pause, letting a sly grin spread across my face. "But after we secure that sweet, sweet funding? You better believe I'll be asking her out. And we'll be giving each other a lot more than just glances."

Reid gives me a high five.

"Which means if we don't get the money, it's because Zack's not packing enough heat," Maddie chuckles.

I scoff. "Whatever. I always bring the heat. I could score with any chick in this joint."

"Except me," Maddie smirks.

"Ugh, enough shit-talking," Cosmo groans. "It's time to get shit-faced!"

Reid glances around the bar. "I thought your boyfriend was coming tonight."

"Yeah, Cosmo, where's your secret lover?" Wes needles.

Cosmo levels them with an icy glare. "You will never meet him. You'll never know his name. Do not seek him out online, and this part is important—do not fuck with me. It will never happen."

Wes taps the table, a playful smile on his face. "Knew it! Cosmo's boyfriend is a Russian spy."

"Or a time traveler from the future, here to prevent a robot uprising," Reid adds.

Cosmo throws up his hands in exasperation and stalks off, muttering, "Let it go."

Wes and Reid have been on a months-long mission to uncover the identity of his mysterious partner. It's become their strange and amusing little game, playing amateur sleuths lacking both experience and success.

I turn my attention back to the knuckleheads. "You two players have your own love lives, right? You can't hide behind your computer screens tonight, so what's your plan?"

"Oooh yes, pecker jockeys, you talk a big game. Let's see it," Maddie says gleefully. She scans the dimly lit bar, pointing out two women chatting by the front window—a leggy blonde and a fiery redhead. "Try and flirt with them. I dare you."

Reid puffs out his chest, not one to back down from a challenge. "Watch how it's done, you lip-flappin' sad sacks. I suggest you take notes." He and Wes saunter off, leaving Maddie and I alone.

Maddie looks spectacular tonight. I want to tell her how attractive she is, but I know she'll only brush it off or make things awkward.

"Time for another round," Maddie announces. "This one's on me!"

As she struts up to the bar, hips swaying with that trademark confidence, I can't tear my eyes off her.

In the decade I've known Maddie, she's never once had a serious boyfriend, just like she vowed back in college. A casual hookup or one-night stand now and then to scratch the itch? Sure. But the only constant man in her life is me. Other guys shoot their shot, crash and burn, and get sent packing. Just like this jerkoff at the bar in the too-snug polo.

I watch Frat Boy's fake smile as he attempts to win Maddie over. She angles herself away, her lips pursed in a clenched expression as she waits for Mr. Polo Dick to take the hint and back off. A protective instinct hits me hard, despite knowing Maddie has many scathing remarks locked and loaded.

She's the most important person in my life, and caring for her has become second nature to me—whether she's technically mine or not.

Fueled by chivalry and one too many IPAs, I slide off my stool and go to her. I drape an arm around Maddie's shoulders and turn to the polo-wearing tool. "Hey baby cakes, who's this guy?"

Maddie instantly gets the hint, snuggling up to my side and batting her eyelashes at me. "Well, sugar dick, this is Gavin. Gavin, meet my boyfriend, Zack."

Gavin's face falls, but he recovers quickly. "Sorry, man, didn't realize she was taken. Can't blame me, though—your girl is smoking hot."

"Oh, I'm well aware," I say, kissing Maddie's forehead. "I wake up to this stunning, brilliant ray of sunshine every day."

A genuine smile lights up Maddie's face. She doesn't deflect the compliment or make a self-deprecating joke for once.

Gavin, gracious in defeat, offers to buy us a round. Before I can accept, Maddie's phone lights up with a FaceTime request.

"Hi, Abigail," Maddie smiles. Her sister's face, all smoky eyes and glossy lips, fills the screen. She's wearing a skintight hot pink dress.

"You're at a bar? On a Friday night?" Abby gasps in mock horror. "Blink twice if you've been kidnapped."

Maddie rolls her eyes. "Ha ha, very funny. What's up?"

Abby responds with an exaggerated pout, batting those heavily mascaraed lashes in an obvious play for sympathy. "My douche of a date stood me up; I need you sis. No way am I going out to a concert alone. Come through for me!" She pauses for dramatic effect. "Heartland Haze is performing at this tiny little dive bar on the Pier tonight at 1 a.m."

Gavin, shamelessly eavesdropping, leans into the frame. "Heartland Haze? I love that band!"

Abby's eyes zero in on the fresh meat, her mouth quickly curling into a predatory little smirk. Her voice drops to a sultry purr. "Heyyy, what's good, hottie? I'm Abby—Maddie's lil sis and the ultimate party starter. What's your name?"

"Gavin," he replies, instantly interested. "Can I just fucking say, you look fire in that dress."

Maddie passes her phone to him, then "finger guns" her brains out behind Gavin's back as the two exchange flirtatious banter.

"Be there in fifteen, Abby," Gavin says, handing Maddie back her phone. "Thanks for the hookup!"

I turn to Maddie and grin. "Looks like Abby scores again! Guess you're stuck with me."

Mads bumps her hip into mine. "I mean, there are worse fates a girl could suffer. Like being mauled by Gavin's Old Spice deodorant."

I wrap an arm around her shoulders and give her a reassuring squeeze. "You know me, I'm always here for you. If you want, I can keep roleplaying as the overprotective alpha male, and you can hang on my shoulder as my ride-or-die bitch."

"Thanks for the offer, but no," she says, grinning. "And if you refer to me as bitch again, I'm kicking you in the nuts."

"Noted."

We're still laughing when my phone buzzes with an unknown number. I answer, my voice rising in pitch when I hear Lexie's honeyed tones. "Lexie, hi! Let me just go outside where it's quieter."

I clamp my hand over the mic and turn to Maddie; my eyes widen. "It's Lexie."

Maddie starts making over-the-top kissy faces. I swat at her, trying to fend off her childish antics while straining to hear over the bar noise.

"Zack, you're fine. I'll make this quick," Lexie trills, her voice bubbling. "I couldn't wait 'til Monday to share the good news. Roland and the team loved your pitch. We think this app is groundbreaking. It's going to transform the dating scene. The firm wants to invest..."

I hold my breath, crossing my fingers and toes.

"Ten million dollars?" I exclaim so loudly that Maddie spits her drink all over my shirt. I'm too stunned to care. I'm seeing visions of LoveScore going viral, our scrappy startup rivaling the likes of Tinder and Bumble.

But then Lexie's voice turns serious. "There's one condition."

I hear it, and my heart plummets. I lock eyes with Maddie as Lexie outlines the unforeseen stipulation attached to this transformative sum of money. My mind is on fire.

How the hell am I going to deliver this bombshell news to Maddie... and what will she say when I do?

***

"THERE'S NO FUCKING WAY!" Maddie yells, her voice echoing through the coding cave at LoveScore HQ.

"Come on, guys. Launching the app in six weeks is a good thing!" I say with a confident smile.

The team needs to see the bright side of the investment firm's demands. Of course they want us to debut at the AppVerge Expo, the biggest tech convention in the country. The hottest new apps and gadgets are announced there, so landing a keynote spot to introduce LoveScore to the world is a dream come true. This has to happen. *If only my genius coders could see the potential.*

"You're all insanely talented. We can pull this off," I say, more upbeat than usual.

Cosmo snorts. "Spoken like a true corporate suit."

Maddie leans back in her chair and sighs. "You can't be serious? We're busting our balls to get this app out in six months. Six weeks? Come on, we're still knee-deep in debugging the core algorithm."

"Not to mention we don't have nearly enough user data to train it properly," Cosmo adds smugly.

An idea hits me. "Then let's pay for a focus group."

"Zack, dating apps like this aren't built on a single focus group," Maddie explains patiently. "We're talking about a dozen different groups and hundreds of personalized interviews."

Reid leans back in his chair. "Which ain't cheap, man. We need hundreds of thousands of dollars."

The realization sinks in, twisting my stomach. "Money we don't have," I admit, rubbing my temples as the headache kicks in.

"Zack, it's like this. The algorithm needs a shit-ton of data from a fuckload of random people to work out compatibility ratings," Wes pipes up. He gestures to his expressionless girlfriend propped in the corner. "Linda's face says it all. Impossible."

They're right, which pisses me off even more. I've been busting my ass with charming investors and perfecting pitches while they're obliviously glued to their screens coding. Sometimes it feels like we're from different planets on opposite sides of the galaxy.

"Look, guys, I know the first date rating system is our golden goose," I say, on edge. "But without funding, we're dead in the water. We've got to find a solution."

Maddie's eyes flash with frustration. "The algorithm is the freaking heart of LoveScore—the secret sauce that sets us apart from every other dating app. And it *requires* a diverse enough pool of user data to train it. Without that, it's basically a steaming pile of dookie."

I throw out one last Hail Mary. "What about doing a soft launch? Release a beta version, get some early adopters on board providing feedback—"

Cosmo cuts me off. "You get one shot at a first impression. If we put out a half-baked turd, we'll get crucified. Game over."

"He's right," Maddie says, shaking her head. "Shitty reviews would tank the whole thing before it even has a chance."

Slumping in my seat, I stare in defeat at the scribbled equations covering the walls, the stacks of takeout containers, and the piles of energy drinks. We're so close I can taste the triumph, but the ten million dollars will slip through our fingers if we don't agree to McBurney Financial's impossible terms.

I pray that somehow, someway, the code gods decide to smile down upon us. Because right now? We need a miracle.

***

MADDIE CUDDLES UP TO ME on the couch, dozing off on my shoulder.

The crook of my neck is like a custom-made pillow for Maddie's head. I love how she relaxes and is simply herself around me; it's like we're two parts of a whole that fit together perfectly. She gives our shared blanket a little tug as she snuggles in. She's a squirmer.

Our living room is a total disaster area, a metaphor for our lives. A hodgepodge of secondhand furniture has produced a chaotic mess of faded fabric and lumpy pillows. Maddie and I are sprawled out on the least uncomfortable cushions of the bunch, watching an episode of Star Trek: The Next Generation.

Maddie's wearing my Northwestern hoodie, the sleeves flopping over her hands. Her pajama pants have llamas. That's Maddie for you—brilliant, driven, and unafraid to rock some llama pajamas.

The guys conked out hours ago, but Mads was determined to keep going. She's hoping for a eureka moment to save LoveScore, but even her stubbornly genius mind is coming up short. On the TV, Captain Picard faces down a swarm of Borg, his bald head gleaming with righteousness.

"You know what I just realized?" I say, nodding at the TV. "Picard is like the ultimate example of never giving up, no matter how impossible the situation seems."

Maddie lets out a huge yawn. "I'm not giving up, just rebooting my brain box." She cozies in closer, hogging the blanket. "Resistance is futile."

I tug it back, trying not to get distracted by her body pressed against mine. I attempt to downplay the way she feels... and smells.

"As your number one, I'm here to advise you."

"Number two is what we'll be stepping in if this app tanks," Maddie sighs, her warm breath tickling my neck. "You don't fully grasp what you're asking. Even if we work 24/7 for the next six weeks, pulling this off is almost freaking impossible."

My eyes light up. "Almost? You said almost. I heard it! So it is possible?"

"I'm saying *you're* impossible," Maddie groans. "And I'm too exhausted to argue against your toxic positivity."

She squirms again, burrowing into my side and cocooning herself in the fabric. I try to pull some over me, but she holds it tight.

"Share the blanket, or I swear I'll let one rip right here," I joke.

Maddie wrinkles her nose in disgust and reluctantly untucks a tiny corner.

She yawns again, her eyelids drooping. "I'm too tired to walk to my room," she mumbles.

My eyes drift over Maddie's face, taking in her messy hair and the dark circles under her eyes. Even worn out and wrapped in a ratty blanket, she's so damn beautiful. Being with Maddie feels like home. She's 100% real with me, no filters. And I get to be myself around her. Well, except for the whole secretly-in-love-with-her thing. Those feelings stay locked away where they belong.

Maddie's phone beeps with a text alert. She groans, fumbling for the device.

"Who's messaging you at this ridiculous hour?" I ask.

"Abby, of course, thanking me for setting her up. Apparently, the blind date was a hit—five stars."

Maddie's eyes widen, and she bolts upright. "Jerk nards! That's it! We can contact people we've previously dated and get them to complete the surveys!"

I frown, thinking it over. "Maddie, no offense, but do you have a lengthy list of exes I don't know about?"

She waves me off. "Nah, but my sisters do. And there's you and the guys. I bet between us, we can scrape together enough data to make this thing a go."

A grin spreads across my face. "Mads, you're a genius. A crazy, sleep-deprived genius."

Maddie sits back down and stretches her arms wide. The movement causes her hoodie to ride up slightly, exposing a strip of smooth skin. I force myself to look away, focusing intently on a mysterious stain on the couch cushion.

Maddie declares. "And as a reward for my brilliance, I'm claiming the blanket. All of it." She quickly retreats under the fabric.

"Hey!" I protest, shivering slightly. "I'm freezing my nuts off!"

Maddie smirks. "Should have thought of that before you mocked my dating history."

God, how I desperately wanted to drift off to sleep with Maddie's warm body cuddled against mine. But I know better. Getting too cozy and letting myself slip into that fantasy is dangerous. Mads is oblivious to the very real, very overpowering feelings I've been harboring for her, and I intend to keep it that way.

If I tell her the truth, there's no happy ending. If she knew my heart, she'd be hurt, betrayed, and probably disgusted that I've been lusting after her this whole time. My honesty would mean losing my best friend forever.

So, I'm gonna stick with my two-part game plan: burying my messy tangle of emotions and unrequited desires while amping up my go-getter attitude.

Starting tomorrow, LoveScore's success will be the only thing I'm chasing, but tonight—just for a moment—I'll allow myself to get lost in the most perfect of dreams, imagining myself being truly, completely loved by her.

CHAPTER FIVE

MADDIE

"THAT WAS A HUGE-ASS WASTE OF TIME."

I collapse into my chair with a groan, surveying the pitiful stack of completed first-date surveys scattered across the table. The entire team looks beat, and don't even get me started on the stench. This place reeks like a jockstrap banged a dumpster behind a 7-Eleven.

Cosmo's rocking his daily dose of sarcasm, a T-shirt that reads, "I put the 'Pro' in procrastinate." And then there's Wes, a lava lamp come to life in his neon orange paisley shirt matched with—wait for it—plaid pants. It's like he got dressed after a bender at a My Little Brony convention.

Zack and Reid have somehow stayed impeccably put-together, while I, Maddie, the coder bridge troll, showcase my signature look: a stained hoodie, bird's nest bun, and chic "haven't slept in three days" under-eye bags. Suck it, fashion world.

Saturday was jam-packed with contacting exes and begging them to fill out our surveys. Oh, the delight of texting, emailing, and awkwardly coaxing past flings to rate our tragic dating skills. I even roped my sisters Nora and Abby into this insanity. So, how many completed surveys did we manage to scrape together after this herculean effort? Drumroll, please... a whopping fourteen. Nowhere near enough.

Zack snatches up one of his reviews. "Now, here's a satisfied customer! Five stars all around for yours truly. 'Zack was charismatic, attentive, and oh-so-dreamy. The perfect gentleman.' Oh wait, there's more... 'Until he ghosted me like a spineless fuckboy. I hope his dick shrivels up like a raisin.'"

The guys crack up laughing while Zack's ears turn an amusing shade of pink. I join in with a little chuckle. *Sue me.*

"Find something funny, Mads?" Zack asks, grabbing one of my measly two surveys. "Let's see what Tanner from Bumble had to say about you."

I shoot him a warning glare, which he ignores.

"'Maddie talked about work. The. Entire. Time. I felt like I was being interviewed for a shitty data entry job, not dating a female human. Two stars instead of one because she's got big tits.'"

The guys snicker as I scowl. "Yeah, yeah, yuk it up jerk stains."

Naturally, Zack's a hit with the ladies—I've been his wing-woman more times than I can count and seen him lay on the charm—all smooth-talking and active-listening—but later on, when it's just us, he'll pick apart every little flaw.

Over the past ten years of our BFF-ship, I've seen a never-ending catwalk of women trying to snag a piece of his heart and a spot on his mattress. Zack will romance 'em with fancy dinners, whisper all the right sugar-coated lines, and maybe, just maybe, they'll stick around for a month.

Sometimes, I wonder if I'm to blame for Zack's perpetual bachelor status. He and I, we're like PB and effing J, stuck together like glue since college. We're each other's number one, a package deal, and there's no breaking us apart. Some of the women he's dated have freaked out about our friendship, like they're competing with me for his time and affection.

There was one girl in particular, Dana, who I thought was the "one" for him. Perceptive and pretty, those two had sparks flyin' like the Fourth of July. But then she issued an ultimatum—Maddie or me—and he chose me. As effed up as it is, that gave me a twisted little thrill.

Don't get me wrong. I don't resent Zack's love life or wanna hog him to myself. I'm well aware of the white picket fence fantasy dancing in his head—the dutiful wifey, the 2.5 kiddos, the damn golden retriever fetching his loafers.

Logically, I'm prepared for it.

When that fateful day arrives, I'll deal. I'll squeeze into some ugly-ass bridesmaid dress, fake a smile through my tears, and watch him promise eternity to someone else.

The idea of losing Zack—watching him create a life without me—was not something I dwelled on, at least not until a few days ago—not until Zack met Lexie. The way he looked at her—he was hypnotized—it was like he could drop to one knee right then and there and put a ring on it. *WTF is this crazy, intense energy between them?*

More importantly, why do I care? I'm incapable of being jealous with Zack, because that's not really our relationship. So this queasy, icky feeling in the pit of my stomach is new, and I'm not a fan.

Cosmo scans the stack of papers and smirks. "I see a review here for Wes..." He clears his throat and reads in exaggerated falsetto. "'Crooked wiener, made me gag. Too much tongue, tasted like stale

Cheetos. Farted while orgasming. Two thumbs down. Sincerely, Linda.'"

The room explodes in laughter as Wes sneers. Wes turns to Linda. "Sweetheart, I thought my wiener curves were our little secret!"

Reid giggles. "Bro, your dick is so bent, it could double as a lock-picking tool!"

"Okay, zip it, cockweasels," I interject. "Let's cut the crap and focus. Bottom line—we're nowhere close to having enough data."

Zack chimes in, "I'm no coding guru, but couldn't we just buy some third-party user data and fill in the gaps after we launch?"

I want to smack my forehead in exasperation. I adore the hell outta Zack, but sometimes his naivete about the technicals makes me bonkers.

"Zack, it's not just users' profile information we need. It's the af-ter-first-date feedback. No other company has that kind of firsthand data for sale. It doesn't freaking exist, which is why it's the secret sauce of our matching algorithm."

Reid stands up, grabbing a Hulk and Princess Leia action figure off the shelf. *Oh boy, here we go...*

"Imagine Hulk and Leia going on a date, okay? But Hulk's got major roid rage, all pissed-off in traffic. Then later he's ready to Hulk Smash a slow-ass waiter into a ficus, you feel me? Not exactly a panty-dropping first impression."

I bite back a groan as Reid continues.

"But Leia's a classy broad who has no interest in dating that toxic masculinity bullshit. LoveScore is the only app that could have warned her—could've saved her from getting green-dicked."

Cosmo sneers, "Reid, you're a bona fide dweeb. But I'll begrudgingly admit your explanation was straightforward and concise. Four and half stars."

He turns to Zack, ticking off on his fingers. "We need ratings on the core factors: compatibility, chemistry, conversation, and overall impressions. The more data on people's quirks and how the dates went down, the smarter the algorithm. Better algorithm means better dates."

Reid concludes, "Suddenly, a take-charge woman like Leia sees that a well-endowed Thor is a much better match."

Wes knocks the Hulk aside, straddling the Thor figure onto Leia while adding all-too-real kissing sounds. The lovemaking scene looks as painful as Wes' Thor impression as he bellows, "Get ready to see my big hammer, Leia, cause now I'm gonna lay-ya!"

Thankfully, Wes's simulated sex moans are drowned out by the groans of the group.

"The point is," I say, focusing on the somber reality, "no first-date-feedback data, no functioning algorithm, no LoveScore."

Zack's shoulders slouch, the gravity of our situation finally penetrating his titanium shield of denial. "So exactly how many of these surveys do we need to be expo-ready in six weeks?"

"A thousand... a hundred at minimum," Cosmo replies flatly.

Zack blanches, "A thousand? In six weeks?! We barely scraped together fourteen!"

"Now he gets it," I mutter.

Cosmo throws up his hands in defeat. "I'm calling it. LoveScore time of death, 4:32 p.m."

Ever the bro, Reid claps a sympathetic hand on Zack's shoulder. "It's all good, man. Bright side—no more 'conflict of interest.' Now you're free to bang that hot investor chick!"

The mere mention of Lexie makes my eye go twitchy. "Banging our heads against the wall clearly isn't working, so let's take a break, and maybe it'll shake some ideas loose."

I observe the squatter's paradise we're living in. "On second thought, let's make this place look a bit less like the inside of a used condom, yeah? Maybe then our brains will shower us with sublime intervention."

I can't say it out loud, but Cosmo's right—we're majorly effed. I've got nothing left in the idea department to save LoveScore. Our dream is slipping away.

I push down the panic that's doing the freaking cha-cha in my chest, grab a garbage bag, and start furiously cleaning up the junk on the table as if tidying this mess will magically fix the dumpster fire we've made of this company.

There's got to be some kind of solution hiding in plain sight. Because I refuse to let LoveScore—the awkward love child of our blood, sweat, and carpal tunnel—come to an end.

***

OUR KITCHEN LOOKS LIKE A POST-APOCALYPTIC WASTELAND.

Dishes piled high in the sink, strange odors wafting from the fridge, and enough leftover pizza boxes to build a fort. It's time to go full-on psycho den mom.

"Alright, peeps, listen up," I announce, hands on my hips. "Reid, you're on dish duty. Wes, do the counters and floor. Cosmo, you're tackling trash and clearing out the fridge."

Reid pipes up, crossing his arms. "Who died and made you queen of the chore chart?"

"I did, butt nugget," I say, shutting them down. "This place is a biohazard. There's some funky-ass shit breeding in this sink that would make a scientist crap their pants."

Cosmo gags as he begins the horrifying task of cleaning out the fridge, unearthing fossilized takeout containers and unidentifiable lumps wrapped in foil.

"It's like the Addams Family's crypt in here!" he exclaims. "I wouldn't be surprised if I found a severed head next to that expired yogurt."

"Even the Addams Family wouldn't consider this food," Reid chimes in, poking at a container filled with a mysterious substance.

Cosmo holds up a shriveled, blackened object. "What the hell is this? Voldemort's turd?"

Wes studies it. "Pretty sure that's an apple, dude. Or it was."

The humor is a welcome distraction, but it doesn't last long as my eyes drift to Zack, his handsome face scrunched in concentration as he jots down ideas on the whiteboard.

With a heavy sigh, I approach him and read his ideas out loud, "Sell my car to raise money for focus groups. Ask dad for a loan."

I snatch his dry-erase marker. "I appreciate how committed you are, but I could never ask you to put more money into this venture."

Zack turns to face me, his brown eyes filled with emotion. "Maddie, I—."

"90% of startups fail," I remind him gently. "You and your dad aren't on the best of terms, so it means a lot that you'd even consider asking him for money. But I will not have you jeopardize your financial future for me."

"Mads, I dropped the ball. I'm sorry."

"Are you kidding? I scoff, placing a hand on his muscular forearm. "You've gone above and beyond. It's incredible that you got someone to offer us ten million dollars. I'm fucking amazed by you."

Zack shrugs, a small smile tugging at his lips. "I guess. I just... I want this to succeed so badly. For you. For both of us."

I wave my hand at the surrounding chaos. "Stop and take a look at this shitshow. Does this scream 'smart investment'? One peek at Linda and those suits and their money would hightail it out of here."

Zack's jaw tightens. "I've been crunching the numbers. The rate we're burning through cash..." He hesitates. "Either we get funding soon, or it's over."

A sense of dread washes over me. I knew things were unraveling, but hearing it out loud makes it real.

Tears prick at the corners of my eyes. I blink them back. I refuse to let Zack see me cry, even if it feels like my heart is being put through a freaking wood chipper. All those late nights, the endless lines of code, the sacrifices we've made—*what was it all for?*

"Zack," my voice cracks. "No matter how this whole clusterfucked situation shakes out... I'll always be thankful that you believed in me."

Before I can blink, he pulls me into one of his signature hugs—the kind where his strong arms wrap so tightly around me that I instantly feel protected, even as my world crashes down. We cling to each other, my head buried in his chest as he soothes me with gentle strokes of my hair.

For a moment, I wish we could stop time.

Stay in this comforting embrace.

Pretend there's no disaster waiting for us.

Too soon, I pull away with a heavy sigh, breaking our intense connection. "Enough with the mushy crap, Hanley," I mutter, swiping at my treacherously damp eyes.

I look over at the brogrammers, who are in the thick of yet another pointless squabble—this time over the "correct way to load a dishwasher." Wes is sword-fighting with a spatula, while Reid, the self-proclaimed expert, is yapping Cosmo's ear off about the wonders of rinse aid.

My hysterical, frustrating man-toddlers.

I motion to the kitchen and say, "I know what'll cheer us up. Let's roleplay. Who do you wanna be?"

Then it hits me. "Holy fuckballs! I know how we can get the data!"

***

"ALRIGHT, PISS MONKEYS, PAY ATTENTION, I'll say this one more time."

I throw my arms in the air, completely fed up. I'm this close to slapping the stupidity off their faces. Seriously, how can these big-brained nerds be so clueless?

I've got action figures lined up on the table in front of me. I grab Wonder Woman and Iron Man and start explaining, "Zack and I are gonna roleplay as different characters and act out a bunch of dating situations."

Cosmo snatches up Luke Skywalker and Lara Croft. "So you want us to create fake profiles and date scenarios? Then you two jokers actually go out and pretend to be those made-up people on legit dates?" He pauses, thinking it through.

Wes adds, "After the date, you fill out the surveys for the algorithm?"

"Ding, ding, ding, yes, that's right!" I do a little shimmy. "The fake dates will give us the random, unbiased feedback we need."

Cosmo gives a considering nod. "You know, that batshit crazy idea just might work."

"We'd go on allll the dates! Coffee dates, hiking dates, whatever basic date scenario you can think of. That way, we can properly evaluate the person's behavior and rate the overall experience." I nudge Zack. "You know, important stuff like—did they put their elbows on the table?"

"Did they overshare personal information," Zack adds.

"Did they viciously double-dip?" I gasp in mock horror.

"Did they floss while still eating?" He chuckles.

"That was one time, Zack!" I protest. "But yes! All the dirty deets!"

Wes arches one eyebrow. "No disrespect, Mads, but you know how to date?"

Reid adds, "You're not exactly what dudes envision as their ultimate arm candy. I'm not sure you can pull off the whole 'smokin' hot fantasy chick.'"

Oh, this dickchunk just signed himself up for a master class in *Maddie Proving You Wrong.*

Watch and learn, boys.

A switch flips. I whip off my glasses and chuck them to the side, morphing into a new persona— transforming plain ol' Maddie into a seductive temptress—I prowl over to Zack.

Beneath my lashes, I shoot him a smoldering look and drape myself over his chair; my body molding to his. Leaning in close, my voice goes all breathy and bedroom-y. "Well, helloooo there, handsome. Fuck, you're even hotter in person."

I lazily trace a finger along his arm, feeling the heat of his skin beneath my touch. "I've been fantasizing about your panty-melting smile, all... week... long." Slow and deliberate, I slither my way around to face him head-on, my lower lip trapped in a gentle bite, my hands skimming over the muscles hiding under his shirt.

Then, *BAM!* I straddle his lap like I was born to be there, fisting my hand in his hair and tilting his face up to meet mine. "I'm so fucking excited for our date. I've been wet with anticipation all day, if you know what I mean." My voice is pure sin, dripping with promise.

I hold Zack's gaze, his eyes darkening with a hunger I've not seen before. I don't break character, though, 'cause I never back down from a challenge. I stroke his chiseled cheek with the back of my hand, the gesture both tender and sensual. "In fact, let's skip dinner tonight so I can be your dessert."

We're so close I can feel Zack's breath tickling my lips, and suddenly, I'm consumed by this overwhelming, desperate need to lean in and claim his mouth with my own.

"Point made!" Reid yelps, grabbing his keyboard to hide the growing situation in his pants.

I quickly scramble off Zack's lap, clearing my throat awkwardly and putting on my glasses. "Let that be a lesson to you, gentlemen, never mansplain what I can and can't do."

Wes tentatively raises his hand. "Uh, so you two aren't like, worried about going on all these dates and accidentally falling in love?"

I bark a laugh. "Yeah, right. Zack and I have managed to avoid catching feelings for over a decade. We're good." I look at Zack, but he's purposely avoiding eye contact with me.

Finally, Zack meets my eyes, and his entire demeanor shifts. He flashes me a big, goofy smile and jokes, "I'm already in love with that hot blonde, remember?"

My teeth clench at the thought of Lexie, but I promptly dismiss it, sensing Zack's reservations.

"Mads, isn't it a bit... unethical to train the algorithm on fake data?" he asks carefully.

I sigh. Leave it to Mr. Boy Scout to be the moral compass. "It's slightly unethical," I concede. "But we're only using it to train the algorithm until launch. Once we get real user data, we will delete all the fake date info." I give him my most convincing smile. "I promise. It's just to get the infrastructure in place. Fake it 'til you make it, right?"

Zack doesn't look entirely convinced, but he nods reluctantly. I'll take it.

"Even if you two go on multiple dates every single day, it still won't be enough data," Cosmo points out skeptically.

"I've got it!" Wes jumps out of his chair with excitement. "I'll create a website with sample surveys and questionnaires. I can close the data gaps by tapping into my extensive chat room network."

I quip, "Translation, Wes will round up the eccentric crew and we'll represent the more mainstream people in society."

"I'm happy to step in and take on some of Maddie's coding responsibilities," Reid offers. "That way, she'll have more bandwidth to concentrate on dates. Besides, it's no secret that I'm the fastest coder here."

With a theatrical groan, Cosmo playfully tosses a crumpled ball of paper at Reid.

Zack frowns. "Mads, when will you have time to sleep?"

"I'll squeeze in some shut-eye here and there, and if I need a boost, I'll just hook myself up to an espresso IV! Hell, I'll raid Abby's stash of magic pills to keep me in the game or knock me out cold!" I stand tall. "I'm all in on launching this app in six weeks and securing that funding."

Zack meets my gaze, searching for something. "You promise we'll delete all the fake user data after launch?"

"Cross my foul-mouthed heart," I vow solemnly.

A slow grin spreads across Zack's face. "All in favor of launching LoveScore in six weeks or die of exhaustion trying?" he asks, raising his hand.

I lift my hand excitedly, flashing a grin at Zack.

Cosmo smirks, "I was waiting for you all to realize we can do this. I'll easily finish the backend and security in six weeks. I'm in."

"Count Linda and me in," Wes chimes in, raising Linda's hand alongside his own.

Reid snickers. "I'm down, but we've got to level up our coffee game."

With all eyes on Zack, he flashes a cocky smile. "Oh, I'm definitely on board, but make no mistake, I'll be the real MVP of this operation. I have to romance the un-romance-able, Mads."

The guys burst into laughter as I poke Zack in the ribs. "Get ready for some scathing reviews, Mr. Perfect First Date," I tease.

Let the fake dates begin.

CHAPTER SIX

ZACK

I JOLT AWAKE FROM THE WETTEST OF WET DREAMS.

Nah, not just a dream—a mind-blowing, vivid-as-hell fantasy—overloading my brain. My heart's rumbling like a racecar, roaring at breakneck speeds inside my rib cage.

I squeeze my eyes shut, but Maddie's still there. Gloriously laid bare and sprawled out—her body curving in sinful invitation—as my hips roll over hers again and again, and she exhales my name like a desperate plea... *Yes, Zack.*

Damn. I've been all kinds of wrecked since Maddie's little *seductress* show yesterday. The way she nibbled on her lip—those smoldering looks beneath her lashes—the heat from her fingers as she drew invisible maps on my chest. Maddie wanted to prove she could charm the pants off any guy. Well, vision... er, mission accomplished.

I groan softly, pressing a pillow over my face as if it'll erase the X-rated highlight reel in my head. How can I not obsess over the way her hungry core rubbed shamelessly against my aching...

Snap out of it, Zack!

She's your BFF.

Your business sidekick.

The girl you swore was hands-off.

Yet I still sense the ghostly warmth of her breath brushing against my lips yesterday. I wanted to lunge forward and claim her mouth with mine, to satisfy a burning curiosity that I've locked down for years.

I imagine losing myself in her soft, velvety heat, letting my deprived fingers roam over the hidden curves of her body while we share hot, open-mouthed kisses...

Enough! Cold shower, stat.

The icy water jolts me to reality. It figures this would go down now, right as we start this crazy-ass scheme of fake dating and forced intimacy. Six weeks of suggestive glances, phony sparks, and teasing touches loaded with empty, filthy promises.

How the heck did Maddie talk me into this? I've spent over a decade fortifying these ironclad friend zone walls around her. But one pouty look of possibility and I'm setting detonation charges on every barrier I've built.

I need to bury these off-limit cravings, and protect our friendship at all costs.

But goddamn, those lips...

***

"JESUS TITS! IS THAT THE JAVA JUGGERNAUT 3000?" Reid lets out an actual squeal, crushing me in a bear hug. "Zack, you gorgeous devil, I could kiss you!"

"You're welcome, but," I wheeze, "personal space, Reid, remember?"

Reid lets go apologetically, then tears into the packaging like a rabid wolverine.

After my frigid shower last night, I laced up my sneakers and hit the pavement. Before I knew it, I found myself standing in the fluorescent aisles of a 24-hour Walmart. Remembering Reid's plea for better coffee, I splurged on the fanciest, most expensive machine they had.

I admire the hell out of these guys for their commitment to our crazy dream. The next six weeks require intense, nonstop coding, which means my non-techy ass is pretty much useless.

We gather in the kitchen, waiting for Maddie to show up. Reid is a zealous preacher on his soapbox, lecturing Cosmo and Wes about his prized Java Juggernaut 3000.

"Guys, seriously, this is not a toy," he says, his voice laced with an air of superiority. "It's a feat of engineering brilliance, a work of art."

"Yes, brewmaster general, we mere mortals shallst not invadeth your caffeine cathedral," Cosmo mocks.

Reid replies, "I mean it, no touching! I am the only one qualified to operate this baby. Keep your greasy meat flaps off the intricate buttons."

"Sorry I'm late!" Maddie says, bursting through the front door with several bulging garbage bags. "I raided my sisters' closets for my roleplay characters. Nora was way too enthusiastic about helping."

My heart sings at the sound of her voice, but I avert my gaze, pretending to be engrossed in my phone. "Sounds good. Just sending off a quick email. I borrowed some clothes from the guys, so I'm all set."

I sense Maddie staring but fight the urge to make eye contact.

Cosmo claps his hands. "Great, let's go over the ground rules before we dive crotch-first into this mad science experiment."

He explains that we'll each get two profiles for our dates—a basic one we can both see and a detailed secret one for our eyes only.

"The secret one has all the extremely messed up stuff," Reid says gleefully. "Things you lie about to get that initial date—criminal records, secret spouses, alien abductions, you name it."

Wes nods knowingly. "It's like a behind-the-scenes look at all the red flags you ignore when your little general is in command."

Maddie slow claps. "Wes, if you could somehow capture your charm in a bottle, you could sell that shit to desperate guys everywhere."

"Well said, Mads," I chuckle, briefly locking eyes with her. She flashes me a smile, and warmth spreads through my body.

Cosmo explains that they've mined data from social media to create the most common personality profiles. "We got your basics—introverts, extroverts, shut-ins, attention whores. But we got your niche markets too—disco yoga freaks, breatharians, guys who are weirdly into horses."

"Green card hunters," Wes says, getting a quizzical look from the group. "I know, it's hard to believe, but I once showed up to a first date at the courthouse. What I thought was 'love at first sight' the immigration office called 'marriage fraud.'"

I pat Wes on the shoulder, "A little advice... stick with Linda."

As if I should be giving love advice.

After last night, I've enacted Code Red on any fantasies with Maddie. I've promised myself I'd maintain a professional distance, regardless of how captivating she is on these pretend dates.

Maddie is right back where she belongs... in buddy jail.

"Children, can we focus?" Cosmo groans. "The success of LoveScore hinges on you two fully embracing your roles, so no half-hearted crap like Reid's Tinder dates."

"Hey! I've never half-assed anything in my life," Reid protests. "I whole ass my dates... I mean, I put my entire ass into my dates... NO—"

"Definitely using that against you later," Wes says. "But now, lovebirds, it's time to get ready for your first date."

"Hold on to your panties, Mads, because this guy is about to work his magic and leave you begging for more," I say with a wink.

"In your wet dreams, Hanley," she smirks.

If she only knew...

***

```
<!DOCTYPE html>
<h1>User Profile</h1>
</div>
```

NAME: Derek Dorkinson

AGE: 30

OCCUPATION: Professional Nerd Herder (IT Technician)

INTERESTS: Board games. Comic books. Did I mention comic books?

ABOUT ME: When I'm not rescuing lost data or battling the blue screen of death, you can find me exploring the

LATEST SCI-FI CONVENTION, GEEKING OUT OVER CLASSIC VIDEO GAMES, OR PERFECTING MY CHEWBACCA IMPRESSION. YES, I CAN DO A MEAN WOOKIEE GROWL! IF YOU'RE UP FOR LAUGHS, OBSCURE TRIVIA, AND THE OCCASIONAL LIGHTSABER DUEL (I PROMISE NOT TO LOSE A HAND), LET'S GO ON AN ADVENTURE TOGETHER!
</div>

<h1>User Profile</h1>
NAME: DIAMOND MCJUGGS
AGE: 27
OCCUPATION: PROFESSIONAL JUGGLER (YES, REALLY!)
INTERESTS: BALLS OF ALL SHAPES AND SIZES. BALLOONS. RUBBER CHICKENS.
ABOUT ME: I'M YOUR NOT-SO-AVERAGE GIRL NEXT DOOR WITH A TALENT FOR JUGGLING BALLS (BOTH LITERAL AND METAPHORICAL). WHETHER JUGGLING FLAMING BATONS OR JUGGLING DEADLINES AT MY DAY JOB (YES, I HAVE ONE OF THOSE, TOO), I'VE GOT IT COVERED. I'VE BEEN DESCRIBED AS A DIAMOND IN THE ROUGH—SPARKLY AND A LITTLE ROUGH AROUND THE EDGES. IF YOU'RE LOOKING FOR SOMEONE WHO CAN JUGGLE YOUR HEARTSTRINGS, SWIPE RIGHT AND SEE IF WE CAN ENTERTAIN EACH OTHER!
</div>

<h1>Date Information</h1>
DETAILS: BREAKFAST AT "THE SYRUP SHACK."
</body> </html>

BEING EARLY IS BUILT INTO MY DNA.

I'm all about showing up first. I arrive at the greasy diner and spot a sweet booth by the window. I instantly claim it because I get a sick view of the street, plus it's right by the door in case I need a quick getaway. This may be a first date, but it's not my first rodeo.

As I scan the menu, this place transports me back to the first 'not-a-real-date' Maddie and I had in college. I remember the raw fun of getting to know each other, and of course, Maddie's infectious laughter. A goofy smile springs across my face, which pairs perfectly with the clown clothes that Wes lent me.

A rubber duckie button-down shirt with neon orange plaid pants is an unholy combination no adult should wear, but I'm committed to my character, Derek Dorkinson, IT Tech extraordinaire.

I'll never forget Maddie's eyes lighting up when we first played her silly role-play game. Now, it could be the key to scoring millions in funding for our startup. *Go figure!*

That night, we talked and laughed for hours, and it hit me like a freight train carrying a cargo of *holy crap, I'm an idiot*—I wasn't just crushing on Maddie, I was head-over-heels, can't-eat-can't-sleep, in-the-end-zone-of-the-Super-Bowl kind of in love with her. But just as I was ready to tattoo her name on my ass, she drop-kicked my dreams into the friend zone.

It's been a decade, and Maddie has never wavered in prioritizing her career over love. "I'm still convinced that opting for friendship with her was the way to go, even if it means constantly keeping my heart in check."

"Are you Derek?" a sultry voice purrs beside me.

My gaze travels up endless legs encased in shimmery fishnets, over dangerously feminine hips and a microscopic neon pink dress that's painted on. Then my eyes land on the face of... Maddie?!

But not Mads as I've ever seen her. This Maddie is a showstopping vixen with crimson lips, smoky eyes, and tumbling curls straight out of a strip club.

She smirks, clearly aware of the effect she's having. "Well? Are you?"

I gulp, "Uh... y-yeah. Derek, hi... Derek Dorkinson," I say, shaking her hand... and shaking... still shaking.

Let go of her hand, Dorkinson!

With a dazzling smile, Maddie slides into the booth opposite me. "I'm Diamond McJuggs," she says with an exaggerated wink. "It's a thrill to see you in the flesh, handsome."

Diamond McJuggs? Reid's grimy fingerprints are all over this. That perv better cool it with the porn star names, *or else.*

Maddie leans her impressive chest in, grabbing a menu, and my eyes whimper. The glimpse down her shirt, surreal and sublime, has me making direct boob-to-eye contact with her ample, black-laced cleavage. All the blood leaves my head and rushes southward.

"So Derek, you're in IT, huh?" Her impossibly sultry voice is doing insane things to my body. "I bet you're like me... naturally gifted with your hands."

She emphasizes her point by dragging one sharp fingernail down my arm, leaving a trail of fire in its wake.

Calm down, dude. You are seeing major sideboob right now, but you cannot take the bait!

Shifting in my seat, I plaster on a goofy grin. "Yup, that's me. Good with the hands. Real... handsy, I mean handy."

Nice save, genius. You deserve a trophy: "Most Intelligible Reaction from a Guy with a Boner the size of the Washington Monument."

My fingers are twitching. The urge to touch her is too much. I'm fantasizing about feeling the weight of those incredible breasts in my hands. I can *not* believe how badly she's turning me on.

"You look... I mean, you're... wow." *Shit. Did I just say that out loud?*

She throws her head back with a wicked laugh that makes my traitorous dick jump. "Well, sugar, I have a reputation for making jaws drop and eyes pop."

Mercifully, our food arrives before I can continue making an idiot out of myself. Maddie starts fork-and-knifing some sort of gooey cinnamon roll monstrosity with velvet frosting, and then I see... a stack of pancakes topped with... pickle slices?

Huh, that's weird. I don't remember ordering th—

Oh, right. The whole 'being a gross eater' is part of my character's backstory. This'll definitely help me with Operation: Dong Deflator.

I dive into my meal with gusto, smearing syrup all over my face. With each bite, I let out a symphony of obnoxious gulps and lip-smacking sounds. Maddie watches in disgust as I chug an entire cup of egg yolk through a straw, then douse my pancakes in soy sauce and yellow mustard.

"So, you're like, a juggler or whatever?" I mumble through a mouthful of partially-chewed food.

Her brow furrows in revulsion. *Progress!*

With a sly grin, she grabs a pickle off my plate. "I don't know what it is about pickles, but they're just like dicks."

My jaw drops as she deepthroats the pickle in one gulp. If this is just an act, she's performing it a *liiiiiittle* too convincingly.

"Honey, I'd love nothing more than to give you a private show," she says in a breathy whisper. "You know... juggle your balls."

The little minx has to go and run her foot up the inseam of my jeans.

In a panic, I jostle the table, knocking over my water glass. I scramble out of the booth. "I just remembered I've got this... thing!" I yell, fumbling through my pockets. "Here, this should cover it!"

Throwing a crumpled wad of cash onto the table, I make a hasty retreat toward the door, tripping over my own feet as I flee the diner, rock-hard boner and all.

***

I STORM INTO THE DINING ROOM. Maddie is hot on my heels, her chest doing some impressive bouncing and heaving in that skintight pink number. The guys mindlessly peck at their keyboards.

"Diamond McJuggs? Maddie shouts. What kind of demented MANtasy was that?"

Their heads snap up in unison, eyes immediately drawn to the physics-defying amount of cleavage smuggled into Maddie's dress. Reid can't help himself—he gives her a full-body once-over, tongue lolling out like a dog.

He smirks, gesturing towards her chest. "I'd say the name fits."

As I resist the urge to bludgeon his horny eyes out, Wes pipes up, "If the app investment craps out, Maddie can bring in the cash with OnlyFans."

I'm boiling with rage.

Maddie lets out a frustrated groan, grabbing a baggy hoodie off her chair and quickly covering up. As Wes and Reid let out disappointed whines, I breathe a sigh of relief. With her tempting assets under wraps, focusing on the problem is much easier.

"Listen up, peckerheads!" I bark out. "We're supposed to be doing normal, run-of-the-mill dating scenarios. That... was basically porn!"

"I shit you not," Wes says. "I went on a real date with a juggler named Diamond McJuggs."

"Wes, what in the abject fuckery are you talking about?" Cosmo asks. "Even for you, that's weird."

I add. "Yeah, what kind of sketchy-ass meat-market dating apps are you using?"

Cosmo waves me off. "Zack, I'll double-check their work from here on out. No more wasting time—you two fill out these dating surveys, then get changed for the next scenario."

Maddie plops down at her laptop station, and I follow suit, pulling up the official Post-Date Survey. I'm kinda curious—and kinda terrified—about the dirt Maddie's already spilling for my 'Derek Dorkinson' persona. I'm really, really hoping she hasn't caught on to the fact that my mind's been going to some pretty R-rated places when I look at her.

"Finished," Maddie mutters, heading for the hallway to shed her scandalous outfit. Her hips hypnotize me as she walks, and I'm not the only one staring at that tight dress clinging to her lush tushie.

"Last look, boys, There goes Diamond McJuggs!" Reid hoots.

I'm gonna punch him in the dick.

I groan, dragging both hands down my face. The image of her in that dress has been seared into my brain. At this rate, I'd better schedule two frigid showers a day, or I'm gonna spontaneously combust.

I close my eyes and picture Maddie... bent over that diner table, the dress barely covering her luscious, jiggling backside as I crowd in behind her. I slide off her thin straps as she turns to me, wantonly with a coy smile.

It's official: my overactive dick has taken my brain hostage.

CHAPTER SEVEN

ZACK

"MY LEGS ARE JELLO... FUCK THIS RUN... I'M DONE!" Maddie groans dramatically, collapsing onto the pavement.

"You know, the first step to getting in shape... is admitting you're out of shape," I chuckle, stopping beside her. "Doing more cardio would be good for you." I take her hand, helping her sit up on the curb.

"Why do I let you talk me into this shit?" Maddie pants, her face a cute shade of pink. "I'm a coder with zero desire to be fit. Just give me a sec to catch my breath—or puke—whichever comes first."

"Okay, Fast and Furious. Take a breath." I plop beside her, our thighs pressing together.

With Cosmo's oversight, the guys dialed back the over-the-top sexual characters like 'Diamond McJuggs'. It's been a week of fun, low-key dates—I've pretended to be a hotel manager and a video editor while Maddie's been playing various roles like school teacher and veterinarian. We've explored much of Chicago, hitting up new hole-in-the-wall spots and doing more touristy stuff like the zoo and that silly mini golf place downtown.

But at this moment, I'm enjoying hanging out with Maddie instead of her different personas.

She sits up and leans her head against my shoulder, taking a long swig from her water bottle. "Any minute now," she stammers.

"No rush. I'll wait until you're ready."

We're not even halfway through this wacky experiment, and it kills me to see her so tired. I'm not about to say anything, though, because she's a hard-headed firecracker, and if I suggest pumping the brakes, she'll only crank up the intensity to prove me wrong.

So while she stays laser-focused, I've been stepping up, helping do various unnoticed tasks. She's powering through late-night coding marathons, and I'm making sure she has clean towels and clothes, a stockpile of her go-to junk food, and plenty of chilled energy drinks.

And, uh... I may have washed her old, ratty bra. But only because it was dirty, I swear! There's nothing weird about a dude washing his best friend's bra. Nope, nothing to read into that at all.

"So, which of these dates has been the most Zack-esque?" Maddie blurts suddenly.

"What do you mean?"

"You've never broken down your flirting game," she explains. "It's like you only want to share the worst of the worst with me. I never hear about the good dates."

"Seriously? We've definitely discussed this already."

"Nope," she says, shaking her head. "Over the years, I've seen chicks throw themselves at you like your penis can do magic tricks. But after this week of 'dating sprees'... I don't know, you're pretty... meh." She wrinkles her nose.

I straighten up indignantly. "Meh? You think I'm meh?"

"You're nice," she amends. "Pleasant. Punctual. But I dunno. I thought you'd be more... wooing? You know, romantic and shit."

A grin tugs at the corner of my mouth. "If it was really me dating you, not these personas, then yeah... you would've felt the romance."

"Ooh, are you saying I haven't been Zacked to the max yet?"

"I'm not wasting my best moves on fake dates."

"Date moves are inherently cheesy."

"How would you know?" I challenge. "You've been on more dates this last week than your entire adult life."

"Rude. True, but rude." Maddie fires back, tilting her head cockily. "Then again, that's because the dudes you're pretending to be are as basic as the ones I've been dodging. You've confirmed what I already know—dating is a cringefest."

My smile falters at her dismissive scorn. Holding her stare, I drop my voice. "My moves are anything but cringe-worthy."

"So confident." she counters smugly. "Then show me some of these moves."

"Let's just say I've toned things way down for our dates and drop it."

Maddie playfully walks her fingers onto my shoulder, pricking up the hairs on my arm. "Seems like Lil Zacky is scared to show me his secret moves?" she mocks. "Come on, Hanley, give me a taste. Is it paying extra for the guacamole? You smoking hot studmuffin."

She's dramatically overperforming and I have no complaints, especially when she purrs my name, "Oh, Zack. Don't look at me like that... with your raw, sexual energy. Your gaze is lighting a fire between my thighs. Oh my God, it's consuming me." She runs her hands over her curves like a sexy little cat in heat.

Of course Maddie would mock the raw, animalistic lust of another person—having never experienced the intoxicating rush—never known the attraction between two people that's so damn palpable it's a drug.

She can't fathom the addictive power of a touch, a look, a whispered word at the right moment.

"Okay, let's dial it back," I mutter, trying to shut it down before things get weird. *Well, weirder.*

But Maddie's in full swing now, really hamming it up. "Zack Hanley, your touch makes me want to rip my clothes off," she says, grabbing my hand and then recoiling like it's burning her. "I can't handle it; if you touch me again, I'll lose control and ravish you right here on the table, on top of this bowl of chips and salsa!"

I roll my eyes, but secretly, I'm loving this. She grabs my hand again, placing it on her thigh. "Oh, sweet Jesus!" she cries out, over-acting like a B-movie actress. "Don't stop, I'm almost there!"

Her moans intensify, getting more explicit by the second as she gropes her tits and throws her head back in mock ecstasy.

Sarcastic or not, my jaw clenches at the seductive thought, desire surging through me. God, I'd love to pin her down, exactly like my dream, and ride her into the night. Her vivacious hips bucking against mine, as her inner muscles cling to me tightly. I watch her moaning mouth and long to take possession of her soft lips. I'm ready to devour every sassy syllable that's spilling out, letting her feel how much I fucking want her until she's dizzy and clinging and—

STOP! I grit out internally, squeezing my eyes to shut off the vivid fantasy. This is Maddie—there's no road to even go down with her. She has no idea what she's doing to you. I need to pull the plug ASAP. If I act impulsively, the only thing I'll be kissing, is our friendship goodbye.

But as I consider Maddie dismissing my skills with women, picturing me as some hopeless loser, using cheesy pickup lines, it's humiliating. And it pisses me the fuck off, as if I'm the one who put us in the friend zone. Fueled by arousal and my competitive streak, the blood in my veins roars to life.

Don't do it, Hanley. Don't you dare—

I inch closer to Maddie, my eyes darkening with smoldering intensity as I lock them onto hers.

"I don't waste time with insincere flirtations. I only pursue women who fascinate me," I rumble, letting the words roll off my tongue in an alluring tone.

Maddie blinks up at me, sensing the tension in my voice. "Okay, so hypothetically... show me the moves you would use... if I was such a lady?"

Move carefully, Hanley. Dangerous territory ahead.

I slide nearer, gliding my fingertips along the delicate line of her jaw. Her lashes flutter, and she shivers slightly, her body giving her away as she tries to maintain her sarcastic demeanor.

"That's the thing, Mads. It's not about lines or moves," I say softly, my face inches from hers. "It's about connection. When I'm into a woman, it's because she's the complete package—beautiful, sure, but also intelligent and fierce. An equal."

Trailing my fingers down the pale column of her throat, I relish the way her pulse quickens beneath my touch. "And when I meet an extraordinary woman like that... one who sets me on fire..."

Maddie swallows hard, her chest rising and falling quickly. My fingers trace her collarbone, and she makes a small, desperate noise that turns me reckless.

"When it comes to a woman that captivating, I don't need corny lines," I say, my voice thick with desire. "I just lay it all out there. Her body pulls at me like a magnet, and I respond with every heated glance, every possessive caress…"

Unable to resist, I cup her face reverently, tilting it to mine. "She can feel how badly I want her in the burning sensation of my fingers on her skin. She knows she's an addiction I can't kick… that I crave every delicious inch of her…"

Maddie meets my blazing stare, her lips parting in a trembling sigh. "And if she wanted you to… would you kiss her?"

"I'd pull her against me… trace the seam of her lips with my thumb… then claim her mouth with my own," I rasp, my voice raw with want. "I'd pour every ounce of pent-up longing into that kiss, branding her with my desire. The world would fall away until nothing existed but her, me, and the electricity surging between us. I'd kiss her until she understood, bone-deep, that she was mine. That I was ruined for anyone else."

The charged moment lingers. Part of me aches to close the space, to finally taste her luscious mouth. But I can't… I won't cross that line, not without her consent. With tremendous willpower, I tear my gaze away and force a chuckle. "So yeah, unless the girl is really something special, no kiss on the first date."

Maddie's hazy eyes snap to attention, and she clears her throat with a sly grin. "Sorry, Hanley, but I'm not buying it. You didn't kiss Diamond McJuggs, and she definitely caught your attention," she teases, pointing to my groin.

"That's because my dick has a sixth sense for trouble," I say with a laugh.

I spring to my feet and extend my hand. "Come on, Mads. We should go get ready for the next round of dates. Plus, I did you a solid. You've got some fresh towels waiting for you at home."

She accepts my hand, and I help her up. She surprises me with a powerful hug. "You did my laundry? Zack, you're the best!"

My arms wrap around her instinctively in an all-consuming embrace. I whisper softly, "Anything for you, Mads."

Looks like I'm due for another round of ice water therapy.

***

```
<!DOCTYPE html>
<h1>User Profile</h1>
</div>
NAME: Shane Miller
AGE: 35
OCCUPATION: Risk Analyst
INTERESTS: Reading. Financial Planning. Silence.
ABOUT ME: I enjoy analyzing data trends, playing chess,
and delving into thought-provoking books. I value
intellectual discourse and seek a partner who's risk-averse
and will prioritize goals over frivolous pursuits.
</div>
```

<h1>User Profile</h1>
NAME: Allison Anderson
AGE: 33
OCCUPATION: Corporate Lawyer
INTERESTS: Reading. Running. Yoga.
ABOUT ME: In both my career and personal life, I believe in setting goals and working hard to achieve them. On our first date, I'll ask questions to see if 1) we share similar values and 2) if we have a shared life vision. If you're not afraid of a woman who knows what she wants, let's chat and see if we click.
</div>

<h1>Date Information</h1>
DETAILS: Afternoon coffee at "The Perky Cup."
</body>
</html>

"COFFEE FOR SHANE DRILLED HER," the barista barks out as she sets my cup on the counter. I laugh at the name faux pas and hope it's a good omen. The Perky Cup is a cozy coffee shop with hipster vibes, bright colors, and mismatched furniture. I spot Maddie at a corner table, scowling at a yellow legal pad like it's a hostile witness. She's rocking a pencil skirt and tight blouse that screams "corporate shark"—a far cry from her usual hoodie and sweats attire.

"Allison Anderson, I presume?" I say, sliding into the seat across from her.

She extends a hand, her grip firm enough to crush bones. "And you must be Shane Miller. Iced coffee, no creamer? How... practical." She makes a note on her pad. "So, Shane, what are your long-term career goals?"

I clear my throat. *Is this a date or a job interview?* "I'm a risk analyst now, but I'd like to get into Fintech eventually. Might launch an investment firm of my own..." I trail off as she tsks and scribbles furiously.

"Speculative income potential. No definitive plan," she mutters. "Not ideal."

I laugh internally. This must be what it's like to date Nora, Maddie's notoriously picky sister. *No wonder all the guys run for the hills.*

"And how do you envision your career supporting a family?"

"Kids?" I splutter, eyes widening. "Wow, you move fast..."

She stares me down, unblinking. "I'd like two children, possibly three if we have the resources. My fertility window is closing, and I need to know if you're a viable candidate for procreation."

"Procre—what now?" I stammer. "Lady, I just met you. How about we begin with favorite movies and work our way up to baby making?"

Again she tsks, writing rapidly on her notepad. "Evasive. Immature. Not a promising debut."

"Whoa, slow down. Here's a... less intense topic. What's your favorite color?"

She sighs heavily. "Fine. Blue. Now, back to the important questions. What's your family medical history? Do you have any genetically inherited conditions?"

"Uh, well, my grandpa had a long, weird middle toe, but I'm pretty sure that's not fatal."

She makes a note, frowning. "Flippant attitude towards health. Concerning." She rattles off a series of rapid-fire questions, from my retirement plans to my criminal record.

I hold up my hands in surrender. "Okay, time out. This feels like an interrogation. Can't we just, I don't know, have a normal conversation?"

"Hmm, you mean small talk, as in superficial, meaningless exchanges that dominate our society and don't determine long-term compatibility? No, we can not." She slides her legal pad across the table. "As you can see, you've failed to meet several key criteria on my checklist. This is not going to work out."

I shrug, taking a sip of my coffee. Checklist or not, it's clear that Shane Miller is *not* going to drill her.

***

```
<!DOCTYPE html>
<h1>User Profile</h1>
</div>
```

NAME: KYLE JOHNSON

AGE: 34

OCCUPATION: HIGH SCHOOL FOOTBALL COACH

INTERESTS: FOOTBALL. FANTASY FOOTBALL. GRILLING.

ABOUT ME: I'VE GOT LOVE FOR THE GAME BOTH ON AND OFF THE FIELD. WHEN I'M NOT COACHING, YOU CAN FIND ME GLUED

TO THE TV, WATCHING FOOTBALL HIGHLIGHTS OR STRATEGIZING MY FANTASY FOOTBALL LEAGUE. I STAY ACTIVE, AND YOU BETTER LIKE THE CHICAGO BEARS, OR IT AIN'T GONNA WORK BETWEEN US. IF I'M NOT HITTING THE GYM, I'M FIRING UP MEAT ON THE GRILL. </div>

<h1>User Profile</h1>
NAME: EMILY SANDERS
AGE: 29
OCCUPATION: POTTERY ARTIST
INTERESTS: CERAMICS. ART. NATURE
ABOUT ME: I'M A FREE-SPIRITED POTTERY ARTIST WHO LOVES THE OUTDOORS, POSITIVE VIBES, AND DEEP CONVERSATION. WHEN I'M NOT CRAFTING, I'M SOAKING IN THE SOUNDS OF THE FOREST OR BASKING IN THE SUN'S ENERGY AT THE CLOSEST PARK. I ENJOY QUIET REFLECTION AND MEANINGFUL CONNECTIONS. </div>

<h1>Date Information</h1>
DATE DETAILS: EVENING DRINKS AT "TACKLES & TAPS SPORTS BAR."
</body>
</html>

"TOUCHDOWN!" I SCREAM, JOINING the roar of the crowded bar, clinking my beer, and high-fiving the guys around me. This sports bar is decked out in Northwestern's signature purple and white colors and glowing with big-screen TVs. The air crackles with energy.

I sit back down, grinning at Mads... er, Emily. "Did you see that touchdown? Gawd, that was epic, bro!"

She stares, her lips pressed in a tight line. "Yes, Kyle. The whole bar saw it."

"The Wildcats are on fire! They're gonna dominate this season, don't ya think?!"

My dating profile specifically said to "act like a one-dimensional jock". Why do I love how much Maddie is hating this?

Maddie takes a dainty sip of her beer. "Mhm. Sports. Yay."

A massive order of wings arrives, and I flag down the waiter for another beer refill. "Emma.... you good?" I ask, nodding at her drink.

She holds up her beer, the liquid barely touched. "It's Emily, actually, and yup, I'm savoring it."

She's just not that into me. Imagining artsy, nature-loving "Emily" on a date with a real meathead is hilarious. I know it's taking everything in her not to tell me how dumb I'm acting. But honestly, I do follow the Northwestern Wildcats, and they really are kicking ass this year.

Still, I can't resist egging her on. Time to be an even bigger ass of a jock.

I dig into the wings like an animal, my mouth open and chewing loudly. Maddie's disgust is evident, but she soldiers on. "Any chance you've seen the new Picasso exhibit at the art institute? I find his sculptures to be more groundbreaking than his paintings."

"Nah, not really my thing," I say, chugging my beer and letting out a belch that rattles the glass.

She's seconds away from politely ending our date when the Wildcats score. I jump up, hot wings in hand, and violently throw my fists into the air. "Touchdown!"

Looking back at Mads, I see that I've splattered her with spicy wing sauce. "Oops, my bad," I say, grabbing a napkin. I try to wipe the sauce off her chest, but I'm rubbing my hands over her breasts.

Oh geez. I'm really being an asshole.

Her eyes flash with anger. "Oh, hell no, pecker jockey! Keep your meat hooks away from my tits. Date over!"

Football, wings, and a boob graze? 5 stars, Emily. Would date again!

***

```
<!DOCTYPE html>
<h1>User Profile</h1>
</div>
```

NAME: Finn Thompson

AGE: 34

OCCUPATION: Chef & Owner of "Finn's Flavorful Food Truck"

INTERESTS: Foodie. Live Music. Outdoor adventures.

ABOUT ME: When I'm not cooking in my food truck, I'm enjoying nature's simple pleasures. I think the best moments are spent laughing with good company, over a meal or a picnic. I'm ready to build a long-term relationship built on trust, respect, and love.

```
</div>
```

```
<h1>User Profile</h1>
NAME: Chloe Evans
AGE: 30
OCCUPATION: Landscape Architect
INTERESTS: Art and design. Food adventures. Travel.
ABOUT ME: I'm an outdoor enthusiast and lover of
all things food-related. Professionally, I create beautiful
outdoor spaces, and I'm always ready for a wilderness
adventure. I believe food is the way to the heart. I love
exploring new restaurants & food festivals. I'm seeking
someone with travel experience.
</div>


<h1>Date Information</h1>
DETAILS: Lunch at the "Santorini Grill" restaurant.
</body>
</html>
```

I GRIN IN MY CHAIR, PATTING MY STUFFED BELLY.
"Damn, Chloe, that lamb was even better than when I had it in
Greece. The flavors were just..." I kiss my fingers like a cartoon chef.
"Mwah! Perfection."

She arches an eyebrow, "Oh, you've been to Greece? Impressive,
Finn."

Time to turn on the charm, baby. I flash my most dazzling smile.
"Maybe I could take you there, and you can taste for yourself."

She moves in closer, her smile turning suggestive. "I'd love that. I've never experienced the wonders of Greece."

The waiter interrupts, dropping off our bill. Maddie reaches for it, but I wave her off. "No, no, allow me. A gentleman always pays on the first date."

She shrugs. "If you insist. You did order a lot of alcohol."

Okay, Zack, time for the big finale. Let's see how Mads handles this curve ball.

I pat my pockets and fake a bewildered expression. "What the... Oh no. No, no, no."

"What's wrong?" she says, frowning.

"I can't believe it. I forgot my wallet at home."

"Oh. Well, that's okay. We can use Apple Pay, or Venmo, or—"

"Yeah, no... listen, sorry, that's not gonna happen," I say, holding up my hands in defeat. "I just declared bankruptcy on my business and needed this lunch. So, uh, thanks for the free meal."

Maddie's jaw drops. "Excuse me? You're gonna dine and dash!"

"Hey, I'm being upfront about this." I stand, giving her a cheeky grin as I turn for the door. "If being honest doesn't mean anything to you, then maybe I misread you."

"One-star review for you, asshole!" her voice rings out.

A dick move for sure, but hey, all's fair in love and fake dating, right?

***

<!DOCTYPE html>
<h1>User Profile</h1>
</div>
NAME: ALEX WARD
AGE: 30
OCCUPATION: CORPORATE STRATEGIST
INTERESTS: DEEP CONNECTIONS. ADVENTURE. ROMANCE.
ABOUT ME: I'M LOOKING FOR SOMEONE SPECIAL. LIFE IS ABOUT MOMENTS SHARED, SO I NEED A PARTNER WHO APPRECIATES MEANINGFUL RELATIONSHIPS AND IS ON THE SAME PAGE

FOR ROMANCE. WHETHER IT'S EXPLORING NEW CITIES, MAKING A HOME-COOKED MEAL TOGETHER, OR CUDDLING UP FOR A MOVIE NIGHT, LET'S MAKE SOME MEMORIES.
</div>

<h1>User Profile</h1>
NAME: ELLIE MORGAN
AGE: 29
OCCUPATION: MARKETING DIRECTOR
INTERESTS: READING. DEEP CONVERSATION. TRAVEL.
ABOUT ME: I'M A HOPELESS ROMANTIC. I BELIEVE IN SOUL-MATES, SERENDIPITY, AND GRILLED CHEESE SANDWICHES. DO YOU APPRECIATE A GOOD BOOK, ENJOY ROMANTIC WALKS, AND VALUE EMOTIONAL INTIMACY? LET'S SHARE LIFE'S SIMPLE MOMENTS TOGETHER.
</div>

<h1>Date Information</h1>
DETAILS: Upscale dinner at "The Skyline Room on 85th."
</body>
</html>

SHIT, THIS PLACE IS INTIMATE.

Dressed in my favorite black Armani suit, I perch on a barstool and nurse a whiskey, soaking up the restaurant's ambiance. It's like stepping into a bygone era. The dim lighting casts a warm glow over everything, and tables are scattered around a small dance floor. A trio of chamber musicians play soft music in the corner. This place is cozy, more suited for a marriage proposal than a first date.

How is Mads gonna play this whole "hopeless romantic" thing? I'm intrigued.

Is she gonna be all lovey-dovey and doe-eyed, swoony, and batting her eyelashes? That would be ironic coming from the girl who never runs out of sass.

But then Maddie, or should I say, Ellie, steps into the restaurant, and I'm completely mesmerized.

She's wearing a rich purple A-line dress that looks custom-tailored, accentuating her curves and flaring out perfectly. That plunging neckline is a straight-up heart-stopper, giving just the right amount of tempting cleavage. Her chestnut hair is swept to the side and pinned back. Whoa, wait a second—she's not wearing her glasses. Her eyes are dazzling drips of dark chocolate, drawing me in.

I'm blown away. She's striking: setting a new definition of beauty.

Our eyes meet and hold, the air suddenly charged. "Wow, you are... breathtaking," I breathe, drinking her in.

A rosy flush colors her cheeks. "Thanks, Alex. You're looking pretty sharp yourself," she returns, eyeing my suit.

Regaining my wits, I grin. "Your profile said you're a hopeless romantic. I figured candlelight and music checked the romance box."

"Yes, consider me officially romanced," she says with a coy smile. "So far."

There's my Maddie.

The second her arm is linked with mine, a force like gravity pulls us into each other. It's as if we're both orbiting—me around her and her around me—I can't fight it. I'm under her spell. I accompany her to our corner table and then hold out her chair, scoring an appreciative look.

"My lady," I offer.

"Why thank you, kind sir," she chimes back.

I offer her my hand as she sits down, and once she's settled, I don't let go—our palms are pressed together, creating this exhilarating friction. Maddie's gaze locks onto our hands, her teasing expression fading away into something softer, warmer.

When Maddie's eyes meet mine again, a raw, unguarded look of longing makes my heart pound. So I take it slow, running my thumb over her knuckles in this gentle caress, never breaking eye contact. I watch her pupils widen, and her lips part with this soft, shaky intake of breath.

A sudden, ear-splitting pop of champagne shatters the thick tension between us. Our heads whip toward the commotion as a woman nearby squeals, "Yes! Yes, I'll marry you!"

Maddie and I exchange an amused smile. "Don't worry, I'm not going to propose tonight," I say, chuckling as I take my seat.

Maddie raises an eyebrow. "So you don't believe in love at first sight?"

I lean in, my gaze wandering to her full lips before meeting her eyes again. "I absolutely believe in love at first sight," I say.

The deliciously loaded statement hangs in the air between us.

Her lips curl flirtatiously. "Hmm, spoken like a man who's been struck by Cupid's arrow. Tell me, who was this mystery girl that stole your heart?"

I let out a soft laugh, feeling the tension ease. "I'm here with a stunning woman. I'd like to keep the conversation about her, don't you agree?"

Maddie's gaze is curious. "Oh, I get it. This girl you fell for... she's someone you're currently in love with, huh?"

Our waiter rolls up just in time to save me from Maddie's probing questions. Dude's going all out with the evening's specials, like he's performing a one-man show. He drones on about the fancy-schmancy foie gras and imported truffles. One look at the menu, and I'm immediately calculating how many ramen noodle dinners we'll be eating to make up for this.

Mental note—tell the guys no more five-star splurges for fake dates.

We get our orders in, and Maddie picks right back up without missing a beat. "Okay, spill—where did you first meet this woman you instantly fell head over heels for?"

No good can come from this conversation.

But the need to express myself and let it all out is overwhelming. To unleash all the feelings I've kept hidden. Because it's not me saying it, it's Alex Ward, the character I'm playing.

"If you must know," I begin, my voice wavering slightly.

"Ooh! Let me guess, you were instantly blown away by her beauty," she teases with twinkling eyes.

My mind screams at me to hit the brakes.

"Actually, no," I go on. "It was her quick wit. She's drop-dead gorgeous, sure, but she's also genius-level smart. She's the most compelling, honest, fascinating person I've ever encountered. Until... I mean, until I met you, of course."

"Obviously," she says with an adorable little wink. "So what's the one thing about her looks that has you swooning?"

"The way she smiles when she laughs—it's unreal. It's mesmerizing; she just glows from the inside out."

"Dang, she sounds special. So what's the deal? Why haven't you swept her off her feet yet?" Maddie asks.

"Uh, well... it's kinda complicated. We... we work together. Soooo, it's just not the right time. It might never be."

"Guess that means you're stuck with me then? I'll try my hardest to hold a candle to this captivating woman you speak of," she says with a playful smirk.

"You and her, you've got more in common than you think."

"Really? Like what?"

I'm dying to tell her the truth.

Because it's you, Maddie.

You're the most stunning woman I've ever seen. You're the one I want to spend the rest of my life with. It kills me that you don't feel the same. You give me purpose. My whole world is you.

I casually reach over and take her hand.

"Your eyes," I say. "They sparkle just like hers."

We share a charged look for what feels like forever, the flickering candlelight reflecting in our gaze. I wonder if she can feel the weight of my stare, the yearning that's consuming me.

Soft notes of the piano float through the air, joined by the cello's rich tones. The musicians perform a tear-jerking version of "A Thousand Years" and couples make their way onto the dance floor. I rise from my seat.

"Let's skip the small talk and have our bodies do the talking."

"I'm, uh, not much of a dancer," she says, glancing anxiously at the swaying couples bathed in soft spotlights on the patterned floor.

"Trust me, I won't let you fall. Come on, it'll be the perfect chance for a little romance," I say with a flirtatious grin.

I lead Maddie into the flowing crowd, moving with her to the soft music—the intimacy and closeness of her body to mine—I'm entranced.

If I could stop time.

As we flow to the rhythm, we're surrounded by other couples lost in desire—steamy embraces—stolen glances—secretive touches.

I resist the temptation to pull her in, instead twirling her body so that her dress swirls around her. My eyes drink in her voluptuous form, unable to hide the thirst that she's meant to quench. Maddie's eyes dart, suddenly coy under my smoldering look, but she can't hide the rapid pulse of her heartbeat against my chest.

Gradually, her cheek rests on the contour of my neck, soft and warm. "You truly are breathtaking," I murmur against her ear, letting my lips teasingly brush her smooth skin.

"You've already said that," She whispers back to me, her voice low and alluring. "If you say it again, I might think you mean it." Her fingers glide down the back of my neck, lighting a fire within me.

Screw it. I let my hands wander lower, tracing her sensuous, mouth-watering waistline and pulling her flared hips closer. We rock silently, our breaths intermingling—every subtle movement heightening the sensation of how well we fit together.

Our eyes meet, and I detect a subtle flicker in her expression.

Nervousness?

Unease?

Craving?

Lust!?

Oh my God. Does Maddie want to kiss me?

Neither of us dare break eye contact, the atmosphere heavy with the weight of unspoken words *(and desires)*. I don't resist the impulse to feel the smoothness of her skin beneath my fingers. With the gentlest touch, I guide her face towards mine, my heart racing.

"Breathtaking," I murmur, my voice heavy with want.

Time slows to a crawl. Maddie tips her head back, a dreamy smile curving those full lips I've imagined tasting so many times. Her eyes drift shut, lashes fanning across flushed cheeks as she waits for me, breathless, to make my move.

And damn, how I want to. Every ounce of me strains toward her, desperate to stop retreating and crash our lips together.

I can't. Not like this—not when she's playing some role, pretending to be someone else.

Gritting my teeth, I disregard the powerful pull of her sultry expression and instead graze a light kiss across her forehead. It's a poor, pathetic substitute, but it's all I will allow.

The moment I make contact, she stiffens—eyes flying wide with shock and disbelief. A range of emotions plays across her face—hurt, confusion, a betrayed flash of longing. Before I can speak, she shoves me away and flees the dance floor.

I'm left confused, frustrated, and lost. Worse, I suddenly feel alone.

CHAPTER EIGHT

MADDIE

POD PEOPLE HAVE TAKEN OVER MY BODY.

Some sort of hormonal, biological poisoning is consuming my every thought. All I can think about is Zack—what is he doing—what is he wearing—is he thinking about me?

STOP IT BRAIN!

I'm lying in bed, breaking down what happened on our romantic "date" last night. My mind flashes to our dinner—Zack pulling out my chair—his fingers delicately tracing my skin—those intense stares. The way he held me close when we danced, I can still feel the ghost of his touch, my body heating at the memory.

Zack was going to kiss me on the dance floor. Electricity was crackling between us. But he didn't.

Whyyyyyy???

All the signs were there.

Why didn't he put his mouth on my mouth?!

I sigh. *Ugh! Why do I even care if he kisses me or not?* I rub my thumb over my bottom lip. God, I wanted to feel his lips on mine. I bet his mouth is like a gift from the orgasm gods.

Get a grip, Maddie!

Zack was obviously just pretending for our app, for the sake of this ridiculous dating experiment. But still, I can't stop wondering why he doesn't think about me that way. You'd think over the last ten years, there would be at least one drunken "oops we accidentally kissed" moment... but no, not a single one.

Zack is repulsed by me.

He thinks of me like a sister—like a girl without a vagina—a plastic Barbie doll with smooth parts down there. I'm his completely asexual, vagina-less BFF...

But wait—what about the boner Diamond McJuggs gave him? Except that wasn't really me, was it? I was some fishnet-wearing ditzbag literally stroking his biological urges! I smash my pillow against my face and groan.

My thoughts race to visions of Zack's intensity. I did not imagine those looks he gave me. And the memory of his "fuck me" eyes triggers an immediate desire between my thighs. It was the same smoldering stare he gave Lexie...

"Of course, you dumbbutt! Zack likes Lexie."

Duh! When I questioned Zack about love at first sight... he was talking about her. No man fantasizes about a vagina-less coding geek, not next to a blonde bombshell oozing sex appeal like her.

It shouldn't bother me that Zack doesn't find me attractive, but it does... and I hate that it does. I've never needed a man to make me happy. I have a vibrator for that. These fake dates are clearly messing with my head, blurring lines that should stay firmly drawn inside the friend zone.

Screw this. I need to focus on work and getting our app ready for the expo, not obsessing over why my best friend thinks I'm just his buddy without lady parts.

***

END ME NOW.

I've been analyzing code for so long today... is it tomorrow... *what day is it?* My eyeballs want to shrivel up and roll out of my head. On a regular day, I would've decoded this tech lingo in an hour, but today? Zippo. Nada. I'm running on negative sleep and a caffeine high that could resurrect King Tut.

The endless lines of code on my computer monitor make me snort-laugh. This jumbled jargon must be what Zack sees when he looks at my screen. Andddd there goes my brain again, merrily skipping back to Snack, er... Zack. *Ugh.*

Thankfully, his gorgeous dumb face isn't here to distract me. He's off at a meeting, schmoozing it up, putting the moves on Sexy Lexie. He's probably blinding her with his panty-melting grin while she not-so-subtly drops innuendos about her lack of a gag reflex.

Okay, that may not be what's happening, but my scumbag brain won't stop conjuring up images of Zack drooling over Lexie like a dog in heat. Girls like Lexie, with their perfect blowouts and fuck-me stilettos, have dudes tripping over their dicks for a taste of their coy, hair-tossing charms.

The annoying clatter of my coding crew's keyboards hits me like a fucking symphony. I glance down at my ratty hoodie, the scent of cheesy popcorn and desperation wafting to my nose. I can't help it. I have to ask, "You guys know I'm a woman, right?"

"Only way to know for sure is to strip down and prove it," Reid smirks.

"Mads," Cosmo states in a matter-of-fact tone, "And I mean this in the nicest way possible, but Linda is more of a woman than you."

Wes sighs dramatically, wrapping his arm around his blow-up doll, "Thanks, man. Linda appreciates finally getting a little respect around here."

I faceplant on my keyboard—stupid *Sexy Lexie.*

"Knock knock!" Nora sing-songs through the door, brandishing a bag of groceries. "I come bearing gifts of the non-processed variety."

It's as if my younger sister Nora stepped straight out of a fashion influencer's Instagram. Her blonde hair falls in glossy waves, her makeup is flawless, and somehow, even in freaking athleisure, she looks both casual and polished.

She hands me a fresh apple, and I side hug her. "You are my favorite sister."

"Well, duh," she smirks. "Sissy and Abby don't take care of you like I do."

She sets the bag down and surveys the carnage that is LoveScore's headquarters. "Cheese and crackers, it smells in here! You guys ever heard of Febreze?"

"That's the smell of genius," Wes chuckles.

She picks up trash as she speaks, "Ya know, if you need some dating scenario ideas. I'm an expert."

Reid flashes her a flirty grin. "How did you get to be so knowledgeable, gorgeous?"

Nora arches one perfectly tweezed brow. "Not to brag, but I'm out on dates at least three times a week."

"Are there any single men left in Chicago?" Cosmo inquires, deadpan.

Nora shoots him a withering glare. "I'm very selective with my suitors. My future husband needs to be emotionally intelligent, financially stable, and good with kids and animals. Ideally, he'll appreciate fine dining and know his way around a kitchen. And, of course, have a solid skincare regimen. I don't mess around with subpar pores."

Wes waggles his brows suggestively. "I mean, minus the financial stability and culinary skills, I'm your man."

Nora takes one look at the blow-up doll propped up beside him. "Uh-huh. No offense, but you're giving off major 'call the authorities' vibes. I wouldn't let you within fifty feet of a playground."

Time to intervene before Nora verbally castrates the guys. "Oookay, let's give the awkward flirting a rest. Nora, can I talk to you for a sec? In private?"

I grab her hand and tug her to my cramped disaster of a bedroom. "I need your opinion on something for Mom and Dad's anniversary party," I lie.

The door clicks shut. "Okay, that was total bullshit. I need your advice."

Nora's eyes light up as she perches on the edge of my unmade bed. If there's anyone who lives for secret sister heart-to-hearts and gushy feelings, it's Nora—the hopeless romantic to my love cynic.

"I'm all ears. Lay it on me, sis. I could sense your vibes were majorly off."

I take a deep breath, steeling myself. How the hell do I even put these swirling thoughts into words? *Fuck it, I'm just gonna rip off the feelings Band-Aid.*

"Nora... do you think I'm sexy?" I blurt out.

She blinks at me, stunned. "Wow. That is so not where I thought you were going. But heck yeah, you're sexy! You're the total package, Mads: boobs, butt, brains. Seriously, if I had your awesome rack, I'd already be married."

I cross my arms over my chest self-consciously. "Okay, see, that's easy for you to say, we're sisters. But spending all this time with Zack, pretending to be in love or whatever... it's got me feeling like the fugliest coding bridge troll to ever roam the land. I'm completely unfuckable."

Nora snort-laughs, her hand flying up to cover her mouth. "Maddie, I love your way with words. Wait! Hold up. Are you... do you have the hots for Zack? Like, legit feelings?"

"No!" I shout, my cheeks flushing hot. "That's absurd. I just want him to recognize that I have a vagina... and I dunno, maybe that I'm also attractive. But that doesn't mean I want to jump on his manstick."

"Maddie, any dude would cut off their left nut if it meant a chance to grope your boobs."

I chuck a pillow at her pretty face. "Gee, what a fairy tale romance. Consider my panties officially wet."

She tosses the pillow back with a grin. "Can I be real with you? I think it's amazing that you and Zack have maintained such a close, drama-free friendship for so long. The fact that he's never tried to drunkenly stick his tongue down your throat or hump your leg speaks volumes. He respects you and your boundaries."

I feel my cheeks heat up again as I process her words. Maybe Nora's right... these fake dates are messing with my head. Zack's a hottie, and I'm a passably attractive female. Surely, there's been a moment or two where he's thought about jumping my bones... right?

"Ooh, I have an idea!" Nora beams, now in her element. "Let me share some of my foolproof tricks for grabbing a man's attention. I've got it down to a science."

"Let me guess, it involves a fifty-point rating system and color-coded charts?"

She sticks out her tongue playfully. "You definitely need my help, but do you deserve it?"

"Sorry, sorry. Enlighten me with your man-snaring wisdom, oh great one."

"I'll let the sarcasm slide because you're obviously feeling insecure right now," Nora says, giving me a sympathetic look. "Getting some manly attention will fix that. When's your next date?"

"In one hour at some dumb bro gym."

Nora's already rummaging through my closet like a squirrel on crack. "It's all about the look, girl. And you're in luck because I've already lent you the perfect activewear for landing a man... ta-da!"

She clutches a scrap of fire-engine red fabric that looks better suited for a street corner than a gym.

Ten minutes later, I'm staring at my reflection in utter terror, trying in vain to adjust the whisper of cloth Nora picked out. The cherry red sports bra has a cutout that is tempting a nip slip if I breathe, and the booty shorts could double as underwear. There's no way in hell my ass cheeks aren't going to be hanging out and about when I bend over.

"I don't know, Nor. I feel like a reality show contestant on Slut Shame Island." I whine, trying in vain to adjust my tatas in their spandex prison. "This can't possibly be gym attire for normal humans."

"Shh," she says firmly, smacking my fidgeting hands away. "Quit fussing with it, you look banging. Every dude in there will be drooling over your slayin' body, Zack included. But it's not enough to look the part. You've got to act the part."

I gulp. Nora explains that being sexy means inserting the idea of sex into a guy's brain at every opportunity. Like by bending at the waist to showcase my plentiful behind or by making lingering eye contact while I chug water. She playfully demonstrates how to do a sexy squat, drawing attention to her ass and cleavage.

"Don't forget to throw in a little lip bite and hair toss," she coaches, flipping her shiny mane over her shoulder with a come-hither smile. "Oh, and if you want bonus points? Make sure you're in his line of sight when you stretch those hammies. Guys can't resist it, trust me."

My head is spinning as I try to absorb her rapid-fire instructions. Flirty touches, intense eye contact, subtle porny poses. It'll be a miracle if I don't trip over a barbell and give everyone a front-row seat to my vajayjay.

"I appreciate the life coaching session, but I gotta go," I say, glancing at my phone. "I'm supposed to meet Zack at the gym in twenty. If I'm late, he'll think I'm bailing."

Nora claps her hands and lets out a girlish squeal, ambushing me with a tight hug. "Ooh, I'm so excited! Okay, wait—don't leave yet. Let me just zhuzh your hair and spritz you with my Scent of Seduction perfume."

I dutifully hold still as she spritzes and fluffs, my stomach churning. I recap her sexy checklist. Arch back, stick out ass, flip hair, bite lip—rinse and repeat. Now I understand why Nora made me a flowchart.

"It's official. You're a sexy gym goddess," she declares, shoving my gym bag into my hands and rushing me towards the door. *This is a wardrobe malfunction waiting to happen.*

Nora gives me a playful smack on the ass. "Don't be surprised when you get a huge reaction from Zack. One so massive he won't be able to lift it, if you know what I mean."

***

<!DOCTYPE html>
<h1>User Profile</h1>
</div>
NAME: Noah Cole
AGE: 27
OCCUPATION: Fitness Model & Influencer
INTERESTS: Weight lifting. Photography. Fashion.
ABOUT ME: I'm an Instagram model, always posing for the camera, pumping iron at the gym, or jet-setting to exotic locales. I'm devoted to fashion, to wowing my followers, and to curating jaw-dropping content. Partner must have passion for fitness and their physique. </div>

<h1>User Profile</h1>
NAME: ZOE RICHARDSON
AGE: 25
OCCUPATION: PERSONAL TRAINER
INTERESTS: WEIGHTLIFTING. YOGA. HEALTHY COOKING.
ABOUT ME: WHEN I'M NOT IN THE GYM LIFTING WEIGHTS, YOU CAN FIND ME PERFECTING MY DOWNWARD DOG OR TRYING NEW HEALTHY RECIPES IN THE KITCHEN ISN'T JUST A HOBBY. TO ME, IT'S A LIFESTYLE. DO YOU HAVE WHAT IT TAKES TO KEEP UP?
</div>

<h1>Date Information</h1>
DETAILS: MIDDAY WORKOUT: "SWEATIN' TOGETHER GYM."
</body> </html>

I STRUT INTO THE GYM LIKE I'M WALKING THE GODDAMN RUNWAY.

My hips sway with each confident step. It's the lunchtime rush hour, and this place is packed tighter than a bodybuilder's glutes, all grunting muscles and spandex, as far as the eye can see.

I catch more than a few eyeballs dragging over my scandalous workout getup, lingering on my pushed-up cleavage and booty shorts *(basically a thong)*. Normally, I'd hide myself in a hoodie to avoid the blatant ogling, but today?

Bring.

It.

On.

I spot Zack, *er, Noah*, by the free weights, his deliciously toned arms flexing as he cranks out bicep curls. Watching him lift the barbells, I'm shook. The man is sexy. I've always known Zack was hot, objectively speaking, but now there's an urge in me. I feel different, and I want to act on it.

I saunter up, cocking a hip and trying to channel my inner Nora as I purr, "Hey, hot stuff. I'm Zoe."

Poor guy's so stunned, he nearly drops his load *(heh)*. He coughs as he takes in my scantily clad bod. "I, uh... damn. I mean, hi. I'm Noah. You look... Jesus."

"You started without me," I tease, reaching for my own weights. "Don't worry, I'll catch up real quick."

I bend waaaay over to snag the weights at my feet, giving him an eyeful of my fun bags. Straightening back up, I start curling, "accidentally" arching my back to thrust my tits front and center.

Zack's eyes nearly pop out of his head as he swallows hard.

Who's got no vagina NOW, sucker?

"Are you doing full body or just focusing on upper?" I ask.

He manages to croak out a strangled, "I'm a full-body kinda guy."

"Perfect! As a personal trainer, I can help you hit those hard-to-reach places. If you can handle it, that is?"

Noah's eyes flash with challenge. "Let's do it... not it... I mean, let's work out."

"Mmm, I do love a man who can get sweaty." I lead Zack over to the preacher curl station and take a seat. "Just watch my form." I lean to grip the bar. My boobs mash against the padding. I start curling slowly, making my chest heave.

His eyes bore into my cleavage, mesmerized by my nipples that pucker against the skimpy material. I finish my set, hop up, and gesture for him to sit.

"Let's see what you're packing, big boy," I purr, sauntering to take my place behind him. The moment he starts curling, I smoosh my breasts against his muscular back, ensuring he feels every tantalizing contour of my lush curves. I angle over his shoulder and let my ample bosom spill onto him. Then I trail a teasing finger down his straining bicep.

"Here, let me help you with your grip," I growl, running my provocative fingers along his hands. "Nice and slow, squeeze like you mean it..."

"Fuck," he mutters, his muscles quivering under my touch. "Yep, uh-huh, definitely feeling... something."

I hide my grin, enjoying my effect on him. But then, he stands up, nearly knocking me over. "Are you a little warm? I'm burning up."

He whips off his shirt like the Hulk, and... *guh. His body is a sexual weapon.* My insides instantly feel all kinds of tingly and hot.

He smirks and flexes. "Gotta let the skin breathe, y'know?"

I nod stupidly, my eyes glued to his glistening torso.

Holy hell, I want to lick him like a popsicle. Focus, Mads!

Nora's voice echoes in my head—*always be touching!* I stroll right up to him, my hands itching to explore. "Speaking of breathing, I know a great stretch for opening up the chest." I splay my palms across his rock-hard pecs.

I start kneading his sculpted chest muscles, feeling his heart hammering beneath my fingers. "You're so tense," I say playfully, letting my nails graze his nipples. Zack hisses, his abs clenching. "Maybe we should move on to legs, give your upper body a break?"

"G-good idea," he stammers, looking like he's about to pass out. *I'm basking in my ability to reduce him to a quivering mess.*

"Let's do some squats and warm up those glutes," I suggest, not so innocently. "You should watch my form from behind, make sure I'm doing them right."

I position myself in front of Zack, hiking up my shorts until my ass is eating the fabric. I sink into a deep squat, giving him a perfect view of the goods.

"You want to feel the burn right here," I say, reaching back and grabbing a handful of my own booty. "Ready to squeeze?"

Zack blinks rapidly, snapping his jaw shut. "Yep, squats. On it, let's do this."

He's squatting like his life depends on it, but his hungry eyes never leave my backside.

How's that for an object of desire? Ready to kiss me yet?

I reposition myself, now standing behind him. *I should not be enjoying seeing him squirm so much.*

"Keep your shoulders back," I instruct, running my hands down his sweat-slicked spine. "And engage those tight glutes of yours."

I give his perfect ass a firm squeeze, delighting in the way he jumps. Then, just for funsies, I smack it hard, the crack echoing through the gym.

"Time for inner thighs!" I announce gleefully. Zack looks like he'd rather walk over hot coals, but he dutifully follows.

I lead him to the altar of seduction: the inner thigh machine. I mount up and spread 'em wide, giving him a beaver shot that would make a gynecologist blush. Time to prove to Zack that I'm not his vagina-less BFF. I'm the Mads he desires, the one he wants to get all up in and...

Kiss.

Those.

Lips.

Zack's eyes are heat-seeking missiles to my cooch. "The key is to find that sweet spot, y'feel me?" I whisper seductively. "You'll know you've hit it when you feel that deep, delicious burn." I move my legs faster.

"Mmmm, fuuuck yeah, right there! God, that's good! Harder, faster, don't stop!"

"Oh God, oh God, oh God!" I let out a porn-worthy moan, throwing my head back in ecstasy. Zack looks ready to fall to his knees and worship. I congratulate myself on a hoo ha well played when—

"Hey, this was fun, but I need to jet," he says, awkwardly rubbing the back of his neck. "I'll, uh, see you around?"

And just like that, he's gone, exiting like his ass is on fire.

It's confirmed, my vajayjay is the Pennywise of private parts; a scary clown that terrifies all men who consider approaching it.

***

```
<!DOCTYPE html>
<h1>User Profile</h1>
</div>
```

NAME: Max Hunter

AGE: 29

OCCUPATION: Outdoor Adventure Guide

INTERESTS: Extreme Sports. Skydiving. Rock Climbing.

ABOUT ME: I'm an adrenaline junkie! Whether it's jumping out of planes, scaling cliffs, or exploring the wildest places on earth, I live for my next thrill. But don't worry, I prioritize safety—I'm not reckless, just fearless! I need someone with a love for adventure and who isn't afraid to take risks.

</div>

<h1>User Profile</h1>

NAME: Ruby Collins

AGE: 26

OCCUPATION: Personal Assistant

INTERESTS: Knitting. Jogging. Trying new foods.

ABOUT ME: Yarn is my relaxation therapy, but I also love the rush of a jog in the park. While I enjoy comfort foods, I'm on a mission to try cuisines from around the world. It's the year of yes, so I'm stepping out of my comfort zone by spending more time outdoors.

</div>

<h1>Date Information</h1>

DETAILS: Ziplining at "Treetop Thrills Adventure Park."

</body>

</html>

THIS IS HOW I DIE.

I peer over the platform edge, and my stomach plummets. Holy mother of vertigo, I can't even see the ground through the tangle of trees!

What in the flying fuck were the guys thinking? This isn't a first date. It's a death trap. Seriously, who is the sick freak that came up with the idea to strap people to a glorified clothesline and hurl them off a cliff?

Zack... Max, has barely said a word to me since we arrived. I'd be thrilled he's not staring at my obvious camel toe in this ridiculously tight harness... if I hadn't already confirmed he sees me as vagless.

The zipline attendant, a lanky guy with a mop of curly blonde hair and a lazy smile, waves Zack forward. "Alright, my man, you're first. Let's get you strapped in." He looks like the human embodiment of a weed gummy, his eyes half-lidded and glazed.

"I am so stoked!" Zack says, preparing his phone as if he's about to livestream this death jump.

If Zack wants to splatter his brains all over the pavement for an adrenaline high, that's his prerogative. I, for one, value my life and limbs.

My pulse races. I'm hyperventilating. I ask the worker, "Has anyone ever died on this course?"

The worker's marijuana-glazed eyes hesitate before answering, "No?"

My confidence shot to shit, I press on, "Has anyone been maimed, lost a limb, a finger, had their eye poked out, gotten brain damage from slamming into a tree?"

Zack drops the gung-ho adventurer act. "Mads? You okay?"

I shake my head. "No, Zack, I'm not okay. You know I'm not. I hate shit like this."

He puts a comforting hand on my shoulder, his brow furrowed with concern. "Hey, you don't have to. Just make it part of the dating data and have your Ruby character back out. No biggie."

His soft touch sends a mix of familiar comfort and instant arousal through me. *Seriously? I'm getting the tingles now? Why the fuck do I care more about making out with Zack than dying!*

Let's be real, if I die, maybe Zack would *pity kiss* my corpse. Of course, I wouldn't be alive to feel it. Ugh, I know I'm being morbid. I won't die. I'll just be permanently paralyzed by a tree. Oooh, but Zack will give me CPR. I can see it now, my mutilated body and mangled lips, as he kisses me to bring me back to life. *Still counts as a kiss.*

What the hell is wrong with my kiss-crazed brain!?!

"No, I'm gonna do it," I say weakly.

Zack takes my hand and turns to the stoner, "Hey man, she's kind of nervous. Is it cool if you strap us in together?"

Next thing I know, Stoner Steve is securing Zack and me into the safety harness face-to-face. He does a half-ass safety check with the enthusiasm of a sedated sloth. Zack's strong arms wrap around me. His tempting lips are dangerously close to mine—*fuck me.*

"I got you," Zack's eyes sparkle in a way that makes me feel safe. Until—

HE STEPS OFF THE LEDGE!

The zipline catches, and we're flying. The wind whips through my hair as we zoom over the treetops at breakneck speed.

And... it's fucking exhilarating! The thrill whips through me like a freight train, my entire body vibrating with euphoria. Holy shitballs, I feel invincible!

"WOOOOO!" I holler, throwing my head back as I soar through the sky. "FUCK YEAH, BABY!"

I'm facing my fears.

I'm lost in the moment.

I'm crashing my lips into... Zack's lips in a fiery kiss.

His mouth feels incredible.

It's pure bliss for a split second. But then... he's not kissing me back. He's stiff as a board.

I jerk away as if scalded, my cheeks flaming with humiliation. Zack is gaping at me, his eyes round with shock and something akin to sheer horror. *Well, fucking ouch. Message received, loud and clear.*

"Oh God, sorry!" I babble. "That was just, uh... heat of the moment, y'know? Thought I was gonna die, didn't die. Yay for not dying!"

Real smooth, Mads. A+ recovery.

I avoid his eyes; it's awkward as fuck. We can not hurtle to the landing platform fast enough.

"Well... I'm gonna go," I blurt out, unhooking my harness. "Thanks for the date. Fun date. Memorable date. Sooooo... bye!"

I run off wearing my helmet, unable to stay a second longer. Zack's calling my name, but I don't stop.

Once safely in my car, with shaking hands, I fire off a text to Nora.

Maddie: *I kissed him.*

Nora: *What?!*

Maddie: *He didn't kiss me back.*

Nora: *Are you sure?*

Maddie: *He froze. Just stared back at me like I mouth-raped him.*

Nora: *Maybe he was just playing his character for the date?*

Maddie: *No. I saw his eyes. It was him. He's repulsed by me.*

Nora: *You should come over. We can talk it out.*

Maddie: *No… if Zack thinks I'm unattractive, then fuck Zack and fuck all dudes. This is why I'm single. I'll lie to him later. Say it was my nervous character and never speak of it again.*

Rage boils in my gut. I want to scream. I want to… smack the ever-loving shit out of Zack for making me feel this way.

CHAPTER NINE

ZACK

<!DOCTYPE html>
<h1>User Profile</h1> </div>
NAME: Ethan Larson
AGE: 29
OCCUPATION: Barista at EarthSip Sustainable Café
INTERESTS: Hiking. Meditation. Eco-Friendly Living.
ABOUT ME: By day, I'm brewing coffee and promoting a green lifestyle, but when I'm off-duty, I'm exploring nature trails or meditating. I believe in living sustainably and reducing my carbon footprint. I'm looking for someone who shares my values of caring for the planet. </div>

<h1>User Profile</h1>
NAME: Harper Mitchell
AGE: 27
OCCUPATION: Environmental Scientist
INTERESTS: Yoga. Painting. Sustainable Living.

ABOUT ME: I'M AN ENVIRONMENTAL SCIENTIST WHO LOVES YOGA AND MAKING A DIFFERENCE. AT WORK, I'M DEEP INTO RESEARCH, BUT AT PLAY, YOU'LL FIND ME ON MY YOGA MAT WHERE I FIND BALANCE AND INNER PEACE. I WANT TO MEET SOMEONE WHO LOVES THE PLANET AS MUCH AS I DO.

</div>

<h1>Date Information</h1>
DETAILS: A.M. COUPLES YOGA AT "NAMASTE NOOK STUDIO."
</body>
</html>

"LET GO OF ANY DISTRACTIONS AND FOCUS ON YOUR BREATH."

I'm sitting cross-legged on my yoga mat, eyes shut. Our instructor, a hipster in a ponytail, calmly tells us to quiet our minds. My racing thoughts didn't get the memo. I glance at Maddie, who looks unfairly sexy in a simple black tank and leggings, her dark hair pulled back in a messy bun.

Since arriving for our fake yoga date at this trendy studio, Maddie has spoken only three words to me: "Hi, I'm Harper," before setting up her mat and meditating.

I'm at a loss for what the hell has come over her these last couple of days. That flirtatious little display at the gym, she was clearly trying to get a rise out of me, or rather, out of my pants. And then, she goes and kisses me on the zipline. Mads kissed me. Was it a real kiss or just part of her roleplay? I don't know if I'm supposed to be confused or turned on.

The instructor's soothing voice pulls me from my brooding thoughts. "Now, stand side by side with your partner in tree pose."

I rise and bring my right foot to rest against my inner left thigh, hands pressed together at my heart. Maddie mirrors me, and for a brief, peaceful moment, we're a harmonious pair planted in a forest of tree couples.

Then Maddie wobbles, overcorrects, and smashes into me with a startled yelp. I topple sideways, crashing to the mat in an ungraceful heap.

"Oops," Maddie says flatly, not sounding sorry at all as she glares down at me. What the—?

The instructor tells us to shake it off and flow into downward dog. I hold the pose, feeling the blood rushing to my brain.

There is no way in hell that kiss was real.

If Maddie's system detected a single love molecule, her body would hunt it down and annihilate it with extreme force before the love cancer could spread.

Guys have one thing on the brain—Maddie has another—her career. Once we land this funding and LoveScore takes off, she'll be back to her driven, sarcastic self.

We move into a standing forward fold, hinging at the hips to touch our toes. I'm just starting to feel the stretch when—*THWACK!* Maddie's hand smacks me across the face. I jerk upright.

"What's your problem?" I hiss.

Maddie arches an eyebrow, all frosty politeness. "Uh, we just met. Why would I have a problem with you? I'm just uncoordinated."

Rubbing my stinging cheek, I mutter, "Your profile claimed you loved yoga."

"Then maybe my partner just sucks at it?" she snarks back.

We sweep our arms overhead, and—*WHAP!* She hits me again, harder this time. If her eyes were lasers, I'd be vaporized.

"Okay, enough!" I snap. "Why the hostility?"

"Oh, I'm hostile? That's rich, coming from Mr. Freeze himself."

"Mr. Freeze? What are you—"

"Forward fold, my friends!" the instructor interjects with a smile.

We bend over again, and Maddie nails me with a swift kick to the ass. I jerk upright, whirling to face her.

"Whoopsie," she smirks. "Foot slipped."

I'm starting to think it's Maddie who's pissed and not Harper the character she's playing. Either way, this mental game is getting old.

The instructor guides us to kneel facing each other, pelvises touching. *Oh, hell no.* I know where this is going, and Little Zack is already perking up in anticipation.

"Actually, I think I'm gonna duck out early," I mutter.

Maddie's eyes narrow. "Aw, yoga too hard for you, tough guy?"

I grimace and stay put. We grasp forearms and slowly lean back, our pelvises pushing into each other, stretching our spines. I ignore the proximity of Maddie's hips to mine, disregard the heat of her skin, and refuse to enjoy the thin sheen of sweat at her collarbone...

KAPOW! Maddie topples backward, slamming her knee full force into my nuts. I collapse in a pile of absolute agony. Even the damn yoga instructor winces.

"This isn't going to work out," Maddie announces sweetly, standing over my crumpled form. "I need a man with stronger balls who can keep up with me. Namaste, fuckboy." she snarls, flipping me off.

Not sure how I pissed her off, but my testicles just paid the price.

***

I GRAB A FROZEN BAG OF PEAS from the freezer and gingerly place it on my throbbing balls as I limp into the coding cave. Cosmo and Wes are huddled around their screens, furiously typing away.

"Downward dog crush your nads, Zack?" Cosmo snarks without looking up.

I lower myself onto a chair, wincing as I adjust the makeshift ice pack. "Apparently, couples yoga is code for Twister for your nutsack."

Reid enters from the kitchen, smirking. "Bro, this is why I can't do yoga. My dick's too big. It's like trying to balance a watermelon on a chopstick."

Groans of disbelief fill the room.

"Here, this'll help bring the feeling back to your cojones." Reid hands me a steaming mug. "New cappuccino flavor I whipped up—Vanilla Berry Blissplosion."

I take a sip, and he waits for my approval. It's surprisingly tasty. "Good stuff, Reid!" He beams, and then I lower my voice. "Hey, uh, is Maddie back yet?"

Wes, hunched over his keyboard, mumbles, "She's in the shower."

I nod, then clear my throat. "Say, have you guys noticed Maddie acting a little... different lately?"

Reid cocks an eyebrow. "Different, how?"

"I dunno... angrier than usual?" I ask.

"Not that I've noticed," Cosmo says flatly.

"I showed her logo options yesterday," Reid adds, and she was like, 'I'm not here to stroke your ego or listen to you manblaming your coworkers. Figure your shit out, brosif.'"

Wes shudders. "That's nothing. Mads walked in on Linda and me watching "The Boobyguard" and she totally freaked. She called Linda a bitch and told me to keep my 'creepy sex doll antics' in my room. Said the living room isn't my personal porn space."

"She called Linda a bitch?" Cosmo says with a frown. "Harsh."

Wes nods solemnly. "I know, right? So undeserved."

"Sounds to me like the regular rage-fueled Mads." Cosmo deadpans.

I wince, shifting the peas on my crotch. Maybe I am reading too much into things.

"Hey, Cosmo, I need to see Maddie's date reviews."

Cosmo fixes me with a hard stare. "I have little to no principles, but I'll go to war for our users' right to privacy."

"But they're not real users," I argue. "They're our fake profiles, so technically—"

"I'm not some pawn in your game of corporate espionage," Cosmo cuts me off. "I'd rather face a horde of angry hackers than deal with the true depths of Maddie's rage."

I slump, defeated. I guess I should just shut up and fill out these dating surveys. Instead, I grab my phone and shoot Mads a text.

Zack: *Hey, are we good?*

Maddie: *Yeah, why?*

Zack: *Um, and don't take this the wrong way... you seem a little more annoyed than usual.*

Maddie: *I'm annoyed you're bothering me in the shower... again.*

Zack: *Ok. Just making sure we're good.*

Maddie: *You threw me off a cliff. I kicked you in the balls. We're even.*

The guys are right on the money. I'd better hold on to my nutsack because she's the same ol' sarcastic Mads.

***

```
<!DOCTYPE html>
<h1>User Profile</h1>
</div>
```

NAME: Lucas Knight

AGE: 30

OCCUPATION: Sales Shark

INTERESTS: Winning. Fitness. Fine Dining.

ABOUT ME: I'm a beast in sales—I only settle for first place. I give my all in everything, including relationships. I'm fiercely competitive and don't like to lose. Seeking a woman who can handle my ambition and appreciates my winning mindset. </div>

```
<h1>User Profile</h1>
```

NAME: Scarlett Sanders

AGE: 28

OCCUPATION: Event Planner

INTERESTS: Dating. Dancing. Travel.

ABOUT ME: I'm all about fun, flirting, and being playful.

I'M THE LIFE OF THE PARTY AND LOVE EXPLORING EXOTIC DESTINA-
TIONS. I'M SEEKING A CONFIDENT MATE WHO CAN KEEP UP WITH
ME AND KNOWS HOW TO FLIRT BACK. LET'S SHARE SOME LAUGHS
AND EXPLORE OUR CHEMISTRY OVER COCKTAILS.
</div>

<h1>Date Information</h1>
DETAILS: FINE DINING AT THE "EVENING STAR TERRACE."
</body>
</html>

I'M OVERWHELMED WITH THE NEED to claim this
woman completely.

"The lobster risotto seems delish," Maddie says in a breathy voice.
My dick twitches in my pants like a trained show dog.

"Get whatever you want, babe. I like a woman who can eat," I say
in a controlled, confident tone.

Behind her menu, Mads shoots me another seductive look. She's
been throwing nonstop flirty vibes my way since we got to this
boujee-ass restaurant, which has me adjusting my pants under the
table every five seconds.

And don't even get me started on that dress. It's a skintight little
number, flesh-toned and sprinkled with black lace. The fabric is so
scandalously short and low-cut, it's practically lingerie. I can't stop
picturing peeling it off her, inch by tantalizing inch...

We're seated on a semi-private outdoor terrace in this upscale
restaurant, making my dirty thoughts a very real possibility. The
twinkling Edison lights and the intimate flickering candles are

enough to turn even a cynical sales shark like Lucas Knight into an incurable romantic.

But I've got a KISS strategy to keep my dick in my pants and her mouth off my face. K.I.S.S.—Keep It Simple Stupid. We'll talk, eat, and immediately part ways. I'll head straight for the shower and indulge in all of my carnal desires that Mads created with that sinfully sexy dress.

Looking is allowed. Touching is not.

I feel compelled to repeat myself. "You are absolutely ravishing tonight," I say, drinking her in.

She's about to respond when we're interrupted by our waiter.

Maddie shifts forward, and her tits nearly fall out of her dress. "Oh my God, I'm so sorry, but have I seen you before? Are you a model?"

Our clueless waiter, who has the physique *(and brains)* of a Ken doll with extra muscles, pauses. He runs a hand through his artfully tousled blonde hair. "Thanks, but nah. Just a working college student."

"Really? Because you are so freaking hot, it's insane!"

Maddie's now licking her lips slowly, deliberately, and... her eyes are roaming up and down this douche nozzle's body. *Is she kidding me? Her lewd perusal, so glaringly aimed at another man, is making me...*

Shocked?

Furious?

Jealous?

She continues, purring, "I want that snatch-seducing mouth to be part of my eating out experience, if you get me... I think I'm going to become one of your regulars."

"I'd like that," he winks.

Fuck this guy.

"Hey, Don Juan, can we order some drinks?" I snap.

Maddie puts her hand on his arm, and I glitch. "What do you recommend for little ol' me?"

He leans in close. *Too fucking close.* "For a hot bod like yours? An Appletini. It's sexy, sweet, and packs a punch."

Mads giggles. *Fucking giggles! Fake date or not, I'm insulted.*

My blood pressure skyrockets.

"Mmm, it's like you know me already. Sounds positively orgasmic. I'll take one," she moans.

And... I'm picturing them having sex. The unwanted images bombard me—Maddie arching beneath this overly muscled d-bag—him pounding into her—her nails raking down his back—sinful noises erupting from her lips.

Jealousy... an emotion I never let take root with Maddie. A few pangs of it came and went alongside her random hookups, sure, but nothing like this all-consuming rage. Picturing her with someone else is agonizing, and it's all I'm thinking about.

My knuckles turn white, gripping the table. "Whiskey, neat," I growl so the waiter finally acknowledges me.

"Excuse me, I need to go to the ladies," she coos to the waiter, winking.

I hate how her phenomenal ass commands my attention when she walks away.

Blondie boy better take his eyes off her caboose. Prick.

"Hey, asshole," I say with narrowed eyes. "I'm gonna give you your tip now, don't fucking flirt with another guy's girl."

***

<!DOCTYPE html>
<h1>User Profile</h1>
</div>
NAME: Jason Reed
AGE: 32
OCCUPATION: Real Estate Agent
INTERESTS: Clubbing. Cocktails. Socializing.
ABOUT ME: I work hard, play harder. After a hectic week with clients, I enjoy unwinding at clubs. I love the energy of the dance floor and the freedom of movement. I'm all about having fun and making memories. Come dance with me, then relax in a VIP booth with a cocktail. I'm seeking someone with nonstop weekend vibes. </div>

<h1>User Profile</h1>
NAME: Amber Johnson
AGE: 25
OCCUPATION: Makeup Counter Associate
INTERESTS: Clubbing. Dancing. Mixology.
ABOUT ME: I'm your go-to girl for a night of drinking, dancing, and fun! WARNING: When I hit the dance floor, I let loose. I live for the club scene and I love the thrill of dancing until dawn. I need someone who can keep up with my party spirit and isn't afraid to get wild! </div>

```
<h1>Date Information</h1>
DETAILS: 2 A.M. DANCING & DRINKS AT "THE MIDNIGHT CLUB."
</body>
</html>
```

I STEP INTO A CLUB PULSATING with enough energy to vibrate my molars loose. The place is a heaving mass of gyrating bodies—the dance floor, a sea of tight dresses and overpriced hair gel.

I'm late, thanks to a last-minute dinner with Roland and some executives he wanted to impress. I didn't have time to change out of my work clothes, so I rolled up the sleeves of my navy button-down, popped a few extra buttons, and declared it club attire.

I scan the crowd for Maddie, but she's nowhere. *Damn, did she bail?* In character or not, clubs aren't her scene—too loud, crowded, and far too much human contact.

I elbow my way to the bar and order an Irish coffee shot, downing it in one burning gulp. The caffeine and alcohol hit my bloodstream like a double roundhouse kick to the face.

That's when I see Maddie, dancing as her character Amber, gyrating her hips and running her hands all over her body like she's trying to seduce herself.

My jaw drops so fast, I'm shocked it doesn't crack the grimy floor. She's wearing a super short black dress that looks like it was painted on, all daring cutouts and flimsy fabric. It hugs her curves like a possessive boyfriend, putting her tits and ass on full drool-worthy display, and... *Sweet Jesus, is that her actual ass cheek peeking out?*

Holy shit. She's never looked sexier. All I can think about is ripping that scrap of a dress off to see if she's wearing panties underneath.

Then I realize she's not alone. Some oily assbag is grinding on her like he's trying to start a fire with his dick. White-hot fury surges through me. I storm over before I can stop myself, my hands curled into fists.

"Maddie, what the hell?" I yell over the eardrum-shattering music.

The greaseball scowls, his arms tightening around her waist. "Whoa, back off, bro! We're dancing here."

I grit my teeth... hard. "She's with me, asshole."

He looks at Maddie, eyebrows raised. "This your boyfriend?"

Maddie giggles, her words slurring together like a drunk toddler's. "Nooooope," she singsongs, popping the 'p' obnoxiously.

I clench my jaw, fighting the urge to deck this fucker in his smug face. "I'm her date, actually."

He smirks, his hand sliding down to Maddie's hips. "Sorry, pal, but right now, she's dating me!"

Red bleeds into the edges of my vision. I want to break every single one of his greedy fingers for touching her like that.

Maddie sways unsteadily, leaning back against his chest. "This... this is Stefan," she hiccups. "Stefan thinks my tits are squishy. Don'tcha, Stef?"

"Fucking perfect, baby. And your ass," Stefan continues, grabbing a generous handful of Maddie's backside. "Damn, girl. That thing is juicy as fuck. I just wanna bite it, like... chomp chomp, nom sayin'?"

I nearly vomit on his cheap-ass sneakers. "Maddie, how much have you had to drink?"

She dissolves into giggles, holding up three fingers. "No, five. Wait, seven? Math is hard."

Jesus, she's shit-faced. Maddie is the world's biggest lightweight. I've seen her drunk one time before, and she was comatose after three weak-ass light beers.

"Mads, we need to get you home," I say firmly, grabbing her elbow. "You're wasted."

She pouts, her unfocused eyes narrowing into a glare. "Nuh-uh! I don't wanna go anywhere with you, Zack. You... you think my pussy is gross!"

"What? Maddie, that's not—"

"I bet your cooch tastes sweeter than honey, princess," Stefan croons, nuzzling into her neck.

I want to fucking throttle him.

Maddie beams up at him, her smile sloppy and lovestruck. "You're sooooo nice, Steffy. Not like dumb, sss-stupid Zack. He won't kiss me, even when I wear fancy underwear!"

Stefan wiggles his eyebrows lecherously. "Oh, I'll kiss more than just your pretty mouth, baby. I'll eat you out like it's my last fucking meal."

Bile rises in my throat. I'd rather set my dick on fire than let this STD factory anywhere near Maddie's panties.

"Time to go," I snarl, tightening my grip on her arm.

Stefan sneers at me, puffing out his scrawny chest. "The lady wants to stay and party, bro. Don't be a fucking buzzkill."

"Yeah, Zack," she slurs belligerently. "Stefan is my new best friend. He's gonna m-make me feel really super good. He sss-said so."

"That's right, baby. I'm gonna make you feel fucking amazing. Open wide, princess," Stefan gets in my face, then gives me a shove. "Now go crash someone else's party, dickweed."

I stagger back, thinking I was pissed, until I see him pull a baggie of white pills from his pocket and dangle one in front of Maddie's face like a dog treat. *Hell fucking no!*

I lunge forward, my fist connecting with Stefan's jaw with a sickening crunch. He staggers back, the baggie flailing and little white pills scattering over the dance floor.

"Those are expensive, bro!" He's already on all fours, scrambling to save what he can.

I throw a swaying, incoherent Maddie over my shoulder like a sack of intoxicated potatoes.

"We're leaving," I growl.

The jealous monster inside me boils. *If I can't have Maddie, no one can.*

***

I GENTLY LAY MADDIE DOWN on her bed.

She's out cold and snoring softly; her hair a wild, sticky mess around her face. I gently touch her, shuddering at the thought of what could've happened if I had gotten there any later. Even in her drunken stupor, she's got a hold on my heart... my Maddie.

There was no way in hell I was leaving her at that club.

I slip off her heels, my fingers grazing the smooth skin of her ankles. I allow myself one last lingering look before tugging the blanket over her.

I turn to leave when Maddie's hand shoots out, grabbing my arm.

"Zaaack," she slurs, her eyes half-open. "Why d'you think I'm ugly?"

I'm taken aback by the vulnerability in her voice. "What? Mads, that's ridiculous. You're beautiful."

"No, I'm not. You think I'm fugly and that I don't even have a 'gina. But I do! I totally have one!"

I bite back a laugh. "I know you have a vagina, Mads."

"Then prove it!" She demands, sitting up and startling me. "Prove you think I'm pretty!"

Before I can process what's happening, Maddie starts tugging clumsily at her dress.

"Whoa, hey, what are you doing?" I ask, alarmed.

"Showing you my sexy underwear! I wore it just for you." She pulls the garment up, and it gets stuck on her head for a moment. She flails around like a boozy, half-naked muppet.

"Help, please!" She whines, her voice muffled by the fabric.

I hesitate, then cautiously sit on the bed. I slowly pull her dress off, trying to ignore the miles of smooth, perfect skin I'm unveiling.

And hot damn, her lingerie is a work of art, covering curves and contours meant for my eyes only. It's black lace and tiny bows, barely covering anything. I can see the outline of her nipples through the sheer bra and the thong... *Jesus fuck, the thong.* It's a whisper of fabric, held together by a prayer and a dainty little pink bow.

I want to rip it off with my teeth.

Maddie presses her hot, vodka-laced lips up to my cheek. "Your mouth is soft," she says, tracing my lips with her finger.

She's making it hard, and I mean way too *hard*, to be a gentleman right now.

"Maddie," I croak out. "You're drunk. Let's talk about this tomorrow."

She pouts, her lower lip jutting out temptingly. "Why? 'Cause I'm ratchet and rep-repuls... a gross cave troll?"

"Maddie," I exhale, my eyes hungry for her body. "You have no idea how much I want to touch you."

Her eyes light up. "Then do it! Touch me, Zack. I want you to."

I clench my fists, digging my nails into my palms. It's taking every ounce of willpower not to give in. I want to run my hands over that creamy skin, and feel the heat of her through that barely-there lace.

No. I can't. Not like this. She's wasted and vulnerable—she needs me—trusts me—to be a friend right now. Not some shithead who takes advantage of her.

I spot my old Northwestern hoodie on the floor, grab it, and offer it to her. "Put this on."

She sobs, "I'm so hideous, I know cuz you didn't kiss me on our date! You told me you only kiss girls you're attracted to!"

Oh, come on. That's what this is about? Our idiotic fake dates?

I tilt her chin up, forcing her to meet my gaze. "Maddie, listen to me. I am insanely attracted to you, but if you don't cover up, I'm going to do something really selfish. You're gorgeous and sexy, and desirable, so fucking desirable."

"Then prove it," She whispers. "Kiss me."

We stare... for a long, charged moment.

I can feel myself giving in, my lips tingling with anticipation.

I can't stop. I trail my fingertips across her lips and then along her collarbone, reveling in the buttery softness of her skin. She lets out a shuddery sigh, her eyes fluttering closed. Emboldened, I skim my hand lower, grazing the lacy edge of her bra. Her breath hitches, and I can feel her heart hammering beneath my palm.

"You drive me crazy," I whisper. "I'm obsessed with you, Mads. Your body, your sass, your everything."

She arches into my touch as I drag my fingers down her stomach, the muscles jumping and quivering. I'm painfully hard now, my cock straining against my zipper, begging for friction.

I dip just the tips of my fingers beneath the waistband of her thong, feeling the maddening heat of her, before pulling away. *Fuck, what am I doing?* I can't believe she hasn't smacked me yet. I need to stop before I do something we both regret.

But then Maddie's hand is on my thigh, achingly close to where I'm throbbing for her. She runs her fingers along the outline of my erection, and I nearly bust right then and there.

"Still don't believe you," she whimpers, looking at me through her lashes. "Cause you haven't kissed me."

I swallow hard, my resolve crumbling. "Because I'm scared that if I start, I won't be able to stop."

Her eyes darken, and she boldly places my hand on her breast. My fingers mold to her form, grazing her nipple through the thin lace. One of us moans.

"Then don't," she breathes, her lips parting invitingly. "Don't stop, Zack."

Fuck it. I'm only human.

I surge forward, claiming her mouth. She opens for me instantly, our tongues tangling, hot and hungry. I press her back into the mattress, crawling over her, desperate to feel every inch of her against me.

I break away to trail kisses down the column of her throat, my hand kneading her breast, rolling her nipple between my fingers. She cries out, her fingers sinking into my hair.

"God, yes," she pants as I close my lips around the outline of her nipple, the lace rasping deliciously against my tongue. I suckle her through the fabric, teasing the sensitive bud until she's writhing beneath me, her hips rocking urgently against my aching cock.

I trace my tongue over the swell of her cleavage, tasting the salt of her sweat and the sweetness of her perfume.

"Your skin," I groan, nuzzling into her. "Fuck, it's like silk."

My hands explore every bend and crevice of her body as I kiss my way down her belly, adoring her with my lips, tongue, and teeth. This is my wildest fantasy come to life. How many times have I imagined this? Dreamed of tasting her, of feeling her come undone under my mouth?

Oh. My. God. It's happening. She wants me back.

I settle between her thighs, dragging my lips along the edge of her thong. I can smell her arousal and my mouth waters. I need to devour her. I blow a stream of hot air over her cloth-covered clit, imagining how good she's going to feel against my tongue, how sweet she'll taste when I—

A loud, rumbling snore cuts through the charged silence.

I freeze, my heart plummeting. No. No fucking way.

"Maddie?" I whisper, nudging her gently.

Nothing.

"Mads?" I try again, a bit louder.

Another earth-shattering snore.

"Fuck," I groan, dropping my forehead against her hip. She's passed out cold, dead to the world. The sexiest, most frustrating cockblock in history.

I ease myself off of her, taking a shaky breath. My balls are screaming in protest, but I force myself to ignore them—to tamp down the raging inferno she's ignited in my blood.

This is a sign. A cosmic "fuck you, keep it in your pants" from the universe.

I pull the covers over her once more, tenderly brushing a strand of hair off her face. She's so peaceful, so unguarded.

I bend down, my lips grazing the delicate shell of her ear. "You're my whole world, Maddie. My everything."

I selfishly press one last soft kiss to her lips, relishing how they feel. And then I walk away, each step a painful reminder of my unsatisfied desire.

CHAPTER TEN

MADDIE

ATTRACTIVE PEOPLE SUCK. HARD.

I feel like a third wheel as Zack and Lexie dry hump each other at this prototype meeting. Okay, maybe they're just sitting side by side, but looking across the table at them, that's what my mind keeps envisioning.

Zack's rocking the suit with no tie, top buttons popped to put his broad and powerful chest on full display. And don't get me started on Lexie. Strutting in here with her tight black pencil skirt, her white blouse unbuttoned dangerously low, and those sky-high red heels that match her deep crimson lipstick. Could she be any sexier?

Ugh. They really are the perfect couple.

I glare out the window, trying to focus on the Chicago skyline instead of their soft-core porn vibes. I'm fresh off the hangover from hell. So. Much. Vomit.

I spent Sunday hungover and trying to piece together my Saturday night shitshow. I'm no detective, but I was definitely grinding on some skeezer named Stefan because I woke up to a phone full of dick pics. *Classy.*

I must have done some horribly embarrassing shit because Zack is being super weird about it, and barely telling me anything. The details are fuzzy—vodka shots—dancing like a maniac—a pair of lips. I woke up hornier than I've ever been in my whole fucking life. But that yummy sensation spewed out of me as fast as the nonstop puke train that followed. *Blech.*

Zack fires up his laptop and grins at Lexie. "These are the logo options and color schemes we're tossing around. I'd love to get your opinion."

Lexie gently tucks a strand of blonde hair behind her ear, her eyes meeting Zack's as she moves closer. "I'm so excited to give feedback. It's incredible watching this app come together!"

She's positively giddy. Gag me.

Lexie, or rather her cleavage, hovers over Zack's laptop, so much so that her red lace bra is blinding me. Zack's eyes keep darting downwards, so he's definitely getting an eyeful.

Could you be more obvious with your flirting, Lexie?

"Hey, Mads, come weigh in on this."

"Nah, I'm good. I've seen it," I reply flatly. Zack is confused but continues his presentation.

"Can I see the interface on a phone?" Lexie asks. I coldly hold out my cell. Zack stands up and grabs it.

Lexie quickly pops up next to him and smooshes the curves of her cleavage into Zack's arm as she leans over to peer at the screen. She giggles, "I love it!"

Eager much? Why not just stick Zack's hand directly on your boob? Picturing that summons a foggy memory... hazy images from Saturday night... blurry hands were groping my breasts... and I liked it!? *Eww. Did I let that Stefan creep feel me up?*

Zack closely interacting with Lexie is pissing me off. I don't know why. She keeps finding little ways to touch him, and I keep imagining laxatives in her coffee and severed brake lines.

Calm down Mads, you're being irrational.

"What about orange for the logo color?" she purrs. "It's like fire or passion."

Is Zack blushing? Oh, he is so into her.

Then, Lexie bends way over the table to reach for a pen, and her fingers "accidentally" graze the front of Zack's pants.

Right. Over. His. Dick!

"OMG, sorry!" she giggles, getting what she wanted, *which was not the freakin' pen!*

SLUT! Whoa, brain, not cool. That's very unfeminist of me. I'm not tearing her down for being assertive. I'm angry that she's being unprofessional.

Since when are client meetings code for jerk-off-the-hot-ceo?

"What if we added a camera feature with filters? Users could take pics right in the app?" Lexie suggests.

"We aren't a social media app. We're a dating app," I blurt out.

Zack shoots me a look, then quickly adds. "I like it. It's innovative and something my team overlooked."

Traitor! He knows that idea sucks! Stop thinking with your schlong.

I sink lower in my chair, silently stewing as they engage in a nauseating corporate mating ritual. Zack's full-on staring at her tits now, and Lexie no longer bothers with an excuse to touch him... *girl has no shame. Alright, universe, you win. I'm outmatched and outmaneuvered.*

Finally, the agonizing meeting ends and Lexie saunters out, her high heels clicking on the tile. I glare as the door closes.

"What was with you two getting so handsy? My eyes need a shower after watching that!" I snap.

Zack takes a step backward, raising his eyebrows. "What are you talking about, Mads? We were discussing the app."

"Puh-lease. The only app Lexie wants to download is the one between your legs. I felt like an unpaid extra in some crappy corporate sex tape."

Zack's utterly speechless; my cue to continue.

"This is not about shitting on your love parade. You just can't rub it in my face like that. I need you to think about me for once. And how I feel."

I storm out before Zack can argue.

Why do I even give a shit if Zack bangs Lexie? As long as we get funded, he can dip his wick wherever he wants.

But damn, the jealousy is real.

***

"DID SHE LIKE THE LOGO?" Reid asks eagerly as Zack and I barge into the coding cave, fuming.

I snort. "Yeah, she basically tattooed it on Zack's dick."

Zack shoots me a glare. "She accidentally grazed my pants reaching for a pen. Mads keeps turning it into a porno."

"Oooh, can I be in it?" Wes chimes in, grinning. "I could be the sexy pool boy who sticks the leaf skimmer—"

"Finish that sentence, and I'll stick my foot up your ass," I warn.

Reid sighs dreamily. "What I wouldn't give to have Lexie's foot up MY ass..."

We pause and stare. He blinks. "What? Don't kink-shame me, bros."

"Forget kink-shaming, I'm Reid-shaming," Cosmo says, fake gagging. "Now, for the love of shit, let's move past your perverse foot fetish."

"Agreed," Zack says. "Cosmo, update on the algorithm?"

Cosmo laces his fingers behind his head. "It's chugging along nicely, adapting to all the new dating data. Even Wes's special brand of input."

"I've been gathering some valuable info," Wes adds. "Which includes vibing with a really cool chick on our website. I can tell she's hot based on how she types. We chat for hours."

Reid snorts. "You're being catfished. I bet it's some dude named Chuck who lives in Ohio."

"Nah, definitely a bot," Cosmo argues. "A real woman, Wes's weirdness. No way!"

I tap my chin. "My money's on a bored Ukrainian hacker waiting to unload his spam scheme."

Zack grins. "How does Linda feel about you flirting with another woman?"

Wes's eyes widen. "We're not telling her! Linda stays in my room until I see where this thing goes."

Reid perks up. "Is she up for grabs then?"

A collective groan...

I turn back to Cosmo. "How many more dates do we need, realistically?"

"I'd say a few more outlier personality types and some niche scenarios. We're in the home stretch." He frowns. "Interface is still buggy as shit though."

"I'm putting in extra coding hours this weekend," I promise. *My carpal tunnel can deal.*

Zack checks his watch. "Maddie, we're gonna be late to Sissy's if we don't go now."

I address my pack of wild code monkeys. "You heard the man. Take the night off, get weird, you've earned it."

"Damn straight," Cosmo says, cracking his neck. "I've got a spicy evening planned with my man. And don't even think about tailing me, dipsticks."

Reid and Wes suddenly find the ceiling very interesting. I narrow my eyes at them. "Wait, is that what you jackasses were doing last week? I thought you were just being your usual creepy selves."

"We're not stalkers!" Wes protests. "We're simply trying to get to the bottom of Cosmo's love life. But tonight, I've got my own hot date with my online mystery lady."

Reid pipes up. "I've got a date too! With the Juggernaut 3000." Off our confused looks, he clarifies. "It's not a sex thing. I wanna learn foam art."

I smirk. "That's a new word for cum I've never heard before."

"And on that disturbing image, we're out!" Zack announces, steering me towards the door.

LoveScore is in the homestretch. AppVerge Expo is mere weeks away, and then we'll unveil our baby to the world.

***

DING DONG!

Zack and I wait on the porch of Sissy and Ben's giant historic brick home. This place is an HGTV reality show come to life, with its fancy-ass columns, perfectly trimmed hedges, and vintage charm. Witnessing this joyful suburban jail cell is birth control in itself.

"Holy shitnuggets, stop staring!" I snap.

"I'm still racking my brain. What did I do to piss you off?"

I blow out a frustrated breath. "Drop it, Zack."

"No." He shakes his head adamantly. "I wanna talk about it. I wasn't flirting with Lexie. It was just—"

The door flies open, and I'm bombarded by two squealing, sticky-handed tornados. "Auntie Maddieee!" Violet and Hazel chorus, nearly toppling me over with hugs.

"Wow, you girls are gonna be taller than me soon!" I exclaim, wrapping my arms around them.

Sissy appears behind them, looking like a human friggin' Pinterest board in her *I'm-boho-but-not-too-boho* tunic and her *I'm a statement, bitches* necklace.

"Girls, let them come inside." She ushers us in, pulling me into a vanilla-scented hug. "Hey, Mads! I love seeing your smile in person instead of on a screen."

She turns to Zack with an apologetic smile. "I'm sorry, hon, but Ben just called. He has to stay late at the office."

Zack nods understandingly, gesturing to the magazine-worthy interior. "Hey, no sweat. Guess a life like this requires clockin' some serious hours."

Hazel tugs on Zack's sleeve, her eyes wide. "Zack, wanna play a new brain game on Roblox with me? I'm so good. I bet I can totally beat you!"

Zack winks at me conspiratorially and turns to Hazel. "I'm sure you will, kiddo. You're like your Auntie Maddie... she wins every game we play."

Violet bounces on her toes and chants, "Roblox! Roblox! Roblox!"

Sissy shakes her head. "Alright, alright. You can have extra screen time tonight. Go have fun."

The twins drag Zack, giggling, to the family room. I turn to Sissy, arching a brow. "Ben's working late again? He's been putting in a lot of overtime lately, huh?"

She sighs, tucking back her strawberry-blonde hair. "Zack's not wrong. It takes a lot to maintain a lifestyle like this. C'mon, Nora's in the kitchen."

Mother, wife, and perfect life. Harddddd pass.

Nora is a whirlwind of veggie-chopping efficiency in the gleaming chef's kitchen, her glossy blonde ponytail swishing as she works. The second she spots me, she abandons her cutting board and barrels over for a hug attack.

"Mads! Oh my gosh, how are you holding up after *the kiss*?" She gushes, squeezing me tight.

Sissy's head snaps up from the chips she's pouring into a decorative bowl. "Whoa, whoa, back up. What kiss?"

Nora's eyes widen. "Uh, Maddie kissed Zack."

"Nora!" I whack her on the arm. "Zack is literally in the next room. Zip it secret spiller!"

Sissy pouts, arranging tortilla chips in a bowl. "It's not fair! You guys always leave me out of the juicy gossip! I need every scandalous detail, stat."

"Fine," I groan. "I kissed Zack. But it isn't what you think. We were a pretend couple on a fake date, so basically... it meant nothing."

"Maddie's feeling super insecure about it like she's not pretty or desirable," Nora says, lowering her voice to a whisper, "She's worried that guys think she doesn't have a vagina..."

Note to self: do not, I repeat, do NOT confide in Nora ever again.

"Aww, Mads." Sissy coos, draping an arm around my slouched shoulders. "You're drop-dead gorgeous, totally screw-worthy, not to mention brilliant and hilarious... And I know you have a vagina because I've seen it."

"That's what I said!" Nora chirps.

I shrug away from Sissy's grip, my face on fire. "Okay, new rule: no more discussing my love life, real or imaginary."

Sissy and Nora exchange a meaningful look—some sister ESP passing between them.

"Fine, I'll drop it..." Sissy says, rearranging Nora's taco bar setup. "But let me ask one thing: you're not developing actual feelings for Zack, are you?"

Nora's eyes light up and she claps her hands. "I asked the same thing!"

"Jesus H. Christ on a cracker, NO! Zack and I are friends. Now, always, forever. We're frriiieeenndddzzzz!" I emphasize, drawing out the syllables.

Sissy hums skeptically, moving the guacamole and shredded cheese for the third time until Nora repositions them back.

"Uh-huh. I've said it before, and I'll say it again—men and women can't be 'just friennddzzzz.' Not in the long run. Eventually, someone catches feelings."

I cross my arms. "Like I've been telling you for an entire decade, that's a bullshit notion."

Sissy turns to Nora, her brow arched. "Nora, honey, have you ever had a dude-pal who didn't try to get in your britches?"

Nora shakes her head and moves the guac and cheese back to their original spots. "Nope. Any guy claiming he wanted to be buddies wound up either banging me or ghosting me."

Sissy smirks triumphantly. "See? Told ya." She moves the bowls once again, ignoring Nora's exasperated huff.

A tousled Abby staggers into the kitchen, her eyes bloodshot and puffy and her blonde hair going every which way. Her glitter-smeared mini-dress is as short as her attention span, and it's clear that she's not wearing a bra. "Taco night? Fuck yeah, I'm starving!"

"Nice of you to finally grace us with your presence, Abs," Nora says with a pointed look.

Abby shoves a chip in her mouth, crumbs spraying as she talks. "Chill, Nor. Cool people show up fashionably late. You should try it sometime."

Sissy steps between them, her voice stern. "Alrighty, you two. Play nice-nice." She squints at Abby, her nose wrinkling. "Abigail, are you stoned outta your gourd right now?"

"Relax, Mom-bot, I'm a little buzzed," Abby scoffs. "But you can bet your basic ass I'll be gettin' turnt at Midnight Club later. Gotta get my vibe on!"

"Ugh, been there, regretted that," I cut in with a shudder. "And lemme tell ya, nothing's worth the skull-splitting hangover."

Everyone freezes, and three pairs of eyes bore into me...

"No fucking way! You went clubbing without me?!" Abby gasps.

I shrug. "I was fake clubbing for one of our fake dates. If it makes you feel better, I wore your slutty black cutout dress. So it was like you were with me... in skank spirit."

Abby whistles, eyeing me appraisingly. "Dayum, girl! I bet you had the man-meat swarming. Did your giant tits stay contained in that bad boy?"

"Actually, funny story..." I say. "I might have locked lips with a club rat named Stefan. Details are muddled, but the dude flooded my inbox with a slew of dick pics the next day."

Abby and Nora exchange a glance. "We want to see!"

I reluctantly pull it out *(so to speak)*. My phone reveals one unsolicited text-icular message after another.

"I want to see some ding-dongs!" Sissy squeals, her curiosity winning against her better nature.

A wave of revulsion washes over us as we see Stefan's not-so-impressive manhood.

"Ew! I'm adding a new dealbreaker to my ideal man checklist," Nora declares. "No scraggly pubes. Manscaping is a must."

Abby snickers. "How did Zack react when you were getting your grind on with Dick Pic Stu?"

I rack my brain, trying to push back the alcohol-induced haze. "Honestly, I can't remember much. Zack must have brought me home... I know I woke up horny as hell."

"Yep, the 'club hangover hornies' are a real thing," Abby confirms. "That's why I always try to score some vitamin D before passing out. Rise n' shine, get mine, roll over, and snooze s'more."

Sissy sighs wistfully. "God, I'd give anything to go out dancing and wake up feeling like I got hit by a truck... but, you know, in a sexy way!"

Abby pats her shoulder. "Those days are long gone. Now you're stuck in the 'better or worse' life. Every morning you're thirsty AF while Ben snores next to you like a freight train."

I high-five Abby, laughing. "Ha! See? Abby gets it. Happily single fo' life!"

Sissy shakes her head. "Oh, just you wait, little sisters. Love comes for us all, usually sweeping you off your feet when you least expect it. Then... it's ring-a-ding-ding time!"

I make a holy cross with my fingers. "Take back your evil curse!"

Nora frowns. "I, for one, can't wait to get wifed up! Bring on the baby making and minivan driving."

Nora and Abby carry plates to the dining room as Sissy pulls me aside, her expression serious.

"Mads, sweetie..." she says, her voice warm. "We don't always agree on love, but please tread carefully with Zack. You two are the very definition of inseparable. Throwing nookie into the mix can have some serious consequences."

She bulldozes her way through my objections. "You haven't had a ton of experience with guys. With Zack, there's always been clear boundaries—a big ol' line in the sand. But now, kissing him, even as a joke... I'm concerned for you both."

"Sissy, trust me, it's all good. Zack and I are like two peas in a non-sexual pod, now and for-ev-er."

We join the others, but her words echo in my mind, creating an unsettling feeling in the pit of my stomach. She's right. Zack and I have a good thing going, and I shouldn't lose my best friend over some stupid, horny urges.

No matter how tempting it might be to climb him like a tree.

***

"OH, STOP, PLEASE, I'M GONNA PEE MY PANTS!" Sissy clutches her stomach and squeals.

"And then, I shit you not," Zack says, "Maddie saunters up to me with her best sex kitten impression and purrs, 'I'm Diamond McJuggs. Wanna juggle my lady melons?'"

My sisters erupt in laughter, rattling the plates on the table. Nora wipes her tears.

"I totally peed!" Sissy gasps.

My cheeks take on a feverish red. "Zack, I did not say it like that, you jerkwad."

He grins and shrugs. "That's what I remember. And that, ladies, is the story I'm sticking to."

"Speaking of Maddie's sexiest hits," Nora starts, "Zack, didn't you just die over her little red workout set the other day? How poppin' was her booty in those tight shorts?"

"It was... damn!" Zack agrees way too enthusiastically. "Have you seen your sister's badonkadonk? That thing is an ASS-terpiece. It should be bronzed and displayed at the Louvre."

Did he just compliment my ass?

Abby giggles. "Zack's got a point, Mads. Your booty is a vibe. Michelangelo could only dream of sculpting something so fire."

"Can we please stop talking about my butt?" I plead, burying my flaming face in my hands. "I beg of you."

Zack smirks. "Nora, let's just say that little red gym getup was about to catch fire it was working so hard. Mads' boobs were seconds away from going rogue and smacking me in the face."

"Ha ha." My eyes narrow as I point to his crotch. "I saw your little soldier standing at attention. So clearly, he wasn't laughing."

"Ooo," my sisters say in unison.

"And here I thought you were part of the no-boner squad when it came to Mads," Abby chuckles. "Nice to know she can get you hard after all these years."

"Abby! Shut it," I hiss, sneaking a glance at Zack, but he seems unfazed.

"What can I say? It's been a wild ride seeing Mads play all these different characters," he agrees with a shrug.

Sissy grins and shakes her head. "I still can't believe your little role-play game is helping LoveScore get financing. Did you know Maddie forced us to play that all the time as kids?"

Zack meets my gaze, his brown eyes filled with warmth and affection. "Maddie's never had to force me. We've always had a blast roleplaying together."

There's something in the way he looks at me, that lingering stare, holding a beat too long. It steals the air from my lungs. My sisters exchange knowing glances, but I refuse to acknowledge them.

Sissy taps her chin. "Zack, we were having an interesting conversation earlier about men and women being friends. Do you have any close female friends besides Maddie?"

Zack pauses, considering it. "Uh, no. Just Mads, I guess."

"Huh. Interesting," Sissy arches her brow at me, putting herself into the crosshairs of my icy glare.

"Actually, Zack has his eye on a girl named Lexie. She's like, perfect for him." The words taste bitter on my tongue, but I barrel on, desperate to divert the attention off of us. "Zack, tell them about her."

Zack blinks at me, surprised. "Sure, yeah. Lexie is a financial analyst we're working with to secure funding for LoveScore," he explains awkwardly. "She's great, except that I have a strict policy to not mix business with pleasure."

I nod along like a bobblehead as jealousy claws at my gut. *Why the fuck did I bring up Lexie?*

"Hypothetically," Nora says smugly, crossing her arms, "if you two weren't working together, would you ask Lexie out?"

Zack hesitates, running a hand through his hair.

"Maybe? Probably. She is pretty cool..."

Hearing him say he wants to date Lexi makes my stomach drop to my toes. But I cover it with a smile, to remind my sisters *(and myself)* for the gazillionth time that Zack and I are just friends. Best friends. And as much as it kills me to admit it...

Zack wants Lexie. Not me.

CHAPTER ELEVEN

ZACK

"FUCK! I LOVE THIS LEATHER," Abby exclaims from the backseat, running her hands along the upholstery. "For real, Zack, you ever get freaky back here?"

"Abs!" Maddie shrieks, whipping around and glaring at her sister. "He's giving you a ride. Just say thank you like a normal human."

Abby puts on a ridiculous posh British accent. "Ever so grateful for the carriage ride, good sir. I do apologize for my elder sister's lack of propriety. She's quite the ill-mannered spinster, you see."

"Hilarious," Maddie deadpans, rolling her eyes.

God, she's cute when she's all riled up.

"Any time, Abigail." I glance at Maddie in the passenger seat, her brow furrowed as she taps on her phone.

"Abby, what happened to your car?" Maddie asks, not looking up.

Abby leans forward. "Don't tell Mom and Dad, but it got repossessed."

"No. Seriously?"

"When the 'rents cut off your fun-money stream, monthly payments are a bitch," Abby says, shrugging. "If you narc, swear to God, I'll tell Nora you're finally ready to do a juice cleanse."

"You evil wench wagon!" Maddie says, shaking her head, but I can still hear the love in her voice.

"Abby, why don't you move to Chicago?" I chime in. "Isn't Evanston a little too... cardigans and soccer moms for you."

Abby scoffs. "Because mooching is fucking free, bro. I can stumble in at 3 a.m., reeking of questionable choices, and no one gives a shit." She grins wickedly. "Sure, Mom's gagging for me to bounce, but I love my cushy setup. It'll take a crap ton of lube and the fucking jaws of life to kick me out."

I shoot Maddie a teasing look, but she averts her eyes.

"Although," Abby continues, "Mom's been crankin' the horny GILF routine to eleven lately. She and Dad are bumping uglies round the freaking clock. It's like an old people all-you-can-eat buffet to the ears."

"Jesus tits!" Maddie claps her hands over her ears. "I'd rather bob for apples in a port-a-potty than picture that. New topic! Can you believe the mountain of bullshit errands Sissy threw at us for the anniversary party? And right before we left, what the balls?"

"Typical bossy, Sissy," Abby snorts. "We were promised tacos, not chores."

Maddie groans. "And she rented out the Ladies Club banquet room for the party. Ugh, could that place be any more up its own ass?"

As they go back and forth, I know something's off with Maddie. Getting her to open up? Well, that's a story I doubt I'll hear anytime soon.

My mind goes back to that night after the club, Maddie's smokin' hot body in nothing but lingerie, pressing up against me. The salty-sweet flavor of her skin, her soft little moans, her pleading for me to touch her, taste her... consume her. If she hadn't passed out, hell, my face might still be buried between her thighs.

But Maddie appears to have no memory of it. I'd like to straight-up ask her, but that would mean a bunch of awkward questions. And I'm not sure my cojones are up for that conversation, especially if Mads doesn't like what she hears.

What was the deal with Maddie acting all jealous during the meeting with Lexie? I mean, sure, Lexie was basically hurling herself at me, and I had to keep subtly rejecting her advances. But Mads was ready to claw Lexie's eyes out.

And then after the meeting, her saying I was *rubbing it in her face* and *not thinking about her feelings... What the actual fuck?* Maddie's never cared who I've dated before.

Maddie's voice pierces my thought tsunami.

"Abs, you should work at a club. You practically live there already."

Abby replies, "Nah. I'm building up my stylist portfolio, tho. Even got a few gigs from my Insta,"

An idea hits me. "You should style us for the conference, Abby!"

"That's a great idea, Zack!" Maddie's whole face lights up, igniting a warm swell of affection within my chest. *God, I've missed that smile. I've missed seeing her happy.* I could fix it if I knew what's been making her so hot and cold lately.

"Red light! Red light!" Abby screeches.

I jam my foot down, the brakes screaming in protest as my arm whips sideways, stretching across Maddie's body like a safeguard as the car screeches to a horn-blaring stop.

"Everyone okay?" I ask, pulse pounding.

"I'm good," Abby says.

I turn to Maddie and realize my hand is resting on her chest. Our eyes lock, and she places her hand over mine but doesn't move it. I can feel her heart racing beneath my palm.

"Are you okay?" she asks.

I nod, searching her face as she clasps my hand tighter, holding it protectively to her breast. And just like that, the pieces click into place.

Those hungry stares... her irrational jealousy.

Begging to be kissed.... pleading for me to rip off her clothes.

Urging me to ravish her body... the death grip she has on me now.

Could it be?

HONK! HONK!

"Green light, Zack," Abby singsongs. "Yo, when you wreck this Tesla, can I have it?"

I remove my hand from Maddie's soft curves, gripping the steering wheel to ground myself.

"Yeah, sure," I mutter.

As I push on the gas pedal, the mind-blowing reality seeps in. All the glaring signs were there, I just didn't pick up on them.

Holy shit! Maddie's falling for me.

***

"THE FORCE IS STRONG WITH THIS HAND." Cosmo holds up his cards, a smug smile playing on his lips.

I stare from behind my own cards. "Make it so, Number One—I'm all in."

Cosmo scoffs. "You see, that's how I know you're bluffing. You come at me with your inferior Star Trek lines when I'm clearly intimidating you with my superior Star Wars quotes."

Abby glances between us. "I don't know what either of those are. Aliens or something?"

"Blasphemy!" Cosmo and I shout in unison.

Abby shrugs and triumphantly lays down her cards. "Whatever, geeks. Straight flush. I win again!"

Abby and the whole LoveScore team are gathered around a folding poker table that's taken over the living room. Instead of poker chips, we're using Maddie's gourmet popcorn flavors to up the ante.

The group groans as Abby rakes in her giant mound of popcorn "chips". It's roughly the size of a small mountain, with no signs of stopping.

"How are you so damn good at this?" Cosmo demands.

She shrugs. "I usually suck. But my astrology app said 'an unexpected gift will bring a smile to your face today'. Guess this was it."

Cosmo snorts derisively. "Technically, it's tomorrow. It's after midnight."

"Technically, the game started yesterday, so it still counts," Abby fires back.

"I think she's cheating," Reid chimes in. "No way someone as hot as you is this good at poker."

Maddie gives him a death glare. "Make a move on my sister, and I'll knot your dick into a freaking pretzel."

My face sobers him. "Trust me, man. Don't tangle with Maddie's wrath. My coconuts still quiver at the mere thought of her fury."

Maddie flashes me an appreciative grin—it's a strange way to win her favor, but damn if her approval doesn't make my heart race. I gotta tread lightly, though, because if I push too hard, I'll spook her and blow my shot. A slow approach will ensure her guard is down and open her up to the idea of us... of love... of how perfect we are together.

My mind races to formulate a game plan as I deal out the next round. Everyone antes up.

"Is Linda wearing my hot pink dress?" Abby asks, eyeing Wes's inflatable girlfriend propped up in the corner.

"Maybe... is that okay?" Wes asks hopefully.

Abby waves him off. "It's cool. Looks better on her anyway."

"See, Abigail? You're already killing it as a stylist," Maddie teases. Everyone tosses their initial popcorn bets into the pot.

With his cards apparently even worse than his poker face, Reid folds. "I'm out. Gonna go make a cappuccino. Anyone want one?" No one responds.

Things are getting interesting as people fold one by one until it's just Maddie and me.

She angles her body toward me, a flirtatious gleam in her eye. "Well, well, Hanley. Am I bluffing?"

I match her coy smile. "Probably. But I'm all in." I slide the rest of my popcorn to the middle.

Maddie meets my bet, flips her cards, and... *Shit, It's a full house.*

"You can't read me at all, can you, Hanley?" she taunts, collecting her spoils.

"I'm not showing all my cards just yet. I'm playing the long game, biding my time. And when the moment is right, I'll strike and take it all." I say cockily.

I'm gonna prove to you just how fantastic we could be together, Mads.

The next round starts, and Cosmo can't wipe the grin off his face as he deals.

"I've got a good feeling about making the expo deadline, guys. Two and a half weeks to go, and things are pretty solid."

Abby gasps. "Quick! Knock on wood, Cos. Don't jinx it."

"Astrology isn't science, Abby," Cosmo says dismissively. "Good luck and bad luck? It's superstitious garbage."

"Hey now," Wes pipes up. "Ya know the girl I've been chatting with online, she's way into that stuff."

Reid snickers. "For the last time. That girl is a dude. And he's definitely not your soulmate."

"Uh, pause, homies," Abby interrupts. "Wes, if you're talking with someone, then nut up and make a move already. Ask her out on a real date! Go have some legit sex!"

Wes's eyes widen. "Uhhh... we could go on a date because she's a real person, but that wouldn't automatically mean sex."

"For sure it does," Abby counters. "I always smash on the first date. You can see if you mesh, if there's a vibe. How else do ya figure out if you even want a round two?"

Reid gapes at her. "Always?"

"Yah," Abby confirms with a nonchalant shrug. "Always."

I watch as Reid quietly mouths, "I love you."

Abby glances down at her cards and pushes her entire popcorn stash into the middle of the table. "All in, losers."

The room is deathly quiet.

You could hear a mouse fart as everyone tosses in their cards, fold written all over their faces.

"Oh. My. God!" Maddie grinds her fists into her eye sockets.

Abby glances around, confusion etched on her pretty face. "Why's everyone bugging out? Did I miss some tea or something?"

Maddie lifts her head, looking like she's aged ten years in ten seconds. "The dating survey. We're such geeks. We didn't include anything about kissing or physical stuff."

"Back up the truck!" Abby shouts, hand flying to her collarbone. "Is this app some retro throwback dating thing? Like you're waiting for marriage or some shit?"

She gives Maddie a skeptical side-eye. "Is that how you smart people do it? No action on your dates, just chatting about algorithms and equations?"

We're supremely fucked.

Wes grabs his laptop and starts frantically typing. "Let me ask the chat group. See what they think."

His eyebrows shoot up to his hairline. "Um, guys, we've got a metric fuck-ton of responses pouring in. And they're all backing up Abby's opinion."

He reads the messages. "Why didn't you include anything about physical contact? What about kiss ratings? Is the person good in bed? Did they initiate sex on the first date? How was the sex? Flirty? Sloppy? Holy shit, the chat is blowing up. Everyone's saying they would not consider using the app unless sexual information is part of it."

I risk a glance at Maddie, who's melting onto the floor like a rogue ice cube on a hot summer day.

Cosmo nods solemnly. "The masses have spoken. They want a physical love score of the person they're gonna date before they commit to a swipe."

I frown. "This isn't right guys. Where does it end? Are we gonna have fields for 'dick sizes' and 'how quickly he comes'?"

Abby scoffs. "Welcome to the 21st century, Zack. People want the dirty deets. The juicier, the better."

I turn to Maddie, panicking and not hiding it well. "Mads, real talk. How much trouble are we in here?"

She runs a hand through her hair, and it looks like she's gonna yank it out by the roots. "If we don't add the sexual shizzbits to the survey, the app is gonna implode faster than a Hollywood marriage. Users will roast us alive in the reviews."

"She's right, it's like the movies," Reid explains. "Bad reviews on opening weekend? Might as well be a death sentence. Same goes for apps."

The full weight of the situation hits me like an elephant unloading a dump truck of Taco Bell. "The app can't tank. We'll lose the funding."

Shit, we're totally fucked!

"Let's all just take a breath," I say, projecting a calm energy that I definitely don't feel. "What do we need to fix this? More specific survey questions?"

Cosmo nods. "For starters, yeah. We need to drill down on the physical chemistry stuff. First kiss timing, intensity, tongue action, wandering hands, the works."

Maddie, rubbing her temples in pain, says, "For reals, we're back to square one. We need an assload of user data for this algorithm to spit out any decent matches."

"Alright, fearless leaders," Cosmo sighs. "What's your fix for this clusterfuck?"

Abby huffs out a laugh. "Um, hello? It's so obvious. Zack and Maddie need to get freaky and fuck, stat."

Maddie freezes in place, her eyes wide in absolute shock.

Reid raises his hand. "I agree. Time for our co-CEO's to start banging."

Wes adds, "I've got people in the chat agreeing to edit their surveys if we add the physical fields. That would drastically increase the user numbers."

Oh man, this is not good. Not good at all. I just found out that Maddie is catching feelings. I wanna go slow, super slow. And now these clowns are saying we need to get down and dirty for the app?

Nope, not happening.

Maddie covers her ears. "Can you all just shut your fucking yap holes for one goddamn minute? I'm trying to think of a plan that doesn't involve me getting impaled on Zack's beef stick."

I stand up abruptly, knocking over my chair. "Mads, can I talk to you for a sec? In private?"

The room erupts in a chorus of *"ooohs"* and exaggerated kissy noises.

"Calm your tits, jerk-offs. It's just a meeting," Maddie grumbles.

My thoughts whirl chaotically as I trail after Maddie. I wanted to take things to the next level with her, but this? This is a fucking disaster.

Shit. Shit. Shit.

***

"COME HERE." I PAT the bed beside me, a casual invitation for Maddie to sit.

"Is that a 'let's get it on' pat or a 'let's have a chat' pat?" Her gaze darts to my bed, then back up to my face.

I roll my eyes, chuckling. "Oh my God, Mads. We're just talking."

She hesitates before plopping down next to me, her body tense. "Are we seriously talking about having sex?... together?"

I take a deep breath, trying to find the right words. "We're discussing our options."

"What would that even be like? We'd be naked... at the same time." She glances down at my crotch, extending her hand like she's going to shake it. "Hello, Zack's penis. Nice to meet you. I'd like to introduce you to my hairy lady rug."

We both laugh nervously.

But then her mood shifts, and she starts to spiral. "If we don't give each other a little sumn sumn, I think it's game over. And all this was for a big fat nothing." She keeps babbling, her words spilling out in a frantic jumble. "Abby's probably right, it's just banging. People bang, you bang, I bang, the team bangs, apparently my parents bang all the time... bang, bang, bang." She's using finger guns and hyperventilating.

"Stop saying bang and breathe, Mads. It's fine. We're going to figure this out," I say, placing my hand on her shoulder.

She looks at me with hurt in her eyes, her voice soft. "Zack, I can't ask you to do this. You didn't even want to kiss me, and now we're talking about sex."

That confirms it. She definitely has no memory of our steamy makeout session or my admission of how badly I want her. Sober

Maddie hides her emotions. It took a drunken Mads to let her guard down and expose her true feelings.

Dammit, this is all moving too fast.

But then her eyes spark with an idea. "We could pretend, you know... to have sex and kiss and all that crap. We can just lie on the form."

"Sure," I encourage, intrigued by where she's going with this. "Lay it on me. Paint a picture of what shaking the sheets with me would be like. What would you write on the date survey?"

She looks embarrassed, fidgeting with her hands. "Well, okay. I'd say on our date when we were getting frisky... it felt like a horny Rottweiler was trying to eat my face off with all the slobber. And, uh, then during sex, your, um... dick was all floppy and jiggly like a jellyfish? You were thrusting and grunting like..." She does some cringy hand gestures and growls to illustrate.

I place my hands over hers, stilling her awkward gestures. "Dear God, please stop." I shake my head, my voice serious. "I promise you, if we had sex, that is not how you'd describe it."

She rolls her eyes. "Oh, is that so? Okay, Mr. I-Know-Every-thing-About-Seggs, how would you explain it?"

Tell her, Hanley. Don't hold back.

Dropping my voice to a low, seductive tone, I edge closer until we're inches apart. "You'd describe being ravaged with an absolute hunger from my mouth." I turn her face toward mine, my thumb slowly tracing the tempting curve of her lip. "How the sensation of my fingers on your neck sent your nerves into a frenzy. How your body ached for more."

I softly pull back the neckline of her top and lean in, exhaling a slow and tantalizing breath, sensing the warmth of it on her skin, just below her ear. Maddie's breath catches as I delicately graze my lips across her vulnerable skin.

"You'd describe in vivid detail how I stripped you down reeeal slow," I murmur in a gravelly voice. "How I took my sweet time covering every inch of your smooth, silky skin with hot, wet kisses, making my way down to get a taste of you."

Her tongue sneaks out to wet those full lips as she imagines the scene I'm laying out. I can see her breathing pick up, her chest rising and falling.

I pull her closer, my breath hot on her ear—my voice a sexy rumble. "And when you described how I fucked you, you'd get all flushed and flustered, remembering every detail about how my thick cock filled you up completely, taking over every inch of your snug little pussy."

Maddie lets out a soft whimper, her body squirming restlessly against me as her eyes stay tightly shut.

"You'd recall the sweat glistening from our tangled bodies," I rasp. "How you wrapped those luscious legs around me tighter, taking me deeper, letting me thrust harder until I had you coming so hard and so loud, the neighbors called the police on us."

She bites down on her juicy bottom lip.

I crave her more than anything, but I know she's not ready for that yet.

Clearing my throat, I force myself to pull away, shattering the intense moment. "So I don't think lying on those surveys is really an option to help the algorithm."

Mads blushes fiercely, looking away as she tries to get a handle on herself. "Yeah, definitely not," she murmurs. "Since I've never, you know... felt like that before. Ever."

Her eyes meet mine again, expression turning serious. "So are you saying if we... I mean, that you'd want to kiss and be touchy and um... have sex? Just for the app's data, I mean?"

Yes! Fuck yes! I'm ready to rip your clothes off and worship every gorgeous inch of your body right here. I want to have mind-blowing sex with you every single damn day for the rest of my life.

"Maddie, I'm not trying to sway you one way or the other. This is completely your decision, and I'll support you whatever you decide," I say somberly.

Her eyes flicker, that blazing mind of hers considering every possible angle, every potential risk and reward.

"Technically," she says slowly, deliberately, "WE wouldn't be the ones actually... having sex."

"I'm not quite following, Mads."

She draws in a deep breath. "I'm saying we will roleplay the sex part. Like with our fake dating profiles—it's not really us. It's our characters going at it." She grimaces at her own words. "Getting all... freaky. With their... you know, bits and things."

I bite back a grin. "Wow, I think I should make you a cheat sheet on sex slang." My gaze becomes serious. "Honestly Mads, are you sure about this?"

"We're already balls deep in this shitshow. No point in backing out now," she smirks.

Oh my God, this is it!

This insane plan, as nuts as it sounds, is the answer. The key to tearing down the massive walls around her heart. I'll let her slip into a new persona and blow her mind one orgasm at a time until she's forced to admit that we're meant to be together.

"Well, Mads," I joke. "As the better actor, I guess I can pretend to like you enough to enter your body."

She smacks my arm, laughing. "Gross! And you think *I* need a better sex vocabulary?"

Her voice turns serious again. "To be clear, the sex between us isn't real. We're only playing a part. Like Abby said, 'it's just banging', so we compartmentalize it. We can do that, right?"

"You and me? We can handle this. We can handle anything together."

Maddie nods firmly before sticking out her hand, all business-like. "Alright then. We stick to the dating profiles, stay in character at all times—that's the rule. Two and a half weeks, and then this nut-so-rama experiment is dunzo."

We make it official with a handshake, and I'm taken back to that night when we vowed to be just friends. *But this time, there's a flicker of hope igniting inside me.*

I love you, Madeline Denton. I've always loved you. I just need you to realize that you love me too. And if you let me, I'll be yours forever.

CHAPTER TWELVE

MADDIE

I WANT TO FUCK MY BEST FRIEND.

Sex, sex, sex. It's taken up residence in my brain like a full-time RVer in a Walmart parking lot. After Zack gave me an X-rated peek into what doing the nasty with him would be like, it's been a non-stop carnal carnival up in here.

The memory of his sultry breath lingers on my neck, and I'm a little mortified to confess that I was mere moments away from a personal fireworks show; ignited by his words and feather-light brushes against my skin.

So either Zack's some kind of sex Jedi, or I've been living in a serious sex desert. I'm gonna go with option C: both.

MOTHERFUCKER! I shut my eye after jabbing it with the freaking mascara wand. I survey the damage of black smudges around my eye. I snatch a makeup wipe... looks like we're starting from scratch.

In the decade we've been besties, the thought of doing the dirty with Zack or imagining him with other women has not crossed my mind. But hot ziggity! Is that the sexual roller coaster all of

Zack's girlfriends get to enjoy? Since we've been roomies, he's only brought one woman home, and she unleashed a soundtrack-worthy moan-a-thon all night. I assumed she was just being theatrical for his benefit.

As it turns out, I was dead wrong.

The picture of freaky deaky that I painted for Zack was based on my own sloppy hookups. Always clumsy, never hitting the spot. That's why I ctrl+alt-deleted myself outta one-night stands and went on playful, waddling adventures with my trusty sidekick, the Pleasure Penguin. But holy fuckballs, what Zack described...

I want it.

I want to feel it.

And I want Zack to be the one to do it to me.

I scrutinize my makeup in the mirror, blinking my mascara dry.

Not too shabby, Maddie. Sexy enough—that was the goal.

I stare at my reflection, focusing on Zack's vintage Northwestern hoodie. It's insanely soft and smells like him—that fresh laundry aroma with a touch of his cologne. I might have swiped it from his room... again.

Don't judge.

Weed whacked the bush? *Check.*

Hair waves? *Flawless-ish.*

Nora's man-eater perfume? *Spritz.*

I take a deep breath and shed the hoodie, unveiling the black skintight jumpsuit I've got going on underneath. The plunging V-neck puts my girls on display, and the stretchy fabric skims over my body, defining every contour, especially my butt.

I know, I know, I'm coming on strong—but I gotta use what I got, right? After Zack pledged his allegiance to my ass at dinner with my sisters, I know the man likes curves, so hell yeah my assets are on full display.

I give myself one more spritz of perfume, just to be safe. There. I'm as fuckable as I'm gonna get. But all of this effort isn't a guaranteed ticket to Bone Town... and why? Well, the geniuses on the team decided we still need to have randomized results. Meaning the date could end with a full-on makeout session to third-base action to actual sex.

But there's also the possibility of zero physical contact. *Can you say mind-fuck?*

According to Cosmo, the algorithm needs that anything-can-happen-vibe, just like in real life. So now Zack and I have these secret extended date profiles that come with a "desire" or "anticipation" for how the user hopes the physical stuff will play out.

Tonight, my user profile 'Sarah Lewis' is hoping to get lucky... *because girl, same.*

I just hope Zack's 'Jake Parker' is feeling as frisky as me.

I slip on my heels and take one last look in the mirror. "Okay, Mads. Time to give these hormones the release they've been begging for. But, remember, this is just about getting physical... no gooey feelings."

Now, let's go have some sex.

***

```
<!DOCTYPE html>
<h1>User Profile</h1>
```

</div>

NAME: Jake Parker

AGE: 32

OCCUPATION: General Contractor

INTERESTS: Home improvement. Skiing. Live music.

ABOUT ME: I turn houses into homes. Originally from New York, now in Chicago. Seeking a passionate someone who isn't afraid to get their hands dirty. Up for new adventures and being yourself? Let's build a strong foundation together!

</div>

<h1>User Profile</h1>

NAME: Sarah Lewis

AGE: 30

OCCUPATION: Physical Therapist

INTERESTS: Volunteering. Long walks. DIY projects.

ABOUT ME: I'm dedicated to helping others live their best lives. My work is challenging and thrilling. When I'm not in the clinic, I love to explore vibrant neighborhoods, try new restaurants, and hit hiking trails. I admire ambition, kindness, and passion in a potential partner.

</div>

<h1>Date Information</h1>

DETAILS: Dinner "The Cozy Cannoli Italian Ristorante."

```
</body>
</html>
```

"IT'S INCREDIBLY SATISFYING TO USE YOUR HANDS to shape something and feel it come to life under your touch," says Zack *(aka Jake)*.

"I bet those strong, skilled hands of yours could make anyone's fantasies a reality," I say, sensually sipping from my straw.

The conversation has been like this all night—flirty, with a hint of innuendo. We both use our hands for our character's jobs, so the double entendres are begging to be said. We're speaking in code, but the code is just *let's smash*.

This restaurant is a relic, and not in a good way. The decor looks like a decrepit Hollywood film set from an old mafia movie, layered with dust and grime. The lighting is dim, mostly because the light bulbs are burned out, and nobody bothered to replace them. The *could-have-been-charming* Italian melodies sputter and crackle from the ailing speakers, a distorted echo of their former glory.

But the food is orgasmic!

If I could bathe in this marinara sauce, I would.

Creating a sexy vibe in this place has been a struggle, but obstacles be damned. I've made it crystal clear that I'm all fired up and down to be clowned in V-town.

I'm doing what I can to get Zack thinking about sex. Eyelash flutters, flirty hair flips, pouty lips.

I even sucked olive oil off my finger like it was a freaking sch-long. He thinks he's been slick, stealing glances at my tits, but I've clocked him every time. And when I excused myself to the restroom, I dropped my handbag *(oops)* and bent over to give him a show.

God, I'm revved up; Zack looks absolutely delicious tonight.

The check comes.

"Let me take care of this," he commands with smoldering dark eyes and a possessive voice that melts my panties. "It's the least I can do after such an incredible evening." Leaning in conspiratorially, his voice drops. "And besides, I'd much rather have you handle something else."

Oh, hell yeah, I'll handle anything you want!

"Can I walk you to your car?" His tone is pure, liquid seduction.

This is it, bitches—go time!

The inside of that place was too risky with all those families around, but out here, in the secluded parking lot, it's prime hookup territory. My heart's racing like it just stole something, a tingling sensation floods my body.

We reach my car and I couldn't be more ready.

Lip gloss on.

Condom in purse.

And I may have removed my panties in the bathroom.

I wait impatiently for him to make his move—to take my hand, pull me flush against him, anything. Zack looks into my eyes earnestly.

"I had an amazing time tonight. You are a treasure. I'm delighted we got to do this."

While my brain wrestles with whiplash, my lady bits are staging a protest. Are you freaking kidding me? This was just a friendly date?! I'm a pissed-off, unsatisfied mess.

"So that's it?"

I notice Zack licking his lips, his eyes smoldering with raw need, and my breath catches.

"I had a really good time," he says, moving in torturously slow.

The kiss starts gentle but quickly blazes hotter, more urgent. I can't get enough, blatantly curving myself against his solid frame. My breasts press against his chest as I seek more of that delicious mouth.

He tastes better than my dirtiest fantasies. I wonder for a millisecond if we've crossed a line, but my thoughts vaporize under the scorching heat of his mouth on mine. All I want is more, more, more.

Zack's hands drift down to my backside, gripping and pulling me impossibly closer. I experience heaven when his impressive manhood makes itself known on my stomach. Our tongues duel furiously, and I'm consumed by—

ZACK!? Where is he going?

He pulls away, leaving me swaying and breathless in his wake.

"Can't wait for our next date," he chokes out.

I'm staring at the massive bulge straining against his pants, and I have to clench my thighs together.

Friction, I need some fucking friction!

But he's already acting as the perfect old-timey gentleman, opening my car door and sliding me into the driver's seat.

Fogged over with frustration, I start the car—my heart still pounding wildly from Zack's volcanic kiss. Every nerve ending in my body craves him like a drug. I've got a full-blown addiction.

But all of it is a cruel tease because THERE IS NO NEXT DATE. That's not how it works. Our characters are burnt. They are one-and-dones. The next date will be a clean slate with two totally different people. I race out of the parking lot.

I swear Zack's eyes had a devilish grin when he pushed me away. Like he got off on getting me all wrecked and ravenous.

What a douche nugget!

I shaved my woo-hoo for this!?

***

```
<!DOCTYPE html>
<h1>User Profile</h1> </div>
NAME: MIKE MURPHY
AGE: 31
OCCUPATION: Mechanic
INTERESTS: Motorcycles. Tattoos. Bar hopping.
ABOUT ME: I love riding my motorcycle almost as much
as I love women. My bike's my first love. You could be
my second. I'm either out riding or at the tattoo parlor,
adding to my ink. Think you can handle a wild ride with
me? Let's grab a drink and see where the night takes us.
</div>

<h1>User Profile</h1>
NAME: LILY COOPER
AGE: 28
OCCUPATION: Waitress
```

INTERESTS: EXPLORING NEW BARS. LIVE MUSIC. KARAOKE.
ABOUT ME: RECENTLY SINGLE AND READY TO MINGLE. I'M SEARCHING FOR A ROMANTIC SOMEONE WHO SHARES MY ZEST FOR LIFE. BUT REAL TALK, I WANT A MAN, NOT A BOY, WHO WILL MAKE MY EX-BOYFRIEND JEALOUS. IF YOU'RE CHARMING, WITTY, AND LOOK LIKE A BADASS, COME SWEEP ME OFF MY FEET.

```
</div>
```

```
<h1>Date Information</h1>
```
DETAILS: DRINKS AT THE "KISS & TELL TAVERN."
```
</body>
</html>
```

ZACK'S TONGUE IS DOWN MY THROAT!

My back's pressed against the grungy wall as Zack's mouth ravages mine. For the last hour, we've been making out in the corner of this dingy tavern like horny teenagers. I'm absolutely dripping over it.

This is hands down my favorite friggin' roleplay ever!

"God, you're hot," he growls against the column of my neck, sucking hard enough to leave a mark.

"This is so fucking sexy," I pant out, feeling like a contortionist the way I'm angling my body against his.

I'm convinced Mike Murphy is Zack's alter ego, from his snug white tank that displays his inked-up arms down to his shredded, form-fitting jeans accentuating his mouth-watering package. Those phony tattoos should be a turn-off, but something about them, releasing the darker side of Zack, is making me wetter than a water park.

His rough stubble keeps grazing my tender skin, making me crave the oddly delightful sensation. It's the way our roughness and softness brush together—the delicious, addictive harmony and friction—that's driving me mad. His gifted mouth moves to my collarbone, and I'm yearning for that luscious scrape. It's got me hoping and praying that this ends with Zack diving headfirst into my lady town.

I opted for a low-cut, flowing dress *(allowing for easy access)* in case that's where this date is headed. I'm fully aware that sex is off the table tonight. And why? The user profile for my character has coochblocked me.

```
<!DOCTYPE html>
<h1>Extended User Profile</h1>
NAME: LILY COOPER
BACKSTORY: FRESH OFF A BREAKUP AND LOOKING TO MAKE
HER EX JEALOUS.
PHYSICAL INTEREST LEVEL: OPEN TO KISSING AND GROPING.
WILL NOT HAVE SEX ON THE FIRST DATE BUT DOWN FOR "OTHER
TOUCHING."
</body> </html>
```

I could give two shits about restrictions right now, not with Zack's talented tongue dancing against mine and his fingers making demands of my body. If he wants to make out until they kick our asses to the curb, I'm totally down.

"I can't believe your boyfriend dumped you."

"He couldn't kiss for shit. Not like you, baby."

His mouth meets mine again, all heat and demand. I'm on the verge of erupting when he catches my lower lip between his teeth, tugging indecently before giving it a soothing swipe of his tongue.

Setting foot in a cesspool-of-a-place like this would normally be a hard pass. Calling this shithole a "dive bar" is like calling a sewer a "water treatment plant." Even first walking in, my senses were assaulted by the disgusting stench of stale vomit, beer, and body odor that blended into one toxic fume. But all that and this rowdy crowd, who look like they escaped from a maximum-security prison, have been replaced by my state of arousal. I'm going to stay in my happy place, even if an entire biker gang is openly ogling Zack and me like we're the evening's entertainment.

"You really turn me on," he rasps, sucking on that sensitive spot below my ear that has me wriggling against him. "Your body is flawless, babe."

A breathy whine escapes my bruised lips. "Fuck you're such a good kisser," I pant, grabbing his head and angling his greedy mouth right where I want it.

I've never made out like this before, all fiery and feverish, exploring each other's crazy desires without the pressure of going all the way. In high school, I remember my sister Nora kicking me out of our room, dry-humping her latest crush for hours, and asking if she was done yet. I never understood the hype.

But now, with Zack's hard man-meat grinding shamelessly against my cooch through his tattered jeans...

I get it.

I so get it.

"You know what would make your douchebag ex insanely jealous?" Zack whispers sinful suggestions in my ear.

A jolt of excitement zings straight to my pulsating vajayjay. "Stop talking and show me..." I purr, chewing greedily on his bottom lip before releasing.

A feral groan vibrates through his broad chest before he firmly takes my hand, leading me with purpose toward the back hallway of the unruly bar. Before I can catch my breath, he's shutting us inside the seedy bathroom, the rickety door closing out the rowdy noise and leaving us blissfully alone.

"God, I want to lick these gorgeous tits," he rasps, roughly cupping my heavy breasts.

"Do it," I beg.

Zack doesn't hesitate, yanking down the top of my flimsy dress until my lace bra is exposed. He cups one boob, pulling it free, and then starts devouring my nipple like it's his last meal. His tongue flicks and swirls, and I'm gasping for air, my bud lavishing all the attention.

"God, yes," I cry out as he travels to my other breast, sucking and nibbling as my skin erupts in goosebumps.

Zack's deep guttural grunts spur me on, and I hastily untuck his snug tank top, dragging my nails up the ridges of his back. He arches into me with a hiss.

"Your breasts are perfect," he groans, pinching and rolling my pebbled nipple between his thumb and forefinger.

A fresh gush of wetness drenches my quaking snatch. I've never been this horny in my entire freaking existence.

I should totally be losing my shit over this! Getting down and dirty with my bestie. I'm supposed to feel at least a little bit of hesitation or awkwardness, right? But instead, it's like Zack's lips are some sort of magic eraser, making all my doubts vanish.

This isn't just hot—it's a raging wildfire—consuming me from the inside out.

How the hell have I gone the last ten years without experiencing this fuckfest of a man who's reducing me to a shameless, panting, lusty puddle?

This nasty-ass bathroom is the epicenter of sin, and I fucking love it.

"Can I touch your pussy?" he asks, with a tone that's more Zack than the character he's portraying.

I can't even respond. I'm so close to the edge. I manage a small nod, and he takes the cue, hiking up my dress and pulling my panties aside. The second he touches my clit, I let out a moan so loud, it echoes off the bathroom walls and makes him moan too.

"Fuck! You're so wet for me, babe."

Something primal just takes over, and I roughly undo his pants, wrapping my hand around Zack's thick, rock-hard cock. He breathes out sharply at my touch, his eyes burning with pure lust.

I start stroking him, matching the fevered pace of his fingers circling my throbbing clit. Our arms entwine as we pleasure each other, the scorching heat between us climbing to unbearable. My orgasm is building, so I pump him harder, using my thumb to tease his sensitive underside.

Zack starts thumbing my clit as he drives two fingers knuckle-deep inside me. "God, yes! Fuck, right there!" I cry out, my walls clenching around his fingers.

"Tell me how much you love this," he cries.

"Yes! Don't stop, please!"

His groans fill my ears, matching the rhythm of my own agonizing gasps as we chase our release. Then, with a long, carnal moan, he spills over the edge, his hot release coating my fingers and sending me over the edge with him.

The force of my climax rocks my body, stealing my breath. I feel every muscle as it contracts and loosens, sending shockwaves of pleasure through me before slowly unwinding, leaving me feeling weak and satisfied.

"Fuck, Mad—I mean babe... that was... the hottest thing... I've ever done," he rasps. "We have to do that again sometime."

With his final words he places one last soft kiss on my lips and leaves me savoring the lingering sensations.

This sexual hibernation bear has awakened!

***

```
<!DOCTYPE html>
<h1>User Profile</h1>
</div>
```

NAME: Dr. Tristan Walker

AGE: 34

OCCUPATION: Orthopedic Surgeon

INTERESTS: Fine dining. Chess. Massage.

ABOUT ME: My job is intense with all the long hours. Bad news—I work a lot. Good news—I save lives. When-

EVER POSSIBLE, I BALANCE MY WORK WITH RELAXATION. I'M GOOD WITH MY HANDS SO I GIVE A MEAN MASSAGE. THERE'S NOTHING QUITE LIKE THE HEALING TOUCH AFTER A STRESSFUL DAY. I'M NOT LOOKING FOR ANYTHING TOO SERIOUS RIGHT NOW.
</div>

<h1>User Profile</h1>
NAME: SOPHIA STEWART
AGE: 30
OCCUPATION: FLIGHT ATTENDANT
INTERESTS: PHOTOGRAPHY. TRAVEL. MASSAGE THERAPY.
ABOUT ME: I'M A JET-SETTING FLIGHT ATTENDANT WITH A LOVE FOR ADVENTURE AND SPONTANEITY. MY JOB KEEPS ME ON THE MOVE, SO IT'S A CHALLENGE TO MAINTAIN SERIOUS RELATIONSHIPS. BUT WHO NEEDS COMMITMENT WHEN YOU CAN HAVE FUN BE-TWEEN LAYOVERS?
</div>

<h1>Date Information</h1>
DETAILS: DRINKS AT THE "SAPPHIRE LOUNGE" IN THE REGAL PLAZA HOTEL.
</body>
</html>

MY HEART IS BEATING SO FAST, I'm pretty sure it's trying to make a break for it.

I look at my reflection in the mirror, my eyes trailing over the red lacy lingerie that hugs my curves.

Meeting Zack—no, Dr. Tristan Whatever-His-Stupid-Last-Name-Is—for drinks at the hotel bar was basically a guaranteed booty call. But now that I'm here, standing in his hotel bathroom, I can't help the nerves fluttering in my flippin' stomach.

Sure, Zack and I got all handsy in the biker bar, and yeah, it was an orgasm that rocked my world. But this? This is the main event. We're talking penis-meets-vagina action. Once we cross that line, there's no going back.

Chill out, Mads.

The nervous voices in my head are starting to sound like a goddamn choir, so I push back.

I remind myself that it's all good. I'm just going to bone my best friend.

Balls! Why did I have to say it like that?

Sissy's voice enters the echo chamber—about how things will get all sorts of messy between us.

I wrap the fuzzy hotel robe around my body and take a deep, steadying breath before I lock eyes with my reflection. "You want this."

I do want this.

Want him.

All of him.

Desire flutters and hums in my core, urging me forward as I turn the knob.

The room is dimly lit, a few flickering candles casting a warm glow over everything. Soft classical music plays from Zack's phone, and the gentle melody sets a romantic mood. He stands there in nothing but a pair of boxers, and his toned chest and abs make my mouth go dry.

For a split second, I long for the noise of that rowdy bar bathroom. That was a no-strings-attached quickie, whereas this is different. It's—

Peaceful...

Personal...

Tender...

Not meant for sex but lovemaking.

"I thought we could start with a massage," he says in a low voice that makes my insides liquify. "Help you relax."

An exhilaration runs through me at the thought of his skilled hands exploring my body. "Oh, alright then," I try to sound casual, but my airy voice betrays me. "Where would you like me?"

He closes the gap between us, then, with agonizing slowness, he undoes the knot on my robe, letting it slide off my body and puddle at my feet. I'm left standing in my lacy red lingerie, which suddenly feels entirely too flimsy under his smoldering stare.

"God, you're funny, you're fierce, and you look like this. You're the most beautiful person, inside and out," he says, drinking me in like oxygen.

His words thrill me, even though I know better. This is just an act—his persona is supposed to make me feel sexy and wanted. I shouldn't read too much into it. "You must say that to all the girls," I tease.

But then he's cradling my face in his hands, making me meet his intense gaze. "Never. Just you." The raw honesty in his voice steals my breath away.

A piece of me wants to believe him. If only I was this desirable. I know better than to get lost in this game we're playing, no matter how well he sells it with those soulful bedroom eyes.

Zack caresses my cheek gently. "Now, lay face down on the bed for me," he rumbles, leaving no doubt he has far dirtier things in mind than an innocent massage.

I try not to fidget as I lay on the bed, but the anticipation of Zack's hands on me has me damn near vibrating out of my skin. Instead of going straight for the gold, he starts rubbing firm circles into the arches of my feet.

A foot massage? Really?

Don't get me wrong, his thumbs are working' some serious magic, and I'm melting into the mattress. But I was kinda expecting to go right to the hot 'n' heavy action. The intimate touch is both bizarrely calming and intensely sensual, a strange yet delicious combination.

His hands move up my calves, his palms gliding over my skin and working out the tension. "Is this too intense?"

"No, it's really good."

An understatement—I've never been touched like this before.

I usually go to great lengths to keep people at a distance. Intimacy has always been a hell no for me—a big ol' nope, nuh-uh, not gonna happen kinda situation. But as Zack's talented hands slowly roam over every damn inch of me, I find myself feeling the complete opposite. In fact, I never want him to stop touching me.

He avoids my butt entirely as he works his way up my spine, almost like he's purposefully bypassing all the obvious fun zones. His fingers glide over my skin, igniting sparks along my nerves that have me squirming against the mattress. He works down my arms, his knuckles barely grazing the sides of my breasts—a tease that lights up fireworks in my thighs.

The man is driving me absolutely wild.

"Such a perfect ass," he whispers appreciatively, slowly tugging my panties down over my hips.

Without warning, he flips me over onto my back, leaving me totally exposed and flushed. I suck in a sharp breath, my pulse racing. I'm fucking desperate for him to finally give me what I've been longing for. The delicious torture is about to pay off.

But no, he brushes by my jackpot and slides his palms over the fronts of my thighs, his wicked caresses inching higher and higher toward my hips.

"You're killing me here," I finally growl out, brazenly writhing against the sheets.

My breasts are tingling.

My vagina is pulsating.

I crave him more than I've ever craved anything.

"Spread your legs for me," he commands.

He goes at his own pace, peppering open-mouthed kisses down my inner thighs. When his mouth grazes my pubic bone, I nearly levitate off the bed.

And then he spreads me wide with two fingers and dives his tongue against my throbbing clit in one fell swoop.

"Oh fuck!" I cry out, my eyes rolling back as I forget how to breathe. I have no shame as I spread my legs wider, giving him total freedom to devour me.

My hands fly into his hair, clutching those soft strands as he starts claiming my clit with that expert tongue. He speeds up, flicking me like a madman, and I can already feel myself hurtling toward that edge at full force.

How the hell can he have me unraveling this fast?

I clench his hair tighter, my whole body tensing up as I selfishly rub my pussy all over his devilishly talented mouth. I can feel my orgasm building at the base of my spine, getting ready to explode.

I can't speak.

I can't even think.

All I can do is moan helplessly as the waves of pleasure crest higher.

Zack rumbles against me, "You taste so fucking good," he growls, and those simple words are enough to shove me over that glorious edge.

I'm pretty sure I passed out because my eyes open to fresh ecstasy overwhelming my senses.

I peek down, and *BAM!* Zack's towering over me with an erection that's not just big, but enormous. We're talking thick, colossal, like a sequoia tree. So much so, it's a little intimidating.

"I want you inside me," I plead.

He spurs into action, condom on in a flash. Zack positions himself at my entrance, those piercing brown eyes peering into mine. "Are you sure?"

I can feel how wet and ready I am. I want—no, need—him buried inside me like yesterday.

"Make me yours," I demand, my voice low and unhinged.

The second Zack pushes into me, a whimper escapes my lips. He takes up every inch, his thick cock stretching me deliciously with each punishing thrust. The friction is pure, electrifying bliss, and I never want this moment to end.

"Fuck you feel so good," he groans. He meets my eyes, then quickly looks away.

Wait, why did he just break eye contact? Am I being paranoid, or did he just get awkward?

What the hell is he looking at?

First the nightstand.

Then the ceiling?

And now he's squeezing his eyes shut like he's trying to block out some traumatic memory.

Shit! This is weird for him. He looks like he'd rather be anywhere else but here, doing anything else but this, or maybe doing anyone else but me. Oh God! Please tell me he's not mentally replacing me with Lexie right now.

The realization spears through me like a red-hot poker, threatening to snuff out my growing climax. He still sees me as his schlubby, hoodie-wearing friend. At best, I'm a second-rate stand-in for the woman he truly craves.

Message received loud and clear assbag! Thanks for making me feel like a total reject in the middle of what was supposed to be a mind-blowing experience.

Fuck that!

No freaking way am I letting his lukewarm, half-assed attitude ruin this for me. This might not be what he wants, but it's sure as shit what I want, and he's going to give it to me.

I will have my brain-blasting, core-convulsing orgasms thank you very much.

He can avoid eye contact all he wants. I'm going to seize every electrifying moment, engrave the memory of his thick length pleasuring me on constant replay. He doesn't get to take my ecstasy away.

I'm the boss of my own body, and I say it's time to let go and enjoy every earth-shattering moment of this experience while it lasts.

You hear that, Zack? You don't want me? Sucks for you.

For the next 2 ½ weeks, your dick is mine.

CHAPTER THIRTEEN

ZACK

MY HIPS DIVE INTO MADDIE'S PERFECT PUSSY, and she lets out a hot little gasp. I almost lose it right there. The way her face lights up—a mix of shock and euphoria—I gotta look away for a sec because I don't wanna blow.

God, she's so incredibly tight and warm around me. Fuck... it's a feeling beyond description.

This dream I've been chasing, it's actually happening. I can't believe it's real.

Maddie's body writhing beneath me...

Feeling her struggle with the pleasure...

Knowing I'm the one giving it to her...

It's an erotic new sensation that I'm enjoying *(possibly too much)*. Years of longing and waiting have built up to this impossible, unforgettable moment.

And I'm trying to make it last, but damn. Her soft panting, those delicious little moans in my ears... If I don't think about something else, this will end way too soon.

I SQUEEZE MY EYES SHUT.

Granny panties.

Garbage trucks.

Roadkill.

Earwax.

Dammit! It's not working. Do NOT make eye contact. Just think about... laundry—mundane shit like folding clothes—separating the lights from darks—getting that fabric softener ratio just right. Washing her delicates... Maddie's sexy lingerie... her gorgeous tits jiggling as I pump into her yummy cunt.

"Christ, you're so fucking perfect, baby," I growl against her neck.

"You feel... uhh... uhh-mazing," she whimpers, opening her legs wider to let me in deeper.

I grit my teeth hard, my self-control crumbling. Feeling myself buried in her mound—her inner walls against me. The fuse is lit, and I'm powerless against this raging desire.

"Yesss!" Her silky walls contract around the full length of me.

Oh my God, she's right there on the edge. I've found the magic angle. I grab onto the headboard and give her exactly what she needs. Her nails dig into my back, and I want her to leave souvenirs. We move in perfect harmony, rhythmically rocking until we can't go fast enough.

"Harder, fuck me harder!" Her wish is my command.

I'm unhinged as I hammer into her, holding nothing back. Her impeccable breasts bounce with shockwaves from my powerful thrusts. Her firm nips rub against me, and my pulse goes into overdrive. I hear her breathing become more unsteady. I know I'm hitting that sweet spot. Her urgency builds on my own, and we're both frantic for our release, both volcanoes about to erupt.

In this moment, we are one.

No history. No complications. No explanations.

Two souls, raw and vulnerable, completely present, meeting each other's needs. It's everything I've ever wanted.

Maddie.

Mine.

All mine.

"I'm almost there, baby. I wanna make you come all over me." I can feel my balls tightening, that obvious sign that I'm close.

"Motherfucker!" she yells, her slick walls fluttering and clenching around my rod. Her body suddenly goes still and then starts convulsing wildly under me, her orgasm ravaging her body.

She has me. My dick becomes ridiculously harder as I come, my own earth-shattering climax ripping its way through me. The blazing grip of her pussy squeezes me mercilessly until, at last, she begins to unwind gradually.

I've just experienced all of her, and I will never be the same.

She's wrecked me for any other woman.

If only I could whisper those three simple words—I love you.

I roll onto my side to drink her in, but she bolts upright, jumping out of bed. She swiftly pulls her robe around her and disappears into the bathroom.

Moments later, she's scooping up her clothes and belongings in a flash.

"That was fun, tiger, but I've got a plane to catch," she says far too casually, slipping back into her flight attendant persona.

"You don't want to stick around? Maybe talk for a bit?"

"Sorry, can't." She shakes her head quickly, pulling on her shoes. "Maybe I'll reach out next time I'm in town... yeah? So later, Dr. Whoever... bye!"

And just like that, she's out the door, still wearing the robe, leaving me with a fast-fading boner and a million questions.

Oh, Jesus. She's freaking out. This wasn't supposed to happen. No, no, no!

I swore I had figured out all her signals.

There's no way she wasn't into it. No chance she faked those climaxes. But hell, I don't know, this is new for me. I've never witnessed my best friend melting into an orgasm puddle. *Shit.*

*****

I SWAGGER UP TO MADDIE'S DESK, attempting a casual-and-totally-not-obsessed expression that would hide the fact that we did the devil's tango. "Ahem, Mads, got a sec? I need to talk to you about... stuff."

Nailed it.

Maddie doesn't spare me a glance, her fingers attacking the keys like they owe her money. "Not a good time, Zack. I've got a shit-ton of code errors to fix before our next date."

I fidget nervously, shoving my hands in my pockets. The fact is, Maddie and I haven't spoken since we did the deed. And by "deed" I mean *life-altering, Earth-shattering, what's-my-name-again sex.* And now I'm standing here like a lovesick idiot, desperate to make sure she's alright before our next fake date.

"Can we hash it out in front of the guys?" Maddie asks, finally peeking up and melting my heart with her mesmerizing brown eyes.

No can do, Mads. Our quirky coder crew doesn't need to know if you're emotionally okay after I fucked you so hard I'm still walking like a cowboy. We aren't going to focus group whether you're feeling as sore and satisfied as I am.

"It can wait," I say instead, flashing a laid-back smile.

Cosmo swivels around in his chair, pushing his glasses up his nose. "Great data coming in from the fake dates. The algorithm is humming along nicely."

"So, uh, how's the 'under the covers' Olympics going for you lovebirds?" Wes asks, wiggling his eyebrows.

Maddie gives him a death glare that could make a Navy Seal shit their pants.

I jump in before Maddie lets loose. "Nope. That's a no-fly zone. It's off-limits, not something Maddie and I are sharing with the class. What happens on our dates stays with us."

But trust me, buddy; I'm dying to know what Maddie's thinking too.

Cosmo chimes in. "Agreed. Topic is hereby dead... moving on. Wes, tell them about the chat group surveys you've been collecting."

Wes nods his head. "Right. We've been getting a ton of awe-some surveys from the website, and a bunch of them are from the LGBTQ+ community, which is, like, a huge win for the diversity data our algorithm needs," Wes says excitedly. "Oh, and things with my lady are getting serious. Our sexting game is on fire—emojis galore—eggplants, peaches, clowns. If emojis were STDs, my dick would need penicillin!"

"I prefer listening to your adventures with Linda," Maddie jokes.

Cosmo shivers. "Wes, I say this as a friend—you need Jesus. And probably some sturdy antivirus software."

"Whatever my PB and Jellies, I'm getting more action than a self-serve car wash." Wes grins, waggling his tongue obscenely between two fingers.

"Pretty sure your hand doesn't qualify as a sexual partner," I point out, chuckling a bit.

"Shows what you know. I happen to be ambidextrous." Wes holds up both hands, winking salaciously. "Double the pleasure."

I look to Maddie, hoping to share a private laugh, but she's already back at her screen, engrossed in her work.

I can't shake the feeling that she's purposely ignoring me.

How can she just sit there all cool and collected? I'm going nuts, replaying every steamy moment between us. I can't shake the provocative sound of her moans in my head—can't stop picturing the absolute ecstasy written across her face as she came undone. I'm dying to know if she's as rattled as I am—if she had even half the fun I did—if she's itching for round two like me, or if she's just feeling duty-bound due to our... situation.

She's giving me nothing. No subtle sign, no lingering glance, nada. Like we're two coworkers who had a casual cup of coffee together instead of screwing each other's brains out. The silence is killing me.

My nose is assaulted by Reid, who shoves his cappuccino cup in my face. "Zack, my man! Feast your eyes on this work of art. I call it... Foam Tatas 2.0."

I squint into the cup, deciphering the frothy blobs. "Is that... are those supposed to be nipples?"

Reid puffs out his chest. "Damn straight, you're witnessing the Picasso of breast foam art. Look but don't touch, boys."

"Tits?" Cosmo says with a fleeting glance. "They seem more like a low-quality 3D rendering of Jabba the Hutt's ballsack."

I squint harder, tilting my head. "Sorry, bro. Looks like a couple of bagels to me."

"Hmmm, I'm seeing lumpy butt cheeks," Wes muses.

Cosmo scoffs. "Yeah... but like a saggy, hairy, grandpa ass."

"So you think the areolas are too big," Reid mutters, nodding thoughtfully. "Dammit. Okay, good notes, guys. I can fix that. Thanks!" He hurries off.

"Time to get ready for the next date scenario," I announce to no one in particular.

"Yup, go manscape your balls or whatever it is you do before these dates." Maddie quips with a teasing grin.

"For the record, my balls are always silky smooth." I wink at her, hiding the sinking feeling in my gut.

Looks like I'm headed for another confusing date, trying to make sense of her mixed signals. Who's the poor asshole falling head over hard-on? This unlucky schmuck.

***

```html
<!DOCTYPE html>
<h1>User Profile</h1>
</div>
```

NAME: CONNOR COLEMAN

AGE: 27

OCCUPATION: Production Assistant

INTERESTS: Movie buff. Concerts. Writing.

ABOUT ME: I'm a huge movie fan, and my dream is to be the next Tarantino. If you're a girl who loves cinema and can debate the merits of Milk Duds vs. Twizzlers, I'm interested. Let's hit the theater together!

</div>

<h1>User Profile</h1>

NAME: Avery Vaughn

AGE: 26

OCCUPATION: Actress

INTERESTS: Film lover. Acting. Foodie.

ABOUT ME: I'm an actress. I do indie roles and work in community theater for now. I enjoy acting as different characters and immersing myself in their world. Currently, I'm preparing for the role of Vivian in Pretty Woman: The Musical—she's so sexy and exciting. Heads up, I might go into character if you're a fun date!

</div>

<h1>Date Information</h1>

DETAILS: Matinee movie at "Grandview Cinemas."

</body>

</html>

THIS CHAIR IS A COCKBLOCKER.

If making out was a video game, this theater chair would be the big boss you have to defeat at the end. It's taunting me, "Think you've got game? Just wait till you feel the wrath of our armrest of doom and the leg-crushing lullaby of our sleep attack after 20 minutes. Bwahahaha."

Challenge accepted.

It doesn't matter what we're watching, some sort of slasher flick... because the real action is happening in our semi-private hideaway in the top row, back corner. It's smokin' hot and intense.

Maddie and I have been feeling each other up for the last hour. My second biggest challenge *(after this damn chair)* is keeping things quiet. Thankfully, the first psycho killer with a chainsaw just showed up, allowing Maddie to be uninhibited. She lets out a sexy-as-hell moan that makes me want to go for it, in public or not.

"Do you have any idea what you're doing to me?" I growl in her ear, tasting her neck hungrily.

The second the lights went down and the previews began, I knew I was in for a good time. My dating profile said, "Make a move at the movie," so I was feeling confident. Then, when I put my hand on her thigh, and she didn't push it away, it was more than confidence; it was go time!

No lie, I could spend the whole movie caressing her breasts.

"Aaaaah!" A voluptuous blonde runs for her life on screen as Maddie's touch sends shivers down my spine. She breaks away from our kiss and glances around the theater, a wicked grin on her face.

"Shh," she exhales, pressing a finger to my lips.

In a moment, Maddie sinks to her knees and spreads my legs, her eyes never leaving mine. Before I can process what's happening—she's unbuttoning my pants—pulling them to the floor—and her hand is wrapping around my shaft. I can't help but let out a low groan. *God, I love her touch.*

She licks her lips.

She runs her tongue up the length of my cock.

From base to tip—slow, hungry, greedy licks.

What is that look in her eye? Why does she seem to be enjoying this?

The sight of her on her knees—the sensation of her mouth—I'm entirely at her mercy. We're breaking a dozen public indecency laws, but I don't give a damn.

She swirls her tongue around my tip, and my head rolls back. Without warning, she takes me deeper into her mouth, pulsing up and down, making my whole body sing.

The chainsaw roars on the movie screen as my body roars with pleasure. The screams of the victims echo through the theater as Maddie works her magic.

She groans against my manhood, humming vibrations that send a jolt through me. My orgasm is building, climbing, reaching a fever pitch with every passing second.

She grabs my base, and I grip the armrests, feeling like I'm about to launch out of my seat. And then, pulling me to the back of her throat, she sucks me hard and keeps on sucking.

I'm done for. She's too much... and I love it.

I can feel myself pulsing and coming inside Maddie's mouth, wave after wave. She swallows me whole, and I'm biting my lip to not cry out in pleasure. She gently releases me and sits back down.

"In case I forget to tell you later, I had a really good time tonight," she says triumphantly.

Shit, wait. Is that a line from Pretty Woman? Who just gave me a blowjob?

Maddie?

Avery?

Vivian?

I yank up my pants, suddenly self-conscious, and glance around to be sure no one saw us.

Maddie threads her fingers through mine and leans her head on my shoulder. I look down at our hands, totally lost. It seems like we're a couple in love. She didn't have to take the character she was playing that far. Is this part of who she is now? A sexually liberated Maddie who comes out to play whenever she wants? Or is this about me? *God, I hope it's at least a little about me.*

"What the hell is happening?" The woman on the screen shouts, her voice tinged with panic. "I'm completely lost here! Somebody, help me, please!"

Couldn't have said it better myself.

***

```
<!DOCTYPE html>
<h1>User Profile</h1>
</div>
```

NAME: BRANDON HOWELL

AGE: 30

OCCUPATION: FIREFIGHTER

INTERESTS: WORKING OUT. HIKING. CAMPING.

ABOUT ME: I'M ALL ABOUT ADRENALINE AND ADVENTURE. ON DUTY, I'M SAVING LIVES AND BATTLING BLAZES. OFF DUTY, YOU'LL FIND ME HITTING THE TRAILS, SETTING UP CAMP, AND PUMPING IRON. RECENTLY DIVORCED, I'M LOOKING FOR CASUAL HOOKUPS.
</div>

<h1>User Profile</h1>
NAME: VICTORIA DUNCAN
AGE: 32
OCCUPATION: NURSE
INTERESTS: SWIMMING. CAMPING. PICNICKING.
ABOUT ME: I'M A DEDICATED NURSE AND A PROUD SINGLE MOM. I BELIEVE IN EMBRACING LIFE'S PLEASURES. SO, WHILE I LOVE MY BABY GIRL, I ALSO LOVE HAVING MY SITTER ON SPEED DIAL. RIGHT NOW, I WANT FUN, CASUAL HOOKUPS.
</div>

<h1>Date Information</h1>
DETAILS: DRINKS AT "THE LUCKY LEPRECHAUN" BAR.
</body>
</html>

MADDIE'S STRAIGHT-UP RIDING ME in the backseat of my Tesla, grinding like it's her job.

We shoved our clothes aside earlier, but some are still hanging off in torn pieces as she dominates me with her hips. Maddie's in complete control, and not gonna lie—it's a total turn-on watching her use me for pleasure.

Her bouncing tits hypnotize me, the way they come alive with our movements. And when she adds her sexy sighs, you bet your ass I'm soaking up every damn second.

I want to remember the feeling of her slick embrace wrapped around my hungry cock, her fingernails leaving their mark on my skin, and the softness and intensity of her lips on mine.

For the past few weeks, it's been a nonstop, crazy ride of lust, like two bunnies on Viagra.

But these dates are coming to an end—so I'm committing every freaking detail to memory.

That, and I'm doing my damnedest to hang on. With all this 'practice,' I've become better at controlling my thoughts and making things last.

"Fuckkkkk, that feels good," she murmurs in my ear.

"Let's never stop doing this," I confess.

My comments have become more daring, boldly dropping hints about my feelings for her. She never returns them, instead flashing that sinister smirk and keeping things physical.

"You like it when I do this?" she whispers, squeezing me tighter until I'm helpless against her.

"Easy baby, you're gonna make me come too fast." There's a wicked twinkle in her eyes as I let out a hiss. She knows what she's doing... pushing me right to the edge.

I've caught on to most of her signals by now—how she grinds agonizingly slowly when she wants to savor the feeling. Then, the desperate, wild rhythm she sets when she's chasing her own intense release. This will not be one of our slow, sensual lovemaking sessions.

Not that I'd ever say "lovemaking" out loud. As far as Maddie's concerned, we're just two random bodies—our fake dating personas—satisfying a physical desire that's taken control.

God, she's so luscious and warm... this out-of-body experience has the car rocking so much that I'm worried someone's gonna call the cops. Maddie leans back and grabs onto the front seats, giving me the perfect angle to worship her amazing breasts.

Who am I to deny such an enticing invitation?

I palm her lush mounds, savoring their weight in my hands. So soft and firm it's unreal. My fingertips roll and tug her hardened buds until they're achingly stiff.

"I know what you like, baby," I murmur, swirling my tongue over one engorged nub.

She responds by threading her fingers through my hair, holding me flush against her as she gyrates shamelessly against me. That silent plea speaks louder than words ever could.

As I run my tongue over her firm nipples, I revel in the fact that my mouth has explored every inch of her body. I remember the first time my mouth touched her slit—the taste of her arousal—how my tongue flicked against her clit—her squirming—it was intoxicating. Even now, the memory of being drenched in her is pure bliss.

How the hell am I supposed to return to a life without this?

Without Maddie's succulent pussy milking me for all I'm worth?

Without her uninhibited moans providing the most scorching soundtrack imaginable?

Without those filthy, desperate pleas falling from her lips as she chases her climax, begging me to fuck her harder, deeper, until she completely unravels around my throbbing cock?

I'm going to be a fucking mess.

A broken, lust-zombie no longer fully alive. How can I see her every damn day without being brutally pummeled by these memories?

Christ, I'm addicted to her.

I'm a complete junkie—controlled by her irresistible figure—bewitched by her complexity—humbled by her fierce intelligence.

"Yes! Yes! Fuck, I'm almost there. I'm going to—" Maddie cries out, her fingers holding me as the telltale signs blossom.

I'm also at the point of no return, knowing there's no holding back my impending carnal detonation. My pleasure explodes, and a tsunami of satisfaction crashes over me, surrendering to the searing heat. Her soft, velvety walls quiver and clench around me in a mind-blowing, sinful climax.

Our bodies convulse and shudder together in a wild crescendo of moans and curses. And then Maddie collapses against my chest, loose and limp. Our ragged panting slows, morphing into a series of soft, satisfied hums as the afterglow kicks in.

In a mere matter of days, this will all be over.

Please give me the slightest hint that you love me.

CHAPTER FOURTEEN

MADDIE

MY CLIT IS STILL THROBBING.

This code looks like it's written in hieroglyphics. Usually, I have JavaScript begging for mercy, but today, it's the one dominating me. Seems like all the mind-blowing sex has reduced my brain to a quivering blob of jelly.

And TMI, but my chair is being straight-up hostile to my lady bits. Zack and I have been banging nonstop like we're in a sex tape trying to be famous, and let's just say my hoo ha is waving the white flag.

Wes fumes, "Reid, seriously. Stop smearing cappuccino foam on Linda's mouth—it's like a glue trap in there."

Reid giggles, "Oh, so you can tell the foam apart from your own DNA-infused goo? Interesting."

Cosmo deadpans, "Nothing says 'healthy sexual habits' like the petri dish of bodily fluids on a sex doll."

The guys look at me expectantly... *no witty comebacks today, thank you.* I yank my hoodie strings and hide inside the hood. *Ugh, I live with the seven dwarfs of Dorkdom.* Not sure which one of them is Happy, Sleazy, Doc, or Horny, but I know I'm a little bit Mopey, mostly Grumpy, and my ladytown's feeling Bashful.

The past couple of weeks have been a smorgasbord of sex and confusion. Every damn kiss that makes my lips swell, every frisky caress that sets my skin on fire, and every thunderous orgasm that leaves me gasping for air. Fake or not, my body doesn't know the difference.

And if I'm being brutally honest with myself, my heart doesn't either. I've always found Zack attractive in that abstract "yeah, my BFF is a hottie" kind of way. But now? The way he gazes at me with such tenderness, feeling worshiped and wanted... it lights me up in unimaginable ways.

Which is a huge problem, considering our little love experiment has an expiration date. A few more days, and it's back to reality. No more sexcapades.

The doorbell rings. *God, now what?!*

It must be Nora checking up on me with another bag of rabbit food. I swing open the door, and I'm shocked. It's Sissy on my doorstep; looking like she stepped out of a Stepford wife factory with a built-in Instagram filter on her face. She's holding a garment bag with a knowing grin.

"I brought your dress for the party," she says by way of greeting, breezing past me into the house.

"You didn't need to do that," I mutter, trying to herd her back to the threshold. The last thing I need is my picture-perfect sister judging our frat house squalor.

"I've heard a lot about this place from Abby and Nora; I was curious." She surveys the cluttered rooms, wrinkling her pert nose in distaste. "They weren't exaggerating."

I make shooing motions, no longer hiding my attempts to get her gone. "Thanks for the dress. See you tomorrow at the party!"

Sissy plants her feet. "Don't be rude. Introduce me to your friends... I mean, coworkers."

There's no stopping her now. She marches into the coding cave. "Hey there! I'm Simone, you can call me Sissy. I'm Madeline's older sister," she declares with radiant head cheerleader peppiness.

"Damn, the hot sister train just doesn't stop," Reid whistles appreciatively, openly ogling her perfect figure.

Sissy tosses her hair with a playful flip and coos, "Oh, my gosh, thank you! That's so sweet!"

I groan. Of course, she's eating up their creepster-level adoration.

I glare at the boys. "Put your tongues back in your heads, pervs. She's married with kids."

"A smoking hot mom, nice!" Wes blurts. "You're the MILF that'll be starring in my dreams tonight."

Cosmo, ever the gentleman, stands to shake Sissy's hand. "I apologize for these Neanderthals. They're still evolving."

Sissy waves away his apology. "It's great to meet everyone! I've heard tons about you guys," Sissy chimes, looking around curiously. "And Zack, is he here?"

"Nope," I say, the sound of Zack's name spiking my body temperature. "Let's head to my room. You can show me the dress."

Once we're safely inside the fresh cringe of my bedroom, Sissy hangs the black dress in my closet, smoothes out the wrinkles, and turns, hands on her hips, to give me her "concerned big sister" look (*patent pending*).

"I thought I'd better see you in person since you've been sidestepping my texts."

I collapse on my bed. "I'm fine. Just busy with work... you know how it is."

Sissy settles herself on the edge of my bed, crossing her legs. "I've been hearing all about how you've been 'busy'... or should I say, 'gettin' busy' with a certain best friend?"

My head snaps up, cheeks burning. "Who told you?"

"Abigail spilled the beans about your little sex-periment for the app."

I groan, burying my face in my hands. "Before you start lecturing me—"

"I'm not here for that, Mads; I'm here for you. I popped by to make sure you're okay. I love you, and I'm worried."

I peek through my fingers at Sissy.

Crapballs! Why does she have to be such a good sister?

"Thanks, but really, there's nothing to worry about. I'm a big girl; I know what I'm doing. Everything's totally fine."

Sissy gives me a look that screams *bullshit*. "Are you sure about that? Because from where I'm sitting, this whole situation has 'heartbreak' written all over it. And not the fun Taylor Swift song kind."

"It's fine, Sissy. Zack and I are fine. Not everyone views sex as some grand, meaningful gesture. I mean, look at Abby—she's the queen of casual hookups."

"She's the queen of something, and it's not dating advice. Abigail is a polyamorous free spirit when it comes to relationships. And this is not that. This is wholly different, Maddie. You're getting intimate with someone you care about deeply. I'm not buying that there aren't feelings brewing."

I start to object, but Sissy plows on like a bullet train full of uncomfortable truths.

"And honestly, Mads, you may not be ready to face your feelings, but Zack is already head over heels for you. What I saw at dinner the other night, that boy's eyes were glued to you like you're it—the one person in this world he can't live without."

I scoff, shaking my head. "That's absurd. Zack is totally into Lexie, ultimate wifey material."

"No, he's not. The way he looks at you, the way he talks about you... Zack is in love with you, Maddie. And I think you're headed for a world of pain if you keep pretending he's not."

I feel like I've been sucker-punched. *Zack, in love with me? Dorky, foul-mouthed, never-been-called-a-smokin'-hot-babe me?* No freakin' way. Hell, he barely knew I had a vagina until he went spelunking down there himself.

Sissy must see the doubt on my face because she softens, reaching out to squeeze my hand. "I'm not trying to upset you. I felt like I needed to say something before it went too far. I don't want you to get hurt, and I don't want to see you lose someone who means so much to you."

I'm speechless. My throat feels like it's got a fucking python wrapped around it and the room's doing this spin-cycle thing.

"Mads, I like Zack a whole lot. Since college, you two have always been by each other's side, like some kind of codependent, platonic life partners. But I'm tellin' ya, everything points to him wanting something more."

I clear my throat and attempt confidence. "Cross my freaking heart, I'm solid. I don't have confused or mixed feelings for Zack, and I know he's balls deep in love with Lexie. This shit will be over and done in a few days, and we'll return to our BFF status quo. No heartbreak, no drama, I swear."

"Okay then, I'll trust your instincts. But promise me you'll show up at the party as the real you, not some vixen-ized version of Maddie. And please, for everyone's sake, no hanky-panky at Mom and Dad's anniversary bash."

I lift my hand in a pledge. "No kinky shenanigans, I swear. Although, you should have that talk with Abby. We don't need a repeat of last Christmas when she stole Santa's pants."

"Yuck, don't even get me started," Sissy shudders. "Did you hear about Abigail's car getting repossessed? Mom is pitching a fit."

As she spills the latest family scandal, one I'm already aware of, my thoughts replay her message: *Zack wants something more.*

Could she be right? Does Zack have real feelings for me?

***

LOVE SCORE : QUESTIONNAIRE

First Date Experience

1. DATE DETAILS
Location: Dinner at Dragon Roll Diner
Name of Your Date: Patrick Ross

2. OVERALL SATISFACTION:
- [ ] Dissatisfied
- [ ] Neutral
- [X] Satisfied
- [ ] Very Satisfied

3. CONVERSATION FLOW:
- [ ] Poor
- [ ] Good
- [X] Very Good
- [ ] Excellent

4. CHEMISTRY/COMPATIBILITY:
- [ ] Poor
- [ ] Good
- [X] Very Good
- [ ] Excellent

5. APPEARANCE/PRESENTATION:
- [ ] Poor
- [ ] Good
- [ ] Very Good
- [X] Excellent

6. PHYSICAL CONTACT:
- [ ] Yes
- [X] No

7. WOULD YOU DATE AGAIN?
- [X] Yes
- [ ] No
- [ ] Maybe

"HEY, MADS, CAN WE PLEASE TALK? Just for a sec?" Zack says, approaching my workstation with that sincere look that makes my heart flutter and my stomach churn.

I keep my eyes glued to the computer screen. "I'm exhausted. I need to wrap up this survey, hose myself off, and crash into bed."

We just got back from a 'date' at a sushi joint. No naughty business this time, thank God, but I'm emotionally spent dissecting Zack's every move.

"I miss you," he says softly, tilting my face to meet his gaze.

Damn him and those warm brown eyes, making me feel like I'm the only girl in the world. My willpower is melting.

"Miss you too, pal," I quip, quickly spinning back to my screen before my eyes rat me out. "Everything will return to normal in a few days, pinky promise."

I feel his stare, searching, jackhammering through my defenses. He has questions I'm not ready to answer... maybe ever.

"Let's make time to have a real talk then," he says, disappointed.

"I was thinking we should have a Star Trek binge-fest when we get back from the conference," I deflect. "You know, to celebrate surviving. What do you think?"

He sighs and gives me a small shrug. "Yeah, sure thing. Sounds like a blast. Cool, I'm gonna knock out some emails and then hit the sack."

"Tits-tastic," I reply with forced casualness. "Nighty night, bro."

I listen for his bedroom door clicking shut before letting out the breath I didn't realize I was holding. I tip-toe to my room and crash onto the bed. Thoughts of Zack take over my brain—his electric touch, the sounds of his pleasure. I grab a pillow and scream into it.

You're fine, Maddie. It's fine. Has this been the most emotionally draining experience of your life? Yes! But it's almost over. I hear my mom's voice quoting Simone de Beauvoir #mother-of-feminism. 'The only way to achieve your dreams is to take action.'

Power through a few more days and your future will come true.

Shizznits, I don't know what my future is anymore. I've pro-grammed myself to believe that falling in love is the eighth deadly sin. Love compromises your identity, weakens your life goals, and fucks up your moral compass.

I refuse to lose myself.

But what if it means losing Zack? I don't have the answer, but the thought makes me want to ugly cry into this pillow.

He misses me. Dammit, I miss him too—our snappy comebacks and secret signals—the rock-solidness of our bond. But if I'm being real, I also want him to set my body on fire with his touch. The mere thought of him and I'm tingling. Moments ago, when I called him pal and sent him away, I was secretly yearning for him to kiss me senseless...

I mentally slap myself. And if we did, it would mushroom cloud our friendship, our company, and life as we know it. The fallout would be catastrophic.

Suddenly, I hear the sound of Zack's shower switching on. My disloyal mind imagines every inch of him—water bouncing on chis-eled abs—soap suds sliding down his thighs—steam rising around his powerful shoulders as he...

A force takes hold, compelling me towards Zack's room. Like a magnet to metal, my feet won't stop drawing me to him. I stand outside his closed bathroom door. My heart is racing so fast. This would be an out-of-body experience except for one thing... I'm very, very aware of our bodies.

I twist the knob, quietly stepping inside. A surge of steam envelops me, and it feels like a fever dream.

Shivers race down my spine. Zack is in there.

I quickly shed my clothes, my hands trembling. I take a deep, steadying breath and pull back the curtain, revealing myself to him completely—my body, my heart, and what's left of my soul.

Zack's eyes widen as they rake over me, "Mads? What are you... is everything okay?"

"No talking." I manage to croak out, "I just... I need to be with you. Please."

The infinite depths of his eyes show me he understands. He reaches out his hand and pulls me under the warm spray.

The world as I know it falls away. I gently cradle his face in my palms, cherishing him for the first time—this gorgeous, wonderful, frustrating, astonishing person who's been my foundation, my secret keeper, my co-conspirator, my equal. My everything. I no longer see him as my goofy best friend; he's someone irreplaceable.

Someone I can't imagine my life without.

Zack must feel the weight of my thoughts because he gentles his hold on me, his thumbs now lightly caressing my hips and his gaze wide-eyed with open adoration. No heat or desire taints the innocence of this shared moment. Just soul-deep connection, and... *could it be?*

My heart flutters at the expression shining in his eyes... daring me to put a name to it.

I'm overcome by the need to worship this man who means more to me than my next breath. I clumsily grasp his body wash and squeeze a generous amount into my palm. Slowly, reverently, I glide the velvety suds over every ridge and valley.

Tracing the sculpted landscape of his chest.

The corded muscles of his arms.

The defined ridges of his abs.

Zack watches me work, his intense gaze never straying from my flushed face. Just as I finish, he takes the shower gel into his broad palm and begins his own hands-on discovery of my full figure.

His soapy hands skim the swell of my breasts.

The dip of my waist.

The curve of my backside.

Warmth pools low in my belly. My breath catches, and Zack's eyes ignite with a matching flame. But still, he takes his time, pinpointing every freckle and birthmark, committing me to memory.

After long, charged moments, Zack shifts to angle my body under the spray, rinsing away the remnants of our intimate exploration. The suds circle the drain, and he turns me to face him again, a question burning in his passionate gaze.

Anticipation hums through my veins, every nerve ending igniting with a sudden, exhilarating spark. He cages me gently against the shower wall, the chilly tile a delicious contrast to his blazing body heat. Before I can react, his lips claim mine in a searing kiss that rattles me to my very foundation.

I surrender to the hypnotic slide of his forbidden mouth with a soft moan. I'm lost in him.

I'm about to spread my legs, offering myself, when he breaks our kiss, shutting off the cooling water. A whimper of protest escapes me until I register the raw hunger within his hooded gaze.

"Wrap your legs around my waist." He effortlessly scoops me up, his hands firmly grasping my bottom as I coil my limbs around him like a seductive vine.

The delicious friction of his pelvis against my aching center generates a moan from one of us... or both of us.

He walks us out of the bathroom, his grip never faltering. My heart squeezes painfully at his show of physical and emotional strength.

I've always prided myself on my stubborn self-reliance. But right now, nestled in Zack's arms, I don't need it. I am secure, cherished... *loved?*

The realization steals my breath even as he lowers my trembling frame reverently onto his bed. Zack positions himself with comforting heaviness in the cradle of my hips, his hardness aligning perfectly with my pulsing center. I instinctively arch, craving more exquisite friction, but he soothes me with a tender kiss on my lips.

Drawing back just a few inches, Zack studies my face intently, with more unspoken questions than I can answer in a lifetime. But there's one question flickering in his warm, chocolate-brown eyes I can answer... Are you sure about this?

Wordlessly, I cup his stubbled cheek, my thumb tracing the plush curve of his kiss-swollen lower lip. Holding his gaze steadily, I try to infuse my expression with every ounce of certainty thrumming through my veins.

I nod decisively, lifting my hips in a shameless offering. Determination flashes in Zack's eyes as he reaches into his nightstand, grabs a condom, and expertly slips it on.

With our gazes locked in a heated and intimate connection, Zack tilts forward to unite our bodies in one slow, deep, blissful slide. My back bows at the delicious invasion, a high, fervent cry escaping my lips as he fills me with sublime perfection.

I want this.

I want him.

With every fiber of my being.

Consequences be damned.

***

I WAKE UP CONFUSED.

Then I recognize the room—it's Zack's room. *Holy mother of fuck—I'm in Zack's bed!*

The memories of last night come flooding back. The shower. The bed. Our bodies tangled into each other. Our haze of passion.

Shitnuggets! It really happened.

I'm curled up beside him, our faces so close I could lick his nose if I wanted to. We're like a couple of freaking lovebirds.

Seriously, how is he so goddamn cute even when he's sleeping?

I can't be here when he wakes up.

He'll have me again if I don't slip out of his arms before he opens those pretty eyes. Carefully, I start to pull away, trying not to disturb him. But Zack, even in sleep, seems determined to keep me close. He grunts softly and reaches out, his hand landing on my ass as he pulls me flush against him again.

Does it feel nice? I'm not complaining, that's for sure.

These past few weeks with Zack have been... intense. Mind-blowing. Emotionally fucking atomic. It feels like when I was ziplining. The initial rush was frightening, but then it was pure, unadulterated zen: weightless wonder that pushed the very boundaries of reality. Even when the ground was rushing closer, joyous rebellion filled my gut with a churning mix of excitement and dread. I've never experienced feelings like this; so all-consuming and overwhelming.

I can't get enough.

When I look at Zack now, I can see it all. There's a future with him where I'd tell my plans and dreams to go fuck themselves.

And that scares the ever-loving shit out of me.

I'm caught off guard by my sudden urge to wake him, to spill all these feelings. I want to tell him everything, to open up in a way I never have before. *But... is that really what I want?*

Slowly, painstakingly, I extract myself from Zack's arms, holding my breath as I slip out of bed. He stays asleep, blissfully unaware of my inner turmoil. I spot his Northwestern hoodie on the floor and reach for it instinctively. But then, I stop.

Instead, I grab a blue towel, wrapping it around my body like armor. I walk out the door and don't look back.

***

I CODE LIKE A WOMAN POSSESSED.

My fingers fly over the keys in a frantic dance. If I stop, even for a second, my mind might wander back to Zack. Back to him, inhabiting me again and again...

Nope! Nuh-uh. Not happening. I slam the lid on that mental rabbit hole and all the other inconvenient feelings I refuse to acknowledge. Coding is my solace, my escape. When the world gets too messy, too complicated, I can always find refuge in the clean, logical lines of HTML.

"Mornin', Mads," Wes says as he plops down in his chair and smirks. "So, you and Zack rocked the Casbah last night, huh?"

My fingers freeze. Slowly, I turn to face him with my most withering glare. "Wes, I swear to the coding gods, if you don't shut your pie hole, I will set your stupid blow-up doll on fire, get the plastic burning at a nice 400 degrees, and then shove it so far up your—"

"Hang on, easy!" Wes back peddles. "Sorry, I was out of line. I didn't mean to make you uncomfortable."

I blink, taken aback. Did Wes, the prince of all things inappropriate, just... apologize? Sincerely?

"It's fine," I mutter, feeling a twinge of guilt. "I'm... stressed."

Wes nods, his expression softening. "Look, I know we bust each other's balls a lot, but seriously, Maddie, I respect you. I don't want you to think otherwise."

I stare at him, stunned. Wes has never said anything remotely genuine to me. To anyone, as far as I know. I look around just to make sure the guys aren't screwing with me.

"What? I can be serious. Just don't tell anyone, or I'll deny it to my death," he says, lowering his voice. "I know I'm just a regular guy, but you? You're something special. And I'm lucky... grateful even, that you picked me for your team."

"What? You're a friggin' idiot... we need you," I say fondly. "Plus... you're a good guy. Your fuckery keeps me from losing it when Cosmo and Reid are being their dickclown selves."

Wes grins. "I live to serve."

We ease into a companionable silence for a bit.

"So, are you still chatting it up with your secret online lover?" I ask, in dire need of something to distract my brain.

"Yeah, actually, Mads, I might be in love with her."

"What?! You've never even met her. You don't know what she looks like."

"I don't need to," Wes says simply. "Physical stuff fades. I mean, you've seen my awkward mug. Who knows what fresh horrors await me in middle age?"

I laugh.

"There's just something magical about getting to know someone, like really connecting with them, without all the superficial crap getting in the way." He lets out a deep breath, a man completely smitten. "I think I've met my soulmate."

"Soulmate? Like, getting hitched, popping out Wes-ta-kins... the whole suburban thing?"

"In a heartbeat," Wes says immediately. "I want it all. The house, the kids, the scheduled sex on Tuesdays because we're too exhausted from adulting to be spontaneous."

"Ah, the American dream," I deadpan.

"Maddie, I'm for real. Don't you want that stuff too? Love, marriage, and the baby carriage?"

I let out a heavy sigh, slumping back in my chair. "It's a whole different story for women. Men can have both the high-powered job and a picture-perfect family. But women have to choose."

"That's bullcrap," Wes argues, shaking his head. "You can have both."

"Can I? Really?" I counter. "Because every career-driven woman I know has had to make serious sacrifices for love."

"So, marry a woman," Wes casually suggests. "Problem solved."

I laugh. "After these last few weeks, I'm 100% certain I'm a penis-loving gal."

Wes chuckles. "Yeah, even the neighbors three blocks over know that."

"Oh my God, that is beyond embarrassing," I say, unable to contain my giggles.

"Maddie, if anyone can rewrite the rules, you can."

"Thanks, but I want to make my mark on this world. And right now, that means pouring everything I have into LoveScore. No bullshit, no distractions."

As the words leave my lips, I realize the weight of them.

This thing with Zack is precisely that: a distraction… a fantasy. It's a beautiful fucking fantasy—a wish even—but I know better. What I just told Wes sucks, but it's true. I have plans, dammit, and I've busted my ass to get where I am. I won't be throwing it all away for some dude, even if he's been the best lifelong friend a person could ask for.

I have a mission: to make LoveScore the next unicorn startup.

Nothing's changed, and no one will stand in my way.

CHAPTER FIFTEEN

ZACK

I GOTTA STOP PACING. Everyone is staring at me.

I'm outside the grand entrance of the prestigious Ladies Club, and I feel like a human vibrator stuck on ludicrous speed. *Why can't I quit futzing with my tie?* This isn't just your average, everyday anxiety; I'm having a next-level, full-on freakout.

When I woke up this morning, Maddie was gone. Poof! And I don't just mean *gone* from my bed—she straight up fled the house like a criminal. She fed Wes some lame excuse about helping her sisters with the party, but that's bullshit. I know Maddie. When she's not down to talk about something, she'll do whatever it takes to avoid it. And not just a casual sidestep. I'm talking special-ops-level evasion.

I can't shake last night from my brain—a slow-motion highlight reel replays in my head. I'm transfixed by every little detail, savoring each sensation and analyzing our movements. It was everything I've been dreaming of, everything I've been too afraid to even hope for. And now, I'm terrified to find out—did it mean just as much to her?

I walk through the towering doors and Maddie wasn't exaggerating when she said this place was boujee as balls. Crystal chandeliers drip from the ceiling like oversized diamond earrings. Champagne linens drape gracefully over the tables, and vibrant colors burst from the ornate flower arrangements. This place screams *old money*.

"Zackman! There you are!" I turn to see Sissy's husband, Ben, arms spread wide. He pulls me in for a hug, giving me the classic bro double tap on the back.

Ben's one of those guys with a talent for making everything feel more laid-back. From the moment we met, the dude made me laugh. He's got a smile that disarms, a quip that charms, and an air of cool that makes everybody want to be his friend. His messy brown hair is movie-star-disheveled, and his green eyes flow naturally between amusement and deadpan exasperation.

But don't let that relaxed vibe fool you—Ben's as sharp and devoted as they come, especially regarding his family. The guy's a total dad hero, super fun and always lavishing his family with gifts. He'd walk through fire for Sissy. Their relationship is the real deal.

"Ben! Missed you the other night at dinner. How's it going?" I ask with a grin.

He lowers his voice. "Hey man, let me level with you. This party is gonna be a real snoozefest. We're surrounded by a bunch of stuffy old folks who are going to talk our ears off about grandkids and arthritis creams. My advice is to get liquored up. Immediately. Trust me, it'll make the party bearable—hell, maybe even enjoyable."

"Hi, Zack." Sissy approaches us in a knockout emerald green dress that flows seamlessly along her slender figure. "Maddie's already inside, mingling like a proper co-host."

I swallow hard at the mention of Maddie's name.

Ben lovingly puts his arm around Sissy's waist and says, "I was just telling Zack about the open bar. I'm gonna go show him so we can grab a drink together."

"Okay, but first, honey, please go save mom. She's been trapped talking to Professor Harris for the last twenty minutes, and he forgot his hearing aid."

"Happy to, sweetie," Ben says, kissing her cheek. He saunters past Sissy and sneakily mimes, shooting himself in the head, complete with a dramatic eye roll and his tongue lolling out.

I stifle a laugh. Sissy quickly looks behind her, but Ben's gone.

"Listen, Zack. Tonight is about our parents, no funny business, okay?" Sissy says, eyeing me in a way that suggests she knows EVERYTHING.

I give a little mock salute. "Best behavior, I promise."

I'm about to ask her where Maddie is when—

"Dean Simmons, so nice you're here," Sissy says, greeting a man with a cane.

The two of them start a conversation about the weather, so I set off to find Maddie, my nerves still on edge, wondering how the hell I'm going to navigate this whole mess.

The party is in full swing, a sea of wrinkled faces and silver strands as far as the eye can see. Waiters weave through the crowd with trays of hors d'oeuvres that look more artistic than edible. I snag a mini quiche and pop it in my mouth. *Damn, that's tasty.*

Where are you, Maddie? I do a lap of the main ballroom, peeking into various nooks and scanning familiar and foreign faces alike, but I come up empty.

The embers from last night's fiery connection refuse to fade; Maddie's scorching presence is raging flames in my heart, her words echoing in my head: "No talking, I just need to be with you."

She stood there—naked and vulnerable—a version of her I'd never seen before. Her fortress had collapsed, revealing the authentic, hidden Maddie. But now, those barriers appear to be back in full force. And I'm scratching my head thinking I hallucinated the whole damn thing. Maybe it was momentary madness, and now she's wishing she could take it back.

I don't know where we stand.

I'm dying to open up, bare my soul until she gets it through her stubborn head that I'm madly in love with her. That I have no future without her by my side.

God, it's hot in here. That or my thoughts are suffocating me. I need some air.

I exit a side door into the gardens and I'm smacked in the face by the cold night air. It's peaceful out here. The manicured hedges, the structured pillars, and the dangling lines of sparkling fairy lights are a total 180 from the turmoil inside my brain.

I turn to face the party, and that's when I see her—Maddie, standing by the bar, a head-turning goddess in black. Her floor-length gown is cinched at the waist with a thin black satin belt and a plunging V-neckline. Her brunette hair is in a perfect updo with soft, bouncy curls cascading down her shoulders. She's not wearing glasses, and even from here, her eyes sparkle from the glow of the chandeliers.

She leaves me speechless.

With a tug on my tie and a quick run of fingers through my hair, I strut over, fueled by a surge of adrenaline. Maddie sees me, her eyes widening as she gives me an obvious once-over. I'm about to compliment her when she cuts me off.

"Zack! Meet Mr. and Mrs. Henderson. They're friends of my parents. This is my... friend, Zack."

Mrs. Henderson smiles. "So nice to meet Maddie's boyfriend!"

Maddie quickly blurts out, "Oh, no, he's not my boyfriend. Just a friend."

I shake the Hendersons' hands, flashing a dazzling grin. "It's a pleasure to meet you both."

Sissy taps a spoon against a champagne flute; the clinking sounds rise and fall like waves. "Attention, everyone! Dinner is served in the ballroom. Please make your way over and find your assigned seats!"

FRIEND?! After last night, she said friend? Well, that's a kick in the nuts.

***

MADDIE'S TREATING EYE CONTACT LIKE A GAME OF DODGEBALL, expertly avoiding my gaze.

We're sitting next to each other at a table with "No Date Nora" and "Definitely Drunk Abby." If not for the tatted-up DJ on stage, Abby would stick out the most at this fancy gathering. I look over and of course Abby's sending him *let's hook up* vibes with the subtlety of a flashing neon sign.

Nora jabs her fork into her salad. "Stupid men. Canceling at the last minute. No reason, no apology. What a colossal jerkazoid!"

Abby slurs her words as she leans in. "He was probably ss-scared shitlessss by your sky-high standards. Poor dude couldn't handle the pressure."

"People don't rise to low expectations. It's how I weed out the losers," Nora replies smugly.

"I ain't settling for just anybody," Abby fires back. "They need to have a pulse and a functioning set of genitals."

Nora nods disapprovingly.

"Let's end your bitchy manless misery," Abby announces loudly. "We'll snag you a date in this room of old farts. There's gotta be a grandpa moneybagsss here with swag and a need for a hot young piece on his arm."

I almost inhale my drink, coughing and choking as I attempt to control my laughter. Abby jumps up and squints her eyes, scanning the room. Nora swiftly yanks her back down into her seat.

"Did you see one that has a working wiener?" Abby asks with a drunken giggle, taking another swig.

Sissy appears like a ninja, her voice a fierce whisper. "What is wrong with you all? Shush the naughty talk and get ready for the toast. We're here for Mom and Dad, remember?"

As soon as Sissy's gone, Nora and Abby start giggling like a couple of stoned sorority girls.

"I dare you to say fuck in your ss-speech," Abby jokes as the two stand and make their way toward the stage.

I sneak a peek at Maddie, who's uncharacteristically silent.

Without warning, I feel her fingers touch mine under the table before pulling away. Wordlessly, she rises from her seat and follows her sisters.

Wait a second.

Was that hand touch intentional?

Or am I overthinking this?

The entire Denton family occupies the stage, with Sissy holding court at the mic. Jerry and Cheryl sit regally in their chairs, clearly the stars of the show, while their daughters stand at the ready, waiting their turn to make a toast.

Maddie's parents are the picture-perfect example of a couple still crazy in love after all these years. Jerry, with his distinguished salt and pepper hair and warm, crinkly eyes, looks at Cheryl like she's the most precious thing in the world. And Cheryl, with her immaculate blonde hair and radiant smile, rests in Jerry's arms like she was made to fit there.

Sissy's been on the verge of tears during her entire speech, and she wraps it up by saying, "Mom, Dad, your love is what dreams are made of. Your romance is the inspiration for my marriage. Thank you for being incredible role models for Ben and me."

Nora grabs the mic, her eyes already glistening with unshed tears. "I've always dreamed of having a love like yours," she begins, her voice shaking. Then her emotions come hard. She bursts into sobs. "I don't know if it will ever happen. At this rate, Maddie will probably get married first. Which isn't fair. She doesn't even believe in love."

She pauses for a moment, tears streaming down her face, before asking the crowd, "Is there something wrong with me? I want to be in love. Don't I deserve love, too?"

Sissy takes the mic and pulls Nora into a hug, saying, "I think we're all feeling what Nora is saying. That love is the strongest force out there... am I right? Abigail, how about you go next? Like now!"

Abby clumsily snatches the microphone, clearly wasted. "So, here's a fun fact about me: I'm the baby, and I'm currently crashing at my parents' pad," she slurs. "And let me ss-spill the tea. Those two are still going at it like some thirsssty teens. There's all sorts of suspicious sounds coming from their bedroom. You feel me?"

The crowd erupts in laughter, and I can't help but join in. Sissy looks like she's about to have a full-blown aneurysm, so Maddie swoops in and grabs the mic.

"Hello there, thanks for sticking around through our cuckoo banana pants speeches. I'm Maddie, or Madeline if you're my dad. Fun fact: I'm terrified of public speaking, so buckle up, this'll be quick... and awkward."

Maddie takes an intense swallow, looking like a deer in headlights. She anxiously scans the crowd, and then her eyes lock onto mine. "Nora misspoke... because I do believe in love."

Time slows down to a crawl. Her words hang in the air, charged with meaning, and my heart skips a beat.

Mads takes a shaky breath, her gaze never leaving mine. "Love is... it's a risk. A leap into the abyss. It's like giving someone the password to your heart and then praying they don't plant a virus and mess everything up. It's a never-ending marathon of compromise and selflessness, and it's not for the faint of heart. But when you find your person, the one who makes you want to strap in and jump headfirst... it's worth every gut-wrenching twist and turn."

I swallow hard, my heart hammering against my ribcage. *She's talking about us.*

She continues, her voice softer now, more intimate. "I see it with my parents. They embody love. They're all about give-and-take and mutual respect. They're not afraid to give away their never-ending supply of love. They rely on each other to answer all of life's questions, at least the important ones. I love the way they've got each other's backs through the highs and lows... it's like a big ol' middle finger to anyone who thinks love isn't real."

A muffled chuckle ripples through the crowd.

"For most people, the sacrifice is worth it," she says, still looking at me. "For my mother, I know she feels this was the right path. She's said countless times that loving my father, building a life with him, and raising us assholes... has been the greatest joy she's ever known."

For a long, quiet moment, we are the only two people in the room. The silence is shattered when Sissy loud-clears her throat.

Maddie turns to her parents, a smile on her face. "So let's raise a glass to my mom and dad, to Jerry and Cheryl, and to their incredible, kick-ass love. May we all be lucky enough to find love like theirs. Cheers!"

"Cheers!" the crowd says in unison.

The fervor of applause fills the room, but my eyes are glued to her. Was Maddie trying to tell me something?

I'm at a total loss. I have no idea what to do.

***

DINNER'S OVER, AND I find myself sitting alone at our table, sipping on a whiskey and checking out the dance floor. Maddie's out there with her sisters and their mom, all of them belting out "Independent Women" by Destiny's Child like it's their personal anthem. Even little Hazel and Violet are getting in on the action, shaking their tiny booties.

It's a sight to behold, three generations of fierce, fabulous females celebrating their independence and giving precisely zero fucks.

"Mind if I join you?" a voice interrupts my thoughts. I look up to see Jerry, Maddie's dad, sliding into the seat next to me.

"Of course not, sir," I say, keeping my cool. *I'm only fantasizing about your daughter, no big deal.*

Jerry chuckles, clapping me on the shoulder. "Relax, kid. I wanted to see how the whole 'fake dating' thing is going with Madeline."

Oh shit, how much does he know?

"I, uh... promise it's all Maddie's choice how it's going down," I stammer, praying I don't sound as sketchy as I feel.

Jerry chuckles, shaking his head. "Zack, we both know Madeline only does what she wants."

I nod, relief coursing through me. "True that. She's a force to be reckoned with."

"That she is," Jerry agrees, his eyes softening as he watches his girls on the dance floor. "I hope it works out for you two. I know how badly Madeline wants this company to happen."

We sit in relaxed silence for a moment, enjoying the celebratory atmosphere. I turn to Jerry, raising my glass. "Congrats on the anniversary, by the way. You and Cheryl have built something really special."

Jerry smiles, clinking his glass against mine. "Thanks, kid. It hasn't always been easy to love a woman as independent and driven as Cheryl. But it's been worth every second."

I lean in, curiosity getting the best of me. "How did you two meet, anyway? Did you both fall in love at first sight?"

"Not quite. We met in college, and she was so busy being a champion for gender equality that she barely noticed me. But I was determined. I knew she was the one."

"So what sealed the deal?" I ask. "A love poem? Serenading her in the park? A surprise trip to Paris?"

"I got her pregnant."

He laughs heartily. "But before that, I never stopped pursuing her. When she finally said yes, I promised to support her passions and dreams, no matter what."

His expression turns serious as he looks me dead in the eye. "And I kept that promise, Zack. Through thick and thin, I've been her partner, her cheerleader, her rock."

I swallow past the lump in my throat, my thoughts racing. *Is he... is he giving me the green light? Telling me to go for it with Maddie?*

Jerry leans back in his chair, a knowing twinkle in his eye. "The key is to let them shine, Zack. Never hold them back. Never dim their light. They'll move mountains for the people they love if you're lucky enough to be one."

I nod slowly, my heart racing. "Thanks, Jerry. That's... that's some solid advice."

He claps me on the shoulder again, standing up. "Anytime. Now, if you'll excuse me, I'm going to go show those young'uns how it's done."

With that, he swaggers onto the dance floor, pulling Cheryl into his arms and twirling her around. Her face is glowing with happiness.

That's what I want. A love that goes the distance and only gets stronger with time.

My eyes drift back to Maddie, dancing carefree with her family. Without a doubt, she's the only one I want that with.

Maddie catches my eye from across the dance floor and grins; my stomach turns a goddamn cartwheel.

Screw it. I gotta go for it. I can make her as happy as Jerry makes Cheryl, as loved, cherished, and supported... I'm ready to take the risk and find out.

I knock back the rest of my drink and rise with fresh determination.

It's time to shoot my shot.

***

"DANCE WITH ME," I say, holding out my hand. It's not a question.

Maddie hesitates, anxiously biting her bottom lip. "Zack, I don't think—"

"Please, Mads. Just one dance."

The dance floor's mood has transformed from a lively party to a romantic haven. Etta James' "At Last" echoes through the room. People are ditching their solo moves and pairing up, getting cozy and swaying to the soul-stirring rhythm.

She yields with a slight nod. I pull her close, my arms circling her waist. We move together in perfect harmony. The only sounds are the sweet melody of the music and our gentle breathing.

"You look beautiful tonight," I say, my lips brushing her ear. She shivers. "Zack—"

"I mean it, Mads. You're captivating. Inside and out."

I feel Maddie trying to pull away as we dance, so I dip her slowly, our gazes locked in unspoken desires. For once, I can see through her façade. She's fighting her feelings, refusing to let herself give in. I pull her up, and our faces are impossibly close—her warm breath teasing my lips. The urge to kiss her is overwhelming, but she tenses and pulls back.

"Roleplay!" she says, her eyes darting around for a couple to imitate.

"No, Maddie. We need to talk about us."

"I don't want to!" Maddie yells.

She bolts off the dance floor, scrambling to the exit. I chase after her, my heart thumping, as I spot her running through the gardens. The cold night air nips at my skin, but it's no match for the intense emotions racing inside me.

"Maddie, stop!" I call out.

She maintains her quick pace on the pebbled path as she steps onto the footbridge that curves over the creek. "Go away, Zack! I'm serious."

"You can keep running, but I'll just keep following you," I shout, my voice raw with emotion. "I'm not going another second without telling you how I feel."

Maddie stops in her tracks, but only because the path has ended at a gazebo covered with glowing fairy lights. I catch up to her, finding her standing with her back towards me.

"Please don't do this," she whispers, shaking her head.

Gently, I take her hand and turn her to face me. "I can't push my feelings aside anymore. Maddie, I'm in love with you. I've loved you since college. I've never met anyone like you. I want to be with you, support you, and help make your dreams come true."

I reach out and caress her cheek. "You can have it all with me by your side. I'll never make you choose between your career and us. We can make it work. I know you feel it too. We're meant to be together."

Her eyes well up with tears, but she remains silent.

"Mads, you're trembling. Take my jacket," I insist, slipping off my coat. She rejects it angrily, shoving me away.

"No! We agreed it was sex, nothing more. No feelings!" she cries. "You can't make promises for the future. It never fucking works. It's the woman who compromises. Always! I want things to go back to normal."

I'm done with normal.

"I'm in love with you, Maddie."

"Don't say that! You need to be with someone like Lexie, who wants to give you everything."

Frustration boils inside me. "Dammit! I don't want Lexie. I want you!"

Maddie breaks down, sobbing uncontrollably. "Lexie will make sacrifices for you. She'll cherish you. She'll give you the family you've always dreamed of. I'm not that woman."

I move closer, gently lifting her chin with my fingers, forcing her to look at me. Her eyes are red and puffy, her cheeks streaked with tears. I press my lips to hers, pouring every ounce of love and longing into the kiss. She surrenders for a fleeting second before pulling away and stumbling back.

"It's not weakness to let someone love you," I say softly, my voice choking up. "You don't have to face everything alone."

She gives me a searching look, and I can see the battle being fought behind her eyes. The fear, the doubt, the desperate yearning for something she's convinced herself she can't have.

"You're the strongest, smartest, most incredible woman I've ever known. I love you, Mads. I love everything about you. All I want in this life... is you." The words tumble out of my mouth, raw, honest, and so true that it hurts.

Tears steadily stream down her face. "I already have a plan for my life. This isn't it."

"So, let's make a new plan."

I can feel the weight of this moment, the gravity of what I'm saying. We're standing on the edge of a cliff, and I'm asking her to step off with me into the unknown.

"Tell me you don't love me," I plead. "Look me in the eye and tell me you don't feel this too."

She shakes her head, wiping furiously at her tears. "I... I love you as a friend, Zack."

"Bullshit. You're lying, Mads. I can see it written all over your face. You're scared to love me."

I reach out and take her hand, tears burning in my eyes. "Do you love me?"

"It doesn't matter if I do. I can never be what you want," she whispers.

She turns and runs, disappearing into the night. I'm left standing with a shattered heart.

My partner, my best friend, the woman I love... is gone.

CHAPTER SIXTEEN

MADDIE

MY EYES RAN OUT OF TEARS HOURS AGO.

I've been crying so hard my eyeballs are loose in their sockets. My heart is doing this dance that's more seizure than salsa. And my face? It feels like it's been used as a stress ball.

It's a twisted game, the way emotions can toy with you. They're like puppet masters, pulling your strings and making you dance to their fucked-up tune. And the worst part? You can't even see the strings, but you sure as hell can feel them cutting into your soul.

I escaped Zack and kept running, no idea where I was headed. Hours later, I ended up on Nora's doorstep. She's like the sister version of a therapist, always ready to listen but without the annoying questions. Nora didn't need me to spell it out; she knew it was about Zack.

Turns out, everyone was picking up on the 'more than friends' vibes between us.

Now, we're huddled on her couch, wrapped in fluffy blankets, surrounded by the carnage of our pizza and ice cream bender. Nora had a brilliant idea to watch "The Purge" in hopes it would purge our own shitty feelings, and it's weirdly working. If only I could hit a delete button on the last month of my life.

But do I want to wipe away those memories of Zack? The magnificent display of his naked form, his grinning reaction to me uncovered and bare, the passion in his eyes when we're intimate. The way my body goes nuts for his touch. The warm, safe feeling of being protected in his arms...

Fuck, heartache is some serious shit.

Since her dickwad date bailed on her, Nora's down in the dumpster fire roasting marshmallows with me. No doubt the guy ran screaming when he heard 'parents' anniversary party,' but still—even if Nora sent out *psycho* vibes—he's a douchebag. Nora's letting me wallow in my misery, so I'll let her do the same.

"Mads?" Nora's voice interrupts the TV screams. "Do you think I'm unlovable? Like, I have some genetic flaw that repels men?"

I snort. "Are you kidding me? You're so fucking close to perfection, it's offensive." I take Nora's hand and give her a serious look. "Getting stood up blows, but it's not a reflection on you. What it means is he's a friggin' moron."

"But it's not just this guy," Nora exhales deeply. "It's all of them. I keep opening myself up, hoping for a real connection, but it never works out. Maybe I'm not meant to find love."

I squeeze her hand, reassuring her. "Come on, stop talking like that. You've got so much to offer; one day, some lucky fucker will recognize how incredible you are."

Nora sighs, hugging a pillow to her chest. "Why is my love life such a disaster? Is it wrong to want someone to live up to my standards? Be honest."

I think about it for a second. "Nah, it's not wrong. We get one shot at this life, Nor. We shouldn't accept anything less than our dreams."

She manages a small smile. "You're the best! You never let anything stand in the way of your goals."

The words hit me like a punch to the gut. "That doesn't mean there's not a cost to it."

"Zack will come around," Nora says in a soothing tone. "I know we said no talking about it, but you two have a deep connection. If you want to return to being friends, he'll understand."

Tears prick my eyes again as I shake my head. "That's not what he said. There's no going back."

Nora wraps her arms around me, pulling me into a side hug. "No matter what, you've always got me."

I squeeze her back hard. "Couldn't do this without you, Nor. Thanks for putting up with my shit."

"We can be spinsters together," she jokes, "Like back in Jane Austen's time."

I let out a watery chuckle. "Now there's a true badass bitch who didn't let men get in the way of her dreams."

A quick giggle passes between us before we're drowned out by the screams and mayhem of "The Purge" blaring from the TV.

I'm clinging to this itsy-bitsy, microscopic hope that Zack will have a change of heart and that we can time travel back to our chill, platonic friendship. But it's way overshadowed by a screaming black cloud of *wake the fuck up and face facts!*

Sissy warned me this would happen, but did I listen? Of course not. I just had to go and cross that damn line, blurring the boundaries of our friendship. The innocence of our bond has been breached like a firewall, and now we're stuck in this convoluted crapshow that I'm not so sure we're adult enough to handle.

And the worst part? I have no one to fucking blame but myself.

***

THIS PLACE SMELLS LIKE A FART MARINATING IN ROTTEN EGGS.

The coding cave always smells like ass, but today we're talking weapons-grade stank. Guess that's the trade-off for pulling a balls-to-the-wall all-nighter.

The guys are chowing down on cold pepperoni and typing away like their noses are out of order. *Me?* The lack of sleep, the over-caffeinated buzz tearing through my system, and the stress of our impending expo trip tomorrow have me feeling mad testy.

I march over to the whiteboard and start assigning the next round of coding tasks. Instantly, the guys grumble.

"Switch with me," Wes whispers loudly to Reid. "I don't want to deal with the chat feature."

"No way, brosif. Profile customization is your headache, not mine," Reid retorts.

I whip around and hit them with my best *I will end you* glare. "I don't give a flying fuck who does what. Just make it happen, assfucks!"

Okay, so maybe I might be more on edge than usual with all of the Zack craziness.

The guys don't protest. Instead, they mutter under their breath and return to their work grudgingly. I'm gearing up to throw out an apology when Wes lets out a choked yelp.

"Oh man, she's gonna be there!" he exclaims.

"Who's gonna be where?" Cosmo asks, not bothering to look up from his code.

Wes starts pacing, his hands flailing wildly. "The girl I've been chatting with online. FantasyFae404. She's a fellow coder, and she's going to the expo. She wants to meet me. Face to face!"

Reid and Cosmo exchange a look before turning to Wes with matching smirks.

"I hope you didn't send her some phony-ass, airbrushed photo of yourself because she's in for a major letdown when she sees you in person," Cosmo declares.

"Totally," Reid nods. "And she's gonna catch on quick that your weirdo charm is just plain weird when you're not hiding behind your computer."

Cosmo continues, "Let's have her complete a post-date survey. That way, we'll get valuable information like 'After a month of getting to know each other online, our in-person meeting was a major letdown.'"

Wes flips them off, but I can see the verifiable terror in his eyes—*poor dude.* I want to tell him it'll be fine, but I'm so goddamn sick of talking about love and relationships. What the hell was I thinking, starting a company that centers around dating? It's a cosmic joke, and I'm not laughing.

I might be extra salty because of where Zack is right now—in a meeting with Lexie. A meeting I was supposed to be part of, but Zack coldly disinvited me through a cc'd email. That's the only communication we've had in the last two days.

He's making his move, or he just can't stand my presence. Either way, it's a shit sandwich for me. I'm about to suggest we take a vow of celibacy and become monk coders when Zack bursts through the front door, like a man on a mission.

My disloyal heart does a little flip at the sight of him, all broad shoulders and determined swagger. *Damn, I've missed him.* I quickly cram those feelings back into the *do not open* box in my mind when I catch sadness lurking in his eyes. He purposely avoids my gaze, and it stings.

The guys start whining to Zack, tossing me under the bus like yesterday's roadkill.

"Bro! You gotta help us," Reid pleads. Maddie's been riding us hard and putting us away wet, and she won't even let us take a piss."

Wes nods vigorously, holding up a large bottle filled with a suspicious yellow liquid. "I had to bust out my trusty pee jar."

"Hold on, was that jar in the fridge yesterday? I thought it was effing lemonade," Cosmo says, wrinkling his nose in disgust.

"Guys, shut up. We have a major problem," Zack announces, his voice edged with frustration.

My stomach drops to my toes. *Oh shit, now what?*

Zack's shoulders tense up. "Lexie dropped a bombshell. McBurney Financial Group is hedging their bets and offered the same deal to another dating app. They'll invest in whichever app has the more successful launch at the expo."

Cosmo's eyes widen. "Well, fuck me sideways. Did Lexie say what this other app is?"

"Yeah, it's called MatchMaster," Zack replies, his brow furrowed. We immediately start Googling.

"Listen to this," Wes says, reading off the MatchMaster site. "The app is an old-school matchmaker, determining compatibility between individuals and their families by looking at stuff like social class, values, and background."

I scrunch up my face. "So, it's basically an arranged marriage? What psycho would sign up for that?"

"I'm interested," Reid says.

"Seriously? You'd let some app pick your wife?" I say in disbelief.

"Beats swiping till my thumb falls off," Reid replies. "If someone wants to do the dirty work and find me a smokin' hot missus, then hell yeah, I'm in."

Cosmo breaks away from his screen. "MatchMaster isn't just your average dating app. It's a distinct concept, catering to a different audience. People who prefer a more calculated path to marriage."

"There's more," Zack says, looking grave. "Lexie warned me the investors think our data is too Chicago-heavy. They're not confident the app is ready for a national rollout."

"FUCK!" I yell, slamming my fist on the desk.

"Uh oh, MatchMaster is already beta testing in ten major cities," Wes says.

I pin Zack with a pointed stare. "What the hell did you tell Lexie about our data?"

"I said we're aware of the issue and working on it."

"So the investment firm still thinks we can fix this before launch?" I ask.

Cosmo snorts. "How? We've known this was a problem from the start."

"Well, we tried," Wes says, throwing his hands up. "Guess we're not going to the expo after all."

"Coward," Cosmo mutters. "You just don't want to meet your supposed girlfriend in person."

Reid chuckles. "Aww, Cosmo called her a girl."

"Shut it, everybody!" I bark. "I wanna see a vote. Who here would honestly use LoveScore to find a date? Raise your damn hands."

All hands fly up.

"See? People want choice, not some creepy arranged marriage algorithm," I say, my mind racing. "We still have a chance to beat MatchMaster if we can prove our approach is more appealing to the masses."

I turn to Cosmo, desperation clawing at my insides. "What if we change the date surveys that Zack and I filled out? Expand our city data set?"

Zack's eyes widen. "You want to add even more fake data?"

Reid jumps in with a crazed glint in his eye. "What if we cheat? For launch day only."

Cosmo leans forward, intrigued. "How?"

"We could hack into another dating app, steal their user data, and randomly change the names," Reid explains, his words tumbling out in an excited rush. "Most of our profiles would have a generic icon since we don't have time to generate new images, but it would look like we have a nationwide user base."

Holy shit. It's insane, but it might work.

"We'll get more organic sign-ups at launch and then ditch the hacked data once we have legit nationwide users," I ponder, my mind working in overdrive.

Cosmo frowns. "One problem. We don't have the expertise to hack through another dating app's firewalls in just one day."

Wes agrees, "Yeah, that's a labyrinth of security to break through."

Reid grins, looking far too pleased with himself. "*We* don't do the hacking. We hire Cyber Sphinxx."

My mouth falls open. Cyber Sphinxx is a fucking legend in the hacker world, notorious for hacking everything from corporate bigwigs to government organizations. He even cracked Edward Snowden's burner phone just to prove he could.

Cosmo slow claps. "Damn, Reid. That idea is legit."

Reid basks in the unexpected compliment, but Zack's face is a thunderous scowl of disapproval.

"No way," he says firmly. "This isn't cheating; it's criminal activity. We don't even know who this Cyber Sphinxx person is. It's too risky."

I stand up to meet his eyes. "It's not only your call, Zack. This could save us."

He grabs my arm, his grip just shy of painful. "Maddie. A word. Now."

Zack drags me into the hallway, his jaw clenched tight. I yank my arm free, glaring up at him.

"What the hell, Zack? We need to explore our options."

"Not this one," he growls, his eyes flashing with anger. "I won't let you risk what we've built on some half-baked scheme cooked up by Captain Douchebag in there."

I fold my arms across my chest, my temper rising. "Oh, so now I need your permission? Last I checked, we were equal fucking partners."

Zack runs a hand through his hair, frustration rolling off him in waves. "Damn it, Maddie. You know that's not what I meant. This is crossing a line. If we get caught, we could lose everything."

"What do you think will happen if we do nothing?" I shoot back, my voice cracking with emotion. "I've poured everything into LoveScore. I can't watch it die without a fight."

Zack's expression softens, and he reaches out and gently cups my face. The warmth of his touch sends a shiver down my spine, even as I try to hold onto my righteous anger.

"Mads. I know how much this means to you. To us," he says softly, his thumb brushing over my cheekbone. "We'll figure something out, I promise. Not this though... please."

I close my eyes, leaning into his touch for a moment. The urge to give in, to let him wrap me up in his strong arms and tell me everything will be okay, is overwhelming.

I can't. Not when the future of our company hangs in the balance.

I step back. "I'm sorry, but I have to do what's best for LoveScore. With or without you."

I turn on my heel and march back into the coding cave; my head held high even as my heart cracks a little more with every step.

"Guys, let's find Cyber Sphinxx," I order. "It's time to make a deal with the devil."

***

WE'RE WAITING FOR A FREAKING GHOST TO AP-PEAR.

Cosmo sent out a message on the dark web hours ago. Reaching Cyber Sphinxx is a long shot, but without his skills, LoveScore goes tits up and fails.

I glance over at Zack's bedroom door for the gazillionth time tonight. I want to talk to him, try to smooth things over, but there's no time. We're a category 5 shitstorm, but our app needs to be flawless. Expo first, drama later.

"Any reply from Cyber Sphinxx yet?" Wes asks, spinning around in his chair.

"No, same as when you asked five minutes ago," Cosmo says dryly. "Assume that I will let you know if and when he responds, kay?"

"Come on guys, stay focused," I command. "We're outta here in six hours. Everything on our end needs to be as tight as possible."

Again my gaze shifts to Zack's door as he switches off his light. I hate that he's upset. It kills me that I caused him pain. And I freaking despise my mind for fixating on him.

Is he right? Is this hack a terrible idea? I wrack my brain, but I see no other solution.

As shady as it feels, I agree with Reid—once we get the funding and traction, we'll scrub the hacked data from the app.

No one outside this room will ever know.

Without warning, every screen starts flashing and displaying some creepy-ass code like we've summoned a demon.

"It's a hack! Quick, shut it down!" I yell.

"Wait!" Cosmo shouts. "It's him!"

Straight out of some dystopian Matrix-y nightmare, an eerie synthetic face pops up on every screen, and a distorted, robotic voice booms through the speakers.

"Greetings, denizens of the digital realm. I am Cyber Sphinxx."

"H-hello," I stammer.

"You must be Madeline Denton."

"It's Maddie," I correct him.

"Delighted to meet you all, Maddie, Cosmo, Wes and Reid."

"That's freaky," Reid whispers.

I square my shoulders and look directly into my webcam. "So you got our message about the hack?"

"I don't hack, I enlighten," Cyber Sphinxx declares. "And Maddie, may I say you're the hottest coder I've ever met. If you were a firewall, I'd be eager to see if I could penetrate your defenses."

Hell no. I'm not gonna play into his sleazy come-ons. "So, can you hack it or not? Because we have shit to do."

"Feisty. I like that," Cyber Sphinxx chuckles. "It just so happens I'll be at the AppVerge Expo. I can do your hack... if you meet my demands."

Ugh, of course the diva has conditions. I grip the arms of my chair so I don't start shaking like a leaf. My whole future and the success of LoveScore depend on making this faceless freak happy.

I raise my voice and address the monitors. "Name your terms, Cyber Sphinxx. Within reason."

"It's simple," he states magnanimously. "A private, in-person meeting with the lovely Madeline at the expo. Call it intellectual curiosity."

I grit my teeth but nod.

"I require an Easter egg in your app giving me a slash line in the credits. Something subtle like 'Penetration testing by Cyber Sphinxx.' I have a reputation to uphold."

"Fine, we'll stick it in the Terms of Service that no one reads," I agree.

Cosmo types furiously as Cyber Sphinxx rattles off his stipulations.

"A case of ThriveTonic Power Drink, Mermaid Mingle flavor. Don't get that Unicorn Elixir crap; it's pure hype and tastes like sweaty buttcrack," Sphinxx dictates. "A galaxy mood light, a gallon-size bag full of fresh red rose petals, a forty-four ounce container of bar snack mix with all the pretzels removed, three lavender scented candles, Fifty thousand dollars in crypto, and a creepy baby doll with twenty-five amphetamines and twenty-five quaaludes hidden in its head."

I stare at the screen, my jaw hanging open. This dude is either a certified Einstein or a freaking wackadoodle. Maybe both.

Sphinxx's voice booms, "If my demands are not met when I arrive, I will bail. I'll only reveal myself to Maddie, who must be present during the hack. This offer expires in one minute."

"How will I find you?" I ask. "No one knows what you look like."

"You won't," Sphinxx responds cryptically. "I'll find you."

"And how do we know you'll finish it on time?" I press.

"I never miss a deadline."

Cosmo leans over to me, his brow furrowed. "Shouldn't you talk to Zack about this?"

I grimace. "He said he wants no part of it."

My thoughts are all over the place. This is a gargantuan pile of green—money we don't have. If this plan goes sideways, we'll lose everything. Game over; thanks for playing.

I look around at the guys, all watching me with bated breath, waiting for my decision. What would Zack do?

No, screw Zack.

He isn't here.

He said he'd be by my side.

But he's making me go at this alone.

Fine. I don't need him; I can do this myself.

"We have a deal."

"Can't wait. See you in San Francisco." Sphinxx purrs. "Time to vanish."

His code face dissolves, and suddenly, the power cuts out, plunging us into darkness.

"That was fucking cool," Cosmo whispers as the lights flicker back on and our computers whir to life.

Just then, Zack bursts out of his room, his hair sticking up at odd angles. "What the hell is going on with the power? I'm trying to sleep!"

"Dude, you should've seen Maddie," Wes gushes. "She was a total badass."

"Cyber Sphinxx took control of our systems," Reid chimes in.

Zack turns to me, his eyes narrowing. "So you went with the hacker?"

"I said I'm going to do whatever it takes, and I meant it," I respond defiantly.

Cosmo clears his throat. "We can meet his list of demands. Except for the drugs. None of us know where to get those."

"Drugs?!" Zack shouts.

I wave him off. "Abby can help with that."

Zack's eyes widen. "You're going to have your little sister buy drugs to pay an illegal hacker? What is happening with you? I don't even know who you are anymore."

His words hit me hard.

"Zack, I—" I start, but he cuts me off.

"No. I can't hear anymore. I don't want to be implicated in this." He stomps back to his room. "Airport shuttle will be here in five hours," he throws over his shoulder before slamming the door.

I take a deep breath, strengthening my resolve. Since Zack's not stepping up, it's on me.

I turn to the guys, my expression hardening. "Make me an encrypted phone. I need to reach out to my sister. We don't want any trace of this getting back to us."

They nod solemnly, already getting to work. These jackwads may drive me crazy, but they've got my back.

As I watch them, a sense of dread settles over me. I made this bed, and I gotta lie in it, even if it means risking everything and everyone that matters.

I'm all in.

CHAPTER SEVENTEEN

ZACK

LOVESCORE IS THE MAIN ATTRACTION AT THIS EXPO! Knock 'em dead, Zack!

I'm psyching myself up as the convention hall doors swing open and herds of eager techies descend upon the AppVerge Expo. Our big moment, the LoveScore main stage presentation, is tomorrow at 2 p.m., so today, our tricked-out booth needs to create lots of buzz.

Overhead, colorful banners dangle from the rafters, announcing the latest and greatest in streaming, apps, software—you name it, it's here. The air crackles with anticipation alongside a hint of "do or die" desperation from the vendors.

I survey the crowd of attendees, loaded with swag bags and being ambushed by salespeople pushing products. The sea of booths seems to stretch on forever, each one outdoing the previous with dazzling displays and extravagant offerings, all vying for attention with their "groundbreaking" apps and gadgets. Everyone wants their product to be the next big thing.

Especially us.

"Did you all check out the booth with the smartwatches that can measure the caloric value of your food?" Wes says, fiddling with his neon green tie covered in cartoon bananas. "It's linked to an app. Pretty sick."

"I enjoyed the surveillance app that gets triggered by your pet's mischievous behavior," Cosmo says with a grin. "I welcome the inevitable surge of more awesome viral videos."

I raise an eyebrow. "You watch cute animal videos?"

"I don't hate them. They're proof that naivety and joy still exist in this screwed-up world," Cosmo says nonchalantly.

"You've got layers, don't you?"

"Don't we all," he quips.

Reid barrels toward us and shoves two steaming cups of cappuccino in our faces.

"Guys, I'm freaking out!" he yelps, eyes darting between us. "Are these tits and dicks good enough?"

I peer into the cups, taking in Reid's frisky foam art. One cup boasts a perky pair of breasts, while the other proudly displays a jizzing penis.

Cosmo claps a hand on Reid's shoulder, his face solemn. "Reid, I don't give compliments lightly, but that right there? That is a goddamn work of art." He grabs the frothy dick cappuccino and takes a long sip.

"It's perfect," I assure Reid. "Now go make a thousand more."

As Reid scurries off to craft more custom caffeinated genitalia, I survey our booth. We've got a unique hook to reel people in—a "first date" coffee station where strangers can sit, sip Reid's scandalous creations, and test out LoveScore's compatibility algorithm.

Afterward, they rate each other. It's fun, flirty, and infinitely more captivating than what's going on at other booths.

The gimmick's working because curious expo-goers are already meandering over, drawn in by Maddie's booming voice as she works passersby. My brilliant, vivacious, pain-in-my-ass best friend is a force of nature when she turns on the charm.

"Let LoveScore hook you up with your soulmate!" she yells, beckoning people to the coffee station enthusiastically. "Go on a legit first date right here, right now. What have you got to lose?"

She's killing it with her line of thirsty singles and skeptical on-lookers. I need to step up my game. I position myself on the other side of the booth, ready to lure in my group of potential daters.

"Say goodbye to awkward first dates with LoveScore," I announce to the people walking by. "Our algorithm finds your perfect match. And if you enjoy the experience here, come to the main stage to-morrow to see what other amazing things LoveScore has lined up for your pleasure!"

I glance at Maddie as I hand out flyers and recruit sign-ups. She's looking vibrant in her polished ensemble. I have to give a shoutout to Abby, who wrestled away Maddie's hoodies and styled her with some sweet blouses and blazers. *Damn, she looks sharp, sexy, and confident.*

As much as I want to appreciate her, I can't shake the tension hanging between us. We've yet to talk since our argument about hir-ing the hacker. I'm shocked she blew the rest of our savings without running it by me. I told her I didn't want any part of it, but still... she's backed us into a corner. If we don't lock down this Series A funding, we're screwed.

To make things worse, Maddie swapped seats with Wes on the flight, so we were completely separated. Sure, she's just trying to avoid more fighting, but it still stings. The truth is, everything hurts.

She yanked out my soul and left me without hope.

Maddie's words have been haunting me these last few days. I begged her to admit that she feels the same way and loves me too. But instead, she said, *it doesn't matter if I do. I can never be what you want.*

How can she shut down the possibility of what we could be so easily? She loves me, damn it. *I know she does.* The problem is that she refuses to let herself be in love, and it's destroying me.

I watch her smiling and conversing with people who've swung by the booth, and I can't ignore this twinge of jealousy. She's avoiding looking at me.

Real mature, Mads. Fine.

Two can play that game.

Maddie's not interested in processing our shit. No, she made it clear that this expo is her one-way ticket to Successville, and no former-best-friend-turned-fuck-buddy will derail her ambitions. I get it. I want her to achieve her dreams, too.

I just hoped… I could be part of them.

***

MY THROAT FEELS LIKE I'VE BEEN GARGLING WITH RAZOR BLADES.

It's the middle of day one, and I'm already losing my voice. But I gotta hand it to Reid—his "sexy foam art" is a hit. People have been lining up all day for our first coffee date gimmick. This incredible turnout proves we're on the right track and is surely intimidating our competition.

I'm serving up schlong cappuccinos when I hear Wes trying to sell the app to a cute redhead with freckles, rocking a purple cat meme top. I'm rooting for him, but his game is seriously lacking.

"... and that's the gist of LoveScore," Wes finishes weakly. "So, uh, what do you think?"

"Honestly? I'm not buying it," she says with a skeptical look. "Awkward first dates are inevitable."

I sidle up next to Wes, disarming her with my smile. "Well, hey there! Zack Hanley, thanks for stopping by our booth. And you are?"

"Brenna," she replies, shaking my hand with a grip that could crush walnuts. "I was just telling your friend here that LoveScore sounds as legit as a three-dollar bill."

"Fair first assessment, but you don't know until you try," I say. "Picture this: you, Wes, two steaming mugs of joy and the most enlightening coffee date of your life. Whaddya say?"

Wes gulps, his complexion morphing into a shade of puke green that matches his ugly tie. "Ah, well, you see... the thing is, I'm kind of already, sort of, potentially... taken?"

Brenna snort-laughs. "Cool your jets. It's a demo, not a marriage proposal."

Wes looks at me hesitantly, but I keep grinning and nodding until he caves. "Okay, sure. Let's do this!"

As they get comfortable with their foam-art-decorated drinks featuring boobs and boners, I blatantly eavesdrop.

"So," Brenna begins, stirring her foam penis into a swirl. "You said you were sorta seeing someone? Is she cuter than me?"

"Listen, Brenna. You're a catch—you're attractive, and your red hair is fantastic. It's... well, I'm sorta off the market at the moment, so this feels wrong."

To my surprise, she smiles. "I get it, and actually... I'm stoked you feel that way. Tell me, did Linda pick out your killer tie?" she quips.

Wes' jaw drops. "Oh my God. It's you. You're her... You're FantasyFae404."

"Guilty as charged," she cuts him off with a wink. "But you can call me Brenna. And Wes, your curls are even cuter than I pictured."

"Brenna," Wes repeats dreamily. "That's the most beautiful name I've ever heard."

At least someone gets to be in love. My money would've never been on Wes, but good for him. Since these two clearly don't need me, I turn to Maddie, who's showing off the app to some potential users. She doesn't even glance my way. It's been like this all fucking day.

Suddenly, a lanky guy materializes before me, pumping my hand like a piston. "Hey, so this is LoveScore? Been hearing your expo buzz, man. Trevor's the name, coding's my game."

I size him up, tall and slim, with long, messy brown hair that hasn't been washed in ages and a matching scraggly beard. His wrinkled button-down and even more rumpled chinos scream, "I couldn't care less about my image." He's not ugly, I guess, but his fingerprint-covered glasses and clothes covered in cat hair aren't screaming "date me" to the ladies.

"Are you guys using Server-Side Programming Languages for the app backend?" Trevor says, his eyes scanning the booth.

I shrug, pointing to Mads. "That's not my department. Maddie over there is the creator of the app and head coder. She's the one to ask when it comes to the technicals."

Trevor's eyes widen as he sees her. "That hottie is a coder? Dude, scope out those bazoombas. She's hands down the hottest chick in this sea of sausage!"

I wince at his objectification of her, but I force a smile. "Yeah, we're lucky to have her on the team. Watch out, though; she's a fierce one."

Trevor nods, still staring. "Do you work under her or over her... ya lucky dog!" He eyes me with a sly grin. "Does she have a boyfriend?"

Before I can answer, he shakes his head and laughs. "What am I saying? Of course she has a boyfriend. Hot piece like that, no way those tatas don't belong to someone."

My desire to be professional is being snuffed out by my urge to punch him in the dick. I'm about to say, *She's actually single and despises jackoffs like you*, when—

"Wow, Zack, look at this turnout!" says a smiling Lexie, appearing beside me.

My cheeks soften as Lexie alters my mood like a genie. I try to introduce her to Trevor, but homeboy has vanished. I spot him already putting the moves on Maddie. I want to swoop in and save her, but then, for the first time all day, Maddie glances at me... with a strange expression that reads?

Shame? Hunger? Pride?

Why is she studying me? I assume it's something inappropriate Trevor is saying until I realize that Maddie is not focused on me. She's eyeing Lexie, and the expression on her face is one I've picked up on in the last few weeks.

Maddie's jealous.

I shouldn't gloat; it's petty and immature. I'd typically take the high road, but if she wants to push me away, then this is what she gets—Zack's "moves" being put on another woman.

You want me to be with Lexie? You got it.

I crank up the charm, laughing a little too loudly at one of Lexie's jokes, finding every excuse to touch her arm and lean in close. I assume Maddie will be fuming with envy, but instead... she's smirking? *Why is she giving me that look?*

Maddie flips her hair like she's in a shampoo commercial and plants a whisper in Trevor's ears. He laughs, his eyes flickering down to her cleavage as she shows him the app on her phone.

That prick's eyes are locked onto Maddie's tits, and she knows it. Why is she encouraging him by holding the phone between her breasts?

Oh, you wanna flirt? Challenge accepted!

I slide closer to Lexie, laying my hand on her shoulder as I show her our promo flyer. "Why don't you take a couple of these and spread the love?"

Lexie places her hand over mine, her fingers lightly grazing my skin, eyes twinkling. "I want to hop on the love train."

But Lexie's voice is distant because I'm checking out this Trevor dude, who's lifting his wrinkled shirt and revealing some unexpectedly toned muscles. *Damn, he's got a six-pack hiding under there.* Trevor seizes Maddie's hand and places it on his washboard stomach, proudly stroking her fingers up and down his abs.

Jealousy descends on me like a swarm of angry bees, stinging my heart repeatedly. If Maddie is playing some flirting game, it's taken an awful turn—time to crank up the heat. I guide Lexie over so we can stop Trevor's saucy wink-and-gun show.

"Hey, Mads, look who stopped by!" I announce, draping my arm around Lexie's shoulders.

Maddie turns, her face lighting up with mock surprise. "Lexie, hi! I'm so glad you came by. Did Zack show you his dick yet?"

Record scratch. Silence descends upon our little group.

"Oh God, I meant the dick foam art! On the cappuccinos!" Maddie waves Cosmo over.

Cosmo glides in with a tray of drinks, each one capped with a foamy penis or frothy boobs. Lexie bursts out laughing. "Wow, the pubes are so lifelike!"

"I've seen better breasts," Trevor quips, flashing Maddie a wolfish grin and giving her tits another peep session.

Maddie smiles coyly back at him. *WTF? How is she falling for this hipster's cheesy lines?*

Trevor, the piece of shit that he is, openly lies, "Bro, you told me Maddie was the token female coder on your team, not this one-woman powerhouse. You better hide this chick, dude; every company here will want a piece of her." He winks at Maddie. "I know I do."

Must. Resist. Urge. To. Throat. Punch.

"I completely agree; we definitely need more female CEOs in the tech world." Lexie chimes in. "Maddie, you're an inspiration."

In 0.5 seconds, Maddie's face changes from surprise to glowing. "Jeez, thanks, Lexie. That means a lot. But what about you? Don't you wanna be a big-shot CEO someday?"

Lexie laughs, waving off the notion. "Oh gosh, no. I'll work until I get married, then switch to part-time so I can stay home with the kids. My career will take a back seat once I have a family."

Maddie shoots me a pointed *I told you so* look.

Great, more fuel for her scorched earth view on relationships.

Trevor senses an opening and pounces. "Let's get the convo away from marriage and kids and back to kinky cappuccinos and casual hookups, eh? Maddie, let's go out to dinner. We can interface, dive into each other's source code, and maybe debug our core functions."

He slips her a business card, and Maddie literally blushes.

Oh hell no. No no no no no!

Call it chivalry... or jealousy... or plain stupidity. I reach my breaking point.

I lunge for the card, snatching it out of Maddie's hand. "Great, we'd love to discuss potential business opportunities with you, Trevor!"

Maddie glares at me, tugging the card back. "Zack, I got this."

"No, let me hold onto it for you." I yank harder.

"Find your own prospects, Hanley!" Maddie huffs, pulling with all her might.

Then, my hand slips, flies back, and collides with Lexie's coffee cup. The hot liquid splashes all over Lexie's pristine white blouse. She lets out a yelp, jumping back in shock.

SHIT!

I grab a fistful of napkins, frantically blotting at Lexie's chest. "Oh my God, I'm so sorry! Here, let me help."

"Zack, we got this," Maddie says bluntly, swatting me away. She gives Trevor an apologetic smile. "It was great meeting you. I hope to see you around." She links her arm through Lexie's and marches her to the bathroom, sending me a chilling glare over her shoulder.

Trevor calls out, his eyes now glued to Maddie's ass. "The pleasure was and is mine." He lets out a low whistle. "Damn, can't tell if she looks better going or coming... probably coming. I'll find out later."

Where does this slimy bottom feeder fuckstain get off?

My fingers curl into fists, and I feel the muscles in my jaw constrict. I'm itching to smash this smug bastard square in his stubbly face.

"With bootylicious cake like that, I better move fast," Trevor says, trotting away.

What the hell just happened?

***

I'M LOUNGING ON THE HOTEL BED, digging into leftover fettuccine with a fork in one hand, and seeking distraction with a remote in the other.

Flip. Commercial for a blender that can turn a bowling ball into a smoothie. *Pass.*

Flip. Reality TV show where celebs eat hot sauce and spill secrets about Hollywood stars. *Pass.*

Flip. Rom-com movie where a dude chases after a girl he's obsessed with. *Ouch. Hard pass.*

I shut off the TV.

Once the expo shut down for the evening, Lexie reached out with a networking dinner invite *(thankfully, no hard feelings about the coffee mishap).* I had a blast with Lexie, she really knows how to have a good time. But now I'm back in my hotel room, and Maddie's all I'm thinking about.

Seeing that Trevor guy all up in Maddie's personal space today was more than I could take. There's no way she's interested in him. *Right?* She put the kibosh on relationships, but after a few weeks of hooking up with her, I know she enjoys sex. I bet she's hungry for more good times between the sheets. It makes sense she'd want someone with no strings attached.

My mind drifts to all the intimate moments we've shared, every kiss seared into my memory. I'm lost in it all—her soft skin, our fingers entwined, the intoxicating taste of her lips—my mouth tracing a slow path down her stomach while breathless moans fill my ears. A heat builds inside me.

I ponder if we could sustain a friends-with-benefits-situation... No, I could never. I would always be wanting more.

And then, my visions turn dark. I see myself on top of Maddie, groaning with pleasure as she squeezes me. But suddenly, the face and body are not mine. In this nightmare-come-to-life, it's no longer me but Trevor. He's pushing Maddie into the bed with his hips as she writhes with pleasure. Trevor's getting to do everything I want, everything I've done before. More visions of Maddie and Trevor, sweaty and thrusting, fill my head. Panting and pounding, over and over, no way of stopping them—

God, Zack! Stop picturing Maddie and Trevor banging!

I grab the remote and start flipping again, desperate for a show to claim my attention. But it's no use. Every drama, movie, and commercial reminds me of Maddie somehow.

I'm so screwed. I'm in love with a woman who doesn't want to be in love, but I can't let her go.

I swipe my phone awake, pulling up Maddie's contact. My thumb hovers over the call button, a battle raging between my desire to connect and my insecurities. I miss her so much it hurts, even if she was clear that her rejection of me was final. My head knows this, but my heart hasn't caught up.

I gotta snap out of it... to let go and move on.

But how do you move on from the best thing that's ever happened to you?

How do you let go of the one person you need to feel alive?

I toss my phone aside and open the suitcase for pajamas. I see my old Northwestern hoodie. I don't know why I packed it, maybe because it's Maddie's favorite.

I make a decision. I'm giving it to her as a peace offering. I've been miserable these last few days, so I'll concede to having her in my life as a friend. I'll respect her wishes and hope that time heals my heartbreak.

Before I waver, I stride down the hotel hallway, clutching the worn hoodie. My plan is to knock on Maddie's door and apologize before she can stop me. I'm hoping the sweatshirt peace offering will diffuse any anger, and then we can hang out as friends.

Watch some TV, order dessert, and it'll be like old times.

I get closer to Maddie's room and hear noises behind her door. I stop in my tracks. It sounds like... erotic moans? I hear a barrage of breathy, high-pitched sex sounds. What the fuckery is this?

My thoughts run wild. Anger surges through me. *Is Maddie seriously having sex with that piece of shit Trevor?* The thought makes my blood boil, and before I can stop myself, I'm pounding on the door like a jealous boyfriend.

The moaning noises halt abruptly, and the door swings open a moment later. Maddie, wearing her pajamas, stands there, looking mortified.

"Zack, what are you doing here?" Maddie asks, her voice cutting through my fog of rage and disbelief.

But I barely notice her because my eyes take in the scene behind her. Candles. Mood lighting. And Trevor, the shitweasel, not wearing a shirt, sitting on a bed of rose petals like a scene from a goddamn romance movie.

And he's one ripped hipster—muscles on top of muscles—tattoos snaking up his arms—his long, messy hair in a man bun. I hate that he looks like a total badass rockstar, one that girls go crazy for.

I'm shaken to my core. This is unreal. Maddie can't be hooking up with this dirtbag after everything we've shared recently. But the proof is staring me in the face, and I don't know whether to lose my shit, break down in tears, or start throwing punches.

The jagoff makes eye contact with me, and then... the creepy douchefuck winks at me. He fucking winks at me!

Maddie steps into the hallway and closes the door behind her. We stand there, facing each other; the tension is so thick, it's suffocating.

"Now's not a good time. What do you want?" Maddie asks, her arms crossed over her chest.

I can't think straight. Adrenaline surges through my veins, and my pulse pounds so fast it wants to burst out of my ribcage.

"I can't fucking do this anymore!" I shout, my voice ringing out.

"Before you judge me—" Maddie starts, but I interrupt her.

"Here's what I know. You don't give a shit. About me, about us... I just, I can't believe you would—"

The words get stuck in my throat, choking me. I can't even finish the sentence.

Maddie stands there defiantly, her face a mask of indifference, and it hits me.

It's over.

Our friendship.

Our partnership.

It's all gone.

Everything has been shattered into a million meaningless pieces.

I have to stop torturing myself.

I inhale deeply, attempting to be calm. "I'm leaving the company after the launch… I hope you get everything you're chasing after."

And with that, I toss her my Northwestern hoodie. "Here. To remember me by."

I turn to walk away, every step driving the knife deeper into my back. Maddie's voice stops me.

"Zack, wait! What are you saying? It's over? We're not us anymore?"

I turn back to look at her, my eyes burning with unshed tears. "There never was an us," I say, my voice barely above a whisper.

I leave her standing in the hallway, the hoodie cradled in her palms.

No more clinging to an impossible dream.

CHAPTER EIGHTEEN

MADDIE

I'M COUNTING DOWN THE SECONDS until this is over.

"Thanks a lot, asshole!" I slam the door shut, rattling the pictures on the wall.

I toss Zack's hoodie into my disorganized mess of a suitcase, willing myself to ignore the full-on guilt trip brewing in my chest.

"That was my co-CEO, and he's super pissed," I say to Trevor, hands on my hips. "I don't see why I can't just tell him who you are."

He looks at me with a smug grin. *This shitwad has some balls.*

"No can do. You agreed to my terms—very few get to know the orgasmic being that is Cyber Sphinxx. Even fewer get to know him physically. My offer still stands." He motions to the bed, salaciously waggling his eyebrows.

I can't believe this guy. "Did you ask for all of these weird-ass things hoping I would sleep with you?"

"So, you're a firm no?" Trevor asks, his face falling.

"Firmer than your dick ever gets," I snap.

Trevor shrugs, unfazed. "Then no, I did not. Now I need to focus."

He opens his laptop and starts typing away like an effing machine. "Almost forgot. My thinking sounds." He turns on the porn he was watching earlier, and sex noises fill the room, the same ones Zack must have heard in the hallway.

I sink onto the bed, head in my hands. Cyper Sphinxx or Trevor or whoever he really is... he's a total dickbag. I know how this looked; the moans, the candles, the rose petals... Zack totally thinks I'm boning this schmuck.

I'm desperate to go to him and confess the truth, but I can't because that's the stipulation for working with this cockweasel. Anonymity.

I've never seen Zack so angry and hurt, and what kills me is it's all my fault. I'm the source of his suffering.

I wish I could just throw away my dreams and make him happy. It would be so simple to let him put a ring on it, buy some basic-ass house in the burbs, get freaky on Fridays, and spend Saturdays lazing around in our PJ's.

Sure, a part of me would be blissfully content, but the other half would be miserable. Zack might be confident he can deliver me the perfect life, but let's be real, nobody knows the secret to making a relationship work forever, especially when you're trying to balance careers and family.

You only find out when you're drowning in the consequences of your choices.

We'd end up right back here, a few years older, and I'd be not only bitter, but deeply resentful of him for killing my dreams. There's only forward, even if it feels like I'm ripping my heart out.

My sacrifices mean something.

I won't give up everything I've worked for.

Not even for Zack.

Of course, none of that matters right now. We're hours away from our launch presentation, so I'm going to do my damn job, save this fucking company, and keep dealing with this dickclown.

"So, that guy at the door, you two in love or something?" Trevor blurts out, his fingers never missing a beat on the keyboard.

"What? No. We're friends," I scoff.

"You don't see it, but I do. I see everything. Love is the ultimate hack," Trevor muses. "It bypasses logic and taps into the deepest recesses of the human soul."

I roll my eyes. "Do me a favor and focus on your job so I can do mine."

"A lone wolf then? Like me. I thought I was in love once until she got pregnant and wanted me to be Mr. Dad. Nah. Settling down and all that bullshit ain't gonna happen. I'm a nomad in cyberspace."

"You're a shitty human being. We're nothing alike."

"I told you I see everything. I can feel your energy, and we both want the same things out of life."

Ugh, Zack was right. He's crazy. I shouldn't be working with this jerkstain. *Worst plan ever.* I need to shut it down. There's got to be another way.

"Cyber Sphinxx is in! Protocol overridden. Data unlocked. I am the ghost in the machine!" Trevor announces, his voice oozing with self-satisfaction.

Damn, that was fast.

"Transferring the data to your servers. Give it a few minutes. You think you can pack up those rose petals while we wait? I just hit up a goth chick, and she's down to Netfucks and chill," Trevor says like he's ordering a freaking pizza.

"Sure?" I say, grabbing the plastic bag.

Is Trevor right? Are we alike? Is this how Zack sees me? An uncaring, self-absorbed assbag? I'm not a douche canoe... am I?

Trevor shoves his laptop into his computer bag, holding the creepy doll filled with drugs. He walks to the hotel room door and says, "Last chance to suck the cock of a Cyber God."

"Trust me, you're the one missing out," I say, handing over his "romance-in-a-bag" rose petals and slamming the door in his face.

I hurl myself onto the bed, groaning in frustration. I check the time. 2 a.m. For the next hour, I'm on again, off again about texting Zack.

Do it. He needs to hear from me.

Don't. He's too mad to talk right now.

Do it. He'll understand once he knows the truth.

I concede that with our big day tomorrow, one of us should get some sleep, and it ain't gonna be me. I can smooth things over with Zack later. But for now, I gotta get back to work. I fire up my laptop and start cranking out code.

I'm haunted by an annoying little voice in my head.

You're making a huge mistake.

***

"HEY WORLD, MY DATING LIFE IS A COMPLETE CLUSTERFUCK!"

"Nope, that's not the line." I wrack my tired brain. "Have you ever had a date so bad that you wanted to leave a review as a public service announcement? Shitballs. What's my damn line?"

I read over the script on my phone and mutter to myself. "Ever wanted to break down emotionally 'cause your partner is a no-show, and you fear he's so pissed-off he's gonna make you do the presentation by yourself?"

I fiddle with my tight blouse, unbuttoning the top button. This business suit is squeezing me like a boa constrictor. I inhale deeply, struggling to keep it together.

I'm holed up on a dinky couch backstage in this so-called green room. The cluttered space has a chaotic charm littered with equipment cases and tech gear. It's me and a dozen other presenters vibrating with nervous energy. A huge-ass monitor on the wall gives us a clear view of the main event.

I stand and pour myself another cup of burned coffee. I'm running on fumes and anxious as hell, so this caffeine is my lifeline, even if it tastes like ass.

The frazzled stage manager approaches me with his clipboard clutched in his hand. "You're LoveScore, right? There's supposed to be two of you."

I look around the room. Still no fucking Zack. "Yup, my partner's on his way," I say, trying to sound convincing.

"Hope so. You get mic-ed up in ten," he tells me, then without so much as a see ya, he's summoned by his walkie.

I clear my throat and start again. "Have you ever had a bad first date and—"

Bzzt! Bzzt!

My phone. A video chat. Sissy's calling—worst timing ever. When I answer, all my sisters are on screen.

"We wanted to wish you luck, Mads!" Sissy gushes.

Nora chimes in. "Don't be nervous about the crowd. Remember, they're excited to hear your idea."

"And Zack will help if you screw up," Abby adds with a smirk.

I hear Zack's name, and my face falls. Tears sting my eyes. Sissy immediately picks up on it. "Sweetie, what's wrong?"

Nora asks gently, "Are things still awkward since Zack admitted he loves you?"

"He LOVES you? Oh my gosh, I knew it!" Sissy squeals. "Wait. Why am I the last to know again? How can I be supportive if you keep me in the dark? I swear, I'm gonna start calling all of you every day."

"Sorry," we say in unison.

Sissy quickly switches to a softer, more soothing tone. "Maddie, what happened, honey?"

The dam breaks, and words rush out of my mouth, "Zack isn't here, and we're up in ten fucking minutes. He hates me, and for good reason, I'm a selfish asshole. He doesn't want to be friends anymore. He's leaving the company. It's over. It's all over."

Cue my sisters' feminist rage, bubbling up like a cauldron of righteous estrogen.

"How dare him!" Abby seethes. "Next time I see Zack, I'm going to fuck him up. Or his car. Yeah. Ima key the shit out of his Tesla. Fucker!"

"Unfollowing him on social media as we speak," Nora declares.

"Same," Sissy adds with a nod. "And he will not be getting a thank you note for coming to the party."

"Guys, I'm not usually this mushy, but I love you," I say through tears, trying to compose myself.

"Love you too, Mads," my sisters chorus back.

I'm so grateful for my sisters. They're the only ones who can handle my shit and still love me unconditionally. I may have royally fucked up and lost my best friend, but I'll have them always and forever. If there is a silver lining to my shitburger of a situation, it's them.

Zack materializes. I shush my sisters. "He's here."

He catches their faces on the video chat. "What's up, ladies? Looking lovely as always."

"Fuck you, Zack. Better watch your car," Abby threatens.

"I hope you go bald," Nora adds snidely.

Sissy's voice rises with uncharacteristic anger. "If you screw over Maddie on that stage, I will hunt you down and kick you in the balls so hard you'll be talking in a pitch only dogs can hear!"

Damn. Sissy might look and sound like an angel, but you can kiss your ass goodbye if you threaten someone she loves.

And just like that, she's back to normal. "Okay, good luck you guys! Go crush it!"

"Give us an update on how it goes," Nora adds.

"Kick ass, bitches!" Abby hoots. Then she sneers, "But seriously, Zack, suck a bowl of dicks."

The sisters end the call with a harmonious, "Love you, byeeee!"

Zack turns to me. "What the hell was that?"

I shrug. "I figured you were flaking."

"Why would you think that? I wouldn't abandon you."

"But you are. You said it last night, you're leaving me." I can't mask the hurt in my voice.

Zack sighs. "Mads, I can't keep being your emotional punching bag. My heart can only take so much."

I meet his gaze; those stupid, beautiful eyes pleading with me. I know I've pushed him away, and I don't know how to get my best friend back. I wish we could have it all—to be a couple AND run our company side by side. But at this moment, I'm living my worst fear.

Zack is leaving because he can't manage his feelings and the business.

He's proving my point!

My fears are valid.

I CAN'T have it all.

Even so, Zack thinks I boned Trevor, like I've gone sex-crazy and lowered my standards. The thought makes me cringe. He needs to know I didn't bang that cyber douchenugget.

"Zack, last night, I know it looked like—"

He holds up a hand, silencing me. "I can not hear about your sexcapades right now, Mads."

As if she's been summoned, Lexie skips over, her boobs bouncing like they're in a race to get there first. "Hey guys!" she chirps. "Just popping by to wish you luck! Every seat is taken, and Roland McBurney himself is waiting to be blown away!"

Zack shoots her a tight smile. "Thanks, Lexie, but maybe ease up on the pep talk. Maddie's not a fan of crowds or talking about her feelings."

I glare at Zack.

"Oh, sorry! I didn't know you have stage fright," Lexie says to me. She creeps into Zack's personal space, whispering something as he chuckles like an idiot. He whispers back in her ear.

Cool, I'll just stand here, being the unwanted side dish to your future main course. Prickwad!

Obviously, I'm the only one who gives a damn about the presentation and this company's future. Whatever, I got this. It was my brilliant fucking idea in the first place. I don't need Zack or his bullshit to make it work.

Lexie dissolves into giggles at whatever hilarious thing Zack said. "OMG, stop! I can't believe you did that at the restaurant last night."

Can you guys fucking flirt somewhere else?

I think it but don't say it, instead opting for, "Hate to interrupt this *laugh-fest*, but we need to get ready."

"Of course, how silly of me! I know you'll kill it up there, Maddie. After all, you've got Zack, and he's amazing at pretty much everything." She emphasizes her words with a flutter of eyelashes that would put a hummingbird to shame.

She blushes and strokes his arm.

And then *he* blushes, too.

Oh, hell no.

Something inside me snaps.

"Let me give you a little advice, Lexie," I say with a snarky tone. "Don't put him on a pedestal. He seems 'amazing,' and he'll promise you the world, but if you don't give him exactly what he wants, he'll peace out faster than you can say fuckboy."

Shit. I immediately wish I could take it back. The look on their faces makes me wanna dig myself a shallow grave. *Why did I say that?* I open my mouth to backpedal when a headset-wearing PA interrupts, summoning us to the stage.

Zack and I head to the wings where a stage manager wires us up. Zack glares at me. "You need to calm down."

"You need to stop letting Lexie hump your leg when I'm in the room."

"Oh, you're one to talk."

Cosmo cuts in, hands the remote to Zack, and says, "The presentation slides are ready. Wes and Reid are in the crowd to help with any app download problems." He catches a glimpse of the tension, and raises an eyebrow. "What's going on, guys?"

"Ask Maddie," Zack retorts. "Since her opinion is the only one that matters."

Just then, the host's voice booms through the speakers. "Put your hands together for the visionaries behind LoveScore, the dating app that'll make Tinder seem as outdated as a Blockbuster Video membership card!"

Zack plasters on a smile and strides onstage, waving. I trail behind him with a phony-ass grin. Normally, I'd be shitting bricks facing a crowd this big, but I'm so mad all I wanna do is kick Zack in the nads.

***

ZACK AND I STEP INTO THE BLINDING SPOTLIGHT, greeted by the deafening sound of applause from horny tech nerds. It's like hearing the mating call of the socially awkward as they all wait to see what's next in digital love.

"Hello, AppVerge Expo! Who's ready to get a little crazy?" Zack yells into the mic, amping up the audience like a guru on a mission.

The crowd hoots and hollers, already eating out of the palm of his hand. I turn to face the giant screen behind us, the LoveScore logo projected in all its pixelated glory.

Zack slips into his smooth-talking presenter voice. "Raise your hand if you've ever wished for a crystal ball to predict the success of a first date? Well, wish no more, I give you... LoveScore!"

Suddenly, the room spins, my heart thumping like a coked-out woodpecker. Cold sweat trickles down my back, pooling at the waistband of my power pantsuit. My gaze lands on Lexie and her boss, Roland McBurney, seated front and center like the VIPs they are. My stomach churns. I'm seconds away from projectile vomiting all over this stage.

"I invite everyone in this crowd to join us in launching our break-through dating app," Zack says. "As you can see, we've got real-time download stats rolling in. We just went live three minutes ago, and we're already at... wait for it... two thousand downloads! No, five thousand and climbing!"

On cue, the screen fills with cascading stats, downloading in real-time, with numbers climbing faster than Zack's ego. The audience 'oohs' and 'ahhs' like he's unveiling the solution to world hunger.

"You heard it here first, people. Today we're making dating history," Zack declares. "Grab your phones and join the LoveScore revolution." He pauses, building suspense, then adds, "And if you need a little help getting started, our coding rockstars Wes and Reid are out there in the crowd. Give us a wave, guys! They're on standby to help you pop your app cherry."

I'm witnessing an all-out nerdgasm as the tech crowd hungrily pulls out their phones. Wes and Reid make their way through the crowd like tech support superstars, smiling and troubleshooting.

Zack strolls over to me, draping an arm around my shoulder. "And now, I'd like to present the mastermind behind LoveScore, my partner in innovation, Maddie Denton. She's the brains and the beauty, but don't get any ideas, gents. Maddie's heart is wrapped in barbed wire, and she's allergic to emotions. Isn't that right, doll-face?"

Oh, hell no. He did not just tee me up like that. Game on, bitch.

Through gritted teeth, I elbow him in the ribs. "Thanks for the glowing introduction, dillhole. My not-so-esteemed colleague, Zack Hanley, has asked me to explain the technical side of our app because it's way too much for his itty-bitty noodle to comprehend. Which, coincidentally, is one of the first things I want to know about a potential date."

I look down and smirk at Zack's crotch. "Size: below average."

Zack's eyes narrow, but his grin never falters. "Oh, Maddie, you slay me. Is it any wonder she's chronically single, folks? I gotta hand it to her. She's written the playbook on celibacy."

The audience titters, and my blood pressure skyrockets. "Speaking of celibacy," I grit out, "let's discuss the importance of consent, shall we? Show of hands, ladies. Who here has been harassed at work about their dating life by a male colleague?"

A smattering of hands shoot up, and I nod solemnly. "Thought so. Don't worry, we got you. Our app shows a person's LoveScore, which means no more unsolicited dick pics or coffee room come-ons from Brad in accounting. You'll know to steer clear."

Zack scowls at me off mic, "Really, Maddie? We're going there? Okay, I'll play."

"Guys, who here has been intrigued by a coworker beyond just her looks but then got mistakenly stereotyped as a misogynist asshole who was looking to turn her into a trophy-wife-baby-machine. Hands up, fellas."

More hands in the air, and Zack smirks triumphantly. "See? Not all men are out to destroy the careers of their female colleagues."

I catch Cosmo's eye from the side of the stage. He mouths, "What the fuck?!" *But I'm in too deep now. This shit just got personal.*

I take a beat and keep going. "And that's the reason we created LoveScore. Because let's face it, sometimes people go on dates with completely different agendas. Maybe one person wants to keep things platonic... avoid complications."

Zack scoffs. "Or maybe the other is too emotionally constipated to let someone in, despite them having a deep connection?"

Backstage, I see Cosmo frantically gesturing for us to wrap it up, but Zack's on a roll.

"To illustrate this, let's look at some real-time first-date feedback coming in now," he says, clicking on the first user review on the big screen. "Listen to this: 'Never date this girl unless you enjoy being an unwilling hostage to her motor mouth. She never came up for air once during our date. One star.'" He turns to the audience with a conspiratorial wink. "Been there, am I right, fellas?"

The crowd chuckles, and a dangerous fury builds inside me.

Here comes Maddie... unleashed.

I grab the clicker from Zack's hand and pull up the next review. "Okay, here's a gem: 'Apparently, this guy thinks buying a girl a burger entitles him to a hand job. It's not called McFondles, limpdick. One star.'" I turn to the women in the crowd. "Sound familiar, ladies? When did buying us a Big Mac become a binding sex contract?"

The women whoop and holler their agreement. I feel a rush of satisfaction, but Zack has already taken back the remote.

"I can relate to this one," he says bitterly. "'Met this girl who said she was totally into me. We had an amazing first date, and she claimed to feel a real connection. Then I caught her sucking face with another dude the very next day. One star.' Man, I feel your pain, bro. Some ladies will swear up and down they care about you, then jump on the first dick that crosses their path."

I'm livid. Is he seriously broadcasting our shit to a room full of strangers? Fuck you motherfucker!

"I bet she got tired of faking orgasms and wanted to feel a real one for once," I snap, not even bothering with the pretense of a review.

The crowd shifts uncomfortably in their seats, the air now thick with the stench of impending disaster.

Backstage, Cosmo is openly facepalming, shaking his head in horror. He grabs a mic, sprints onstage, and yanks the remote from Zack's tense grip.

Cosmo's eyes dart between us, his expression equal parts confusion and exasperation. "Hey, let's find some of those coveted five-star reviews, shall we? Really show off LoveScore's matchmaking chops!"

He rapidly clicks through a slew of one-star reviews, each harsher than the last. The crowd's initial excitement has given way to simmering discomfort. An uneasy laughter ripples through the large room.

Cosmo says, "Hmmm, it appears people take great pleasure in leaving negative feedback."

A string of one-star reviews. Click. Click. Click. Click.

Zack rounds on me, mic still in hand. His showman's mask is finally slipping. "Why did you come to me that night, Maddie? Was it just a twisted mind game, toying with my feelings for shits and giggles?"

Blood drains from my face, and the threads of my composure snap one by one. "I told you from the beginning, Zack. Love was never on the table."

"Admit it," he hisses, his eyes wild and pleading. "Admit that you love me, that you're terrified of being vulnerable to someone, even knowing they love you!"

I recoil like I've been slapped. "Was that your grand master plan? Pretend to be my friend for a decade, then guilt me into falling for you? Fuck you, Zack. Fuck you and your fucking fairy tale expectations."

"Jesus Christ, Maddie! I've done nothing but respect your boundaries. YOU crossed the line that night, not me. But sure, keep playing the victim. It's what you do best."

Cosmo's still gamely plowing through user reviews, his voice hitching with barely suppressed panic. "I'm sure we'll find a five-star testimonial any second now, folks. LoveScore is all about... fostering meaningful connections... and..."

Zack and I face off center stage, our chests heaving, a decade's worth of unspoken hurts and misunderstandings crackling between us like a live wire.

"This whole thing was a mistake," I whisper, my voice cracking.

Zack laughs—a harsh, ugly sound. "Of course. Shit gets real, Mads runs away."

"I've told you a thousand times, Zack. I don't love you. I'll never love you like that. Do I need to spell it out in crayon for you?"

"Message received, loud and clear," he says coldly. "I'm done chasing after a woman who'd rather self-destruct than let herself be happy. Have a nice life, Maddie."

He storms off stage, leaving me alone in the spotlight of my humiliation.

I look out at the crowd of stunned faces. Their secondhand embarrassment burns through me.

"Wait, I found one!" Cosmo crows—a captain going down with his ill-fated ship. "A five-star review, hot off the keyboard. 'My date was a total snoozefest, but her smokin' hot mom made up for it. Five stars for the MILF who gives a decent blowie, and a big fat zero for her dud of a daughter.'"

"Thanks, everyone, for coming out to the launch of LoveScore," I say sarcastically. "Where you can be an asshole and troll your dates in real-time. The future of romance is here, and it's a fucking disaster. Enjoy the rest of your conference."

I drop the mic and walk offstage, vision blurred with unshed tears. I can hear Cosmo frantically trying to do damage control, but his voice fades into white noise.

So much for our triumphant tech world debut. LoveScore just crashed and burned like a lit fart out of Satan's bunghole.

CHAPTER NINETEEN

MADDIE

THIS IS THE WORST FUCKING DAY OF MY ENTIRE LIFE.

Here I am, face-planting into this hotel bed, sobbing so hard I'm pretty sure I'm drowning in this pillow. It's like a friggin' sponge for my tears. And of course, my mascara is making a black smear-y mess all over it. My heart? Feels like it got caught in a goddamn bear trap and then mauled by the actual bear.

"Let this be the worst of it," I whisper, "I can't fucking take any more."

Another wave of soul-crushing sadness numbs me. I roll into a ball and cling to my knees like they're keeping me afloat. I want to be strong—unleash a hurricane of fury—but all I can manage are these pitiful, gasping sobs.

I refused to cry until I was away from all the judgmental stares because that's not who I am. But now, in this dull beige shoebox of a room, I'm owning my sadness. My brain won't stop replaying the awful things Zack and I said.

The launch was a massive failure. And not because of any technical difficulties or our less-than-stellar presentation—nope, if anything, our spectacular meltdown made LoveScore the juiciest gossip of the expo. The internet made damn sure I would never live this moment down. Between the viral YouTube video and word of mouth, there was only one reason the app failed... me.

After the presentation, I had to face Roland McBurney alone; Zack having skedaddled the fuck out to God knows where. Roland's faux sympathy was almost worse than the humiliation. "Sorry, kiddo. Them's the breaks," he said with a condescending shrug. "Apparently, people only want to leave bad reviews. Guess if they find a good match, they hold onto that person."

It took all my willpower not to let loose a blood-curdling scream. After so many late nights, endless coding, and gallons of coffee, how did we overlook such a massive flaw? We were obsessed with making the perfect algorithm and creating stupid fake profiles, blind to the fact that users would be dicks and only leave negative, revenge-filled reviews.

After that kick to the ladyballs, I couldn't look my team in the eye. I trudged back to my room, allowing myself a full-on breakdown.

I'm snuggled in Zack's freaking Northwestern hoodie, his lingering scent torturing me.

It's the loser-of-the-year pity party I deserve—just me, the mini bar, and the snack mix Cyper Sphinxx left behind. I'm drinking vodka like it's water and shoving cheeseballs in my mouth like a squirrel preparing for winter.

My phone buzzes nonstop with texts from my sisters and the coder bros, but there's no message from the one person I want to hear from. Zack made it crystal fucking clear—he's done with me and my bullshit.

My priority should be damage control for my career and helping my loyal team that I've majorly screwed over, but my heart's a shithead and only wants to think about Zack.

I could march over to his room and beg for his forgiveness, but no. We took our friendship, stomped on it, and set it on fire in front of the whole damn world.

Another pathetic sniffle, and I bury my face in his hoodie, seeking comfort I don't deserve. Zack was right—I've never let myself be this vulnerable, never allowed myself to feel so deeply. And now I know why.

Heartbreak is a bitch.

A fresh wave of tears threatens to overtake me. I power down my phone, ignoring the onslaught of messages. *I want to sink into oblivion.*

I cling to his hoodie like it's the only thing keeping me alive. I let the tears come. LoveScore's in the crapper. My rep is trashed. I fucked over the people who believed in me. But, the most soul-crushing truth is this:

I'm so fucking in love with Zack.

***

"MADDIE, ARE YOU IN THERE? MADDIE?"

The sound of knocking and Zack's muffled voice rouses me. A few groggy seconds later, my brain accepts that yes, Zack is outside my hotel room door.

Knock. Knock. Knock.

"Maddie. Please open up. Everyone's worried. Your sisters won't stop blowing up my phone. And Sissy threatened to barbecue my balls if I didn't check on you." A pause. "Mads?"

I stumble out of bed, my head feeling like a beat-up piñata. I use the sleeve of Zack's oversized hoodie to touch the door, but I can't bring myself to open it. An immense shame pins my feet to the floor.

"Zack, please, just go. I know I fucked up, and you being nice makes me feel even shittier."

"I need to see you to make sure you're okay." His concern makes my heart clench.

"Why are you here? We're not friends anymore," I choke out, hating how lame I sound.

"Maddie. Can you just open the door?"

"I'm too embarrassed," I admit, fresh tears threatening to fall.

"Fine. Then I'll camp out here. I'm not leaving."

A sob escapes my throat, and I quickly muffle it with my sleeve. I can't let him hear me cry.

I listen as Zack's body sinks to the floor with a thud, his back against the door, and I find myself doing the same. Like a sad mirror image, taking comfort in our plywood-separated closeness.

"I know you're hurting," he says softly. "But you'll bounce back from this, I promise. You'll come out the other side an even stronger badass. I know because, well... you're you."

"I'm not hurt. I'm pissed," I say through the door.

"Mads, you can't control everything, that's just life. None of us could've predicted getting only one-star reviews. Setbacks are part of the game in startups. One day, this will be a funny story you tell."

Silence stretches on as I absorb his words.

"Nobody's perfect," Zack continues. "You're damn close, but you can't beat yourself up over a mistake."

A garbled giggle-sob hybrid bursts out of me. "I'm soooo not perfect, and I'm not angry about the app."

"So, what's really going on then?"

A fucking dam breaks inside me. A tidal wave of feelings shakes me to my core. "I'm so fucking mad that I hurt you! I'm mad that you hate me!" I say through massive, ugly sobs. "I'm mad that... that I've lost you!"

"Mads. Open the door. Please."

But I can't stop. The words keep tumbling out between gasping breaths. "I'm mad that we ever went on those asinine fake dates. I'm mad that I'm selfish. I'm mad I can't muster up the balls to be honest. I'm super fucking angry that I lied to you." I begin to hyperventilate.

"Lied to me? About what?"

"So much shit."

"Like Trevor?" His voice is cautious.

My sobs gradually calm down to pitiful sniffles. "That fuckwad was Cyber Sphinxx, the hacker. Zack, I promise, nothing happened. He was a total shady prick just like you warned me. Clearly over-compensating for his teeny-weeny-peeny."

Zack chuckles unexpectedly at my dumb joke, and for a second, the tension lifts. I want to see his face so badly right now. To reach out and touch him. But I've lost that right.

"What else did you lie about?" Zack asks, serious again.

I inhale a deep, shaky breath. "When I said you weren't smart. Zack, you're brilliant. Your vision, your leadership—it leaves me in awe. Half the time, I feel like a freaking poser next to you."

"Mads—"

"No, let me finish. Please. I don't know shit about running a company. It was you. You made it happen. I'm sorry I ever made you doubt that. LoveScore would've never gotten anywhere without you."

Silence hangs heavy in the air. *Did I say too much? Or not enough?*

Zack chokes up as he speaks, "Thank you for saying that. It... means a lot to me. I often felt like I was more style than substance, like maybe what I brought to the table wasn't as valuable."

"I'm so sorry," I say. "That's on me. You deserved better."

Another weighted pause. "Since we're being honest, is there anything else?"

A hysterical giggle bubbles up in my throat. "I, uh, I lied about faking it. Turns out I'd never actually had a real orgasm before. Not until you. Pleasure Penguin doesn't count."

Zack lets out a relieved sigh. "Fewf. Good to know. You had me questioning my manskills for a minute there."

"Oh no. Your schlong-tastic skills are gold medal-worthy. 11/10, would ride again... if I hadn't, ya know, nuked what we had togeth er..."

"Maddie."

His voice saying my name turns my already broken heart into dust. Fresh tears fill my eyes, making everything look more blurry even as it feels more real.

This is it.

The end of our journey.

Goodbye.

I'm a checkbox on his nice guy list, but now, this is where he walks away, and I'll have to learn how to be half a person.

Because that's what I am without him—incomplete.

A crippling panic takes hold, constricting my chest and sending my heart racing. I have to navigate a future without Zack—never again feeling the happiness and solace he brings. It's unbearable. I'm staring into a black hole, knowing there is no escape from the suffocating darkness once I fall in.

I reach for the door handle with trembling hands, every cell in my body screaming at me to open it, to face him, to lay myself bare.

Slowly, I crack the door open, my heart galloping like a herd of wild horses. Zack leans back, eyes wide with surprise. But he doesn't come in. Instead, we face each other on the floor, sitting cross-legged on either side of the threshold, separated by a few inches of worn beige carpet.

"Hi, Hanley," I whisper.

"Hey there, Mads." He reaches out, tucking a strand of messy hair behind my ear.

"Zack, I..." I swallow hard, forcing myself to maintain eye contact. "I lied about one more thing, and it's a freakin' doozy. I lied... when I said I only love you as a friend." My voice cracks, but I push on. "I was scared that loving you would mean losing myself. But the only thing I lost... was you."

His warm brown eyes search mine, swirling with emotions. "Maddie, you haven't lost me. I'm right here."

And he is. Despite everything, he's here.

I stare into the endless galaxy of his eyes, and I feel something shift inside me, like a key turning a rusty lock. I've always been so hellbent on making my mark, on getting recognition and success, but now, staring at this man who loves me for who I am—not what I can create or build or become—I realize I've been chasing the wrong fucking dream.

Love isn't the enemy of ambition. It isn't an evil force out to steal my identity. Love is magic—it makes life worth living. It's the courage to be vulnerable, to give yourself wholly to another. And without love, it's impossible to build something that matters.

Love isn't sacrifice. It's balance. It's about finding your equal—someone to hype you up—to chase your aspirations with. Zack was never gonna make me pick between him and my career. He wouldn't dare press pause on my life, and he wouldn't fathom asking me to abandon my goals. He's proven he's my rock, my cheerleader, my man through all life's bullshit.

And I want to be that person for him too.

I finally see it—the future I was so scared to admit I wanted: waking up to bangin' sex on a lazy Sunday, schmoopy date nights holding hands and battling over the last fry, stolen kisses during Star Trek binges. Squabbling, apologizing, and growing together. It's messy, it's beautiful, and it's abso-fucking-lutely worth every sacrifice.

Zack saw what I couldn't see.

Love is worth the risk.

"I've fallen for you, Zack. I tried so fucking hard not to, but I did. You're it for me. And I'm done running."

Zack's hand reaches out, his palm warm against my cheek. "I need to hear you say it, Mads."

"I love you." The words burst free, three simple syllables that redefine my world. "I'm sorry it took me so long to get here. But I love you, Zack Hanley. With every broken, stubborn piece of me."

His lips crash into mine like a wrecking ball, years of pent-up longing and desperation pouring into the kiss. I cling to him desperately, fingers twisting in his shirt, dragging him closer. I need to feel him, every hard inch of him until I don't know where I end and he begins.

"Again," Zack demands roughly against my mouth. "Say it again." His hand weaves into my hair, angling my head back to expose the delicate skin of my neck to him.

"I love you," I gasp out as he trails hot, open-mouthed kisses down the column of my neck. "I love you, I love you, I love—"

In one swift motion, Zack scoops me into his arms, kicking the door shut without breaking our frantic kiss. He places me on the bed, then takes a step back to study me, his eyes ablaze with a desire that steals my breath.

I'm a woman on fire, possessed with a single purpose—show him how much I mean it. I rip off his hoodie, exposing my bare chest, and press his hand against my thundering heart. "It's yours," I rasp. "No one else's."

"Mads, you destroy me. You're so goddamn gorgeous." He looks at me with an intensity that makes me want to surrender myself completely to him.

I attack the buttons of his shirt, aching to get my hands on his bare skin. "I love your body," I confess breathlessly, running my fingers down the hard planes of his chest. "I love your kind heart."

Zack's thumb sweeps my cheekbone, unbearably tender. "I love your brilliant, beautiful mind." He presses a soft kiss to my forehead, my eyelids, the tip of my nose. "I love your sexy curves."

I slide off my pajama pants and lie down, a clear invitation. His gaze drinks in my naked form.

"Maddie... if we do this, you have to be all in... tomorrow, the year after, and forever. Otherwise, I won't survive."

"I want you. In every way. Always."

Zack strips down, and I admire the sight of his formidable erection. He produces a condom from his wallet, and I take it, deftly unwrapping it and rolling it down his hardness. I give him a firm squeeze, relishing the sound of his sharp intake.

With a primal growl, he kisses me with a devotion that drives me wild.

"I love your mouth, Zack."

"Say my name again. Please. I fucking love it when you say my name."

"Zack," I moan, rolling my hips to meet his. "My Zack... make me yours."

He glides into me, and I let go, losing myself in the rhythmic sensation as our souls merge. There is only this—the mind—blowing friction where we connect, the delicious rub of skin on skin, the climbing of pleasure, obliterating everything else.

I cling to him, nails marking his back as I utter pleading, broken words while he pushes me to the edge. We're helpless against this lust, ferociously chasing our climax together.

"I love you so much!" I cry out. My voice trembles as his thrusts send me to new heights. "Yes, Zack!"

My unrestrained moans only make him more determined. "Christ! I love you, Maddie," Zack groans, his ragged voice raw and untamed like an animal.

His hips grind into me, setting me off. My nerve endings sizzle with pleasure as my climax rises, everything clenching and curling up inside me.

"I... I... Zack, YES! Zack! Zack!"

"Fuck, Maddie! God, yes."

I feel my insides fluttering and contracting around him as he comes to a halt, his eyes glued to mine, lips parted while he pants through his own orgasm. I lay there, enjoying the rush of my release as it consumes me. His body collapses onto mine, and I feel his jagged breaths against my neck.

This is the start of a life I never imagined.

"I love you, Zack Hanley." I whisper breathlessly.

"I've loved you forever, Madeline Denton," he whispers back.

In the glow of the most intense lovemaking of my existence, Zack rolls onto his side, drawing me close. I snuggle into his warmth, nuzzling my face into the crook of his neck. His fingers stroke my hair, calming me, lulling me into a state of blissful contentment.

"Dang, that was over faster than a virgin on prom night," I joke. "Looks like we gotta work on your endurance, loverboy."

Zack's deep laugh rumbles through me. "Hey, cut me some slack. I've been waiting ten years to hear you scream my name like that. You should be impressed I lasted as long as I did." He presses a soft, long kiss to my lips. "If you give me a minute to refuel, I promise round two will make you forget your name."

I look up at him with a naughty grin. "You better bring your A-game, because I plan on keeping you in this bed until we both die of dehydration."

"And that's why you're the brains of this operation, Mads." He smirks. "You've got the best ideas."

I prop myself up on an elbow, drawing random shapes on his chest. "So, what's our label now? Boyfriend and girlfriend? Boning buddies? Lustful lovebirds?"

Zack catches my hand, bringing it to his lips. "I don't care how you label it, Mads. I just care that you're mine. Nothing else matters."

My heart skips a beat. "I am yours, but are you sure you want my dirty mind to choose?" I tap my chin, pretending to ponder. "How about Sovereign Commander of Zack Hanley's Dick?"

"I love the way your mind works." He hauls me close, burying his face in my neck, his breath raising goosebumps on my skin. "Sovereign Commander of Zack Hanley's Dick it is. I'll have it printed on business cards for you."

Laughter bubbles out of me as he peppers my throat with playful kisses, his stubble scratching deliciously.

"Alright, funny girl." His voice drops, low and rough, as he nibbles on my earlobe. "We have years of pleasure to catch up on. Lil Zack has been waiting forever for this. He's ready for round two, are you?"

And then he's kissing me again, deep and filthy, and I know this is exactly where I'm meant to be.

You don't need a partner to be complete. I could've been a badass, independent woman following my passions and living life on my own terms. But I found Zack. If you're lucky enough to find that person who makes your heart soar—puts your soul at ease—someone who loves you for you, quirks and all—you better lock that shit down.

And when you find love, you take care of it. You honor it. You put in the work, day in and day out. You choose each other again and again. Even when things suck, and the honeymoon phase is over, even when real life starts kicking your ass; you cherish it cause love is a fucking gift.

A crazy, imperfect, life-altering gift.

Zack is mine. My rare-as-fuck, soulmate, can't-believe-he's-mine gift. And loving Zack? Being loved by this incredible man? It's everything I never knew I needed.

Now I have a new dream.

But I'm still the same me.

I'm Madeline Denton. Feminist crusader, coding genius, and Sovereign Commander of Zack Hanley's Dick.

EPILOGUE

ZACK

"I COULDN'T AGREE MORE. Maddie is perfect for the *Wired Magazine* feature on innovative women in tech. My assistant will set everything up," I say, ending the call *(that's right, my real assistant—sorry, Siri).*

I'm strolling around the chic, contemporary office of our newest startup, BFF2bae. The massive open layout is alive with energy as our extensive team collaborates at long, shared tables, their screens facing off. Bright colors pop against the minimalist design. It's a serious step up from LoveScore's cramped coding cave.

After LoveScore's monumental flop, Maddie and I brushed ourselves off and went big on a new dating app idea—one that came from an unexpected inspiration... us. BFF2bae is designed to mimic the journey of falling for a friend, encouraging users to get to know each other before jumping into romance.

Our algorithm works its love magic based on all the stuff that really counts—common passions, goals, and maybe even a few shared kinks *(not judging).* Then you hit the "friend zone" texting stage, bonding over sweet memes and heavy, existential thoughts. After that, it's video chat time with outrageous face filters and voice modifiers to keep things interesting. And finally, when you're sick of sexting and so horny you could screw a pool noodle, it's time for the big in-person reveal.

"Zack! Brenna and I need you to be the tiebreaker." Wes runs up to me, his new girlfriend Brenna trailing behind. They're a quirky duo with a ton of personality, and Brenna has even started copying Wes's style. Today, they're rocking mismatched paisley shirts. The only way to tell them apart is Brenna's fiery red curls.

Wes didn't exaggerate when he said Brenna was a gifted coder. Maddie snatched her up on the spot. In fact, our company now leads the tech industry with the highest number of female coders. 51%, to be exact.

"What's up, lovebirds?" I ask with a grin.

Brenna gives a playful eye roll. "We're fighting over new face filters for the video avatar dealio. Some of Wes' picks are... I'm just gonna say it, bruh, they're creepy."

Wes scoffs. "Babycakes, you said you were into weird stuff! Zack, buddy, back me up."

Brenna sighs, "Pumpkin pants, I'm nutso about your weirdness, but I gotta put my foot down on filters that make users' faces look like sex dolls." She turns to me and whispers. "He's been a little clingy since I put Linda in time-out."

I throw up my hands. "I'm bailing. Leave me out of your naughty negotiations. You maniacs are the app's star couple. I'm sure you'll find a middle ground that won't give our users nightmares."

Wes and Brenna's unconventional romance, born from chatting as friends online, was what made us realize we could take our friends-to-lovers experience and make it digital. They're proof that a unique kind of awesomeness unfolds when people form genuine bonds without obsessing over the physical.

And holy crap, it's a hit. BFF2bae is the hottest new dating app out there, with feel-good success stories flooding in every day. Our couples' match rate is off the charts! Well, except for Maddie's forever single sister Nora. That girl's extensive "future hubby" checklist has guys fleeing faster than you can say "bridezilla."

Wes pulls Brenna into a steamy kiss right in front of everyone, inviting some playful catcalls from coders walking by. I should probably reprimand the flagrant PDA, but it's nice to see Wes so love-struck. I can hardly blame the guy, considering I'm pretty blissed out myself.

Smiling, I make my way to the kitchen for a pre-meeting cappuccino boost. Cosmo's already there, stirring an absurd amount of Splenda into his drink.

"Hey, Cos, we still good for poker night with you and Franklin this Friday?" I ask, snagging the milk frother.

Cosmo sighs melodramatically. "Indeed, but I had to assure Franklin that I wouldn't spend the whole evening revealing his pitiful, bluffing cues. My husband claims I'm 'ruining game night with my excessive competitiveness' or some such nonsense."

I chuckle. Poor Franklin. We finally got to meet the love of Cosmo's life when we were invited to their small beach wedding a few months ago. They are weekly poker night fixtures, and I can vouch for Cosmo's intensity being no joke, especially when Maddie's sister Abby is in the game. Those two face off, and Abby always comes out on top.

"Did you hear about Cyber Sphinxx?" I ask.

Cosmo responds gleefully, "Are you talking about how he hacked Facebook's mainframe? And then Zuckerberg went nuclear on him, plastering the guy's whole life story online."

I can't help but snort. "Yeah, heard that dipshit's locked up in some Russian gulag now." Picturing it makes me smirk.

"Asshole had it coming," Cosmo says, shaking his head.

I reach into the drawer and pull out a "Frisky Foams" XXX-presso art stencil. Reid's a total genius. The guy turned pervy latte art into a multimillion-dollar empire. I place the stencil on top of my cappuccino. A sprinkle of cinnamon and voila—a delicious derriere design.

Cosmo speaks in a hushed tone. "If you repeat this, I'll deny it, but I do miss seeing the guy every day."

"Word is he's dating Lexie now," I say, grabbing a second mug to fix Maddie's usual. Reid's living his dream—a ballin' penthouse, a gorgeous girlfriend, and a paid entourage of 'yes bros' at his beck and call.

I position another Reid original on top of Maddie's cappuccino—a downright dirty take on the Kama Sutra's lotus position. Her favorite. *It's the little things, ya know?*

"Off to eviscerate the ego of our new recruits," Cosmo declares, punctuating his words with a knuckle crack.

I make my way through the lively bullpen, careful not to spill our drinks or ruin the naughty designs. I stop outside Maddie's office door, admiring her. She has a cute little wrinkle between her eyebrows, a few stray hairs breaking free from her messy bun, and she bites her lip as she types.

She's the most gorgeous, intelligent creature I've ever seen. At long last, she's mine.

Bonus for me: Mads now straight-up owns her sexiness. Today, she's rocking a black blazer, dark jeans, and a white blouse that gives me the perfect peek of cleavage. She still keeps it low-key with makeup and those tortoiseshell glasses that drive me crazy. No more hoodies, but when she rocks my Northwestern one to bed, pantless, I know we gettin' frisky.

Just this morning, I watched her get dressed after some incredibly steamy shower sex. We live together in a high-rise apartment conveniently located next to our office. I chose the place specifically so we could stroll to work hand in hand and sprint back home for some midday lovin'. And trust me, it's a lunch routine we enjoy on the regular.

It still blows my mind that we ended up together after a decade in the friend zone. Yeah, getting here took a questionable "fake dating" scheme and some big-time misunderstandings, but I wouldn't trade our crazy journey for anything.

This time, we built the company the right way. It took us over a year to get it off the ground, but once we did, investors were practically tripping over themselves to get a piece of the action. Maddie is more confident than ever in her role as co-CEO, and it's so damn sexy.

Her sisters forgave me once they heard the full story. In fact, they even took my side. They said they knew Mads was into me but was too stubborn to admit it. Sure, Sissy might still throw some side-eye my way, but her hubby Ben swears it's an act. Probably. My balls are taking no chances.

And Maddie's dad was right. I've kept my promise to help her achieve her dreams. In return, she's loved me with a passion I never thought possible. No one in the world makes me feel as special as she does.

Rapping my knuckles lightly on the doorframe, I saunter in as Maddie glances up with a slow smile. "Is that what I think it is?"

"One forbidden cappuccino with vanilla, cinnamon, and a dash of cocoa, topped with my beautiful lady's favorite position," I say, setting the cup on her desk with a grin.

She flashes a seductive smirk that sends a shockwave to my groin and takes a sip. "Did I miss a memo cause it looks like you're trying to tell me something?"

"Just thinking about our meeting later," I say casually, trying to unrev my body. "Unless you want to move that meeting earlier?"

"Zack Hanley, are you hitting on me at work?"

I lean across her desk, my smile widening. "You bet your sexy ass I am." I bring my lips tantalizingly close to hers, then change course and tenderly kiss her forehead.

"You tease." She playfully hits my arm. "I know I'm irresistible and all, but babe, you've got to keep it in your pants. I've got a to-do list longer than your massive meat missile."

"You're my favorite thing to do," I say, pressing her hand to my lips. I kiss her knuckles softly, loving the slight catch in her breath.

Tugging her hand free, she levels me with a look that's an adorable mix of frustration and affection. "7 o'clock, Santoro's. Now beat it before I sic HR on your ass."

"Roger that, boss lady. If you don't get your work done, your co-CEO will be riding you hard this weekend," I say, stealing one more kiss before I hightail it out of her office, grinning like a fool.

"Love you, Zack," she calls after me.

"Love you too, Mads."

I get comfy in my office chair, firing up my computer and signing into the next meeting. Just as I'm about to kick things off, Maddie struts in, sporting a playful spark in her eye.

"It's later," she purrs, closing the door and locking it with a definitive click.

I start to say, "Umm, Maddie. I'm—"

Before I know it, she's spinning my chair around and silencing me with a finger on my lips. "You're the ruthless boss, and I'm your rebellious assistant who secretly has the hots for you. Roleplay!"

In a heartbeat, she tears off her top, unveiling an insanely sexy purple lace bra, and climbs onto my lap. She kisses me like she's starving for me, and damn, and I'm already harder than steel.

Suddenly, a throat clears, and we both freeze. "Mr. Hanley, would you like to reschedule?" a voice asks from my computer.

Maddie's eyes pop as she realizes I'm on a Zoom call with multiple people. She covers her bra with her hands, her cheeks flushing a delicious pink.

"Yes, it seems I overlooked a prior engagement. Let's reschedule," I say, attempting a poker face as I close my computer. With that, I pull Maddie in for a kiss, pouring all my love and desire into it.

"Okay, naughty girl. Now, where were we?" I whisper to her lips.

Maddie grins, settling more firmly in my lap. "Well, Mr. Hanley, you see, I was hoping to get a raise."

I smirk, my hands sliding down to squeeze her perfect ass. "Oh, well, Miss Denton, that'll depend on whether you can negotiate a raise... out of me." I nod down to my crotch, where my bulging erection is begging for her touch.

Maddie unhooks her bra behind her back, letting it slowly slide down to the floor. I'm awe-struck. My heart's so damn full it might explode. She looks at me with passion burning in her eyes, and I find myself completely and hopelessly lost in her.

"I love you with all my heart," I murmur, cradling her face in my hands like she's the most valuable treasure in existence. Because to me, she is.

"I love you more," Maddie says, her lips a hairsbreadth from mine. "Now, kiss me."

I grin. "I thought you'd never ask."

And then I'm right back in it, kissing her with a passion that's wild and untamed, full of what's to come. Because Madeline Denton? She's my forever after.

I can't wait to spend the rest of our lives proving my love to her, starting in this cockblocking office chair *(stupid armrests)* and ending with us rocking side by side on our front porch; old and gray and blissfully happy.

Get ready for the ride, Mads. We're just getting started.

***

WANT MORE FAKE RELATIONSHIP WORKPLACE ROMANCE? CHECK OUT OUR HOLIDAY BOOK: **FAKE IT 'TIL YOU SLEIGH IT**

hey there, hot stuff ;-)

Think Zack and Maddie are done steaming up the windows? Not even close. How's life in their new apartment one year later? Unpacking or roleplaying? Perhaps both?

Find out in this spicy
FREE BONUS EPILOGUE!

Scan code or visit:
MELISARYUN.COM/BONUS

ALSO BY MÉLISA RYUN

HOT MESS SUMMER SERIES

Italy Can Bite Me

Hawaii Can Suck It

Mexico Can Choke On It

THE DENTON SISTERS SERIES

Love, Plus Pixie Rae

Nora's story, Book 2 – Coming Spring 2026

STAND-ALONE TITLES

Fake It 'Til You Sleigh It

a Holiday Romantic Comedy

Live From New York... It's Love

Short Story

AUTHORS' NOTE

Hey there lovely reader! So, where do I even start? I freakin' adore my wife and her potty mouth. When MéLisa hit me with this story idea—a badass, unconventional woman kicking sexism's butt—I was like, "Hell yeah, let's do this!"

Now, let me tell you, Maddie's struggle? It's basically my wife's life story (minus the coding). When she's directing, I've seen MéLisa strut onto sets full of dudes, ready to take charge, only to get eye-rolls and mansplaining. But did she back down? Hell no! She gave exactly zero fucks.

But that's not all they have in common. My wife also:

- Invents cusswords like it's her job (it's impressive, really)

- Has a weird thing about wet hair (thinks it'll get moldy if she sleeps on it—I can't even)

- Gets knocked down, bounces right back up like a boss

- Will make you laugh so hard you'll pee a little

- Puts people in their place (doesn't matter if you're a man, woman, or even a sassy hamster)

- Does all this with a heart bigger than my TBR pile

And don't get me started on the sexism women put up with on the daily. Your tone's "off", you've got "bitchy resting face" (eye roll), you're "weak" if you mentor, but a "bitch" if you set boundaries. And if you dare call out chauvinism, then you're "playing the gender card." *Sheesh!*

We wrote Maddie to be a character saying the things we wish we could in real life—stuff that should be said.

Now, as a girl dad, I gotta say—fellas, we need to step up our game. Let's be the allies these kickass women deserve. Stand up against misogyny, hype up the ladies in your life, be their personal cheerleader!

To my amazing MéLisa, my partner in crime *(and writing):* You're my daily dose of inspiration. This book? It's all you—your journey, your talent, your unbreakable spirit. I'm the luckiest guy alive being the Zack to your Maddie

And to you awesome readers, thanks for having our backs! We hope this book made you LOL, ugly cry into your pillows, and feel ALL the feels during Zack and Maddie's rollercoaster ride.

Sending love, bear hugs, and virtual high-fives,
Ryun (aka Mr. MéLisa)

P.S. Still swooning over Zack and Maddie's love story? Do us a solid and leave a killer **AMAZON REVIEW!** Do it for feminism—stick it to the patriarchy—make some noise because you're a badass who loves empowering stories.

ACKNOWLEDGMENTS

Huge thanks and endless gratitude to all the new friends and mentors who continue to inspire and assist us on our writing adventure.

- All Write Well

- Author Ever After

- Joquena Lomelino

- All the rockstar romance authors we've met since moving to Las Vegas

We're beyond honored to join this fantastic romance community—you've treated us like family from day one. We've found our tribe!

And a massive shoutout to you, sexy reader! Your support is everything. Your reviews, downloads, follows, and messages. We cherish it all. Okay, enough mushy stuff. Back to writing!

ABOUT THE AUTHORS

MéLisa Ryun is our combined pen name, and we're a husband-wife duo who've been finishing each other's sentences (and steamy scenes) for nearly 30 years. We left the glitz of Hollywood for the glitter of Vegas. Despite calling Sin City home, we say what happens in Vegas should definitely not stay in Vegas—not with our scorching hot romcoms.

We spend our days in a death match of yoga and joke-writing. Living out our happily-ever-after while making silly social media videos together. **Snark. Swoon. Spice!**

VISIT MELISARYUN.COM

FIND US ON SOCIAL MEDIA @MELISARYUN